THE HUSBAND DIET

T0017106

ALSO BY NANCY BARONE

THE HUSBAND DIET TRILOGY
The Husband Diet
My Big Fat Italian Break-Up
Storm in a D Cup

OTHERS
Snow Falls Over Starry Cove
Starting Over at the Little Cornish Beach House
Dreams of a Little Cornish Cottage
No Room at the Little Cornish Inn
New Hope for the Little Cornish Farmhouse

THE HUSBAND DIET

Nancy Barone

An Aria Book

First published in the UK in 2014 by Bookouture

This paperback edition first published in the UK in 2022 by Head of Zeus Ltd,
part of Bloomsbury Publishing Plc

Copyright © Nancy Barone, 2014

The moral right of Nancy Barone to be identified
as the author of this work has been asserted in accordance with
the Copyright, Designs and Patents Act of 1988.

All rights reserved. No part of this publication may be reproduced,
stored in a retrieval system, or transmitted in any form or by any means,
electronic, mechanical, photocopying, recording, or otherwise,
without the prior permission of both the copyright owner
and the above publisher of this book.

This is a work of fiction. All characters, organizations, and events
portrayed in this novel are either products of the author's
imagination or are used fictitiously.

975312468

A catalogue record for this book is available from the British Library.

ISBN (PB): 9781803287652
ISBN (E): 9781803287638

Cover design: Nina Elstad

Typeset by Siliconchips Services Ltd UK

Printed and bound in Great Britain by
CPI Group (UK) Ltd, Croydon CR0 4YY

Head of Zeus Ltd
5–8 Hardwick Street
London EC1R 4RG

WWW.HEADOFZEUS.COM

To my *Tuscan Sisters*.

Prologue

'Miss Cantelli?'

I looked up from my desk at the two beaming men in suits. 'Yes, Mr. Lowenstein?'

'Can you see our favorite client out, please?'

'Certainly, sir. This way, please, Mr. Smith.' I obliged with a courteous smile and ushered the satisfied duck with the golden eggs out of the office then returned to my desk.

'Have you locked up for the night, Miss Cantelli?'

'Yes, sir.'

'And have you sharpened all the pencils?'

'Don't push your luck, Ira.'

'OK,' my boyfriend grinned. 'Let's go home, honey.'

Home was just over the threshold of Ira's spare bedroom, from which he operated his newborn company, Tech.Com.

Once in the living room, he slipped his tie off and sighed happily. 'That's two excellent clients in two days, Erica,' he rejoiced as he gave me a smacking kiss on the mouth. 'At this rate we'll be a known brand within a year!'

I smiled. Ira was on top of the world. Was now the time to tell him?

'I need a smoke. Order a pizza or something – we're going to celebrate. Back in a mo,' he promised and let himself out through the back door of the small apartment we'd rented together.

It was the second week of October and the snow had fallen, plunging fall right into the dead of winter. The afternoon before, Ira and I had been sipping hot chocolate by the window, naked under the patchwork quilt, admiring the red-and-orange landscape. And just like the sudden onset of winter had fallen upon us, catching us unprepared, so had some unexpected news of my own.

I sighed, changed into my nightie and studied my stomach. I wouldn't be showing for another couple of months. Could I wait that long before telling him? Slipping into my galoshes and throwing a coat over my bare shoulders, I ventured out into the tiny backyard of our first home together. Not exactly a gazelle, I slipped and slid, desperately trying to stay upright, flapping my arms frantically to stay on my feet. He watched me, puzzled and helpless, and before I could even yelp, I landed on my ass in a heap of snow.

'You OK?' Ira laughed as he ditched his cigarette and came over to crouch next to me.

'Argh,' I huffed. 'Sure.' Considering my ankle hurt, that I'd snapped a nerve in my back and looked like a homeless streetwalker, I was peachy.

He smiled down at me, his face red from the cold. How to tell him? It was way too early in our relationship – he'd only asked me to move in with him and into his company just a few weeks before. How could I spring this on him just as he was starting out, and with minimal damage to our relationship?

I looked around, stalling as he helped me up. Our

backyard had suddenly become a layer cake of mud and snow. Depending at what angle you scraped your boots into the ground, you'd get either dirty wet brown caking or the purest, whitest snow. A bit like our present situation. If I could rub my galoshes the right way, it could be a clean, happy start to the rest of our lives. If I scraped haphazardly, I'd find only mud.

I looked at the love of my life, the man of my dreams. Ira Lowenstein was the one I wanted to be with and if we were going to build a family together, here was step one. A little too early, perhaps, but I knew we'd be OK.

'Come on,' he said with a grin and pulled me up, using both hands for balance, I hoped, and not because I was beyond the one-arm job.

He pulled me close and kissed my lips. His nose was cold. 'It's a mess, this backyard, isn't it?' he said.

I nodded, rubbing my cheek against his shoulder.

'Ira…' I swallowed, my heart rate picking up, already tap-dancing against my ribs and in my ears.

I had to tell him. It was now or never. But I kept holding my breath, hoping I'd turn blue in the face. And maybe even be rushed to a hospital where the doctor would finally emerge and put Ira out of his misery with a 'It was touch-and-go there for a while, but now she's perfectly alright and thankfully, so is the baby.'

To which Ira would blink and whisper, 'Baby? I'm going to be a father?' And he'd be so happy, he'd take me home and we'd celebrate with nice hot chocolate and glazed doughnuts.

Ira chuckled, bringing me back to reality. 'I know, I know.

I've been neglecting the garden. But I promise, as soon as spring comes, I'll put up a nice deck for you and we can have BBQ parties and invite all your friends, OK?'

'Maybe even a swing set for kiddies,' I suggested, watching him as my heart leaped into my throat.

Was that the right way to introduce the news? How was I supposed to know?

A glance in his direction told me it probably wasn't, because his red face went snow-white.

'Well,' he tittered. 'It's a bit too soon to talk about that. Maybe one day – who knows?'

My heart thudded against the bottom of my stomach, dead still. *Geronimo*. 'Ira… I'm pregnant.'

'*What*?' he said.

It wasn't a 'What did you say?' what. It was a 'Please tell me you're joking' what.

'Three weeks at the most.'

Ira scrambled and slipped on the ice. I steadied him. Not a good start. His face was sweaty, his eyes wide.

I sighed. 'Look, I know you're shocked. Even I can't believe I'm going to be a mother. But it'll be OK.'

He looked at the ground for a long time, as if trying to find insect footprints in the snow. After what seemed like forever, he glanced up.

'I'm not sure I'm ready to be a father just yet, Erica,' he said quietly. 'I think we should consider our options.'

I blinked. 'Options?' I whispered, understanding but hoping I hadn't.

'We're much too young to start a family. We have a company – our livelihood to nurture. How is a baby going to get our lives into gear?'

And then, the realization. The painful truth. I was too numb to move. But I could still think, and I could certainly still speak.

'You don't love me, do you?' I whispered.

Any man in love with his woman would have been overjoyed to learn she was expecting a baby from him. At least the men in my historical romances would.

He looked at me for a long moment, like when you examine fruit at the grocer's before buying it. *Please say you love me*, I silently willed. *Please don't tell me I've thrown my heart away.*

Ira sighed and wrapped an arm around my shoulders. 'Of course I do, silly. Now why would you get so dramatic?' And then he kissed me tenderly and broke into a grin. 'Let's do it. Let's get married and have kids.'

I stopped holding my breath. 'Really?'

Ira tapped my nose gently. 'I love you – you love me. Hell, how hard can it be?'

I

Comical Visions of Murder

Time: fast-forward to a few years later, to any night of the year. It doesn't make a difference.

'Ow! For Christ's sake, Erica! Can't you keep this place tidier?' Ira grumbled as he tripped over our son Warren's baseball glove in the hall.

Oh, God. Here we go again. I could have sworn Warren had put the glove away when I told him to. I did tell him to – didn't I? I bared my teeth at Ira in a lame effort to smile. One of these days I'd get lockjaw besides migraines. Had I subconsciously left that glove there to trip him?

Place: our new large white-brick house on 3566 Quincy Shore Drive, Boston. Good piece of real estate. It had taken many years and a lot of sacrifices to buy it and make it our home. Ira's company still didn't earn enough to keep us afloat, despite what he always said. And I was happy to do my bit.

But who knew I'd end up like this? Married with children at thirty-four, with thoughts of comic murder drifting through my mind – like clobbering my husband over the head and shoving him in the oven to roast for a couple of days before anyone asked about him. Not that anyone would miss him.

Have you ever, just for a moment, wished your husband would disappear into thin air, or at least to another country far, far away? Or, more simply, go back to being the guy you married ages ago? What the hell had happened to us? I wondered every day. What had started out with a promise of love had in the end become routine, mundane, deathly dull.

I remembered the days I used to serve him his espresso coffee (in bed) in an elegant cup and saucer, but then we'd gone on to just the cup minus the saucer and after Warren was born, Ira was making his own and using styrofoam cups.

And now I was having murderous daydreams, in which I wiped him out of my sight with a single swat of my hand, or pushed him off a cliff (not that there were many on my daily route to work, back from work, picking up the kids and grocery shopping).

But I wasn't the only one faltering. At least I had a reason – many, actually: a full-time job, two kids, a house to run, meals to prepare, laundry to do. While Ira had become a ghostlike presence, appearing late at night and disappearing in the wee hours.

'Are you having an affair?' I'd asked him brusquely one rare Saturday he was home.

He'd looked up from his paper, his eyes wide, studying me, and finally sighed. 'Erica…'

'Just please tell me, Ira. No beating around the bush.'

'No, I'm not having an affair. Besides, when would I even have time?'

He had a point there. Ira was always at work. Assuming

he was at work and not, say, bonking the cashier from the bakery opposite his office building.

He put the paper down and squeezed the bridge of his nose. 'And thanks for dropping this on me the one time you see me at home relaxing, by the way.'

'When else would I ask you when you're never around? Ira, the kids and I never see you anymore,' I said, lowering my voice from attack mode to a more persuading pitch. 'We *miss* you.'

His face softened. 'I know, and I'm sorry. It's just that I'm always so busy. I'm overwhelmed. There's just so much to do and so little time, and Maxine only has two hands.'

His secretary was a college student who came in after her classes to do the paperwork while Ira concentrated on trawling for new clients. He paid her next to nothing, but it was still more than he'd ever paid me. The story of my life. I sighed. Time to make a deal.

'Maybe we could arrange something. If you could spend one day a week with us – like maybe Saturday – then I'll spend some time on your accounts. How's that?'

His eyes widened. 'Really? You'd do that?'

'Of course. We're a family. And it's time we remembered that.'

Ira nodded, his eyes searching mine. 'OK. Thanks. I appreciate it.'

And then he did something he hadn't in a long time. He folded his paper and came over to kiss me on the cheek. I wished it had been on my mouth.

'Things will get better, Erica. The business will pick up and I'll have more time for you, Maddy and Warren – for all of us.'

I nodded. 'I know. It'll be OK.'

That had been three years ago.

Still today, he'd come home and bury himself in his paper or surf the net (in search of more golden egg-laying ducks that would supposedly save his company), taking little interest in Warren, who was now twelve, and Maddy, who was eight. It seemed at times that he simply endured their presence, always too tired to play with them or help them do their homework. The truth was that by the time he got home, I'd already fed, washed, played and homeworked them, so there was nothing left for him to do. Except to *do me*. Which he hadn't in ages, by the way.

What had gone wrong? Exactly when had we started taking the slide? Ira's work was absorbing him completely, killing any other interest in family life. Not that he'd ever been a real family man. He'd tried. He'd tried so hard. But year after year he became more and more detached from us all. We never went places together anymore. He never came to parents' night or to the family reunions at my aunts' Italian restaurant.

He was always cranky but refused to tell me why, no matter how many times I'd sat him down to try to get to the bottom of it. I'd even suggested marriage counseling, but he always said I had too much imagination.

And then one day, it simply got worse.

'Erica, you know I don't like eggplant! If you can't even keep track of the basics, just quit your job already!'

Yeah. And then with what he earned, for the rest of our lives we'd be having our dinners chez *le* Salvation Army.

I scooped up Maddy's dolls and Warren's baseball glove, plunked them in their toy bins and rushed the kids through dinner and off to bed, anxious for the next day to come. If I could only slow the reel down while I was at work or with the kids and my best friend, Paul, and speed up the dreaded few hours Ira was home, my whole life would be made.

I quickly grilled Ira a steak and defrosted a caponata – my grandmother's amazing onion, potato and red pepper dish, minus the eggplant upon which he frowned. But my homebaked (actually, the hotel's in-house baker's I'd passed off as my own) apple pie shut him up almost instantly and he was happy. Until I'd decided to strike the iron while it was hot (mainly while he was home) and talk to him once again about the major root of our arguments.

Life was becoming too hectic and expensive here in the States. Working hours were longer than downtime. Our work–life balance was unbearable. I wanted to go back to my family's homeland in Italy, Tuscany. At one time it had been our common dream. Tuscany would be our haven, the place we'd planned to move to for a life change.

We'd always wanted to buy an old stone farmhouse with haylofts, granaries and tobacco towers and spend our time restoring them before renting them out to paying guests. We'd produce wine and olive oil, and I'd swap my job as manager of the uber-luxurious Farthington Hotel with hanging laundry and sweeping out rooms, because they'd be *our* rooms, *our* property. And our children would see more of us. *Us.* What a nice ring it had.

As I've never suffered having a boss very well, running my own business felt like second nature. I'd stay at home and run the business, bake pies, get a couple of dogs (or maybe not – Ira's allergic) and watch the kids playing in the open fields. Ira would oversee the crops and boss everyone else around. We'd been determined for that to happen one day. Even the kids had grown up under the idea of Tuscany.

Back then, Ira used to say, 'Wow, yeah, absolutely.' Then he switched to 'Someday,' and finally just to a lame smile without a comment. And lately, the smile had disappeared, too.

But I wasn't giving up on our family dream – he'd have to crack sooner or later. So, to get the ball rolling again, I suggested we enroll the kids on an Italian language and culture course.

'Italian?' Ira folded his paper and sighed his usual sigh that always began an argument. 'You're not still going on about Tuscany, are you?'

Going on? So it was like that, was it? 'Ira, you *know* we'd be so much happier. Why shouldn't we do this?'

'Because this is America! Nobody leaves America.'

'Yes, they do. Lots of people are returning to their homelands.'

'Italy isn't our homeland.'

'It is mine.'

'And when was the last time you went to Italy?'

'Every year up until I met you,' I challenged.

But Ira was shaking his head, completely closed to the possibility. Which wasn't fair. This was my life, too. And the children's. I wanted a more genuine existence. I didn't mean cows and sheep, for Christ's sake, but at least some open spaces where we could go biking and for afternoon walks, where the sun shone ten months of the year. Like one of my mother Marcy's size four designer Versace shoes, the city lifestyle here was too tight for me. I needed space to breathe.

'It's out of the question,' he said finally, throwing his paper down.

I followed him into the bedroom, where he began to rummage through his drawers.

I rested my hands on my hips. 'Why? Why is it out of the question?'

'Because I'll never move to Italy. I'd hate it and the children would, as well. Just accept it so we can get on with our lives, OK?'

It would have been easier just to give up and cry in frustration. But I was a strong woman and a mother of three (yes, I'm counting Ira).

'I'll make a deal with you,' I said, feeling my patience slowly strengthening again.

He watched me warily, his hand buried in a neat pile of socks.

'I'll forget about Tuscany – for now – if you agree to let the kids take Italian lessons.'

He groaned. 'Is this one of your tricks, Erica? Because it won't work.'

'It's not a trick. All I want is for them to learn the language. That's all I ask.'

Ira stalled.

'What difference does it make to you?' I urged in earnest. 'I'll be the one ferrying them back and forth to lessons anyway.' I didn't mention I'd also be paying their tuition, because then he'd get defensive about income again. Tech. Com still wasn't doing well (actually, it was a bottomless money pit), but he never wanted to talk about it. 'Don't you remember, Ira? Don't you remember our dreams?'

He shook his head. 'But that's just it, Erica. It was only

ever that – a dream. It's time to wake up. Besides, have you even *thought* about me? About my company? Or am I expected to ditch everything and chase you around the globe?'

'Would you?' I asked hopefully. 'Like you said you would, once upon a time.'

'That was a very long time ago and our lives have changed since then,' he said, demolishing the neat piles of socks in search of his favorite pair and then starting to upturn the second drawer in search of a pair of briefs.

'Changed for the worst,' I muttered. And when he glared at me, I added defensively, 'You're always saying how you hate Boston.'

'That's only when I'm stressed!'

I raised my evil eye at him. 'Ira, level with me here. You're always stressed. And you're really getting on my nerves. I can't remember the last time you and I had a laugh together, or a decent conversation.' Nor could I remember the last time he'd kissed me – the last time I'd felt any love vibes flowing between us, in fact.

'That doesn't mean that I have to bury myself in the Tuscan hills.'

So, it looked as if Ira would rather drive nine-inch nails into his skull before agreeing to Tuscany. That could easily be arranged.

'Listen to me, and listen good,' I snapped, scaring even myself. 'The only reason I want to go is because I still cherish those dreams, as opposed to *you*! It's not just about money or careers! I see the kids only a few hours a day and it's not enough for me. Before we know it, they'll be off to university!'

'That's because you want to be a *hotel* manager,' he scoffed, now bunching his fists.

'No, Ira. I'd rather stay home and cook and be a full-time mother. But I can't. I need to work to support this family.'

Truth was, without my income, we'd still be living in that shitty flat on the edge of town. And I'd never said anything about how the marriage was sucking my life dry. I'd do anything for my kids. And it really didn't matter who made more. We were a family. Weren't we?

Ira knew I was right but didn't give me the satisfaction of admitting it. Instead, he shrugged.

'Find a part-time job, then.'

'A part-time job isn't enough. We have the kids' school tuition, ballet, soccer, school trips and a gazillion other things, not to mention that gas guzzler you continue to drive around town for God knows whose benefit.'

At that, he turned to me, his face reddening. 'We wouldn't be in this situation now if you hadn't left Tech.Com to have a baby! If you'd stayed by my side like a proper wife should!'

I blinked. So that was what it was all about. All these years he'd resented my earning enough elsewhere. Not sharing his dream with him. And now he didn't want to share mine. But I'd never had any choice to stay at Tech.Com. We had children to feed and clothe and shelter and protect. I couldn't keep up with the romantic and impractical notion of the woman who follows her husband to the edge of the Earth. Unfortunately, I was the only one who saw things clearly. Ira had been blinded all these years by his dream, financed by my job. And now he was throwing all my sacrifices back in my face? He was past delusional if he thought he was right.

'A proper wife?' I said, feeling my cheeks burning. 'I did what I had to do to feed my children, seeing that you weren't capable.' I bit my lip, because I'd never wanted to hurt him but knew now I'd been too kind to him. Besides, Ira had never censured himself to be kind to me. So I let him have it. 'Are *you* a proper husband?' I demanded, getting braver by the second. 'The one who hardly glances at his kids anymore when he comes through that door, who stares at the TV while they're trying to talk to him.'

'I need a shirt for tomorrow,' he said.

'They're hanging in your closet,' I snapped over my shoulder as I turned my back on him and yanked off my robe, sliding under the covers, hoping he'd get the message that the conversation was now over.

'My blue striped one isn't.'

'Well wear another one, then.' For once, I was one step ahead of this crazy game called homemaking and he had to nitpick over one shirt? Give me a hotel crisis any day.

'No. I want my blue striped one,' he insisted, like Warren did when he wanted ice cream for dinner.

'Then you know where the iron and ironing board are,' I bit off. 'I have to get up in five hours.'

With a huff, he stalked off into the bathroom and ran himself a bath.

'Can't even iron me one damn shirt... too busy with her own life,' he muttered, just loud enough for me to hear. 'Some housewife you are.'

'Actually, I'm a career woman and a mother *and* a housewife. And I do my damnedest.'

'Could have fooled me,' he corrected coolly as he slammed the bathroom door behind him.

'I'm the one who plays with them! *I* help with the homework,' I shouted through the closed door. 'I'm the one who cleans the house. Cooks, does laundry, gives Maddy a bath. Have you talked to your son lately? He's growing up, you know. But what male role model does he have at home?'

'Your gay buddy who's always slithering around here for free meals! Why doesn't he go back to his supposed *villa* in Italy and leave us alone?' he spat back through the closed door.

'At least Paul is loving. He doesn't push them away and say, "Yes, that's nice, now let me watch TV." You wouldn't notice them even if they painted their faces green. So don't try to make me feel like a bad parent, because if there's one here – it's you!'

Are you getting a sense of déjà vu, dear reader? Then welcome to my life.

'When was the last time you ever left this house without an ironed shirt?' I demanded as I threw myself out of bed to fling the bathroom door open. He was already lying in the tub in a mountain of bubbles. 'Tell me!'

He crossed his arms. 'Quite a few times, actually. How embarrassing for you.'

I could have killed him on the spot. Charged right in there and smashed his head against the pristine ceramic tiles, a red glob against white. Teach the insolent bastard a lesson.

'For *me*? You're the one who should be embarrassed! You don't even take the trash out.'

'I work like an animal,' he shouted, 'twenty-four seven, and now you *decide* you want to go to Tuscany! When are you going to wake up from your stupid dreams?'

Stupid dreams? I pulled out the hairdryer from under the vanity unit, shoved it in the socket and began to straighten my brownish auburn hair. For no reason at all. At every yank, it was like I was trying to straighten the kinks in my life. Besides, the lovely noise drowned his voice as he went on and on.

I looked down at him and saw a bitter old man who cared only about himself. I saw a bitter old woman who was done trying and fighting. I saw the bitter old woman heave a deep sigh and measure the length of the cord of the hairdryer, gauging the distance to the bathtub. It was enough.

I saw my reflection lift the hairdryer high above his useless body and let go. I saw him jolt, the shock in his eyes as he sizzled, jerked once, twice, thrice, like in a magic formula, and finally slide below the surface of the water, like a sea monster that had finally met its match. It felt fantastic to be finally free.

'Are you listening to me?' he yelled, pulling me back to the here and now.

'I'm done listening,' I replied as I unplugged the hairdryer, wound the cord around it as if it were Ira's neck. 'I take care of you – *and* our children *and* this house *and* everything that comes our way, and I do all this on top of my own job. What the hell do you do? Where are you when your children need you – at parents' night, track-and-field day, Madeleine's ballet, at Warren's big games… at bedtime! Where are you?'

He stared at me and I stared back, my breath sawing in and out of my shaking body. Boy, I could feel it, feel the anger oozing out of every pore, like a thick dark liquid that had been pent up inside a barrel for years, fermenting to its most acidic, unbearable point. That was a frustrated, exhausted and murderous working housewife for you. And boy did I need to de-stress.

'I come home from work and clean up the mess *you've* left the night before. Then I cook dinner. *And* do the laundry. And you can't even iron yourself a lousy shirt?'

He stared at me as it slowly sank in and I realized I'd never given him one of my masterpieces that I'd strictly reserved for my poor staff at The Farthington. Maybe I should be my usual belligerent, confrontational self – the self I'd hidden over the years so as not to scare perspective suitors (ha!) away. It sure made me feel better, more in charge; because if I couldn't be in charge, then I was nothing, nobody.

Ira wasn't used to this side of me. My dark comedy side. If only he knew my real thoughts – how many times in my fantasy I'd left him bludgeoned and bleeding to death. I think he was in shock, actually. Then again, so was I. I'd never expected to react like that to what was a normal routine between us lately. But hell, was I proud of myself.

All these years I'd managed to harness my aggressiveness and channel it only into my work, and never onto him, despite the increasing gap between us. Truth was, the daily domestic grind was wearing me out and more and more often, I imagined my husband hanging from power lines, his electrocuted body swinging in the wind like forgotten laundry.

The scary thing was that I still found it hilarious. Was my murderous potential finally about to surface? Would I soon pick up an axe and wipe him out, and then laugh about it? Why was I having these delicious fantasies all this time?

Was I that unhappy? I was beginning to worry. And then, in an effort to return to normality, I'd go into the kitchen and begin to chop onions, blaming the fumes for my tears.

But then all the kids had to do was show me their appreciation for something I'd done for them or draw me a picture and I was instantly rewarded for all my efforts, and thoughts of bludgeoning Ira to death ebbed, disappearing into the fringes of my unconscious. Not that I'd ever do something like that, mind. (Isn't that what murderers say before they kill someone?) But it's nice to fantasize.

I left the bathroom, slamming the door behind me, and buried my head under the pillows, the beautiful image of his dead body keeping me company.

'You have to do something about that grinding,' he said as he climbed into bed next to me. 'It's annoying. Go see your dentist. Maybe he can fix you. And while you're at it, go see a shrink so you can stop talking in your sleep.'

'Anything else?' I asked, crossing my arms in front of my chest.

'Yeah. Do it tomorrow.'

And that, to me, sounded like an ultimatum.

The next morning, as I was getting dressed, he came into the bathroom wearing the damned blue striped shirt. Rumpled and creased.

I sighed. 'Don't be silly. Take that off.'

He obeyed immediately and left it hanging on the doorknob. I brushed my hair into my usual tight bun, so tight it acted as a natural facelift, and applied a thin veil of make-up. I scooped up my coat, ready to leave, only to find Ira sitting on the bed in his trousers and undershirt.

He blinked. 'Where's my shirt?'

I blinked back. 'Your shirt?'

'I thought you'd ironed it,' he exclaimed, shooting to his feet, his eyes checking the bathroom doorknob.

'What, while I was in the bathroom getting dressed, you mean?'

'You told me to take it off so you could iron it!' he squeaked in a panic. Now, he really was going to be late.

'No,' I said slowly, like you talk to foreigners. 'I told you to take it off because you looked silly in a crumpled shirt – not because I was going to drop everything else because you don't like your other nineteen shirts. I have to go to work. See you tonight.'

I didn't even stay to hear his linguistic masterpiece of a rant, instead hustling the kids out in front of me, but it was loud. On the way out, I gently closed the door behind me, but not as gently as usual, and smiled.

2

Operation Seduction?

Among the *ten* (at least) things Ira hates about Erica, the easiest to solve had to be the teeth-grinding. Right? Because if – and only if – I still thought that this marriage was worth it, I could put up with the discomfort of a dental bite for a bit, especially if the reward was possibly a good solid session of marital benefits.

If I could get Ira back to how it used to be in the good old days, surely all the other sources of tension in our marriage would slowly melt away? If there was any chance that deep down, he still had some love for me, I had to do my best to exhume – and resuscitate, eventually – that feeling. Not for me but for my kids.

So there I was, at stage one of Operation Seduction. And if it meant swallowing the bitter pill, so be it. But the horrendous contraption in Dr Jacobs' hands wasn't exactly the size of a pill. It was the size of a Happy Meal burger.

'Here, put this in your mouth,' he said as I backed off in horror.

'No, thanks. I'm not hungry.'

Dr Jacobs, who never looked down at me unless I was in his chair, let out a laugh, turning the bite in his gloved hands. 'Oh, come on, Erica, it's not so bad. It's flexible and soft.'

'So is a rubber ducky. Would you sleep with a rubber ducky in your mouth?' I asked, looking at the gob in disgust. I might as well have gone to bed with rollers in my hair and slathered brown cream all over my face for the effect that it would have on my sex life.

'Just for a couple of nights, Erica. Try it. What have you got to lose?' he insisted.

What did I have to lose? my will to live? It was a revolting piece of work and it gave me gag reflex, only succeeding in making my mouth hurt along with the rest of my teeth. Can you imagine me with one of these things in my mouth and having one of my nocturnal apnea attacks? Images flashed through my mind of me with my eyes bulging out of my head while the air that couldn't get past my nostrils detoured instead to my mouth, only to find that tunnel blocked by a big fat piece of rubber? I was faced with two choices: either dying of suffocation or never having sex again.

'Alright already. Give me the damn ducky,' I sighed.

'Attagirl,' he smiled.

Operation Recuperation Husband had begun.

Three whole frustrated and horny weeks later, I bravely ditched my favorite cow pajamas and bite for one evening and pulled on a pretty nightgown with a lacy bodice. It was do or die, meaning that if he didn't do me tonight, I'd kill him. He *had* to make a damn effort – it couldn't always be me. I needed some cooperation. And so came phase two of my strategy: the sexing-up of the husband.

I crawled over to his side, pressed against his back and whispered, 'Hello…' like we used to in the days of old.

Nothing.

I caressed his shoulders, just the way he liked it.

Still nothing from the other side.

'Ira…?'

He sighed, more like a groan, and turned over to face me. Involuntarily, I stiffened. Not because the torpedo (him) and the rabbit (me) would make yet another baby (I was on the pill), but because we'd lost our intimacy and were now practically strangers.

But there we were, Ira's hand going south and me suddenly changing my mind, silently willing him to stop.

I heard him pant, huff in frustration and finally roll away.

I lay there, stunned, and then turned on the light.

He groaned in annoyance.

'What? What's wrong?' I didn't smell, did I? I'd showered and BO was one of the few problems that I didn't suffer from.

'It's so awkward.'

He felt it, too, then, the distance between us. Maybe now he'd agree to see a marriage counselor. Long moments of equally awkward silence followed and I waited with bated breath for him to open up to me.

'I can't do it,' he finally said. 'I've tried, but you're way too big and I'm too tired to make the effort.'

'Come again?' I said, no pun intended, my eyes searching for him in the low light.

I could see the silhouette of his head and I was happy I couldn't see his face.

He sighed and was silent before he answered. 'All these years I've been on your case about losing weight. And you never listened, never cared. And now you've blown to a size twenty… and it's just too much.'

I sat in stunned silence.

'Look,' he said apologetically. 'I don't mean to hurt your feelings, but you have to face the facts here. A normal woman is a size ten.'

Had he done a study project on it? What did he consider normal? And was this what he'd been thinking all these years during which I gave birth to and nurtured his children – and him? That I wasn't the size of a normal woman? And that loving the woman who had been by his side all these years required an *effort*?

I stared at him, my heart falling, flailing, to the deepest part of me somewhere inside.

'You won't have sex with me because I'm big?' I said, unable to believe it. 'Don't you think that's being a little superficial?'

He shrugged, his eyes downcast. 'Maybe. But I can't keep lying to you. Your body is putting me off. I've begged you to lose weight. I've tried giving you all sorts of signs to make you understand.'

I snorted, too hurt to show how thin skinned I was. 'You mean being an asshole was a sign?'

'There's no reason to be offensive now, Erica.'

'Oh, because you're paying me a *compliment*? You think living with you and all your hang-ups is easy?'

He shrugged again, unable, or unwilling, to elaborate.

'Do you think it's normal to act like this?' I demanded. 'Do you think every man in the world whose wife is a bit big acts like you do? I've seen other men adore their big wives.'

He sighed. 'Contrary to what big women think, men don't like all that flab.'

I blinked back the tears and his face softened.

'Look, I'm sorry, but for years your mother and I have been asking you to do something about your weight.'

Which wasn't true. They'd been bashing me about it, pushing all sorts of surgery at me. Stomach bypasses. Restrictive rings – the works. At home I had a whole library of brochures and printouts courtesy of the two of them.

'I don't want to undergo surgery, if that's what you're so subtly hinting at yet again,' I snapped.

He groaned. 'You know what? It's late. I have to get up early tomorrow.'

'You can't just drop this bomb on me and then turn over and go to sleep. What kind of a monster are you?'

'A tired, exhausted and fed up one,' he sentenced, scooping up his pillows (all four of them) and leaving our bedroom with a slam of the door.

I sat in bed with my hands over my mouth, staring at my flannel pajamas swinging from the hook on the door. They seemed to say, *See, stupid? You should have stuck with us and saved yourself the embarrassment.*

I'd tried to skirt around the various issues of my teeth-grinding, talking in my sleep, hoping it was just a phase, but nothing. That was it. He'd spelled it out to me, loud and clear. It had boiled down to lose weight or lose him. This was his ultimate ultimatum.

I honestly hadn't seen it coming and now I wasn't sure how traumatizing the latter result would be, to be honest.

When a man is no longer interested in what's under your dress, there's no amount of cooking, ironing or candlelit dinners that will save the day. Once he's off you (literally, too), he's off you for good. Never mind all the efforts you've made to try to see him as George Clooney. Never mind all the sacrifices you've made, period.

Outside, the iris bulbs I'd planted were somewhere deep in the ground, under three inches of the first snow, enveloped in the cold dark earth, practically dead until the first warmth caressed them back to life. In spring, they'd sprout and bloom, as beautiful as ever, right on cue. But it was going to be a long winter.

I leaned out the window, taking in the silent white world that was my dormant garden, and remembered one night on a Sicilian beach when, as a child, I'd had to pick my way through campfires and couples making out. Even my cousins who had brought me along had disappeared. That sense of loneliness had overwhelmed me then and now, instead of snow-filled clouds, I saw starry Sicilian skies and smelled the smoke from the campfires from so many years ago.

My husband doesn't want to make love to me anymore.

How had Ira and I changed so much? There were so many hidden feelings between us and the good ones were rapidly fading like stars at dawn.

Maybe being thinner would make a difference between us. I'd tried everything else and nothing had worked. If I lost weight, it would improve my life on all levels and it would bring me back to life. But would it bring the old

Ira back into my bed? Just how badly did I want him back there? Surely I'd forget him if I had to. Just like my mattress that didn't have memory foam technology, meaning it was as if Ira never had been in my bed at all. I, too, could erase him from my memory, as if he'd never existed. Could I do it if it came to that?

3

Jump to Stage Four?

'Dump him!' my best friend, Paul, exclaimed as we lugged our delicatessen food home.

Freshly baked ciabatta with oregano, stuffed peppers, baked potatoes with rosemary, veal *involtini* parcels simmered in white *inzolia* wine and my favorite, tiramisu. Take *that* to the bank, Ira.

'Don't be ridiculous,' I said as I hefted the bags and inhaled the marvelous fragrances, already envisaging a revenge feast.

Well, maybe a goodbye-to-food dinner, kind of like my own version of The Last Supper or something.

'I can't believe it. What am I saying? Of *course* I believe it. That little shit is capable of anything,' Paul scoffed. '*Too tired to make the effort. Blown to a size twenty.* As if he was Aidan friggin' Turner!'

Paul sooo got me. 'I know, right?'

Every week, the same story – Paul telling me to dump

my husband and me biding my time, waiting for a miracle to happen. Only now I knew it wasn't just our hectic work life sapping the strength out of him that made him always cranky. It was my fat ass.

He no longer saw me as he used to and it was true – I'd gone a long way down from the young preppy, free-spirited and sexy girl I used to be. At least I had been before the kids. Ira couldn't understand why I'd never lost the baby weight. Fact was, it wasn't just the baby weight. It was the doughnut weight, the apple pie weight, the tiramisu. It had nothing to do with the baby fat.

Yes, I'd packed it back on after Warren and Maddy were born, but I was simply returning to my old (big) self who Ira hadn't seen before because he'd met me during my two-year stint of slimness when I'd been a size fourteen. And even then he'd had something to say about it. He'd told me I was pretty but that I needed to lose just a tiny bit of weight. What a joke.

Ira didn't understand me. I was born hungry and nothing could fill me. I liked to blame my mother for never loving me the way she loved Judy and Vince, my siblings. I liked to blame my love for cooking, or Le Tre Donne, my aunts' Italian restaurant. Or even the desserts section at my local supermarket. But in truth, eating made me happy. It comforted me and made me feel like everything was alright. And up until then, I hadn't given a damn about my weight. Inside, I was still me. And I still managed to dress nicely thanks to the plus-size sections in Macy's department store.

But it was soon becoming obvious to me – once my La

Vie En Rose designer shades had dropped off my nose –
that the weight was really starting to weigh me down. I
was a busy working mum who could never go fast enough,
with never a moment to spare, always running late, always
dropping things on the way to the car and wheezing when
I bent to pick them up. Of course if I lost some weight, I
could actually keep up with the kids and face anything they
threw my way.

Who knows, maybe I was hoping I'd lose weight out of
sheer force of concentration and become this irresistible
woman whom Ira couldn't help but make love to. Because
dieting was hard. I was always too hungry and there was
always amazing food around me. If I didn't have time to
bake it or go back to Little Italy, there was always the shop
around the corner.

'I'd say you're at stage four,' Paul diagnosed, which,
according to his scale of one to five in troubled relationships,
was just before divorce.

'Nonsense! We're just in a rut.'

'And you're in denial.'

'Is it really just because I'm big?' I asked.

There had to be more, even if, essentially, Ira had dwelled
on my looks. He'd literally spelled it out to me, but it still
hurt to believe.

He shot me a skeptical glance. 'Sunshine, only a real man
deserves a real woman. That's my official version. My real
opinion is Ira's always been a shit.'

'That's not true,' I countered. When we'd met, Ira was
different. He was sexy, alluring, with so many goals in life.
I huffed. 'He doesn't even want to go to Tuscany anymore.'

Paul had been helping me trawl for farmhouses through an Italian connection of his in Siena but so far, nothing was affordable. He'd suggested settling for a normal house in the country, but I'd put my foot down. No more settling for me. I wanted the real deal this time. I'd earned it.

'Doesn't want to go to Tuscany?' Paul echoed. 'The guy is beyond helpless. What are you waiting for to split the scene?'

I stopped to admire the doughnuts in the bakery window. Paul tugged on my arm.

'Sunshine, *no*.'

I cast a longing look at him, my best friend, the one person with whom I could chew the breeze and be myself with, something we rarely did around anyone else.

'Just one,' I pleaded. It had been ages. Well, two days, really. Oh, the chocolate glaze! 'What's one measly doughnut? Besides, whose side are you on? Why can't I be big and be loved all the same? *You* love me.'

'Sunshine,' Paul said. 'I love you, but I'm never gonna have sex with you. You know I don't do women.'

'If you weren't gay, would you? Do me?'

Paul chuckled. 'And you need to ask? Of course I would.'

'Even though I'm big?' I insisted.

'You're not big. You're beautiful. Like the Renaissance women – soft and squeezable. Who wouldn't want you?'

'Then don't give me a hard time if I want a doughnut.'

Paul looked at me, his eyes shining with what I knew was compassion, and sighed. 'Alright, but only if you promise to leave him.'

'Paul! All I want is a damn doughnut.'

'And all I want is for you to be happy. Erica, you can't go on like this. The kids can't go on like this. You need to send him to hell once and for all.'

As if it were that easy. I remember the old Ira and our evenings together, having a quiet dinner and a chat on the sofa.

And very often, we'd take it from the sofa to the bedroom. Now, there was nothing much left to take anywhere. The person I'd become – although I kept a roof over his head and food in his belly – had *disappointed* him.

I hoped he was just going through a phase. Because I couldn't stand it. And if I couldn't stand by my man in his time of need, then we were toast. I'd promised to love and cherish him. For the sake of our marriage. For the sake of our children. I could deal with it. If I ran a leviathan like The Farthington, I should be able to do everything, including saving my marriage. Provided I still wanted to.

Because sometimes, and it was becoming more often than not, I wished I could just… wiggle my nose and make him disappear. Or at least make him change. But that wasn't happening. He'd spoken his mind. The die had been cast. It was lose weight or lose him – live in Boston or go to Tuscany on my own. But I was no longer sure I wanted to play by his rules.

'So, no doughnuts – are you're saying Ira was right?' I challenged.

Paul rolled his dark eyes. 'It's not your looks or your sex appeal I'm worried about. It's your health.'

'I'm perfectly fine,' I assured.

'You are now. But what about when you get older? A fit body is a successful body. And it houses a happy mind.'

A fit body houses a happy mind... Could he be right? Would I find happiness on the lower end of the bathroom scale? Would being lighter not only make me feel better, but also make me more satisfied about my life? Technically, yes. I'd look better and feel better. Was it really down to being slim again? Yes – I remembered the looks I got when I was thin and it felt great. It had empowered me.

There was no cartwheel I couldn't (in my younger years – I haven't tried lately) accomplish, no race I couldn't win. I'd wake in the mornings thinking, wow! Not only do I not feel like shit anymore, but I also feel good! No headaches, no stomach aches, no backaches that would keep me twisting and turning in bed (thrashing like a pig on a spit, according to Ira). I'd have to grip the bars of our wrought-iron bed to be able to turn over, my back was so bad.

'You're starting to sound like my mother,' I huffed. 'How did we get from talking about your latest squeeze to me?'

Paul shrugged. 'Because for the last few years you've been miserable – and Carl's boring the crap out of me. I'm thinking of a way to get rid of him. Speaking of which, tell me again how you killed Ira last night,' he giggled, suddenly more flippant, and I grinned despite myself.

It was a harmless game, really, but a real sanity-saver. I forgot all about the doughnut as pleasant images caressed my mind, and I brightened and stifled a giggle.

'I hung him upside down to dry in the sun for days, like my nonna Silvia's ham joints,' I answered. 'And when his carcass was ready, I made some real groovy leather bags.'

Paul's eyes flashed. 'That's still too light a treatment for Ira.'

I don't need to tell you that Ira and Paul weren't bosom

buddies. My husband wasn't tolerant of anyone different from himself. It was a wonder he married me, an Italian Catholic, when his family had always hoped that one day, he'd meet a nice thin Jewish girl.

Ira tolerated Paul politely enough when he was around, but in the evening, he'd sniff the air and sigh. 'I can tell by the smell of the cheap perfume that your gay friend's been here again.'

Not even the fact that Paul was a respected freelance costume designer who traveled the world for his living (and whose butt had never seen a desk chair) could sway Ira.

'Sunshine,' Paul said, cupping my clenched jaw with his free hand and bringing me back to reality as we reached my front door without my realizing. 'Instead of having these visions of murder, why don't you just leave him already?'

Why? he kept asking. For two excellent reasons: one was twelve years old and the other eight.

'I can't. He's my husband.'

'What, you don't think you could live without him? Please tell me that not even you are that masochistic?' Paul begged.

Ira's revelation of his lack of desire for me certainly put things in perspective. I was living with a man who didn't find me attractive. How far were we from the end? Were we really at stage four and I was just in denial? Was it worth trying to save a marriage that Ira didn't seem to care about anymore?

After dinner, Paul sat down with Maddy (did I mention I loved him and would marry him in a heartbeat?) and did their usual thing, drawing clothes for her paper dolls. She was becoming alarmingly similar to my mother, who was a fashion victim and the emptiest head on the planet if you didn't count Maddy's paper dolls.

At eight years old, she was so confident, so pretty.

Please, God. Make her as intelligent and grounded as she is pretty, and not an airhead like Marcy or my sister, Judy. Make her be a good wife and mother, if that's what she wants, and spend time with her family. Make her be successful and happy with anything she wants to do.

And please, let Warren be a patient man, and be kind to his wife and children, even if she isn't a raging beauty. Let him understand the beauty inside people.

I sat on a kitchen stool with a glass of wine, observing my mini three-dollar-each succulent cacti plants, perfectly aligned like little soldiers on the kitchen windowsill, their thorns sticking out proudly as if to say, look at us – we don't need Erica's TLC! We can survive without water! And boy, could they. I'd forget to water them for weeks and they'd be there for me, resistant, alive and beautiful, even with little purple or pink flowers sticking out from the top, no matter how much I neglected them.

I wish my poor kids knew the same survival techniques, but I guess I was asking too much. Hell, I wish *I* knew them. Look at me – I can survive without sex with my husband! What doesn't kill you makes you stronger.

Maybe one day I'd have time to plant a beautiful rose bush right by the front door, so every time I came home I'd be greeted by beauty. Roses, the symbol of love. I sighed. Life wasn't perfect and if I had no sex life, there were also other things I still had to master – like being the prefect wife. I was trying with all my heart. In any case, I always had plan B: envisioning the day my fantasies of killing my husband became reality. God, sometimes life was a pain in the ass.

4

Mother Marcy?

'Ira told me you're still refusing surgery. Really, Erica, it's the least you could do to save your marriage,' my mom scolded me as she took a sip of her Martini.

I glared at my mother, sitting in her size four YSL designer number opposite me at lunch at The Farthington Hotel, my domain. She never came to see me at work, so I'd figured it must be something important, namely her next shopping spree in Europe.

Marcy had never really been a hands-on mother, particularly with me. Sometimes it seemed she simply tolerated my existence, from my birth all the way up until… well, now. But at the same time, she doted on her only son, Vince, and shared a fashion fever with my sister, Judy, with whom she still can be seen today storming the designer shops in the city center.

Marcy didn't want to be called mum by any of us and even her seven grandchildren had to call her Marcy. She can't stand the sight of elderly people because she was terrified of aging and had never said anything nice about the way I looked (although I couldn't blame her most of the time) and my lifestyle choices.

At least *I* got out of bed every morning and earned myself a living, as opposed to Marcy, who had my dad to keep her in sexy negligees and shiny kimonos until noon at fifty-nine years of age (I'm not kidding you) and designer numbers in size four. (*Four?* Four! How the hell did she give birth to three kids and stay a size four? She didn't exercise, and she smoked and drank like a stevedore.) And here I was, a glorious size twenty and ever dodging the umpteenth diet.

If it hadn't been for my nonna Silvia and my mum's three sisters, Zia Maria, Zia Martina and Zia Monica, we'd have certainly died. My siblings, Judy and Vince, of malnutrition and me of obesity (I was the only one smart enough to have a stash of junk food under my bed). And here she was talking down to me as usual, under the pretense of exasperated motherly love.

'What will it take for you to understand that you can't keep a man, looking like you do?'

I sighed. Yes, we all knew I was big, thank you very much. But I'd tried to lose weight. God knew I'd tried and tried and tried. And failed and failed and failed. I couldn't seem to stay disciplined. Wasn't I making enough sacrifices in my life as it was? What was wrong with indulging in a little cream puff at the end of a long, hard day during which I'd done both the manager's shift *and* played the homemaker, saving the hotel from yet another disaster while keeping the kids from climbing the walls?

OK, so sweets were killing me instead of helping me improve the quality of my life. Maybe if I renounced one every now and then... No. I had to renounce them entirely. For my health. It was time to admit defeat. Even I could see that. But hell, was it too much expecting my husband still to love me in the process?

It wasn't as if he was an Adonis himself. He was now balding, bad-tempered and almost scrawny – nothing like the guy I'd fallen in love with. Back then, he was good-looking, charming, ambitious and sexy. And so was I. We'd been, I used to think, a perfect fit. But the years hadn't been kind to us – neither physically nor emotionally.

'Don't you think it's time, Erica?' Marcy persisted.

'Time for what?' I replied as I swallowed a generous forkful of shrimp salad. I loved the pink sauce.

She took a sip of her Martini and rolled her eyes. 'To lose weight, of course. Think of how your love life would improve – think of the sex.'

'Eww. I can't believe I'm even having this conversation with you,' I said, raising my evil eyebrow at her.

She shrugged her slim silk-covered shoulders, so glamorous she'd put any Hollywood star to shame.

'I'm just saying. Your whole life would improve if you lost weight. So please at least consider the option of surgery. You'd see the results in a matter of months. And think of the *clothes*.'

I squirmed involuntarily. There it was – clothes. Her dream – my nightmare since childhood. Marcy dragging me to Macy's was still one of my most traumatizing early-life experiences. Nothing pleased her. When I tried something on, she'd tut and shake her head, asking the salesladies, in a very loud voice, if there was a *larger* size. And when they coughed and whispered that there wasn't, she'd check the seams to see if the outfit could be widened (by my grandmother Silvia or aunt Martina, of course – Marcy couldn't sew a stitch to save herself and still can't today).

Then, totally mortified, I'd look at the beloved item and mumble, 'You know, I really don't like it anyway.'

At which point she'd open her mouth to say something but think better of it.

Sometimes there would be a party and I'd have to get a fancy outfit, usually a dress. My after-school look was baggy jeans and a T-shirt, but I wasn't blind. I saw the nice accessories and stuff, and my arty soul was already longingly matching this with that item as I walked past the racks, pretending not to care my size was, for a kid my age, unheard of, nor that I'd forever be Miss Fashion Pariah.

So glitzy Marcy would sigh. 'Go into the changing room, get undressed and I'll bring you whatever I can find.' Then she'd turn to the sales reps. 'Ladies, I'll need *all* the help I can get from you today.'

Do you know how many times I stood there behind Macy's dressing room drapes, practically naked at Marcy's mercy, with that offending neon light and those deforming circus mirrors pointing at my butt, waiting for her to find a piece of cloth that could manage to span the width of my body?

Now keep in mind that it's *my* mom we're talking about and not, say, yours, who was probably thrilled to see you in a nice dress, looking all pretty and waiting for your prom date. (My boyfriend, Peter DeVita, the only one I'd ever had up until then, moved away just before my prom.)

And every season the same story. I was sick of it. As much as I liked fashionable clothes, I didn't want them if they were going to cost me so much pain and humiliation. So in the years that followed, I bought an incredible number of shoes and bags, all cool and fashionable.

I created my 'wear it with your baggy jeans' look. It didn't catch on at school, though. Could you imagine me in an enormous lilac off-the-shoulder dress that 'tapered' down the hips? No, I didn't think so either, unless you figured me as one of the dancing hippos in Disney's *Fantasia*.

Why was it so difficult for Marcy to understand that not every woman could dress and look like a model? That for some people it was difficult even to look decent? She'd been born gorgeous. I hadn't. Why couldn't she just chill out and concentrate on my good qualities, like my excellent communication and organizational skills? The fact that I was a great cook, a great manager and a very hands-on mom. All qualities she'd never had.

And now, at almost thirty-five, I felt like the unhappy high-school girl again. Was this my life, running around in ever-decreasing, sad circles? Was there to be no pleasure whatsoever in my life? Never, ever again?

I turned in my seat to call my head waiter. 'Mitch, can you have someone bring me the dessert cart, please?'

'Of course, Mrs. Lowenstein.'

Marcy's mouth fell open. 'Dessert? Aren't you full enough?'

I looked at her, all dolled up and daintily wiping her mouth. No. I'd never be full, because the emptiness inside me went miles deep. Nothing could sate my hunger for love, my need to feel accepted even if I didn't look like Judy or didn't, not even at ten years of age, fit into Marcy's clothes. I know because I'd tried playing dress-up in her closet once when I was a little girl and had gone back to my room heartbroken. Not even her shoes had fit me.

As she graciously declined the cannoli, the Sachertorte and even the almond parfait, I motioned to Mitch for a slice of tiramisu. Spoonful after spoonful, I could already feel the joy and satisfaction spreading inside me, dissolving Ira's unkind words.

Marcy leaned in. 'I'm talking life-changing surgery to you and you eat life-threatening foods?' she hissed. 'Erica, what is the matter with you? Have you got a death wish?'

And then it struck me that if Marcy hadn't always been so judgmental, making me feel inadequate and blubbery, I might have liked myself a little more, for both Ira and myself. Just enough not to feel ugly or, worse, dull. And then I wouldn't have felt so empty all the time and wouldn't need to comfort-eat to compensate for the pain inside me. If I'd had my mother's life and looks, I'd have been happy. But if I'd simply had her love and support, I'd have been serene and self-accepting.

Most of all, if I could better my life and move to Tuscany (where I'd chase my laughing children across the golden fields), I wouldn't have to sit here and listen to this.

But here I was for now, an overweight, under-loved, struggling career woman-slash-housewife forever trying to finish tasks and keeping on top of it all. Ever trying to lose weight with three-week diets (I couldn't manage for longer) that only made me fatter than before I'd started.

As I sat there and silently ate my tiramisu under Marcy's resigned eyes, I realized that if it hadn't been for Warren's birth, Ira wouldn't have proposed to me in that snowy, slippery backyard thirteen years ago.

And now with one unkind word, I'd been catapulted back to my teenage years, once again conscious of my heavy bum and heavy dark clothes. OK. I was obese. Got it. Now what was I going to do with that information? What was I going to do with all the emotions bubbling and festering, like an infected wound, inside me? With the fear of failing my diet? The anxiety, the humiliation of remaining me when everyone else expected me to look like a model?

And now, after two kids, with years of not being able to get to the gym and eating up everything from the kids' plates as well as mine, here I was, a product of my own unhappy choices. You can't imagine what a big part frustration played. You drink a glass of water and you instantly start bloating, bloating, bloating until you start to leaven like bread. Then one horrible morning, you look down and can't see your feet anymore. And when you search your once pretty face in the mirror, you see two of them, or at least one the size of two.

I desperately looked into myself as I swallowed my dessert and my tears so Marcy wouldn't see, and delved for the me I once met briefly fifty kilos ago. The one who had lured Josh Irons onto a moonlit English beach and driven all those British boys mad. The one who, albeit only for a few years, fit into the coolest clothes. The one with the awesome butt. And the confidence of a lioness.

Now, I was a big, fat clawless cat, meekly wandering through the wilderness, trying to get to the other side unscathed, all the while graceful antelope, sleek wolves, jackals and hyenas were passing me and turning away in scorn. I was an unwanted stray in the jungle of my own life.

And Ira wasn't having sex with me until I fit on his lap

without the two of us bowling over. How could the world want you if your own husband didn't accept you? How could your man love you if you recoiled in horror at the sight of yourself?

Plus, lately I was hungrier than ever because Ira would watch me like a hawk at dinner, scowling if I ever went for a second piece of bread or put too much on my plate. But he heaped his up to the ceiling, because he was skinny. The truth was he had skinny arms and legs and bony shoulders (how come I'd never noticed that before?), and was actually much shorter than I thought.

And so because I had this immense emptiness to fill, when the coast was clear, I'd sneak a snack between doing the dishes and the laundry, gobbling it down in one quick gulp lest he figured me out. Which of course he almost always did. His radar would bleep and he'd sneak up behind me and tap me on my shoulder, growling his usual, 'Christ, you're not eating again, are you?' Ever tried swallowing when someone's just scared the crap out of you?

For a family of no specific religion, Christ had made many an appearance in our house, and in every room, too. In the bathroom: 'Jesus Christ, Erica, why don't you step on that scale and face reality?' In the living room: 'Jesus Christ, Erica, why don't you move over? You're taking up the whole sofa!' And finally in the bedroom: 'Jesus Christ, you're snoring again!'

At the beginning of my diets, I was always a loose twenty, meaning my jeans would fit comfortably. After a stint of dieting, I'd lose some weight, even to the point that I needed a belt, and then, boom – I shot right back up and *over* size twenty. Which meant my clothes became so tight they cut into my waist and stretched across my boobs, buttons threatening to pop, leaving unsightly gaps.

'By the way, are you wearing a nude-colored bra again?' Marcy said. 'Why are you trying your best to look like Mrs. Doubtfire? What about the sheer pleasure of being sexy and beautiful? It's important to a woman, but you don't understand because...' Marcy closed her mouth and took another swig of her Martini.

I looked at her expectantly. 'What? Because I've never been sexy and beautiful?'

And down she went with the 'I never said thats' and 'Why do you have to put words in my mouths?'

All my life I'd had to listen to Marcy praising Judy's mermaid figure and how all the boys went gaga over her and how proud she was of her. Never mind that Judy went through guys like an Eskimo through snow and that she'd have been a high school dropout if I hadn't helped her through that year she came home pregnant. Never mind that prior to that, Judy had been coming and going every evening, and that for her, *every* night was date night. I couldn't even get a friend to come over on a Friday night because they were all busy out with boys as if the world were ending and they didn't want to die virgins.

Was this what it had boiled down to? My own family not accepting me because of the way I looked? Was losing weight really all it would take to make my own mother and my husband love me?

5

Cuts Like a Knife

So at the tender age of thirty-four and because I wanted to be happy again (and possibly have another husband-induced orgasm if I wasn't asking for too much), I accepted it was time. After twelve years of marriage to Ira, and with a great deal of 'support' from my mother, I'd been bullied, badgered and finally blackmailed into it.

For the first time, Marcy volunteered to come over at least once a week and spend time poring over brochures and websites, making appointments for me with doctors of all kinds, psychologists, psychiatrists, as if I'd suddenly become this big case, or someone very important to her. She'd take care of it all and all I had to do was just show up. Like some star on the red carpet.

It felt kind of nice, to have her there, encouraging me, telling me I was doing the right thing for once, and that I wouldn't be sorry, and that I should just wait and see how my life would change. If only she'd been there for me like this when I was a kid and really needed my mother's guidance and not a stand-in crew of relatives. It would have been nice.

So with her support, I was going under the knife to lose weight. And, let's face it, to save my marriage. Now, things were about to change for good. The next day, I was going to have one of those operations that you can never be too fat for and that was supposedly going to change my life.

Who was I doing this for, anyway? For a husband who wouldn't sleep with me, as a form of punishment, until I got down to a size ten? Yeah, like that was happening. Was it even worth it? It wasn't like the final prize was a night with Aidan Turner or something – that sort of fun was still restricted to my dreams.

I picked up the phone and dialed Paul's number.

'Yellowh,' came his beloved voice, and I cracked.

'I can't do it,' I whispered, my voice hoarse.

Silence. A long one.

'Paul? Did you not hear what I just said?'

'I'm thinking, I'm thinking. Just tell me why.'

I swallowed the knot in my throat. 'I'm afraid. What if I die, Paul? Who's going to take care of Warren and Maddy? Can you see Ira raising them? Can you? Because I sure as hell can't!'

'Calm down, Erica. Relax. You know your aunts and I would never leave the kids alone at Ira's mercy. Is there any other reason?'

'Of course not,' I lied. 'What other reason could there be?'

'Oh, just fear of regaining the weight and having to admit defeat and realizing you just missed your last boat to happiness. Or, paradoxically, fear of losing all your protective padding and having to face the world a much slenderer thus, according to your devious mind, more vulnerable woman.'

Good old Paulie had me down pat.

'So? What if?' I sniffed. 'What do I do? The op is tomorrow.'

'Honey, I can't tell you what to do. Is there a distinct possibility you could die? That's why they make you sign a waiver. Are you never going to pack it back on again? Who knows? And probably, if you start eating again, you'll blow the whole operation, pun intended.'

I sniffed and dashed a hand across my eyes. He was right.

'Sweetie, what I *do* know is that if you don't go through with it, tomorrow morning you're going to groan again because tying your shoes requires just about the same effort as lassoing crazy cows – no pun intended this time.'

I nodded into the phone and let out a loud laugh, followed by a howl of pain, humiliation and frustration. Why was being a woman so difficult?

'What does Ira have to say about it?' he asked, and I snorted.

'He's beside himself, of course, as if being thin were a solution to all our problems.'

'Well, Erica, maybe not to yours as a couple, but to yours health-wise, along with other things… Ever think of that?'

Being thin. It wouldn't just be about fitting on Ira's lap or into nicer clothes, of course, or even Marcy's approval. It would mean not worrying that airplane seats are too narrow for my butt, or that the seat belt won't stretch across my belly, leaving me the only person in the craft bouncing around like a rubber ball from wall to wall and, ultimately, to my death (and that of other people's) in case of turbulence or a crash. I could already see the headlines:

Flight 2378: Obese woman bounces passengers to death, then finally slams head-on into the cabin door and dies of severe concussion. Cabin crew safe.

No matter what other things you had going for you, no matter how pretty you were or how good your hair and teeth were, if you were fat, people still looked at you with pity. I hated that. At work, no one looked at me with pity. At work, my size was of no consequence because there, I became a goddess. But once I got back in my car and homeward...

'I *do* want to be slim,' I sobbed finally.

'Sunshine, if you drop – and you will – at least six dress sizes, you'll be able to go cycling with your kids and play tag and everything else without giving yourself a minor stroke every time.'

Again, I nodded, and it was as if Paul saw me over the phone.

'Good. Now, get some sleep. I'll be there tomorrow morning to drive you to the hospital.'

'OK,' I sniffed, drying my eyes for good this time. Enough tears for one day.

But then, eight hours later, as I donned a horrid hospital nightie, the kind that leaves your ass bare and cold, I wasn't so sure again. What would happen if I called the whole thing off? Did I really need to go through with something so big? Or would I rather stay this big?

I could walk away right now if I wanted. I wasn't shackled

to an operating table yet. The choice was mine. But because I was free to make my own decision, I knew that if I really did chicken out now, tomorrow I'd be in the same situation as Paul had said – hating my body, struggling to tie my shoelaces (although I actually bought slip-ons to make my life easier) and panting to keep up with my sporty children.

Now, I had the opportunity to change all that in a snip. I'd spent days running tests: heart rate, blood, breathing patterns and everything else. Shrinks had made sure I wouldn't freak out at not seeing Angelina Jolie in the mirror (which was never going to happen anyway, I was aware) and that I understood the weight loss would take months, etcetera.

Just before my op, Paul came in to sit with me. He saw my family (led by Marcy, for once) come, deposit kisses on my forehead and go. 'Too choked up,' Paul explained lamely, about me getting sliced to pieces, to stay a little longer on such an important day.

'You're still here,' I countered.

'Don't kid yourself. I'm only here for the drama,' he winked, and at that moment I knew Paul, who was as gay as they make 'em, was more man than any other in my life.

Looking into Ira's eyes, on the other hand, I saw myself the way I never had and never cared to. I saw a fat, ugly, pathetic woman willing to go under the knife to keep her husband.

They came for me twenty minutes later.

'Here's for drama,' I squeaked, and Paul squeezed my hand – real hard – and gave me a quick peck on the cheek before they wheeled me away.

'I'll be waiting here. See you later, sunshine.'

I was left in a room all by myself, staring up at the Styrofoam square ceiling panels with no one but the ghosts in my past and the demons of my present. Being dumped there like a slab of raw meat was enough to make me want to jump and run for the emergency exit stark naked (who cared if anyone died of shock or exposure to my blubber?). Also, I couldn't take my mind off Madeleine and Warren. What would happen to them if I croaked on this very table in the next few hours? Ira couldn't cook to save himself, and as far as keeping a household running, forget it. They'd have social services round by the end of the week.

I choked on a lump in my throat and coughed. Who was going to get them ready for school and ferry them back and forth? My mom? Can you imagine Marcy, lumbered with two kids? Thank God indeed for my aunts and Paul.

And now, lying on my back, ready to be diced, there was a distinct, blood-chilling possibility that I wouldn't wake up from the op. Did I really want to be skinny that badly? Hell, yes. I knew that now. I was tired of fighting. I wanted the easy way out now, please. I needed a sign that everything would be OK after this. That there could and would be a new me. And out of nowhere, silly, irrational tears began to trickle from my eyes and sideways into my ears, cold and abundant.

A beeping sound made me jump. Was it my heart monitor indicating something? Maybe an oncoming massive heart attack that would prevent me from going ahead with it... I turned over in the bed, careful not to dislodge the patches above and under my breasts, and touched a solid rectangular object under my sheet. A cellphone? I pulled it out from under the covers and looked at it, frowning. It was

Ira's. He must have dropped it when he bent over to kiss me and now he was texting me to tell me he was coming back for it. Ira couldn't live without his cellphone.

I pushed the button and squinted at the tiny wording:

I'll be waiting for you – stilettos and no panties, sexy boy!

I gasped. Sexy boy? My monitor flatlined for a second, then went berserk as I absorbed the words. *Sexy boy?* Was it just a friend goofing around, maybe? My heart pounding out of control, I quickly texted back:

And what exactly do you want me to do to you, pussycat?

The answer was almost immediate:

Whatever you want. I'm horny.

A lover! Another woman! No wonder he wasn't interested in sex with me, the bastard! It had nothing to do with me being big, or my teeth-grinding or even talking in my sleep! And I was going to have an operation to try and win him back?

Before I knew what I was doing, I'd ripped off my patches and wound the bed sheets around my naked body, almost knocking over the nurse who had come in to prepare me for the surgical banquet. They'd have a long wait, those butchers.

'Mrs. Lowenstein! What are you doing?'

'I'm sorry!' I cried and swiped at my tears as, barefoot, I burst through the doors and down an endless corridor to where Paul was waiting. A myriad of doctors, nurses, interns and patients all turned to stare at the quasi-naked five-foot-ten mountain of flesh blazing a trail past them, followed by a tiny nurse wielding a mask.

Paul looked up from his magazine, his eyes round. 'Erica...?'

'You wanted drama!' I yelled as I darted past him.

'What?' he called after me.

'Just run!' I cried behind my shoulder, scooping up the bed sheets around me, dodging stretchers, wheelchairs and crash carts as Paul, juggling my overnight bag and handbag, caught up.

I hadn't run this fast since I chased my school crush, Tony Esposito, down a back lane to see who he was secretly going out with.

And soon we were out in the parking lot, me pulling my coat on over my quasi-naked body as we dashed past startled faces. I must have looked a sight. It was no wonder Ira preferred some skinny bitch in stilettos.

Once at the wheel, I shifted into Drive and burst into tears.

'Sweetie,' Paul wheezed as he jumped in and I took off with a screech, burning rubber. 'We talked about this. You could have just told me you'd changed your mind about the op. No biggie.'

It took me a few minutes to be able to breathe properly, let alone speak. I rounded out of the parking lot and burst into traffic.

'He's got someone else, the bastard!' I sobbed, tears blinding me so I couldn't see where we were going. 'It wasn't about me being big, it was about her being smaller!'

Paul gasped. 'Shut up! You're shitting me!' Then his eyes swung back to the road.

'I shit you not!' I cried, swerving just in time to avoid an oncoming car. 'She told him to hurry because she was pantie-less and horny!'

'Erica…'

'This is ridiculous. I almost let them friggin' dice me like a chicken. And for whom? For a pseudo-husband who's got a lover in stilettos? God, I'm so pathetic.'

'Erica…'

'What the hell's wrong with me? I could have died on that table, and he knew it! And he sent me all the same!'

'Erica!' Paul screamed.

'What?' I screamed back.

'We're both going to die if you don't slow down and stay in your lane!'

I turned back to the traffic and suddenly, I didn't know where I was.

Paul's hand steadied the wheel as he sighed. 'Pull over.'

I did as I was told (does that surprise you?) and broke down, my head buried in the wheel, my hair in my face, gagging on my salty tears.

Paul sat silently, caressing my nape, over and over. It felt good.

Finally, when I was all cried out, he sighed. 'Come on, sunshine. Switch places.'

I stretched my bare leg over the gearshift and hauled my big ass into the passenger seat as Paul got out and went round. Once in the driver's seat, he pulled me into his arms with a sigh.

'Who is she?' he whispered.

'I don't know!' I bawled all over again, tears blinding me. 'I can't believe he did this to me.'

'Forget him for now. Get some clothes on. We'll go home, have a chamomile and sort this out, OK?'

'No! I want to drive over to his office or wherever he is and emasculate him with my nail file! Have you seen my boots?'

'In your overnight bag.'

I threw my upper body into the back seat as I rifled through my things. Socks, bras, panties (no goddamn stilettos), my Kindle, my favorite family picture, which I threw to one side.

'I don't need surgery,' I mumbled into my bag. 'Or a husband who doesn't love me anymore. I can do it on my own.'

Which, I suddenly realized, was true. It wasn't necessary for me to take such drastic measures to lose weight. I'd do it on my own – change my eating habits and exercise. Maybe a bike ride round the park a couple of times a week, giving up dessert. I could do that. A whole new start! I could take charge *now*. I knew I could.

'Good for you!' Paul chimed, slapping my exposed butt.

I retrieved my boots and stuck a long leg up on the dashboard to put them on, but my feet were swollen.

'Stuck,' I huffed after a few minutes of pulling and wheezing.

'Here,' Paul said, leaning over me. 'Damn, you're right. Hang on a minute.'

And with that, he climbed into the seat behind me and reached around me (he had long arms) so he could pull them on from behind.

'Right this moment, my husband's bonking a bitch in stilettos and I can't even get my own boots on my fat feet,' I bawled uncontrollably as I upturned my bag, looking for a tissue. 'I'm a fucking disaster! A joke. No wonder he cheated on me.'

'Sweetie, don't be ridiculous. You're not a joke. You're a wonderful, well-respected woman. A pillar of the community, you know that.'

Suddenly, sirens blazed out of nowhere and a female cop on a motorcycle pulled up alongside us, peering into our car, wide-eyed.

'What's going on here?' she demanded, and we froze.

We must have looked a sight. I was naked with a coat over me and one leg stuck in the air as Paul grunted and heaved to pull my boot on, my lap covered in dubious-looking cosmetics, creams and magazines. Enough to put you away for good in puritanical Boston.

I looked up at the policewoman and, not finding any words, began to bawl all over again.

'Please, officer,' I heard Paul shout over my howls. 'Don't mind her. Her husband badgered her into going for a stomach bypass while he was screwing someone else.' He looked at the hefty officer and craftily added, 'A skinny bitch.'

The policewoman raised her eyebrows in disgust. 'You're kidding me?'

'I hate men,' I cried.

'Sunshine, you have to leave him,' Paul urged. 'Now is your chance.'

The officer peered closer into the car. 'Lemme get this straight. Your husband cheated on you?'

'Uh-huh,' I sniffed, wiping my eyes and taking deep breaths to calm down.

'After he told her to get a stomach bypass or *else*,' Paul confirmed.

'Divorce him,' sentenced the policewoman.

'I know, right?' Paul exclaimed. 'I've been telling her for years.'

'He should pay you alimony,' the policewoman opined. 'Have you got any evidence? In court you need proof.'

'Proof?' I shrieked, waving the cellphone under her nose. 'What more proof do you want?'

The policewoman's lips moved as she read the text message and then glared at me. 'You should have pulled a Bobbitt.'

'Bobbitt was neutered because he wanted too much,' I corrected her. 'My husband doesn't want... oh, forget it. Take us in, officer, and let's end this shitty day in grand style.'

The woman's big brown eyes softened. 'Tell you what. You put some clothes back on, ma'am, and I'll pretend I never saw you. OK?'

I wiped my eyes and nodded. 'OK. I'm sorry for the hassle, officer.'

'And besides – you're beautiful just the way you are. Happy Bobbitt Day.'

The plump woman smiled. A beautiful smile. Maybe one day, if I ever decided to play for the other team, I could always look her up.

After she waved us off like dear old friends, my cellphone rang.

'Erica, this is Doctor Bowers. What happened?' asked my bypass doctor.

'I'm sorry, I… I panicked.'

A bored sigh. Lots of people jumped ship before the fat feast. We'd talked about it and I'd assured him it wouldn't happen to me. But that was before I knew I had a cheating, no-good slimeball of a husband.

'Alright. It's OK. Let's meet in my office and we'll discuss this calmly. OK?'

'Um… no, I can't.'

'I understand. You need time. Next week?'

'No, I, um… I've changed my mind.'

Silence.

'Gotta go, Doctor Bowers. Sorry! Thank you for everything!'

And I hung up, a new braver, determined me. There was no way I could ever forgive Ira for cheating. There was no way I could forgive Ira for everything he'd done to me. Not even the gaping years of loneliness looming ahead could change my mind.

Erica had literally left the building!

6

One Way (Out)

You can imagine what happened when Ira got home and realized I hadn't gone through with the operation. His eyes widened in surprise to see me there and then narrowed when he saw I was still *all* there. Perhaps he thought I'd come home looking like Miss America, or maybe even his pantie-less lover in stilettos. I don't think anyone told him it would take months for me to shed the weight and that they wouldn't just hack off the fat bits like a cut of meat at the butcher's counter. Like I wanted to do to him right now. All the murder fantasies and I finally knew what my unconscious had known and been telling me all along. My eyes swung to the knife block in the kitchen, then back to him.

The asshole would have let me go through with a life-threatening operation when all this time, he'd had his own skinny-assed floozie waiting for him under the sheets. Bastard. This was the ultimate – the worst offence he could have thrown at me.

And now, just looking at him from across the kitchen

island, I knew I could do it on my own. Not just the diet, but my whole, entire life.

'Erica,' he said. 'What are you doing home so soon?'

'I didn't go through with it,' I answered simply, feeling my cheeks turn to fire as I looked at him superciliously, forcing myself not to hurt.

But who was I kidding? Inside I was dying, tearing myself to shreds smaller than his lover's panties. Horny bitch. Horny bastard. How could he throw away twelve years of marriage and two children for an hour's romp in the sack? Pardon me – eight minutes on a good night.

He frowned. 'Didn't go through with it? What the hell, Erica. We discussed—'

'I know about your affair,' I said calmly.

He sighed. 'Are you at it again? I'm not having an affair.'

'You dropped your cellphone in my hospital bed. She sent you this message.'

He patted his breast pocket and I held the phone out for him to read when instead I wanted to ram it up his nostrils. Dirty, pathetic cheating bastard.

Pale, he looked up at me in shock. I could see his mind churning, looking for another lie.

He swallowed, his eyes wide. 'Erica, we just—'

I exhaled and it hurt like hell, as if an eighteen-wheeler had fallen from the sky and landed smack dab on my chest. 'Don't bother, Ira. I'm not interested. It's done and I can never forgive you.'

Awkward silence. No 'I'll do anything to make it up to you', or 'Can't we just start all over again?' Instead, he nodded, as if he were all too eager to get out of there. How humiliating for me.

'What about the kids?' he asked. 'How... do we break it to them?'

I inhaled – slowly. Exhaled again. How the hell do you tell your kids that mommy and daddy don't love each other anymore? How do you relieve them of the gut-twisting pain and ensure their lives will benefit from it?

I shrugged, feigning indifference. 'We tell them in the New Year. No point in ruining their Christmas. Until then, you stay here and act like a decent father for once.'

He thought about it at length, as if debating, and my evil eyebrow shot up.

'Surely your lover in stilettos and no panties understands you have children who will always be more important than her, no matter how many tricks she turns?'

He blinked at me and I now feigned surprise, slapping my forehead. 'What am I *saying*? That goes for *good* fathers. But you don't care about this family, Ira. All you care about is yourself. And I'm sick of it. The kids aren't idiots. They can see what's happening here.'

'The kids have nothing to do with this,' he spat.

'They have everything to do with it!' I spat back, only louder. 'You're upturning their entire world!' Which was only half true, really.

Sure, divorce was always painful. But in my heart I knew there was nothing keeping us together anymore as a family. All those years, slaving for him, to make his life comfortable, to compensate for his own shitty mother, working day in, day out for years on end to support him... Finally being able to buy Quincy Shore Drive, raising our kids single-handedly, then going to his office on weekends to scrub his urinals and sort out his accounting books... And what the

NANCY BARONE

hell had I got out of it, if not shattered confidence and a broken heart?

Maybe Maddy and Warren would benefit from this separation, seeing mommy and daddy unburdened by love woes. Then a thought. His lover would, if it lasted, eventually want to become part of the kids' life. Or would she? Some women don't want to know. Sooner or later, I'd find out who she was. There was no way I was exposing my kids to a homewrecker.

No. Divorce was the only solution now. Emotionally and financially. Because at the rate he was going, if I gave him the time, he'd wipe me out completely. We had a prenup, the house was in my name. I had Nonna's inheritance. All I needed was to get my life back in gear. And my dream house in Tuscany.

Screw Ira. Somebody screw him, because I sure wouldn't be doing it anymore. Not that there was any danger of that happening. And yet, although our marriage had been sinking for years, betrayal had come as a surprise. And it hurt big time. I should have seen the signs. He liked that I cooked all the time, but whenever I put something in my mouth that wasn't a leaf of lettuce or an apple, he'd go ballistic.

On Fridays, I always baked multiple recipes in my fantastic multifunction oven. Once, I remember I'd made a pizza, a roast with vegetables and an apple pie. Which, out of sheer frustration (or gluttony, call it whatever you will, I don't care anymore), I'd polished off, one slice at a time, in the space of an afternoon. And after dinner, satisfied, he'd pushed his empty plate away and said, 'How about that pie I can smell?'

'Um, didn't I tell you? It was an apple crumble. It didn't turn out... I burned it, so I threw it away.'

Ira had turned in his seat and stared at me. I'd tried to keep an honest-looking face, but I was sweating. That's why I never made the selections for the drama groups at school.

'You ate the whole thing,' he sentenced as if pronouncing someone – or something – dead.

My mouth screwed into a grimace and my eyes fell to my empty plate.

There we went: three, two, one...

Keep it light, Erica, I'd told myself. *Keep it light. Don't let him hurt your feelings.*

What I should have done was read the damn signs of our crumbling relationship. This was the life I'd lived up to that point.

7

The Final Countdown

The next morning – my first as an unburdened woman – I rose extra early, woke the kids and drove them to school, where we parked and ate muffins. We were the first to arrive and would probably be the last to leave after school, because I couldn't envisage going home as long as *he* was there.

A couple more months to Christmas. I could do it. If I'd pretended everything was alright all these years, what were sixty measly days?

As if to speed up time, I worked like a madwoman all day, never stopping once, and at the stroke of three, I hauled my betrayed ass out of the office and picked up my kids. Only instead of taking them home, where Ira was bound to return sooner or later, or to a healthy alternative like my aunts' restaurant, I took them to McDonald's. I was going to turn them into blimps at this rate. They obliviously munched on their Happy Meals as I worked out my war strategy.

Was he going to be a decent man at least now and share the responsibilities? Notice how he didn't ask for my forgiveness. Not that it was happening. Or would he go as far as claiming full custody? That wasn't happening, for two reasons.

The first was obvious and the second was that it would never even occur to Ira. What the hell was he going to do with their continuous arguing, the constant questions (that's the way kids learn, I'd told him) and the howling when he failed to pay them attention? But maybe, just maybe, out of vengeance, I'd reward him with custody every other weekend. That way, he wouldn't be able to flop on the sofa and watch his Saturday games and Sunday reports. It would serve him right. But it would also kill me to think of them abandoned to their own devices while Ira acted as if they weren't even there. To hell with him. It was time for a change. Many changes, in fact.

A week later, when I got home dripping with rain and groceries after a trip to the supermarket (I didn't even look at the snack food shelves!), I hardly recognized our house. I can't begin to describe it. Magazines, head sets, controllers, keyboards, Chinese takeaway cartons strewn all over the floor, the coffee table and even the sofa. A baseball game was on full blast, and so were the kids, hyper to their limit, bouncing off the walls and running around, rolling over my pristine sofa with sticky fingers. The kitchen sink, a glance told me, was loaded to the ceiling with dirty dishes and some dirty clothes even littered the hallway.

'Hi, Mom!' was Warren's greeting as he sped by me on a skateboard.

On my wooden floors. And that's when I realized that smack dab in the middle of it all, sitting in his favorite armchair, was Ira, hidden by his usual paper. So much for his promise to be there for the kids. I preferred it when he wasn't.

Keep it light, girl, went the voice inside my head, and I tried to erase the image of me going round to the local gun shop to buy a bazooka. Just until after the Christmas holidays. Then Ira would be gone and my house would be a nicer one. In every sense.

I put down my bag and he looked up.

'Hey… here's dinner,' he said, nudging a carton of leftover Chinese takeaway (which he knows I absolutely hate) with his foot.

Just two more months, I told myself. *And then I'm really free*. 'Why are the kids still up? It's ten o'clock.'

He shrugged. 'They didn't want to go to bed just yet,' he answered, still camouflaged in his sports section.

'Ira, they *never* want to go. They're kids. It's up to us to set the rules. Just how much chocolate did you let them have? And look at this place!'

Ira glared at me, got up and stalked into the guest room, slamming the door. And to think I'd slept with a rubber ducky in my mouth all night for him.

'I heard,' Marcy informed me as I was chopping parsley and garlic with my brand-new half-moon cutter.

She was pretending to visit her grandchildren. In other words, downing a Martini. She and this conversation were the last things I needed after the day I'd had.

'He told you?' I asked through tight lips, as if she were trying to pull all my teeth out and keeping my mouth firmly shut would actually stop her. I put my half-moon cutter down and speared her with my hairy eyeball.

She took a sip from her Martini and said coolly, 'Ira's not very good at keeping secrets.'

I kept my evil- and suspicious eye trained on her until she buckled and waved her half-empty glass, the liquid sloshing dangerously near the rim, and sighed.

My hands found my half-moon again, squeezing the handles tight. 'Well, he managed to keep one secret. What did he say?'

'Oh, lots of things.'

Christ, if Marcy had suddenly become Ira's confidante, he must have been desperate. Or crafty. She's the only one in the family who would gang up against me. Even Judy and Vince would support me.

'Like what?'

'That you grind your teeth at night. Go see Dr Jacobs, no?' she said simply.

Obviously, he wasn't telling her everything. How dare he talk to my mother about my faults when all I seemed to do was put up with his!

'He also says you're still going on about Tuscany after all these years. What an absurd idea, Erica. What are you going to do in Tuscany?'

I didn't even need to think about it as I chopped away. 'Be happy.'

'But you'd be all on your own. We have very few relatives left there, if any.'

'Suits me,' I sentenced as I began to dice some onions to a pulp.

After all, I wouldn't be on my own. Paul spent six months a year in Tuscany in his own villa.

'Is it because of your bedroom problems?'

'Wha-at? I'm not talking about *that* to you.'

'Oh, get over yourself. You need to learn the secrets of keeping your man. Good sex.'

I rolled my eyes. 'Marcy, get real.'

'I am real,' she assured. 'You think I kept your dad on a leash all these years because I was a good cook?'

Highly unlikely, I thought to myself, and seeing the look on my face, she nodded.

'Exactly. It was the sex.'

Today, singledom didn't scare me. And I definitely wouldn't go back on the shelves again, because I wouldn't be interested in being picked. Not that there was any danger of that happening. I'd probably end up with some deluded divorced guy and we'd end up pouring our hearts out to each other on date one. Pathetic.

Besides, I didn't need a man. I had everything I needed. Great kids. A fantastic job. A good house. And Paul. If I could afford to take the kids to Tuscany now, I'd go in a heartbeat.

'If you'd only listened to me and gone ahead with the operation instead of running like a mouse. Really, you'd have solved all your problems. I told you how important sex is. Why can't you understand?'

Obviously, Ira hadn't confided in her completely, the slimy bastard.

'He was cheating on me,' I said as I chopped away, pretending it was Ira's neck over and over. *Chop! goes the dick's head.*

'What?'

'He's sleeping with someone else,' I repeated, big tears plopping onto my ingredients for tonight's special: Miserable Minestrone.

'You see?' she said simply. 'Sex. It's all men want. And if you can't give it to them, they'll look for it elsewhere. Now, take my advice – go reschedule the op and see if Ira will give you a few months to change.'

I whirled round to look at her. *I* was the one who had to change? On what friggin' planet did she live? In that moment, more than ever, I realized that Marcy and I would never be able to speak the same language and that I was never going back on any of my decisions. Somewhere deep inside me there was an amazing Erica waiting to burst out of my heavy life.

8

Dieting Disasters?

It was like there was this big pink elephant in the room all these years and everyone saw it but me. I was the pink elephant who needed to go on a diet, pronto.

It was never going to be fun, but I started on Monday. And religiously broke it by the time Wednesday rolled around, despite the fact I spent most of my free time with Paul, who was lighter than me, ate properly and in small quantities – not like me, the garbage incinerator. I could eat anyone under the table. Figured I'd meet someone like him.

'You need to do it for yourself, not for Marcy's approval or for a man. Think of a sexy dress,' Paul urged.

I snorted. 'Sexy dresses and I don't mix. Not since I was young.'

'But remember how beautiful you were. Remember how it made you feel.'

Paul had borrowed a dress from The Wilbur Theater in Boston and put a couple of pins in it so my boobs wouldn't spill out. I thought about it. 'Pinchy? Pricked?'

But I had to admit, the dress had been my pass. I sighed. If I ever wanted to be a size fourteen again, I was going to do this properly. Which meant striving for a better quality of life in general. And perhaps even looking in the mirror and finally saying to myself, 'My! aren't you pretty. Where have you been all these years?' But how did people manage it?

Resigned to learn more about skinny people, like fascinated ufologists studying the possibility of extraterrestrial life out there, I subscribed to an online dieting service. Now I'd heard of online dating, but online dieting?

There was so much information on the net – most of it discordant – and cartloads of (again) contrasting rules. Don't drink (water) near your meals... drink lots of water during your meals... drink only before your meals... drink only after your meals... and finally, don't drink *at all*. The same went for fruit: eat fruit only two hours after your meal as it'll ferment in your stomach otherwise. Stock up on vitamins before your meal so your body won't need more. Eat mostly fruit.

Get out on your skateboard (huh?) the minute you finish your meal and burn those calories right off! Rest for twenty minutes after your meal so your blood will go straight to your digestive system and perform better. Chill out with your family before a meal so you don't pounce on your plate the minute it's set before you! Well, nobody has ever set my plate before me. And by the time I've fed everybody else (they do the pouncing), mine is frozen solid again. So don't tell me to chill out.

Who was a gal to turn to?

And then one day, to make things clear, I received an email with The Golden Rules to Being Slim:

Always plan meals.

That was easy. I always planned very rich meals worth living for.

Cut quantities by 50 per cent.

Yeah, and because you're still starving after lunch, have a chocolate bar to fill the void and then eat 200 per cent more at dinner.

Drink water a half-hour before, not with meal.

Glad someone's made up their mind.

Drink water in the mornings and before going to bed.

I can't. I've got a bladder like a sieve and I can't keep getting up in the middle of the night – I need my beauty sleep.

Sit at a laid table.

Haven't you been listening to me?

Chew everything 30–50 times.

This actually works, because once you've managed that, you don't want to swallow it anymore.

Eat everything in moderation.

That simple, huh?

Put knife and fork down between mouthfuls.

That'll be interesting to watch when you have two kids at the same table playing tennis with their food. It's a question of when I can *pick up* said knife and fork.

So there they were – the eight things I'd never, ever thought of and nor had any other woman on Earth. *Really?* If I cut my intake by 50 per cent, I'd swallow less calories? The asshole who wrote this syuff was full of it and had certainly never had to starve himself (a woman, even a thin one, would never have written such bullshit). What was he on? La-la drugs? And where did he live? Down a rabbit hole?

Determined to have a better understanding, I began to observe what thin people ate. Did they really eat less than me? Then how come everywhere I turned in the street there were slim jims gobbling down hotdogs, ice-cream sundaes, nachos – *with salsa* – chicken curries and all the food you could possibly imagine? And at every hour of the day? Once, I had to pop to the pharmacy in the middle of the night and I ran into a man wolfing down something that looked disgusting but smelled delicious. I almost asked him where he got it from.

How was I expected to ignore food that literally surrounded me 24/7, filling my nostrils, day in, day out, from the doughnuts I found at work in the mornings, to the snack trays that passed my office on their way up to the suites? Not to mention the dining hall, laden with delicious fancy foods.

My boss, good old Harold Farthington and owner of Farthington Hotels, had given me access to the same food to which our guests were treated. And everywhere else I went there was great grub: carts with hotdogs on the streets, pastries in shop windows, mouth-watering fragrances wafting out of restaurants and cafés. Making it home clean and empty-stomached was impossible without being ambushed by a drive-thru sign or a plaza teeming with diners, bakeries and restaurants. This was, after all, the United States – land of plenty too much.

Thus, you can understand how grocery shopping was a real torture treat for me. Since Paul was preparing snacks for the kids at my place, having picked them up from school, I shopped alone. Word of advice if you're on a diet: never shop alone. Food will ambush you. So, bring your trusty back-up – someone who will still love you after you've verbally assaulted them for not minding their own goddamn business. And *always* shop on a full stomach. Otherwise you'll get all sorts of food fantasies and end up buying the whole supermarket.

Once, I had a dream that I got locked in this shopping center for a ten-week period of closure. They were the happiest ten weeks of my life. Aisles and aisles of everything I always (and constantly) wanted. Hot chocolate? Choose your brand. Reese's Pieces peanut butter candy? All you can eat. And don't worry about your shrinking clothes – the plus-size department is on the third floor.

So this new me, I'd decided, was going to eat properly. Not to attract Ira, but to look better and feel better about myself. No more caramel-coated popcorn, no more chocolate (I know it sounds heinous and unnecessarily cruel, but that's how I did it the first time), no more bread and butter, no more mayo, no more fried stuff, no more desserts, no more nothing. Just good, wholesome food. Half the quantities I used to eat (see Golden Rule Number One). And a trip to the gym every other day. There was one in the hotel and I'd been given an honorary membership years ago when I went back to work after Maddy's birth. Yeah, as if I had the time.

Maybe someone should invent a washer-dryer that's pedal-powered, or maybe build a 'pedal while you do the dishes' thingy. That would break the world record of the most bought and least used piece of shit ever.

I squeezed my Kia van into a space big enough for a Mini Cooper right opposite Food World, debating whether or not to get a shopping cart. If I was going to buy myself some diet food and eat half as much (was I really sure I wanted to go through with this?), surely I didn't need a shopping cart. But you know me – soon I'd be standing at the checkout, breaking my bladder for a pee and craning my neck looking for a basket, juggling my low- to no-fat items in my arms and evil-eyeing the usual old lady who had bought half the store and wouldn't leave me an inch of space on the conveyor belt.

I decided to do a dummy-run diet first. So I grabbed a small basket and picked my way through the healthy foods section which, in my local supermarket, was way at the back. In fact, I'd never even noticed it before. Right. Here I was. So. Low-fat cream cheese. Rice cakes for when I was sick of melba toast. Melba toast when I got sick of rice cakes. Parma ham? Are you kidding me? Pay twenty-seven dollars a pound when I could get it for free from my dad's Italian shop? Yoghurt. Low-fat, of course. Cereal? Muesli, to help the digestive system, if you know what I mean. Which reminded me. Skimmed milk. Fruit, lettuce, tomatoes (no mayo, no bacon). What else? Not much, apparently. I turned the corner and... ooh! Low-calorie jam? Tucked inside low-calorie *doughnuts*? And, further down, low-fat muffins? Unbelievable!

There were shelves and shelves of low-calorie desserts, from tiramisu to apple pie. How was this even possible? And in the freezer, low-calorie lasagne. *And* cannelloni. Shepherd's pie? Chocolate ice cream? Surely I'd died and gone to diet heaven. How could it be possible to eat all these fantastic mouth-watering foods and still lose weight? And why did it have to come out of a box if I could make my own?

Oh, why was good food fattening? Why couldn't we just live an easy life, eating what we wanted, like animals? Have you ever seen a fat tiger? Or a fat fly? I did everything I could to avoid delving inside me. I ate because I was sad. I always had been. The brief gorgeous stint in my early twenties had simply been a commercial break in the long miserable movie of my life.

Accepting I needed to change wasn't a gung-ho idea or a knee-jerk reaction to Ira's infidelity like it may seem. It was a painful process – a daily ordeal with just me and my shortcomings. Me and my weaknesses. And my goddamn fear of failing again and again. I was sick of failing, sick of trying to lose weight all my life. So in the end, I'd given up.

Skinny women had absolutely no idea what we were going through, every single day of our lives. Therapists made me laugh, especially thin ones. Granted, they were balanced. But I'd be balanced, too, if I'd had a normal life, possibly in someone else's skin.

My mouth already watering, I juggled all my stuff – and there was loads of it – to the checkout, paid and went home. Paul was going on a date and waiting for me by the door.

'I thought you'd gone *diet* shopping,' he sighed, peeking into the bags.

'I have,' I answered, hustling by him in my haste to sit down to a succulent dinner and not feel guilty about it for once.

And so after I'd fed, washed and put the kids to bed, I rubbed my hands together and reached for my succulent, guilt-free foods.

Guilt wasn't the right word. Disappointed was more like it. The shepherd's pie, which I'd had a major hankering for, was about as big as the palm of my hand. All that big, big box and cellophane to protect *this*? I opened the lasagne as well, just to make sure I hadn't been gypped twice. There it was – Golden Rule Number One. This was less than 50 per cent of what I was expecting. Much less. It wasn't fair, considering I'd paid double for it. If I'd made my own, it would have been free. Ah, but my *own*, I argued, wouldn't have been low-fat. So chin up and dig in!

Sighing, I nuked the lasagne and shepherd's pie. There was no point in lying to myself by thinking that the lasagne would be enough. I mean, look at it. I could hide it with my hand cupped over it. At least I was being honest with myself. I know people who would have defrosted one thing at a time, pretending to have good intentions when they knew very well they were going back into the kitchen to nuke the second box as well. At least I was straightforward and I knew what I wanted. And right now, all I wanted was to swing by Le Tre Donne restaurant and have my zia

Maria cook me all my favorites in *my* helping sizes – not this microscopic processed bullshit.

I poured myself a glass of Nero d'Avola red wine and reached for my prettiest place mat, the one with the linen fringes. As per all the weight loss websites, if you set the table nicely, with maybe a candle or a rose and some pretty crystal glasses, you could fool yourself into enjoying your meal. Sighing, I set my place with small plates and cutlery. From Maddy's old plastic toddler set, to be exact, which was the smallest I could find. And *still* it didn't look like much.

Gathering my provisions on a tray, I went into the living room and flicked on the TV just in time for the BBC America program, *Fantasy Homes by the Sea*. People wrote in the requirements of their dream home and every week, searching families would be featured. This week it was a British couple looking to move to Tuscany. The host of the show had found them a lovely farmhouse in Chianti, with acres of vineyards, outbuildings for guests and even a pool. I instantly sat up, ignoring my measly meal. Now that was something I'd swap a tiramisu for.

The host walked us around the property and I found I was hanging from her lips. It had everything I wanted, including my annexes. But when she revealed the price, I winced, thinking that at least once in her life, Marcy had been right. She'd always told me to marry as rich as possible, average-income guys being, according to her, cheaper and much meaner than the rest. Not that she spoke from experience, having been raised in the lap of luxury, with a silver spoon stuck down her throat.

My parents both came from high-income Italian families.

My paternal grandparents, the Cantellis, owned a successful citrus conserve factory in Sicily while Marcy's, the Bettarinis, had olive groves and vineyards in Tuscany – very much like this one on TV – and shrewdly marketed their own brands of olive oil and wine. Then in the Fifties for reasons beyond me, both families had emigrated to Boston. I wish I'd been born and raised in Italy. I wish my nonna Silvia hadn't sold up and invested in the USA. Why the hell would someone want to leave beautiful climes, a simple life and happy faces? I'll never understand. Here in the States, it was always rush, run, rush, hurry hurry hurry. The silence and slow-paced life in Italy was more appropriate to my solitary nature.

The Cantellis had met the Bettarinis at a wedding in Boston a few months after they'd immigrated. You know, those big Italian weddings à la the *Godfather*, where there's enough food for even the relatives still living in Italy. And then amid the singing, the dancing and the food, boy's eyes meet girl's. Only this time it was more complicated.

The girls were four – Marcy and her three younger sisters, Maria, Martina and Monica. And my father was so blown away that he couldn't decide which he liked best. I know that because once I found a picture of a beautiful young Bettarini brunette in his wallet and when I asked which one of my aunts it was, he almost had a fit. I think he was secretly in love with one of them, but for the life of me I couldn't understand which of the belles it was. They were all beautiful and classy and, above all, smart – something Marcy wasn't.

The picture wasn't clear and the four of them were almost exactly alike with their lustrous thick dark hair, ivory skin, naturally full lips and innate class. The youngest and the eldest being ten years apart, sort of like a live demonstration of a camera speeding up through the years, taking you through each phase or season of life, the youngest with a fresh face, the eldest, my mom, bearing the knowing sensual look.

And because she was the eldest, she was the first in line to be married off. Which was good news to her, because she hated living with her sisters. She still hates them today and for the life of me, I can't understand why. Judy once suggested it was because they reminded her of what she used to look like when she was young.

I'd given Judy a jab in the ribs to silence her, but it was too late. Marcy had already heard and had sulked all week, checking her appearance in the mirror more often than usual, which I always thought was an impossible feat.

My aunts were very close but they weren't, as one might imagine, one entity. They all had different interests and personalities. The only thing they agreed on, in fact, was how to run a business and how great my dad was. They were in complete adoration of him. And when he'd chosen my mom, they'd all taken it in stride, fawning on him and doing for us all the things Marcy couldn't. There were never any hard feelings against him for not choosing one of them – just a wistful resignation that immediately amped up to enthusiasm whenever they were needed around the house, which was always. Because, as bright as Marcy's beauty shone, it wasn't strong enough to make the house sparkle.

After my parents had married, Dad opened a store called Italian Gifts. When it became obvious that Marcy wasn't much help behind a counter, Nonna Silvia stepped in and invested some of her Tuscan money in the shop. Nonna and Dad became equal partners, and the business grew and grew until we were the best known and most trusted Italian shop in all of Little Italy and Boston.

Which was great for them. But all my life I'd wanted to reverse family history and go back to Italy. Marcy said that it was selfish of me to nullify all the hard work put in by Nonna Silvia to come to America to give us an opportunity to live the American Dream (even if so far, my life in America had been a nightmare).

And Ira had said, among other things, that it was selfish of me to turn my children into Italians when clearly, they had more opportunities here. Opportunities for what? I wondered. To get stuck in traffic? To breathe exhaust fumes? To freeze your ass off ten months of the year? To look up and see only skyscrapers?

I sighed. Tuscany was *my* dream. My life-long dream. I envisioned what I'd have to go through to get there eventually. Because I had to.

The British couple on TV was shown three more farmhouses. The prices were unbelievably high even for Tuscany, but the woman had followed Marcy's advice. She'd married rich and her dream home in a warm country was only a choice away. While here I was in a cold, cold city with a cold, cold soon-to-be ex-husband and longing for some warmth – any way I could get it.

But for now, I'd have to face reality. Face my life and keep my chin up as always. I looked down at my meal of lasagne and shepherd's pie, and when I tallied the calories I'd eaten, I burst into tears. Another day, another pound on.

9

Spider Man

'God, I hate her,' Lindsay whispered.

The whisper slithered up my back like a traitor's caress.

'I know,' Lesley answered. 'You'd think she owns the joint the way she barks orders.'

I power-smiled to myself to bury the soft-as-mush me, swung round on my sturdy heels without breaking my stride and, raising my world-famous evil eyebrow, retraced my steps toward the doomed girls at the reception desk.

A couple of idle busboys caught in the crossfire started and stood to attention as I brushed past them. The so-called receptionists, both sporting an improbable shade of blonde and still trapped in the Eighties make-up wise, turned crimson as I came to a stop before them, dark and ominous in my perfectly tailored albeit a tad too severe plus-size suit. OK, so maybe I was trapped in something worse than them – my own body.

'Ladies. If you're used to working in joints, then maybe

you should both consider returning to one, which can be arranged in the blink of an eye.'

Not a word. They were too stunned by the fact that I'd heard at all. Was starving making me an even bigger bitch or what? Plus, when you're a mother you develop a bat's hearing. And when you're practically a part-time mom like me you develop all sorts of telepathic abilities, but unfortunately no telekinetic, automatic house-scrubbing or kid-feeding powers. Apparently, my sole strength at work was the fact that I scared the crap out of my staff. Good enough for me.

'It's not your job to like me,' I continued. 'Your job is to mind the front office and at least look professional. Do you think you can manage that?'

Lesley and Lindsay nodded, turning, if possible, a deeper red, making their peroxide manes look almost white.

'Yes, Mrs. Lowenstein. Our apologies, ma'am,' whispered Lesley, the blonde bimbo with less make-up.

They weren't stupid, in all fairness – just very young and too preoccupied with their looks. They'd learn.

'Right. Now, both of you switch your brains on and don't ever let me catch you in an unprofessional situation while in this establishment again. And smile.'

Chef Gordon Ramsay couldn't have done it better. Boy, had I come a long way from my job as junior receptionist on the English Riviera.

Yep, I acted like I owned the joint. Truth be told, in my position as manager of The Farthington Hotel, I was in my element. I could make the five-star, eighty-bed hotel run like Swiss clockwork, day in, day out. I had the entire staff terrified but synchronized. Cooks, cleaners, drivers, accounts, maintenance, the IT team... The madam's flashy girls who appeared in the lobby at cocktail hour... Of course I'm joking, because I chased them away years ago, but I suspect my head chef Juan dabbles in that avenue of pleasure now and then.

If anyone here screwed up, it was my butt. And if we were to live up to our reputation as the best hotel chain, not only in Boston, but also in North America, we needed to keep our socks up every day and every night. An impossible herculean feat for most. For me, it was a cinch. A breeze. It was my personal life that was killing me.

The good news was that Paul had gotten us into tango classes during the two hours that the kids were at ballet and soccer. He'd made me buy a wide skirt that actually hid a few bumps. Now, if you think that all gorgeous gay guys dress like models and dance well, you're absolutely right. Paul already knew all the steps and guided me like a pro, causing the envy of many girls (and guys) in there.

'Hey,' I exclaimed as he pushed me and pulled me around the floor like a light, old mop. He obviously didn't need lessons. 'Where did you learn?'

'My mom was a dance teacher, remember?' he said, winking at me.

And after a moment's shock, I got it and smiled gratefully. He'd enrolled us for *me*. To get me moving, to make me happy and to take me away from my life for a couple of hours a week. I couldn't have loved him more.

Whirling and twirling across the dance floor, I realized it was fun, not having to worry about looking like a respectable kick-ass boss who scared the pants off her staff. It felt exhilarating just to move to the sound of the music. Dancing was carefree and didn't have a purpose except to make me feel good (and shift some pounds, of course). Just moving around for the sheer fun of it and not because I had to hustle and run errands was elating. And how long had it been since I laughed?

I almost felt silly, but I shrugged it off. There was more to me behind the mother, manager and betrayed wife. I was a girl again in Paul's arms, just like twelve years ago, when we were young and wild and free. Paul was still all the above. Me? Getting there, slowly but surely.

I glanced around at all the couples of every color, shape, age and size having a great time, leaving their worries at home. Sure, they were always there when they got back, but at least dancing gave them some happiness and fortified them for the rest of the week until it was once again time to tango. So when in the dance hall, I danced. I danced my heart out, thinking that if this was going to be the new and improved Erica, it wouldn't be half as bad as I thought. I'd missed me, missed the person I once was. The one who used to be able to laugh at anything.

Paul twirled me and swirled me, guiding me through the complicated steps that, after a while, became easy. I relaxed in his arms, confident there was no way I could ever let him down, not even if I screwed up his steps. Paul was my lifeline.

While I was washing-up after the kids' lunch on Saturday, I got a call from Paul. He was in hospital with a broken leg and just wanted me to know in case I needed him. That was Paul for you. The one time he needed a friend, he was worried about me.

Knowing I couldn't depend on my siblings or my aunts, who were leaving for a vacation in Mexico for the week on a trip organized by the Italian community in Little Italy, I turned to my last resort and called Marcy to see if she could babysit. All I needed was an hour or so to run a few things over to him and keep him company.

A sigh. 'Erica, I'm getting ready to go out for dinner (at 1 p.m.?) with some friends. I don't have time to come babysit your kids.'

Why was I even surprised? Did I think she'd managed to change overnight? And did you notice she didn't even ask me what was wrong with Paul?

Didn't she remember when she made me drag my kids across town at night to the hospital for her ingrown toenail op? And now that I needed to rely on someone for a couple of hours tops, I was on my own.

'Never mind,' I snapped. 'As you so often remind me, children belong to their mothers and not their grandparents.' Before she could replicate, I hung up on her for the first time in my life.

I called an emergency babysitter and within twenty minutes, I had a Mrs. Doubtfire lookalike at my door. Ever grateful, I shoved the list of emergency phone numbers (all mine) at her and in three minutes flat, I was out of there. Which was unlucky for me, because five minutes later, I was squirming in my Kia van, dying for a pee. I pulled into a plaza and charged into a nice-looking bistro.

Finally a relieved woman in every sense, I stepped out

of the stall and lathered my hands with some rose-scented soap. Did I remember to get Paul's slippers? I... what the *hell*? A tickling, multi-legged slimy sensation under my slacks made me freeze as my mind knew there could only be one explanation. A spider!

A horrible convulsion shook my body at the realization of my worst phobia. Never mind heights, open spaces or closed spaces! The only thing in the world that scared me to death were those wretched beasts.

I remember screaming and beating my leg to kill said beast, but the thought of it crushed to a pulp against my flesh sent me into a mindless hysteria. I was beyond panicking. I also remember throwing myself on the floor in a fit of terror for what seemed like days because darkness kept washing over me. I must have been near passing out several times until someone – a man – gripped my arms.

'What's wrong?'

'Help! Take my pants off!' I shrieked.

'What?'

'A spider in my pants! Take them off!'

'Your pants?' he asked dubiously.

'Please.'

'Are you sure?'

What the hell was wrong with the guy? 'Now!'

At that, the blessed man obliged and yanked on my zipper. 'It's stuck,' he informed me.

'Just rip them off!' I begged.

'You want me to tear your pants off? Is this *Candid Camera* or something?'

'Just do it!' I shrieked.

Shaking his head, he reached down and easily tore my

front zipper down before pulling them off my legs, checking every inch of wobbly thigh as I frantically kicked, repeating, 'Kill it, kill it!' I didn't give a shit if he saw my flesh jiggling all over the place – I'd never see him again. All I wanted was to be rid of the monster.

At some point, I finally collapsed under him, exhausted but still digging my nails into his flesh, still shaking and bawling and clawing at his shirt until he was half-naked next to me. He felt so safe, so solid, like a nice cozy cabin in the middle of a snowstorm. And he smelled fantastic, like a real man, without the nauseating mist of different colognes I have to fight through to get from the lobby to my office every morning.

But more than anything, I remember how he'd calmed me with his deep, soothing voice and how it had enveloped me, warmed me, like a father's should when you're a scared child or a husband's when you're a woman down in the dumps. I'd never had either source of comfort in my life from my dad or Ira, and it was like the other shoe had finally dropped. This voice, this presence, this kind of man was what I'd lacked my entire life. If I'd had this kind of solid support and understanding all that time, and not for just a few terrifying seconds in the ladies' room, my whole life would have been made. I'd be a different woman today. Sweeter. More self-assured. Less aggressive. More loved.

This was the kind of patience and loyalty that I'd sorely lacked. Someone who would believe me and act upon my fears as if they were as important to him as they were to me. This man had taken me seriously. This man had been my security. If Ira had been here with me, never in a thousand years would he have agreed to rip my pants off in public, just like that.

The stranger put his lips against my ear and whispered, 'It's alright. It's gone. Calm down now.'

'Are you sure?' I croaked, burying my head deeper into his chest, my arms and legs still wrapped around him like a real whack job.

'Absolutely positive. Take a look for yourself – see?'

I stopped and lifted my face to scan the floor with trepidation. He was right. No sign of the thing. The coast was clear. And then I finally looked up at him. And almost fainted dead away again, but for another reason this time.

He was surreal. Handsome didn't even begin to cut it. Wide shoulders. Muscles. Strong. Perhaps enough to lift me. Black hair that fell over his forehead. Big dark eyes and the most awesome, longest lashes. Dark five o'clock shadow. Pure man. Pure, sinfully gorgeous man.

'Hands up!' twin voices echoed in the empty bathroom.

My savior turned toward them and raised his hands, his torso still stuck to mine so that he looked like he was doing sit-ups against my breasts.

'It's OK, lads. It's only me,' he assured them. Then he turned to me. 'I'm a regular here.'

One of the guards re-holstered his gun. 'Sorry, sir.'

'It's fine. A little accident with a big hairy monster,' he explained, tucking his shirt back into his jeans as the two guards looked at me.

I crossed my arms in front of my chest and shot them an evil glare. 'He means the spider.'

One of the guards stifled a snort and I shakily crawled away, making a break for my pants, which were now in shreds, much too humbled to look my savior's way. It was a good thing that Paul always waxed the hell out of me, otherwise the guards would have thought the poor man was tackling a grizzly bear in the ladies' room.

'Oh, OK,' agreed the other guard all too easily.

I hid my face in my torn pants. 'He was just helping out a hysterical lady,' I contributed, not wanting to seem ungrateful. 'Go now, please. I'm in my underwear, in case you hadn't noticed.' And they weren't my best pair, either.

At that, my savior chuckled and wrapped his jacket around me like a kilt. I'm big, but this thing fit all the way around me. My face still hidden, I muttered a muffled 'Thank you,' and skulked back into the stall – a different one, though.

'OK, let's give the lady some breathing space,' I heard my hero say. 'I'll be sitting outside if you'd care to join me for lunch?'

'Uh, I don't know. Thanks anyway.'

A pause. 'OK, then. I hope to see you again soon.'

Yeah, like that was ever happening. 'Me too. Thank you.'

'We're at our desk if you need us, ma'am,' called one of the guards.

'Alright. Thank you. And thank you again,' I called to my hero from over the stall, too embarrassed to show my face.

'My pleasure,' he said in a charming British accent.

I raced home wearing the guy's jacket around my hips, shot up the stairs past the aghast babysitter, who must have thought I was a freak, and hopped back down the stairs, one leg in a new pair of jeans. By the time I reached the front door, I was dressed. When you're a working mom, you learn to multitask quickly.

'I'll pay you the extra time!' I shouted over my shoulder as I catapulted myself out the door and into my Kia, flooring it. No wonder I always got speeding tickets.

Paul was sitting up brightly in bed as if he'd just had a groovy haircut instead of breaking his leg.

'Hey, sunshine, what's up?' he chirped as I kissed his cheek and sank down, winded, in the chair next to his bed, his overnight bag at my feet.

'Are you alright?' I asked in a ragged breath. 'How did it happen?'

Paul shrugged. 'It's nothing. It's not broken, just badly sprained. A sex accident. Carl and I slipped in his shower this morning.'

I raised my eyebrow. I'd never had sex in the shower in my life. Just ordinary bed sex, while it lasted. I wondered if Paul could sense my envy.

He cupped his hands in front of his mouth and said, 'No, Erica, you'll never have sex in the shower until you find yourself a new man.'

I stared at him. He was right. Not only was I not having sex in the shower, but I also wasn't having any sex at all.

'You look more frazzled than usual,' he observed. 'What's up?'

It took a minute to sink in as my mind was still focused on the steamy showers I'd never had, and then it dawned on me. 'Paulie, I've just met the man of my dreams.'

Paul nearly jumped out of bed, but his elastic cast stopped him. He slapped his hands together, his eyes mischievous and excited. 'You're kidding me! What's his name?'

I stared at him blankly. 'I don't know.'

'Well, what does he *do*?'

I thought about it, but could only remember the sensation of pure protector, like in the romance paperbacks I used to sneak behind my chemistry books. 'I don't know.'

'You don't *know*? Can you at least describe him?'

Before his overwhelming beauty, the sensation of manliness and kindness came to mind. 'Tall. Dark. Soft, loose black curls A deep, soothing voice. Big hands. Lean body but strong.'

'Oh, great, that'll help. You've just described half the male Boston population. The gay one, mostly!'

I shrugged helplessly.

'Well, how did you meet him? Tell!' Paul urged, getting as comfortable as he could, considering he was anchored to the bed.

But I was already back on Earth, anchored and grounded to my own reality. Hell, I had kids and already one failed marriage. I couldn't afford to fantasize about the first hunk who tore my clothes off.

'It doesn't matter. I met him. And I'll never see him again. That's why he'll always be the man of my dreams.'

Paul's eyes popped out of his face. 'You didn't get his number? Have I taught you absolutely nothing?'

I shrugged again. All I knew was that he'd enveloped me in such a way, making me feel protected and not silly for my fears. He'd taken control of the situation, but not so I'd feel like an idiot, which I should have. But he'd been understanding, not judgmental. If I'd been single, and younger, and beautiful, and confident, I'd have found a way to meet him again, even if I had to canvass every door in Massachusetts.

Maybe somewhere in this city at this very moment, a

woman was opening her front door to him, arms wide, and I envied her. I'd never know his name. But I did have his jacket to remember him by. Or, if I were my sister, Judy, I'd track him down and bump into him 'by chance'. He'd be charming, protective, kind, passionate – a real alpha male like you see in romance books. He'd be practically perfect. And then, like Ira, he'd get sick of me, start sleeping with someone else and break my heart.

For years, as I was growing up, I'd longed for the dates, the first kiss, the first time, the 'oh my God, my period is late'. All the things I'd seen in my friends' lives. The works. But of course then, there was no danger I'd ever get pregnant unless someone up there took pity on me and sent me the Archangel Gabriel on a mission.

Some of us aren't destined to find love. I'd missed my love boat. But at least I had two children I loved to pieces, Paul, a great job and a lovely house. The rest, well, maybe in my next life.

10

Home Truths

The first thing I did when I woke the next morning was sneeze. My throat itched and my nose was dripping. Shit. I couldn't afford to get sick. I dragged my butt out of bed and took a hot shower to chase away the microbes and I was fine – until I stepped out of the shower. I don't know how I managed to get dressed, because my head was so heavy and my bones screamed in pain at every movement.

Shivering, I opened my wardrobe and winced. I'd forgotten to pick up my work suits at the dry-cleaners. All I had in the house were some sundresses I hadn't worn since before I'd got pregnant with Maddy and some jeans from before I met Ira. Apart from the pants that hunk had torn off me, my only other good jeans were in the wash. None of those fitted, so it was either one of my old track suits or a brown suit that consisted of a wool dress and matching coat that never fit me. And even if it did, it would made me look like a sack of turnips. Marcy had brought it back from France and I'd hated it on sight but never had the courage to throw it away. Why? you may ask.

Because Marcy (who has the key to our place) systematically goes through my closet to throw out things she says are absolutely horrid and that I shouldn't be caught dead wearing. Can you imagine that? Needless to say that she got rid of more than two thirds of my closet in one visit. At first I was shocked. Then I was angry. Then I was resigned. *My mother would never do that*, you may be saying out loud while shaking your head, but come on, don't you know Marcy yet? Don't you know that couture is more important than nurturing your own children?

We were practically specular. Where she was hopeless, like cooking and nurturing, I shone. Where she was polished, like social events, couture and beauty, I was grubby and careless.

Anyway, back to the sack-of-potatoes suit I swore I'd never wear even if I did lose weight. One lesson I'd learned was never say never. I took a step closer. It was my only solution right now. Did I smell *mothballs*? Yep, another contribution from Marcy. But I had no choice but to see if it fit. If it did, I was home free. If it didn't, it really was going to have to be my track suit. Maybe if I kept to my office all day, no one would notice.

I begrudgingly bunched the suit up at the hem and slowly – *slowly* – pulled it over my head. Shoulders clear – that was a first! Oh, God, was it coming to a halt around my waist? No, it was just the lining scrunching, thank goodness. I tugged on it as delicately but firmly as I could, as if this dress were made of paper and the very last one on Earth.

After this it was the proverbial fig leaf. How Marcy hadn't foreseen that this suit wouldn't fit me had been a mystery to me for many years until one day, while scoffing at it, resenting its mere presence in my home, it dawned on me that she'd done it on purpose. To give me a goal in my life. As if wearing this dead ringer for a burlap sack was going to inspire me to lose weight.

At my hips there was a definite stalemate situation. It wasn't going down any further! Panicking, I eyed my track suit and then my flowery summer dresses, and with a grunt, coaxed the suit (the wool stretched easily enough, but it was the damn lining that seemed made for a five-year-old) over my curves. All the while holding my breath.

And yes! Mission accomplished! Here we were, as one, this horrid piece of couture and me. *And* I'd never been this elated before, not even in my wedding dress. I'd finally proved Marcy wrong.

Admiring the way it didn't cling, squeeze or underline anything, I added a shiny burnt-copper beigey-green silk scarf that changed color under the light. I had to compensate somehow for the lack of make-up. There was no way I could wear mascara with these watery eyes today and not look like the actor Brandon Lee in *The Crow*. Besides, I could hardly keep them open. All I wanted to do was crawl back into my nice warm, comfy bed and sleep until Christmas. Or even better, next summer, by which time the divorce would no longer be a novelty to the kids.

I made it to work in record time and, way ahead of my schedule, I plunked myself down into my amazingly comfortable *Star Trekkie* swivel armchair behind my desk, ready to take on the day. If you're a working mom, you know how difficult it is to balance things. If you're a single working mom, I know exactly how you feel, doing everything on your own without a man at your side. My assistant, Jackie, poked her head round my office door. The look on her face wasn't good.

'Uh, Erica? We have a teensy-weensy problem.'

I sighed. 'Just give it to me straight.'

'There's a… um… flood on the third floor.'

'A flood,' I repeated calmly, as if she were talking about some remote, overpopulated and underfed village in some Third World country that I could sympathize with but do absolutely nothing about.

'And it's leaking onto the second.'

'Did you see where it's coming from?' I sighed at the blank look on her face. 'Never mind – I'll do it.'

Jackie was amazingly good with people, but she was a disaster with disasters. Me, I was good with disasters – and people with whom I didn't share a surname.

It was the boiler system. It had sprung a major leak, and there was nothing I could do but call the maintenance team and invite the guests on both affected floors to an improvised mid-afternoon buffet and drinks. In the meantime the in-house laundry service took care of transferring their sodden clothing to be dry-cleaned or washed and pressed, and we upgraded them all to a superior room. On top of that, I threw in a voucher for a two-night stay in any Farthington Hotel in North America, all compliments of the management. By the time I'd finished my reparatory spiel, I'd charmed the pants off them (their only dry pair) and the incident was forgotten. That was my job and I was amazing at it.

And motherhood? I did my damned best. The kids were always fed and read to and everything (well, not quite everything, but at least the most important things) that was natural for a woman to do for her family. I grimly pictured the list of women's chores and compared them to men's. Bit of a chasm there, not to say the entire Grand Canyon.

So, faced with the fact that I'd never be able to check mark all those chores, I did what I'd normally do at work. Prioritize. What was more important – cleaning my windows or helping my kids with their homework? To iron bed sheets, which no one ever sees anyway, or learn to play baseball with Warren – even if it meant knocking myself out and seeing stars in the process – and take Maddy to ballet classes? No contest.

And gosh, the look in their eyes whenever I dropped my vacuum cleaner and sat down to color? Much to Ira's annoyance, of course, because he always thought I did it to show him up, to underline the difference between mommy and daddy. He never understood it wasn't about him. He never understood it was simply about making the kids feel loved, about them coming first – before Sunday brunches, before our own hobbies.

I once had a passion for painting and had been told I was good at it, too. But I hadn't painted a landscape in years, though my fingers yearned to. Every time I saw a beautiful view or closed my eyes, I could see a million things I wanted to paint, could feel a million colors exploding within me, dying to get out. But I settled for coloring and making paper dolls with Maddy.

Ira, on the other hand, sometimes, if at all, paid attention to them the first half-hour he was home, but then lost interest. He was totally unaware of anybody else's needs and he'd slowly worsened over the years. A bit like my mom, in a way. These people lacked the sensitivity gene. They didn't realize what was going on around them or if someone, friend or family, was suffering. They'd never really loved, in my opinion. Never sat up all night worried about someone (Nonna Silvia had told me I was never sick as a baby, so I guess that was my mom's cue to take life easy).

As a child, every time I woke in the middle of the night with a nightmare, it was always, *always* my nonna who came to my bed with a glass of water, a chat and finally a good night hug. She was the only one who ever kissed me and said, 'Sleep well, sweetheart.'

Sleep well, sweetheart. I couldn't remember the last time someone had said that to me.

A few confused, phlegmy and foggy hours later during lunch, as I was writing a list of all the bad words I knew in Italian, like *bastardo* and *stronzo*, and linking them to Ira's name in a sort of spider-gram, I got a personal call from Mr. Foxham, the kids' new school principal.

Shit. He'd sent out a letter to the families with a new mission statement against the spreading phenomenon of bullying and what his main goals were, inviting us in to discuss whether or not our children felt safe, were happy, etcetera. I'd forgotten to RSVP *that* party.

And so, clutching the phone, I feared the worst, conjuring images of Warren hanging from the strip lights or the ceiling beams by his tie, courtesy of an older kid, or Madeleine's dress being torn to pieces by a posse of vicious girls kicking her and her pretty pink raincoat and matching boots around in the mud.

'Good morning, Mrs. Lowenstein,' came the voice of doom, calling me by a name that was no longer mine. 'I'm Mr. Foxham, Madeleine and Warren's principal.'

This wasn't going to be pleasant. Memories of my homeroom teacher, Miss Briton (who was actually Australian), talking down to me in her crisp accent, surfaced and in a single moment, I relived the worst years of my school life.

I felt my own diction tighten accordingly. 'Yes, good morning, Mr. Foxham. Is there a problem?'

A pause. Oh, that deadly pause where I saw at least one of my kids lying lifeless…

'No, no, they're quite alright, Mrs. Lowenstein. Warren's sitting a math test at the moment and Madeleine is doing art, her favorite subject.'

I exhaled in relief. The personal touch hadn't escaped my notice. They were always nice to you before delivering the blow.

'Warren didn't cheat, did he? I told them a million times it's better to get a C that's yours than someone else's A.'

He chuckled. A warm, deep chuckle, and I hung on to it as a guarantee that whatever he had to say couldn't be *that* bad.

'Well, you're right about that. Mrs. Lowenstein, would it be possible for you to pop round here today? Say an hour or so before the last bell? Would half two be alright? That way you'll just be in time to take the children home when we're done.'

What the hell were we going to talk about for an hour? How bad was it?

'Are you going to expel them?' I asked meekly and totally out of context, I don't know why.

'Oh, no, Mrs. Lowenstein. I just need to talk to you, if that's alright.'

Actually, it wasn't. Nothing was alright. I knew they were feeling the strain of the household, even if Ira and I were civil in front of them. It was obvious by the way that they dropped themselves at the kitchen table lately when we all got in: sullen, tired and irritable. They were starting to look more and more like Ira every day. Which was the reason I knew I'd need all the help I could get.

'I'll be there, Mr. Foxham.'

'Brilliant. See you then, Mrs. Lowenstein.' And he put the phone down.

Besides dreading what he needed to see me about, I couldn't stand the sound of Ira's surname next to my name anymore, I realized with a sudden panic. I mean, it really bothered me, *hurt*-bothered me, like salt inflicted on an open wound.

I knew Mr. Foxham was a good principal, but I'd never actually met him, which I knew was bad. I hoped he didn't think I was a terrible mother and that the time had come for my comeuppance.

I got Jackie to take over for the rest of the day and drove to Clifton Street Private School (Ira had vetoed Parker, probably because it was free) with my stomach in my mouth and my heart trying to make its way out through my nostrils. I hadn't felt this nervous since my job interview at the hotel years ago, where I sat before Mr. Harold Farthington, sweating buckets in my navy suit and silk scarf, looking like an inflatable airline hostess. I did that when I was nervous. Sweat buckets. And wear silk scarves. So really, nothing much had changed since then.

In a matter of minutes, I was ushered into the principal's office in a state of sheer terror, clutching my scarf as if it had magical powers. I attempted to breathe normally, hoping my imminent panic attack didn't show too much.

'Good afternoon, Mrs. Lowenstein.' He greeted me cheerfully, extending a large hand.

I held out my own shaky one and looked up at him, and my knees almost buckled as I sucked in my breath. And my tummy. It was *him*, my spider-whisperer! In the flesh. And me looking like crap. It was just my friggin' luck.

I pulled my scarf closer to my throat and my scruffy bag closer to my chest, hoping the floor would have mercy on me and swallow me up. Of all the nice outfits I had for work and out of the 365 days of the year, I had to choose today to look – and feel – like shit.

'G-good afternoon, Mr. F-Foxham,' I stuttered, still holding his hand, hoping he didn't remember me as again that strange heat instantly settled over me.

It was like being in a healing cocoon, where nothing could ever harm me – something I'd experienced only that one time on the floor of the ladies' room in that downtown restaurant. The feeling of being enveloped by the warmth and protection of his large, powerful body had stayed with me while I secretly fantasized about him like crazy for the past few weeks. But what was the point? He was completely out of my league.

More gorgeous than I remembered. A bod like an athlete, with shoulders so wide even I could stretch out on them for a nap, and a chest that looked so lean and solid you could use it as a surfboard.

And his eyes – the color of chocolate. It had been years since I'd been perturbed by male beauty. I mean really overwhelmed. I felt my face catch fire at the thought of him having seen me in my underwear and wished I could vanish into thin air. Now if only he didn't remember *me*, my whole life would be made.

He grinned, and I was awarded with a perfect white dazzle of a smile. He should have been in the pictures, with his athletic physique that only made him look terrific beyond bearable.

I felt as if time had disappeared. How long had he been sitting there smiling at me? Was it still daylight outside? I glanced out of his window just to make sure I hadn't been abducted by a gorgeous alien or something, but nope – here I was, on Earth, still trying to breathe properly, my eyes still glued to his beyond handsome face and my hand still in his.

A slight red seeped into his cheeks as he let go. Oh my God! A blushing hunk. I always thought they were a myth. He was my ideal man, the one with the perfect everything (I didn't get a chance to steal a glance down *there*, but I'm sure it was all in order).

He looked at me with a funny expectant look as I dreaded

the moment he'd recognize me and see my goodnight fantasies of having so much absolutely savage sex with him that it was shamefully greedy.

He cleared his throat. 'Do you, ah… remember me?'

Shit, shit, shit. I pretended to think and then finally shook my head. 'I'm sorry,' I finally apologized. 'No.'

He shrugged. 'It's OK. You were upset. I'm not crazy about spiders, either.'

You know when the floor beneath you opens and you plunge into a black abyss of shame? Multiply that by one billion. Go figure that the one time I'd been naked in public (well, two if you count my hospital escape), a guy like this would see me.

Embarrassment roiled through my every cell as I recalled how I'd begged him to take off my pants, acting like an absolute psychopath, the kind who runs screaming down the main streets and you move off to one side, averting your gaze, trying not to make eye contact. You know the kind. In any case, the jig was up. I could no longer hide.

'You're…'

He grinned shyly. 'The spider bloke, yes.'

Oh, God, please kill me now. Just swat me out of my miserable existence and get rid of me for once. I slapped my hand over my eyes, waiting, *wanting* to die. I peeked up at him through my fingers. 'I'm absolutely mortified you had to see that…'

'Don't be. I never thought I'd run into you again.'

Him and me both. Which was why it had been OK to fantasize about that encounter over and over in my mind, changing the ending to where we wound up at dinner together and then... well, let's just say if you have to dream, dream big.

Now for something intelligent to say. 'You must think I'm a total lunatic.'

He grinned. 'Of course not. Well, maybe just... original.'

'Gee, thanks.'

'So, how are you?'

'Still hating spiders. And you? Still patrolling the ladies' rooms for damsels in distress?'

Why couldn't I just learn to keep my mouth shut? Now, my children's principal would always remember me not only as the woman with the big bum, but also the one with the big mouth. And to top it all, this morning I even smelled like mothballs. Better run to repairs and show my human civil side.

'I'm so sorry to have caught you up in that.' Meaning between my thighs. Not that I minded. 'And to have caused you such trouble with security.'

'Nah they know me. I told you, I'm a regular there. And I'm so glad I got to see you again.'

I swallowed, trying to play it cool as that familiar rushy feeling sent all my blood from my brain, making the rest of my body hum. I can't even describe how his presence overwhelmed me. He was extremely fit and his body reverberated masculinity. All I could do was swallow and stare back at him, my mind experiencing complete shutdown, except for the memory of his arms around me as we lay (him crouched, me kicking at the spider) on the cold bathroom floor, him whispering soothing words and me trembling like Jell-O and begging him to take off my pants. I wondered if that would work on him again, only without the spider.

I said nothing, taking in every possible detail of him, starting with the black hair that curled past his collar and the long dark lashes. Beautiful lips. Square jaw. Kindness. Pure male harnessed by polite manners. If he ripped off a lady's clothes the same way he did mine, then the guy was a keeper for sure. Someone I might have fallen in love with a thousand years ago, before my body was sexually anaesthetized by marriage, children and everything in between.

I noticed he wasn't wearing a suit as principals always do but graced a pair of khaki pants that barely hid the thigh muscles vibrating underneath and a dark green sweater that highlighted the broad shoulders even if it wasn't fitted. You could just tell he was lean and ripped. I tried to remember the last time I'd met someone so gorgeous and kind, and then I knew. Never.

The temperature of my body rose considerably and I began to sweat again, making my skin so slick I almost slid straight out of my coat, like jelly from a tube, and off my chair twice. Almost. How high did this guy *need* his thermostat set? I unbuttoned my collar, then some more to clear my chest, which was swathed in layers of wool, so there was no danger in looking like I was exposing 'the boobs'. That was my sister Judy's department. But I was still boiling.

'So, *you're* Maddy and Warren's mom. What fantastic children you have,' he said.

As opposed to me, I mused, as he certainly looked surprised. 'Thank you, Mr. Foxham—'

'Please, call me Julian. After all, we're acquainted outside school.'

Meaning he'd seen my underwear. I wondered how many other mothers he was acquainted with.

I nodded. 'OK, I'm Erica, then.'

You know those plastic conference chairs, the ones for skinny people, where the only direction you can go is downward unless you plant your ass right in the center and your feet firmly on the ground? At the moment it was the only thing keeping me off the floor. And I looked like a bag lady, perched on the edge of a bridge, ready to jump, with no make-up (not that I wore much these days) as I fretted with my fingernails, conscious that I'd chipped one while backing out of The Farthington parking lot in my haste to get here. Nail polish was a no-no, because it would only be yet another deadline I had to meet. I was a total mess. And my hair – my arch-enemy – was in its usual face-lift-tight bun. I knew I looked like a harpy.

Mr. Foxham – *Julian* – noticed my uneasiness but pretended not to. Oh, he was very smooth. And all this time I'd been pining over someone I thought was a normal guy, not a professional parent-basher.

Why am I here? I wanted to blurt as he professionally assessed me behind a friendly smile. With horror, I felt myself sliding down my torture chair again and scrambled back up into my coat, which stood stiff of its own accord, planting my feet firmly on the carpet once again for purchase.

This could not be good. Something, I knew, was very wrong. And if fate would have it, then Mr. Spider-Whisperer here, who so obviously had it together, was going to give me news that would shatter my world…

'Erica,' he began, and I involuntarily said, 'Uh-oh.'

He smiled, white teeth sparkling at me through dark red lips, supported by a square chin. And despite his effort to shave that morning, I could already see the dark stubble shadowing his cheeks. *Tell me what's wrong, damn you!*

'Coffee? Tea?' he offered.

A basket case by now, I shook my head, wondering how long I could play it cool or whether I was about to fall apart.

'Right, let's not dally any further. Please forgive my bluntness but, in total confidentiality, is everything alright at home?'

There it was. My stupid act of hysteria had returned to bite me on the as. And then, to top it off, it happened. I slid off my chair, landing at his feet with a thud.

In an instant he was kneeling at my side. 'Are you OK?'

Am I OK? My husband has a lover and we're divorcing. I challenge anybody to be OK.

'I'm fine,' I snapped as he moved to haul me up, tears of humiliation pricking the back of my eyes.

I hoped he hadn't caught a whiff of my dingy eau de mothballs. In one swift movement that surprised even me, I lurched back to my feet on my own, saving the remains of my dingity – I mean, my *dignity*.

For good measure, I treated him to my famous evil eyeball, but he didn't flinch, either. It was official – I was starting to lose my touch.

'Now,' I said to the man who had seen my plus-size thighs, 'can you please tell me what makes you ask such a question, let alone pry into my personal life?'

It wasn't me, Erica Lowenstein, the lousy housewife talking, but Erica Cantelli. My brave, haughty alter ego, the super hotel manager, the one who kicked ass and was never talked to without paramount respect. And boy was she angry now.

Julian was thrown for a split second but recovered fantastically. And with such class.

'Erica, it's not about your personal life per se. It's about the children. They're showing signs of abnormal behavior and we're just concerned.'

'Concerned? I see,' I answered, having regained composure and possession of my wits. I didn't care if this gorgeous guy was Mr. Universe himself – he had no right to… to pry into my soul and bring out all the things I was doing wrong.

'I'm not trying to pry into your soul, Erica. I'm just worried.'

I looked up at him in horror as I realized I'd spoken my thoughts. Did I also say the Mr. Universe part? Aww, to hell with it all. I didn't give a damn anymore about anything. I was just tired and wanted to go home to Maddy and Warren. And a cartload of aspirin.

Mr. Foxham – Julian – hadn't returned behind his desk but lingered with his butt on the armrest of a nearby chair, facing me.

I sighed. This guy was like a hound with a carcass. And he wasn't letting go of it. Better get it out, if it helped the kids.

'I'm not… exactly in the best place at the moment,' I managed.

He nodded sympathetically. 'Problems?'

'Just stressed and overworked. I've got so many responsibilities, I'd have to be a schizophrenic to handle every role in my life and not go crazy. Does it show that much?'

He chuckled and peered into my face as if to count how many personalities lurked inside me.

'No. It's just the way the kids talk about you. You're their heroine.'

I sat up higher. 'Hmm,' I said, trying not to sound too impressed, although my whole life had just been made in this one sad but unexpectedly glorious moment.

'If they had to choose between their dad and their mom's, er, many personalities, it would be every single one of yours.'

So not only was the hunk sympathetic, but he also had a sense of humor. Big deal. 'Ah, I'm not sure I'd try to encourage this kind of confession from a pair of kids, Mr. Foxham,' I drawled softly, back in the saddle.

He looked at me squarely with those eyes and the hair on the back of my neck rose. Jesus, if his gaze had this effect on me, imagine if he reached out and *touched* me.

'It was something they revealed spontaneously. I didn't elicit it. No one did. Here, have a look.'

I glanced at the sheets of paper put in front of me, recognizing Madeleine's and Warren's writing. I read Madeleine's first. Her literacy levels were superior for her age, I'd been told time and again. But still, she was a child with a child's thoughts. I smiled at the colored sparkles all over the page:

My mom works all day in a hotel, but she always picks us up from school on time and bakes us a cake and makes us supper. She's never in a hurry to finish our evening bath when we talk and laugh. And when she tucks us into bed, she doesn't read us bedtime stories from a book. No, sir – she tells us about the weird people she meets every day, and she even makes their voices and makes us laugh.

(There was a smiley face instead of a period.)

My friends say she's big, but to me she's a star. I love her better than my dad, who yells at her saying she's too fat and ruins his life. I hate my dad.

Maddy Cantelli

Whoa. The story of my life spread out for the world on one scribbly page. I let out a storm of air, trying to catch my breath at the same time. The result was that I was choking on my own saliva and Mr. Foxham – Julian – had to give me a smart smack on the back. First, he rips my clothes off, now this. Our encounters were destined to be physical. Which, in a parallel life, would have sounded very promising, at least in theory.

'Better?' he asked, offering me a glass of water, which I took gratefully, downing it in one swig.

Maddy Cantelli. She'd used my maiden name, forsaking her own last name. Jesus.

'She gets the long sentences from me,' I tittered, clearing my throat, my eyes still watery from my close encounter with asphyxiation. 'I go on and on, even when I speak, just like I'm doing now, see? And the surname? That's my maiden name. And this is just one of her many Italian moments,' I continued, flashing him one of my brilliant pseudo-smiles. 'I'm Italian and she always wants to hear about Italy. She hates the name Lowenstein. So do I, really, but that's the way it is,' I finally sighed, stealing him a hopeful glance.

He wasn't buying it, of course.

'So, you're Italian? So am I. I mean, my mother was.'

'Oh. I'm sorry. Not that she's Italian – that she's no longer—'

Julian waved it away. 'My adoptive parents are British. My real mother was Italian.'

So that was where his Mediterranean looks came from. I was fascinated. Somewhere, there was a woman who had abandoned her baby. Oh, if only she could see the man he'd become. I shuddered at the thought of abandoning either of my kids.

'Oh. Well, we Italians are a bit... well, you know. Original, to quote you. But we're good, solid people.'

He smiled. 'I'd like to retrieve my roots. Learn to speak Italian, soak in the culture, cook.'

All things I could do with my eyes closed, but there was no way I was offering to help him achieve his goals and spend time with him. I had enough problems of my own.

He cleared his throat. 'So, Erica. The contents of the letter – are they true? Is there a problem at home? Please forgive me, but you know, we are—'

Worried, yeah. No shit. Here I was, sitting like a schoolgirl on detention with this guy trying to stick his nose in my family business. And he actually expected me to pour out my soul to him in one go – all the pain and hurt and humiliation I'd been through because my husband saw me as a walrus and the fact I'd always imagined killing him. Consequently, to keep my family together, I had to jump through hoops, day in, day out. How dare he question my love for my children – my reason for living.

He sat there, his long fingers resting on the edge of the armchair, just waiting, like one would for a cappuccino. Easy for him to be so calm and collected, while inside I was screaming.

I jumped to my feet. 'I'm sorry; I can't do this right now. I'll call back to reschedule if you want, but right now, I can't stay. Thank you for your concern,' I managed as I brushed past him and out of his office, tears in my eyes, clutching Maddy's letter in my right hand and Warren's unread confession in my left.

I wandered aimlessly through the school grounds, watching a game of baseball before finally plopping myself down on a bench, smoothing the wrinkled sheets of Warren's letter over my thigh. Not that I was dying to hear more about my withering marriage or my fat ass, but it was a 'now or never' epiphany moment.

'*My dad is a prick*,' I read and then moaned. I agreed with him fully, of course, but never, *ever* had I wanted my children to wake from their innocent childhood and see the truth.

He never plays baseball with me, goes to the games on his own and always sits in front of the TV watching the pros play. He never smiles, and always says what do we know about his life and dreams. I have a dream, too.

That one day I hit him over the head with a baseball bat. And it feels good. And then we're all free.

Oh my *God* – my poor kid. Was it possible that he'd inherited my not-so-comical visions of murder?

He keeps it behind his bed and at night hits my mother with it.

What?

I know because I can hear her crying sometimes. Even if I give her a hard time, I love my mother. She's cool, even when she tries to play baseball with me. Last week she swung so hard, she fell on the grass and saw stars, but she laughed and asked me to teach her.

I sat there and, as quietly as I could, bawled my eyes out into my scarf. Our deepest, most intimate secrets were now disclosed, splayed wide open for a stranger to see. Worse than that, a stranger whose job was to judge us. But the baseball bat part was all wrong. Ira had never, ever touched any of us. Images of social services carting my kids away shot through my mind, brandishing my brain cells with words like 'incompetent and inept mother', and I was so ashamed. Was I that much of a loser?

'Erica?' came the deep voice of scholarly authority.

I stiffened and swiped at my eyes while keeping them trained on his shoes. How long had he been standing there?

'Are you OK?' he whispered.

'No, not really,' I answered stonily.

'Do you mind if I sit down?'

I shrugged. 'It's your school.'

He sat next to me, looking ahead of him, but, funnily, I felt he was tuned into my situation. All this time I'd been fantasizing about him as my dream man, a fresh start, or maybe just a quick scene, and here he was, with a front-row, humongous panoramic view of me, my life – and my exterior vastness and interior littleness. There was no way I could ever hide from him and pretend I was someone else now.

At least he had the decency to remain quiet. I had to hand him that. I enjoyed the silence for a while. He seemed OK with it, too.

'The baseball bat part – it isn't true,' I finally whispered.

He turned to me. I knew he didn't believe me.

'Really, it isn't.'

Stormy eyes bored into mine.

'The last bell is about to ring, Erica. Why don't you come into my office and freshen yourself up?' he suggested gently and then grinned. 'I have this amazing bathroom with expensive tiles. The previous principal must have splurged the school's yearly budget on it.'

'No, that's OK, thanks. I think I'll go use the little girls' room.'

The last thing I needed was to be seen exiting the principal's toilet. Then, my reputation of lousy mother would be complete. Didn't he know any better?

'Yes, on second thoughts, that's a better idea,' he said, as if reading my mind and offering me his hand to help me to my feet.

I pretended I didn't see it and brushed past him.

The little girls' room wasn't such a good idea, after all. The mirror was too low and I had to squat to see myself. And I almost fell over again at the sight of me. Yesterday's mascara (now how the hell had I missed that?) streamed in black lines down my cheeks. Dried whatever-it-was, hopefully not snot, caked my nostrils and my hair, once in a tight, professional bun, was a mess. Plus, I stank too much to be true. I removed my coat and air-dried my armpits. Then I slicked my hair behind my ears into a semblance of a ponytail and rubbed the various kinds of guck off my face. There. Not pristine, but much better. I left the building without saying goodbye and waited in the car to gather my wits.

'Hi,' I chirped as the kids tumbled in, school bags landing on the back seat.

'What happened to *you*?' Warren asked as Madeleine started pulling her drawings out of her satchel to show me.

There were rainbows and colorful flowers everywhere. The drawings of a happy, serene little girl.

How long would this childhood happiness last if I didn't get my ass into gear pronto? As I turned on the ignition, I realized I need a year-plan with all the things that needed changing, bar none. I'd make a complete list and pin it up in my mind's eye.

Later that night, I went through my precious stack of *Ville & Casali* – a glossy Italian home magazine that had an enormous real estate listing of luxury homes and farmhouses throughout Italy. I flipped to the Tuscany section and feasted my eyes on all the possibilities, my mouth watering every single time, despite the fact that I knew each listing verbatim. And also despite the fact that there was no way on earth I could afford them.

Beautiful two-storey stone buildings, solid like a fortress, surrounded by vineyards and green fields and patios and pools, where I could see my kids frolicking and being happy. Inside, magnificent terracotta tiles and chestnut wood beams on the ceilings supporting terracotta vaults. Large spaces, big, sunny rooms and the cicadas singing outside in the sun. Lazy lunches under the wisteria-laden pergola, sipping a glass of my own wine with Paul (in absence of a proper male lead) as my gaze spread over the land I owned. Day in, day out, just my loved ones and me.

I sighed, flipped the magazine shut, hauled the stack back onto the nightstand and pulled out my notepad to stare at the year-long plan I'd written only a few months ago. It was like someone else had scrawled those hopeful words. How things had changed in such a short space of time:

'Home', I'd written.

OK with grocery shopping and meals. Need to hire a cleaner. I can't do it all by myself.

Job: Fulfilling. Well-paid. But need to cut back on the hours.

Kids: Need to spend more time with them to make up for Ira. Warren needs extra attention. Maddy's a dream.

Now, I scribbled in:

Problem: How to be there for them all the time?

And then I smiled and wrote:

Solution: Leave Ira, move to Tuscany and start my own vacation property business once and for all.

And then my eyes darted to the box at the bottom of the list titled 'Love Life', with Ira's name in it. Tears streaming down my cheeks, I crossed his name out, back and forth, until I made a hole in the page. And then above it, I wrote:

Julian Foxham: in a parallel world.

I I

Turbo-Mama

If it weren't for my job, I'd never see anywhere outside Boston City Center. It had widened my horizons but slimmed (I do hate that word) my chances of being a good mother and wife – according to Ira.

'Erica, you just can't keep going off on business trips all the time,' Ira had curtly said to me during one of my calls home.

'And you,' I snapped back, 'can't keep talking to me like I'm your dumb wife. You lost that right when I opened my eyes and saw you for who you really are.'

He groaned. 'You have to be here every day. Your mother is driving me crazy again!'

I huffed. God, I hated him. One more month to go before the New Year, when he'd move out. But he was right. Marcy wasn't by any stretch of the imagination anyone's ideal babysitter.

'There's no one who can do this job here but me,' I

explained for the umpteenth time in twelve years. That someone was doing a better job than me in the sack was the strong unsaid message.

I heard him snort. What Ira refused to understand was that fieldwork had given me the bonuses that we needed to stay afloat. We were living way beyond our means and at the end of every month, I calculated we'd just made it and breathed a sigh of relief. Until the next month. But next month I'd be free of his car payments and, yes – even the rental of his office space. He was on his own from now on and my purse strings breathed a sigh of relief. Let him finally fend for himself.

Considering he was a 'business expert', Ira had no idea of our financial situation. I was sure he'd screwed up his company because of his lack of organizational skills. He concentrated too much energy on maintaining his IT equipment rather than his clients and services. What Ira needed was to accept advice. If not from me then at least from someone else who would make him wake up and smell the coffee.

'I've got someone else on the other line – I have to go,' he said hastily and hung up, but I knew it wasn't true.

I shut my cellphone, feeling like shit – there was no better word for it. *Hang in there, Erica*, I thought to myself. *These dark days will soon end. They have to.*

I looked in the mirror and saw a young old girl, with bags under her once pretty eyes, a messy head of hair, and a face bathed in anxiety and exhaustion.

I was already going away on business twice a month and had greatly improved the quality of our hotels, much to my boss' joy, so I knew that even more trips would have to be made. But I was missing out on entire days of my children's lives. They were growing up – and I was growing old – away from them.

That night, like every other night I was away, I lay in a luxurious Farthington hotel room, this time in Seattle, Washington, hours before my real bedtime. Sleep eluding me as usual, I stared at the ceiling and listened to the typical hotel sounds: the heating system quietly humming recycled air though the vents, the wheels of the baggage cart softly squeaking through the plush, thick carpeting of the corridors, toilets flushing (no amount of luxury can eliminate that) and the occasional grinding of keys in bathroom door locks. I missed my children terribly.

As I lay there, waiting to fall asleep, Julian, or my projection of him, quietly stepped into the room.

'What are you doing here?' I ask, sitting up suddenly, but he puts his finger against my lips and shushes me gently.

'I'm your erotic dream,' he whispers.

'Oh,' I answer. That made so much more sense.

He sits on the edge of my bed and as I open my mouth to speak, he catches my lips in a toe-curling kiss, his mouth hot, soft but firm on mine, coaxing (as if he needed to) a response from me. Now unless I can get him drunk and abduct him just so I can have that one kiss, that's the kind of kiss that would shake me from my foundations to my roof beams.

'You're so beautiful, Erica,' he whispers, sliding under

the covers, which at this point become redundant, seeing how hot it is in here all of a sudden. 'Can I make love to you, Erica?'

'You need to ask, foxy headmaster?'

'I'm going to have to keep you here all night on detention.'

Okay, it was a lame dream, I knew it, but after all these years without any romance whatsoever, I was easy to please.

A loud screech brought me to my senses, pushing him right off me. *What?* Where had he gone?

I slapped at the alarm clock uselessly and moaned in grievance, leaning over the side of the bed, scanning the carpet, wishing he'd been real, willing him back to me, and willing myself to continue with the dream. But, as a dearly departed one, he was lost to me forever. Or at least until my next erotic dream.

The next day when I got back home, as the first point of my multipoint plan toward happiness and well-being, I decided to face my boss.

'Can't Jackie go to Denver?' I asked him. 'She's never seen Colorado and I really need to stay home with my kids more, Mr. Farthington. Like we agreed.'

He seemed to consider it. 'Jackie's great, but she lacks your flair. I need you out in the field, Erica.'

'You promised it would only be a couple of times per semester. I practically live in my suitcase and my kids miss me. I should be at home with them more.'

He sighed. 'I'm sorry. No.'

And that was his final word. But not mine.

Maddy was a jubilant little girl. Perhaps too jubilant. And she loved the hotel elevators. Just what I'd counted on. Our guests were amused by this charming little thing who hopped on and off for hours on end, striking ballet poses when the doors opened on her. She was a bit too vain for my taste, just like my mother. I hoped it would wear off soon. But today it served my purpose.

The news of the charming miniature ballerina reached Harold Farthington by the end of the day and he called me immediately. 'I run hotels, not day care centers, Erica.'

'I'm sorry, Mr. Farthington, but if you keep me away from my family, I have no choice but to bring my family here.'

There was a long silence.

'Three trips per month,' he said finally.

'No. One,' I bargained.

'Two. That's my final offer,' he bargained back.

'Only if I choose which ones to attend. And that's *my* final offer, Mr. Farthington.'

This time the silence was longer. I found I was holding my breath and I realized I cared about keeping this job more than I thought. It was, after all, our family meal ticket. At least until I could get us to Italy.

'Agreed,' came his final verdict, and I grinned into the phone.

'Thank you, sir. I appreciate it.' It had taken me eight hours to crack the bastard.

12

Ball and Chain

Weeks later and I was still running around like a madwoman. One good thing about splitting up from Ira was that he wouldn't be missed by the kids in the least. He was like a pro-forma father, existent in theory but not in practice.

By the time I got the kids to plunk their rear ends on their chairs for dinner, I was exhausted. I could have easily ordered a pizza or a KFC and called it a night, but it was important for me to do something for them. So together we baked different kinds of pizzas and a chocolate cake and played Twister until they howled with laughter at my less-than-dignified poses while I kept telling myself, *yes, you're heading in the right direction, Erica. This is what life's all about.*

That evening when I put the munchkins to bed, their eyes were drooping but at least their mouths weren't. On her bedside table, Maddy had left me a drawing. Like me, she was very arty. She loved colors and when she had a packet of Smarties, instead of shooting them down her throat missile-style like I did, she played with them, passing them from one hand to the other, watching the flow of blues, pinks and reds, mystified. In dismay, I'd often watched her use hand-paints on the living room walls with vigorous, almost ferocious creativity. And then Paul would come up with some obscure cleaning product that worked miracles, saving the day.

Like me, she was dying to express herself and be free of restrictive boundaries like the lines in her coloring books. Like the thick black lines surrounding my own life.

Maddy was more like me in every way. For this, I have to thank my grandmother's genes and her solid presence in my life. Nonna Silvia taught me everything I know. Thanks to her, I actually had a shot at homemaking. But sometimes, when I dropped the kids off for parties or sleepovers, I craved to be like those slim, suburban cookie-cutter moms in pearls and pastel twinset tops, smiling and waving at me from their pristine doorsteps while I sped past them, still secretly pulling my tights on or applying deodorant. I know, I'm a real class act.

If I had more time, my house could be pristine, too. I was managing to cook meals and give my children quality time and help with their homework and be the mother Marcy never was. Who cared if my windows still needed doing? Sometimes it was easier to watch the world through an opaque glass anyway.

The other moms, who were all stay-at-homes, knew I had a high-power job and I'm sure they had something to say about that among themselves. I didn't belong in their circle and would never be one of those straight-bobbed, tennis bracelet moms. The elitist group of perfect women – helicopter moms, if you ask me – would always elude me, no matter how hard I tried.

But exactly how perfect were they in reality? Did any of them have pseudo-homicidal thoughts about their husbands like me? Did they have satisfying sex lives? Or did they simply survive by taking a lover? I didn't have time for a man unless he wore an apron and an earring, and his name was Mr. Clean. But I always had time for my erotic Headmaster Foxham dreams, which didn't count because they didn't impact on my waking hours.

Sometimes, when I returned from my business trips, I crept to the kids' rooms just to sit and breathe in their fresh baby scent, Maddy would roll over and look at me, eyes huge in her pink princess nightlight, and stare at me as if I were her fairy godmother and not simply her mom. I guess she saw me so rarely lately that she was beginning to wonder if I was just another fairy-tale creature. And if I existed only at night, for a brief moment. She would watch me in awe, before her long baby lashes finally fluttered as she succumbed to her baby dreams.

Now that I was completely on my own, I had to organize a nine-to-five shift, or better, a nine-to-three one, where I could be there to pick up Warren and Maddy after school.

'Why don't you just quit?' my aunt Maria suggested simply one day as she was preparing Le Tre Donne's winter special for the day, the vegetable minestrone. No frozen veggie bags for her restaurant, no sir. Every day, she and her sisters got up at 4 a.m. to make bread, cakes, muffins and serve breakfast, then they'd start preparing lunch. I often came here on my break to grab a quick bite. And for some family gossip that was usually about my mom's latest extravagance, invariably a shopping spree in New York.

'Quit my job?' I could feel my eyes pop out of my head as I drank the coffee Zia Maria had brewed me. 'How would I even manage to survive? Besides, the women in our family have always worked. What if Zia Monica heard you?'

Zia Monica was the youngest of Marcy's sisters and the most progressive. She's a Xerox copy of my nonna Silvia, in both body and soul. She believes in progress, particularly for women, and technology. For a woman to quit her job and be a homemaker was unheard of. Of course, all three sisters were spinsters. The most beautiful spinsters I'd ever seen.

Zia Maria pointed her potato peeler at me and grinned. 'You could always come and work here. Give your mother a heart attack.'

I snorted my coffee through my nose. 'Give me that,' I ordered, taking the potato from her.

'No – start on the onions for me. Would you mind?' she asked.

Mind? I was an expert onion peeler. Plus, I didn't have any make-up on, so nothing to worry about.

'Besides,' I said. 'Restaurant work has no strict hours. I'd merely be changing address.'

'Not if you stick to your hours as a regular employee. Drop everything when the clock strikes.'

'You know I couldn't do that to you, Zia Maria,' I said. 'I can barely do it at the hotel.'

'Which is becoming your second home,' she scolds me.

'I know. That's why I'm going to do something about it.'

'Good girl. I've wrapped up a chocolate cake for you to take home,' she said. 'Think about the job offer.'

'You're nuts. But thank you.'

And so I thought about it. Could I do it? The hours were just as crazy; half of Massachusetts showed up at lunchtime sometimes. I'd see the kids even less. No. I had to find another way.

'No more, Warren, or you'll become a blimp,' Ira said as we devoured Zia Maria's cake after dinner that evening.

What Ira hadn't said was 'like your mom', but I knew that was what he meant. The context was clear as crystal. By now, I was counting the weeks until I'd be free.

Even if we managed to avoid direct confrontation in front of the kids, things were still pretty bad between us. We were at the point where he'd sit at the dinner table and read his paper without communicating for hours while I did the dishes and cleaned up in absolute silence. I was done with him. Finito.

Even on weekends, for which I practically made a pact with the devil to be home, we'd ignore each other. He'd sit at that same table with yet another paper while I played with the kids or did some chores. Let me tell you, if only where he was concerned, it was a relief to go back to work on Monday.

Why was it that I could run The Farthington, a responsibility of titanic dimensions, but struggled to keep my own home, a little dinghy with four passengers, afloat? One thing was for sure – there was one passenger whose head I'd gladly hold underwater until he stopped kicking. But enough of my fantasies...

Luckily, at home I had Paul, who was living with us more often than not. He took care of the kids until I got home, and then we had dinner and exchanged gossip.

One evening, we were sitting on the sofa drinking a lovely Sicilian Corvo Novello, kids in bed, glad to have some 'us' time with my second ideal man (minus the sex). Every time I was sinking and needed a hand, it was Paul, and not Ira, who reached out for me, pulling me back above the surface, bless him.

'So, how's your hunky headmaster?' he asked.

You can imagine how he'd flipped when I told him Spiderman and headmaster were one. He'd professed that it was fate and what the hell more did I need to understand that? I only wished.

'I haven't seen him for a while, but I'm assuming he's as delectable as ever,' I answered as I took a sip of one of Sicily's miracles.

He shook his finger at me. 'You shouldn't be wasting your time like this. Things don't happen without a reason and even you said he was the man of your dreams.'

'Dreams – exactly. This is reality, Paul, and men like that aren't interested in women like me.'

'Meaning?'

I thought about it. As it turned out, dieting wasn't impossible and I was getting into the swing of things, especially with Paul power-dancing me a few hours a week, along with brisk walks in the park. Slowly but surely, I was starting to see the weight go, ounce after aching ounce. It was slow, like watching paint dry, but it was happening. It was ghastly work, resisting my favorite foods and only having this one glass of wine a week, but every time I stepped onto the bathroom scales, it was pure, unadulterated (if you'll pardon the pun) bliss. Even if I'd never be a supermodel, who cared? I was me and was happy to be me. I only wanted to be a healthier, fitter me. For myself and my kids.

I huffed. 'Meaning, Paul, that most men don't like women who are big.'

'Oh, big, shmig,' he said with a wave of his perfectly manicured hand. 'What's wrong with having some fun? Look at you, almost thirty-five, two kids you're raising on your own, a job that totally absorbs you and your soon-to-be ex-husband can't be bothered to'—he hooked his fingers into quotation marks in my face—'make the effort.'

Ouch. Put like that, it sounded like pure hell. I gave him the hairy eyeball and crossed my arms in front of my chest. 'What's your point?'

He looked at me, unperturbed. 'That you're looking better and better every day, and that you should have a fling.'

Of course he was right, but I wasn't ready to admit it yet. 'I don't want a fling.'

'That's because you don't remember what it feels like. To feel your insides go all jittery and your heart flutter. Oh, the ecstasy!'

'You've been reading too many romance novels,' I quipped.

'I love Carl and I'm going to miss having him around,' Paul confessed in a sigh. 'With all his uptightness and dedication to those stupid scripts and no time for me... I still think we were made for each other.'

I smiled, thinking how similar we were, even if he didn't realize. 'Then don't leave him, Paul. Give him a chance. Everybody loves somebody, like the song.'

'No, honey, the song I remember says "everybody needs somebody". And you need this principal–spider guy to give you a good—'

'Quit saying *spider*. I hate that word and I hate thinking about that episode.'

Which was bull. I thought about him all the time, reveling in the feeling of his strong arms around me, protecting me, his lips against my ear, soothing me. And now Principal Foxham had gone and spoiled even my fantasies by being a respectable man and not a sex toy for my...

I sat up and listened, my ears pricking while mother instinct (even I had it by now) told me the house was too quiet. I listened some more, waiting. Nothing. But a trip down the corridor was enough to kill me.

All over the walls, at Maddy-level, were big bright wax lines of every color imaginable. She'd been trying every single one of her new 64-pack Crayolas. As I stepped toward her, she turned and gave me one of her sweetest smiles. I wanted to cry on the spot, but instead I scooped her up and put her back to bed, while Paul came to the rescue with a sponge, chasing all the drawings around with the bottle of Fantastic he'd bought and put under the sink, where I'd be sure to see it, eventually.

'It's OK, see?' he said. 'All gone.'

'Marry me?' I said. 'Now?'

He slapped my shoulder with a giggle. I didn't care if he

was gay, didn't care if we wouldn't be having sex. He'd be a major improvement on my present marital situation, as we were way more intimate than my husband and I had ever been. All I really needed was someone on my side.

'We're already married, remember?' Paul soothed, running a hand up and down my arm.

The first adult male contact I'd had since Spider Hunk's hands around my arms weeks ago. I wondered where he was and what he was doing, and what his girlfriend or wife was like. Was he nice to her, or had the daily grind beaten them both into the ground, too? I couldn't imagine someone so kind telling his wife he didn't like the way she looked or anything. I was sure that if he had kids, he'd be a great father. Kind and dedicated.

'But I'll forgive you if you sleep with another man. Invite Julian out for a coffee. Go out and have fun.'

Fun? I looked up at Paul. He was right. I was going to try to raise the amount of enjoyment in my life. Screw the walls, the windows, Ira and his scowls. From now on, I'd start thinking about me as well. And the little things in life that *I*'d always wanted to achieve. Like… growing real live flowers and not just my cactus-like succulents, for instance. And start painting again. And maybe, just maybe, have a fling…

13

Two Beds are Better Than One

I soon discovered that although at first humiliating and painful, separate beds actually meant oodles of freedom. You get double the space, you can watch late-night movies, make long-distance calls (it was irrelevant that I didn't know anybody long-distance apart from my fellow hotel managers scattered across North America), eat in bed, receive a booty call or whatever took your fancy.

A week later, I had to leave the safety of my car and venture into the school yard with the risk of seeing Julian. The school was having a bake sale and baseball match, and I'd had the suicidal idea of volunteering, just to show Julian Foxham I wasn't the total loser of a mother he thought.

Don't ask me why – they say the heart has reasons that reason cannot comprehend – but that day I took extra care with my grooming. I guess I wanted to make sure I looked tidy, clean and stable – the exact opposite of Julian's first impression of me – so I wore my best (and smaller-sized) skirt and a nice green top. Proper, but still casual and not trying too hard. I'd got over my cold and sent that damn burlap sack-of-potatoes suit to the dry-cleaner, hoping maybe they'd misplace it for me.

I baked the biggest and prettiest cake I could and after greeting everyone politely (*him* included – I didn't want him to think I was a nasty grudge-holder), I clung to the cake stand and served fruit juices: strawberry, orange and even a green kiwi that matched my top.

And then he came to stand next to me and helped with the drinks (personally, I could have used a Bloody Mary), making apparently harmless chit-chat. He told me that he'd moved to Boston from England when he was a *lad* and that he was bullied because of his accent.

'No, what accent?' I said, and he grinned, his eyes twinkling, reaching some deep, deep layer inside me.

I found myself smiling back and gulped down an entire glass of kiwi juice in one swig. He seemed to have that effect on me – the dry throat, I mean.

So far everything was going OK, he informed me. The kids (my kids) were having fun and had I said or done anything in particular lately, because they seemed happier.

'Mr. Foxham,' I said softly but with an edge of impatience, like when I told Ira off on one famous evening way back into the annals of our story. 'They *are* happy kids. Maybe a bit wiser than those who come from more solid couples, but I can assure you that everything is going to be alright.'

'What happened to calling me just Julian?' he asked quietly.

The same thing that happened to my erotic dreams about you and my desire to lick you from head to toe would have been an honest answer, but I shrugged, and he paused awkwardly. Boy, was I being difficult or what? But he could hold his own, too.

'So then the letter – the part about you and your husband – it isn't true?' he asked softly.

I turned to look at him and tell him it was none of his business, but the look in his eyes made me laugh. 'Like I said before, not the baseball bat part, no. I mean, we do have one in the remote chance someone tries to break in. He's still a Jersey guy at heart, but Ira would never ever hurt us. And before you ask, the kids are in no kind of danger. Ira isn't a violent man.' At least not physically, I thought to myself.

And I realized that Julian Foxham didn't need an office and a big desk to make me feel like I was under a microscope. He managed to do it right here in the open air on a sunny day, with his sexy yet professional gaze (how did he *do* that?) sweeping across my face. Oh, sure, he was pleasant and all that, but I knew what was going on behind those bedroom eyes. His personal Spanish Inquisition.

I pictured him and his perfect looks, his perfect job and perfect life, retiring in the evening to a practically perfect woman.

A sigh escaped me – a deep, sad one, as if I were moaning, crying and gasping for air at the same time. It was all I could do not to break down in tears. I took a deep breath and choked on my saliva, gasping for air, and he swatted – again – a hand against the space between my shoulder blades. One sharp blow, but it didn't hurt.

'Are you alright?' he whispered, and I nodded and blinked him an apology as I drank to the end of my juice.

To avoid looking at him, I filled a few more cups, lining

them along the edge of the table, pretending to be absorbed by the task. But all I could think of was the effect his hand had had on my back.

He looked at me kindly, his eyes soft, almost like a friend's.

'Erica Lowenstein,' came his deep, sympathetic voice.

I knew in a way he felt sorry for me and it annoyed me tremendously.

'*Cantelli*,' I said, warding off that dreaded surname.

'Cantelli,' he repeated musically.

It sounded nice, the way he said it, with that British twang. Ira always made it sound like *Erica can't tell yeh*. If he was questioning my using my maiden name, he didn't show it, the poker face.

'You're undeniably a good mother. One of the best, judging by those letters.'

I lifted my head. 'Really? You're not just trying to reel me in?'

'Erica, I just want you to know that I'm very sorry for upsetting you the last time we met. But you see, we were very—'

'Yeah, yeah. Worried about the kids. I get it. OK, Headmaster, what do you want to know? If my marriage is a happy one? No, it's not. Then again, I...' I stopped, biting my lip. This was none of his business anyway – nosy, gorgeous bastard.

'What? What were you going to say?'

'That if you want, you can come by any time after school to check on us. Then you'll see that they live in a comfortable, warm and loving home. Feel free to bring your social services, your guidance teacher or anyone you like.'

There. I'd said it. And then he was blinking at me. Finally, he sighed and took a sip of his juice as a kid approached with some change to buy a slice of cake.

'Did you bake that?' Foxham asked me, reaching into his pocket to buy a slice for himself.

I nodded and as he offered me a slice, I shook my head. I was still as disciplined as could be. The two most delicious things in the whole wide world were at that table and I was struggling to keep my hands off both of them.

He sighed. I knew I was being difficult, but this guy was really getting on my nerves, what with the prying and the unsaid sentences left hanging. I preferred him when he stuck to killing spiders.

'Mmm... delicious. From scratch?'

I nodded.

Julian pointed toward the baseball diamond. 'Look at Warren – he's just stepping up to bat, see? He's a real champion.'

Sure enough, Warren was readying himself, his legs finding their right stance, his hands testing his grip around the bat, his little face pale and his lips tight. This was going to be one of those historical moments in his life where his reputation would be made or broken.

I truly felt for my little guy and I know it's corny, but in that instant, as he stepped up to bat, I saw the first steps he ever took, and the look of sheer stupor on his toddler's face, followed by pure joy. The same look he had now as he hit the ball and sent it right out into space.

I squealed and cheered for my boy with the rest of his team and everyone else, so happy that I managed to punch my son's principal in the chest with all my strength, but he didn't flinch. Instead, he grinned and pulled the trophy off its stand to present it to Warren and his team.

'Great game, lad,' Mr. Foxham said, slapping Warren on the back.

I watched the exchange from afar, so proud of my boy I thought I'd burst into tears right there and then. The principal wasn't such a bad guy, after all. And he liked his students. He knew everything about them – and the parents. It occurred to me I knew absolutely zilch about him.

'If you don't mind my asking…' I said to Julian later as we were all saying our goodbyes and slowly making for our cars.

'Anything,' he said with a good-natured grin.

'You mentioned you were adopted. Have you ever thought about contacting your real parents?' Now where the hell had that extremely personal question come from?

'No.'

'Don't you want to?'

He thought about it. 'I don't want to break my mother's heart.'

'You could always do it secretly. Who'd know?'

Julian shook his head. 'If my real mother wanted to find me, she'd be able to trace me. Besides, I'm a bit of a mess with lies, I'm afraid. I tend to forget what I've said so just don't bother.'

'The ideal husband, then,' I said on instinct, and he flinched. 'Sorry.'

'No worries. I told you Warren's a trooper,' Julian exclaimed, changing the subject masterfully.

'Sorry about the punch, by the way,' I said.

He grinned and I grinned back, and together we charged

for my son, along with his teammates, who threw themselves all over him again. Warren caught my eye and winked, like I'd taught him when he was little. My little guy. It was all I could do from bursting into tears all over again.

'You're a fine mother,' Julian beamed at me, and I said, 'You know what, Headmaster Foxham? At times like this, I think so, too!'

'And, Erica? Do call me Julian. We are, after all, acquainted outside the school.'

What he was *really* thinking was, after all, I've seen you in your underwear – and they weren't the prettiest I've ever seen, either.

I shrugged. If he could call seeing my worst underwear being acquainted, I wished I had a chance to get to know him very well.

14

The Superman Syndrome

In the month leading up to Christmas, I was so miserable I barely ate, losing, as a result, two dress sizes. I'd gone from a size twenty to almost a sixteen without even noticing. Now *that* was a diet I wouldn't recommend any woman – *The Husband Diet*. It was so sad, I burst into a hysterical fit of laughter. Would it ever stop hurting? Would I ever be able to forgive myself for losing my husband, my children's (albeit absent) father?

But on the other end of my roller-coaster feelings, being lighter made me feel lighter *inside*, like those infomercials where you see a woman stepping out of a rubber flab costume to reveal her splendid new self. I was still far off from splendid, but even I could see how much better I looked. It was a great feeling.

Losing my weight as a teenager had implications nowhere near the ones I was experiencing now. Now, I was a woman with so much more at stake. It wasn't about chasing my crush down the street anymore. This was about the direction my life would be heading. I was now the one in the driver's seat. And although I hadn't had much control over my life in years, I was beginning to recognize the familiar flavor of freedom. Only back then, I'd called a lack of a man loneliness. What a difference an unloving, cheating husband made.

When I got home from work, I found a simple but pretty bouquet of wildflowers wedged into the door knocker with a note: *I think you're great. One day I hope to be able to tell you in person.* I stared at it blankly. Paul. Or a joke? It had to be. You, a smart chick, might have figured out already who it was, but believe me, it took me months to put two and two together, and even then, it still made no sense to me.

On parents' night, I masterfully avoided speaking to Julian, although I saw him excusing himself from a couple when he spotted me. I really didn't need anymore encouragement or sympathy, so I whirled around and pulled out my cellphone to dial Ira, who was supposed to be here.

'Can't you handle it?' he said tiredly.

I closed my eyes and swallowed. 'Of course.' And then I hung up.

We'd only communicated for the benefit of Maddy and Warren. Now, there was nothing else to say.

When I managed to get home without meeting the object of my erotic dreams face-to-face, I sent the babysitter home and looked in on the kids, who were sound asleep.

Contrary to what Ira had always thought, my bed was the best place on Earth and I fell into it without even getting undressed. If I'd figured it out right, the minute I closed my eyes my projection of Julian would come into my room as usual, slip under the covers and hold me, caress my hair and whisper sweet words of encouragement. That would gradually become more heated until I clung to him and he'd initiate crazy-amazing sex, and soon we'd be swinging from the chandeliers and bouncing off the walls. And that was when I'd knock my head against the headboard and wake up alone, drenched in tears.

On our way to Italian lessons (yes, we were finally getting a hold of our own life), I caught a glimpse of Judy, in a plaza, coming out of a supermarket. Before I could call her, she jumped into a shiny new jeep, and the man inside grabbed her and kissed her at length. It wasn't her husband, Steve. What the hell was wrong with everybody? Was betrayal contagious now? I was so shocked I rammed my Kia van straight into a parked car.

'Mo-om!' Warren wailed.

Shit.

'We can't be late! We can't be late! Please, Mom!' Madeleine begged. 'We're doing *colors* today!'

I dared a glance in Judy's direction. My little crash had brought her back to Earth and she turned to look at me in surprise. For a moment our eyes met. She had a look I'd never seen before. She spoke to him quickly and they drove off. Meanwhile, my crash victim had materialized, yelling and cursing at me.

'What the hell, lady! You blind or what?'

I guessed I was. More than I thought. Judy had a lover. After three kids and an eleven-year marriage. *And* a fantastic husband like Steve.

I sat there, stupefied, and when things couldn't get worse,

who (you guessed it) happened to come out of the sports store but Julian Foxham! He spotted me and the yelling man, and instantly came over to see what the kerfuffle was all about.

'What's the problem here?' he asked. 'Erica, are you OK?'

'Hi, Mr. Foxham!' Warren and Madeleine chimed in unison.

And then Maddy added, 'We're going to be late for our Italian lessons.'

I sighed as my hand drove through my hair. 'We've just had a little fender-bender, that's all.'

'This chick ran into my car!' the man spat.

Julian turned to him. 'Easy, mate. Let's see your insurance.'

Oh, just great. The last thing I needed was Julian coming to my rescue. 'I can handle it, Julian, thanks.'

The man stared at him. 'You're Julian Foxham! The former Red Sox baseball champion! Man! I can't believe it. Can I have your autograph, sir?'

Huh?

Julian grinned. 'Absolutely, just as long as you don't give my friend here any grief.'

'Nah,' the guy said as he disappeared to rummage through his glove compartment for pen and paper.

I stared at him in disbelief, then at Julian, who shrugged his shoulders with the cutest, most annoying grin.

'Glad to help,' he said.

'Gee, thanks,' I said more sarcastically than I meant, and Julian studied me with a strange light in his eyes.

It was my turn to gape. I was standing elbow to elbow with a sports star and I'd had no idea.

'All this time and I've been acquainted (my underwear flashed through my mind) with a baseball star?' I asked.

He shrugged. 'It was a long time ago.'

'And now you are a principal? Why?'

Julian shrugged again, turning red as if I'd caught him stealing. 'I broke my arm a few years back, lost my swing and eventually decided to use my degree in education, after all. My dad is a die-hard scholar. He teaches English literature in London. Plus, I like kids.'

'I just called a tow truck – for both of us,' the man volunteered as he returned, and Julian paused before signing his autograph.

'What's your name?'

'Larry. Larry Dignam. Thank you, sir. Wow. You just made my day. Is there any chance you might be considering a comeback?'

Julian stilled. 'I don't think so, mate.'

The man looked into his eyes and it was as if there had been an understanding that would have gone way over my head if I hadn't understood the pain he'd been through. Losing your status as a champion must have been hard on such a young man.

Julian then turned to me. 'Erica, why don't I take the kids to their Italian lessons? It's the one on Sudbury Street, isn't it? I'll be back in five minutes. OK?'

I couldn't argue with him. But when Julian drove off with my waving kids in his jeep, I resented it. This was *my* family, *my* problem, and it was up to me to solve it on my own.

Julian came back in time to take me down to the mechanic's. I'd totaled the front and the radiator, as well. Taking the bus home or calling a cab wasn't an option, according to Julian.

'I live right near here,' he said. 'I can drive the kids to school in the morning and then take you to work until your car's ready,' he said as he was driving me home.

I turned to look at him. Either he didn't have a life or was trying to fix mine.

'Uh, no, that's OK, thanks.' That was all I needed – Headmaster Foxham on 24-hour guard duty.

'It's no trouble at all.'

'I have a husband, you know,' I lied, then turned to check his face.

Did I mean I had a husband who could drive me or a husband who wouldn't appreciate me driving around with a good-looking guy?

He nodded dutifully and said, 'If you don't mind my asking...'

I sighed. 'Let's have it.'

'When the mechanic asked for your registration document, I couldn't help noticing you had a lot of parking tickets in your glove compartment.'

And his point was? Why did everybody think I didn't know how to park? This guy was worse than a damn bloodhound. Why was he constantly on my case?

'Speeding – *not* parking tickets,' I corrected tersely, then shrugged, because I knew he was going to ask me anyway. 'And they're paid, in case you're wondering about that, too. But yes, I'm always in a hurry – and always late.'

'Not picking up the kids you aren't,' he said kindly.

I smiled. At least he noticed the good things, too. 'No, and work. Except for those two, I'm late everywhere else. You name it – the beautician, my dentist appointments. So eventually, I stopped going. To the beautician.'

Not that that was info he needed. Besides, it showed big time. I sighed. I was still – always – a mess. Why didn't I just keep my mouth shut?

He turned to grin at me. I know it was intended to be a friendly one to put me at ease, but the fact was that I found it – him – sexy as hell. Now *that* was pure unmotherly behavior, forget skipping a school meeting or whatever.

'Where am I going?' he asked, tearing me out of my reverie.

'Oh. Uh, Quincy Shore Drive. Make a left at the lights. It's all the way down, number 3566.'

I was sure he'd already driven past the house to make sure it wasn't a dump or a fake address. Some principals could be real paranoid. Some mothers, too.

'Can I ask you a stupid question, Julian?'

He threw me a wry grin as we crossed a busy intersection. 'Of course.'

I hesitated. It wasn't any of my business. 'Are you sure you can't go back to playing baseball? Or at least coach outside the school? Or give the kids counseling or anything baseball-related? Warren tells me you're the best coach a boy could have.' There. I'd been as nosy as him. But it felt right to reciprocate, to show some level of caring.

He chewed on his lower lip for a while before answering and I could tell it was costing him a big effort. Why couldn't I keep my mouth shut?

'That part of my life is over, Erica. For good.'

Wow. That sounded pretty final. 'Don't you miss it?' I insisted, getting braver by the minute.

He hesitated and then shrugged. He was worse than me, this one, and I could tell by the angle of his shoulders it wasn't his favorite topic of conversation.

'Every day,' he whispered. 'But life goes on.'

I gaped in surprise. I hadn't expected such a candid admission from a guy who seemingly had it all together. I opened my mouth to say something equally intelligent and honest, but he looked out my window and I turned, too. We'd arrived.

'Nice,' he said.

He means the house, not you, you idiot. 'Thanks,' I said as I catapulted out of his car as if the seat had suddenly caught fire. At least mine had. The physical attraction for this guy was becoming more and more unbearable by the day. Funny, when you think he thought I was a real mess. And then I put my foot in it. 'You really should come by – for coffee. And to see that I'm not such a bad mother, after all.'

He searched my face to see if I was serious and finally grinned. 'I'd love to, thank you.'

I slapped my forehead. 'Aw, crap.'

He sat forward. 'What's wrong?'

The kids. I'd almost forgotten them. Where had the time gone? Great. Now I'd never get him off my case. There was no way I was going to confess him that much. 'Er, what time is it, please?'

'Six. What time are the kids done at Sudbury Street?'

'In five minutes,' I said meekly, knowing I was never getting rid of him now.

He grinned that oh-so-sexy grin at me again, motioning me back in with a flick of his head as if beckoning me back into his bed after a hot session of no-limits sex.

'Hop in. I know a shortcut.'

I eyed him, embarrassed, then obeyed. 'You're right – I am the worst mother in the world. But I swear I've never, ever—'

'Erica,' he said softly. 'I've never indicated anything like that. Why would you even think that?'

'Hello? All those questions about my family life?' I said defensively.

'I'm sure you make everyone's life better,' he said as he turned to look at me, his eyes X-raying me to the core.

I swallowed. It wasn't fair that he was so hot and in a position to judge me. Normally, I can pulverize any hot man who tries to make me feel uncomfortable, but Julian – how do you pulverize your kids' principal, especially when just looking at him makes your skin tingle?

When I got in with the kids, who were still waving Julian off with big fat smiles, I made an insane dash for the house phone that was ringing on the hook.

'Oh, it's you,' I said to Judy, who had undoubtedly called to secure my silence.

Who did I think it was? Julian calling me from his jeep thirty seconds after dropping us all off, saying, *Hi, I just wanted to tell you what a great time I had acting as your cab driver today?*

'Oh, lighten up, Erica. Everyone nowadays has someone,' she drawled. 'You could use some *umph* yourself,' she said. 'Get yourself a lover.'

I was surprised Marcy hadn't spread the word about my marital problems yet. Maybe she was mellowing a bit. 'A lover?' I said. 'I'd never do that.'

'Of course you wouldn't, lest you actually find some happiness.'

Judy was right. The kids were still oohing and aahing

about being picked up by their champion principal, and I had to admit, I wasn't totally unaffected, either. Maybe Judy's wandering eye was contagious. Or even genetic. It hadn't manifested itself in twelve years of marriage, so why was I suddenly feeling jittery and breathless after sitting next to my kids' principal in his jeep? Just because my marriage was over didn't mean I was going to throw myself into another relationship. I was done with love. But the erotic dreams of Julian were mine forever.

I heard my sister take a drag from a cigarette and puff out.

'When did you start smoking again?' I asked in surprise, happy to get my mind off that afternoon that had started like hell but ended very nicely. Too nicely for my sanity.

She inhaled again and muttered, 'You see? You're the world's biggest prude. I wonder why Ira hasn't left you yet.'

I bared my teeth, even if she wasn't there to see it.

'So, still no sex?' she asked and exhaled after my long, long pause, and I closed my eyes, regretting that one evening of closeness that my sister and I had shared and during which, while she'd poured the Corvo Rosso, I'd poured my heart out to her.

Paul and I always talked about the sex I was missing out on, but strangely, I'd never shared my problems with her.

'Judy...'

'See? Prude.'

Indeed I was. But I still wasn't ready to tell the world my problems. Nor could I understand her. If she didn't love her husband anymore, why didn't she just leave him instead of screwing someone else? Why hadn't Ira had the same courtesy for me instead of screwing around behind my back? I wondered who it was, what she looked like, if she was as thin as a rake and younger than me. Who was I kidding? Of course she must have been all the above.

'This guy is sooo ripped, Erica!' Judy assures me. 'Like nothing you've ever seen.'

It was true, I'd never *seen*. My own husband had never been ripped and wasn't suddenly going to start developing a six-pack, just like I wasn't going to become Angelina Jolie overnight. Or ever. Not even after ten stomach bypasses.

'I mean, even the size of his—'

'Got it!' I said before Judy could continue.

She laughed. 'I was going to say "his hands", but while you're on the subject, yes – he's very well endowed.'

Good for them.

'And he takes me places and we do it wherever and whenever we want. This morning we did it—'

'In his car – I know.'

'Silly,' she said warmly, and I realized she'd never spoken to me warmly.

Had sex with a guy finally mellowed her?

'He's… wonderful. He makes me feel like a queen, you know?'

No, I didn't know. I had absolutely no idea what it felt like to be treated like a queen. I'd never been treated with consideration by Ira. I was lucky if he simply put the toilet seat back down. That alone would make my day. But other women around me, starting with my sister, were getting it all. The security from a loving (although unwittingly betrayed) husband, the luxury of waking up in an amazing house and not having to go to work, a housekeeper to take care of them and the kids, a cook to prepare meals.

Yes, Judy had it all – and now she even had the extras on top of the extras. But she hadn't called just to boast. She wanted to make sure I wasn't going to sell her off to the highest bidder.

'Your secret's safe with me – don't worry,' I assured her.

'Good. Gotta go now. I'm seeing him again in half an hour. Bye!'

And she hung up before I could answer. On one hand, I hoped it wasn't going to end in tears for her as well. On the other, I envied her ability to have fun.

During my lunch break the next day, I wolfed down a sandwich over my keyboard (whoops, a bit of crust stuck between the N and the M) and looked up some more Tuscan properties in my budget, as I'd been doing for the past few months.

I wanted a farmhouse, so I typed in *casolare* and Val d'Orcia, because that was my favorite area in Tuscany. If you Google Image the Val d'Orcia, you'll see loads of amazing pictures of green valleys and yellow hills and majestic 20-meter-high cypress trees coasting winding roads. The ultimate dream.

I needed a house that was at least 300 hundred square meters, 150 for us and the rest for paying guests. I had two options. Either I bought a cheap ruin and restored it, putting in a pool and everything else, or I could buy a renovated one with all the mod cons at double my budget. So I did an advanced search.

One caught my eye. Quite old, with a sturdy-looking wide staircase going up one side (separate entrances, that's great) and an annex (to be restored as well), just the right price. I scrolled down to the floor area – 75 square meters – just about enough for the kids' toys and nothing else.

My eye swung to another property. *Beautiful stone farmhouse with swimming pool and completely restored.* Yes! *Floor area 350 square meters.* Yes, yes!

Price – triple my budget. *Crap.*

And then another one, to be restored, and enormous. Which would cost me its price again in renovation. Even with the sale of the house, I'd be short. I'd have to apply for a mortgage, which I'd pay with the rental income, sure, although it would take me forever. But how the hell was I going to get all the restoration work done? By using the kids' college funds? I sighed. There had to be a way.

15

Spiderman Meets Family

The next morning, I got a call on my cellphone. Now, I normally don't answer private calls when I'm at work, unless it's someone important, like my family or Paul. But today I had a gut feeling I should. My heart skipped a couple of beats when I recognized Mr. Foxham's – I mean Julian's – voice, but the other half of me was experiencing the naked terror that something had happened to one of the kids.

'Hi. Is everything alright?' I asked straight away.

He chuckled. That same warm, deep chuckle that made my skin tingle, and I relaxed.

'Of course everything's alright. But you owe me a coffee, remember?'

I did? Then I remembered my invitation, or more like my challenge, to drop by any time after school. Shit. I hoped I'd have a few days to clean up first.

'Of course,' I said, cool and composed by now. 'Any time.'

'How about today? Say four o'clock.'

Damn. 'You bet,' I confirmed with utter confidence.

As I hung up, I gulped. He sure wanted to catch me with my pants down, and not in the good way. A few days' notice would have at least allowed me to wash the windows.

But what worried me more was the kids' reaction to having their principal around our house twice in a week. I didn't want to scare them. They were so protective of me they'd think we were in some kind of trouble. Of course Julian gave me no way out. I couldn't say no, could I?

I needed a remedy, something to boost my confidence. So I went into the hotel kitchen and snatched the simplest-looking cake I could pass off as my own and put it in a fancy box (which I'd have to get rid of if I wanted to get away with this).

I parked at the school gates and looked up as the car door opened and my gang tumbled into our courtesy car.

'Hey, guys,' I said cheerfully. I couldn't wait to get the news off my chest. 'Guess who's coming after school for a slice of cake?'

'Mr. Foxham,' Maddy chimed.

How did she know?

Warren buckled his seat belt and turned to me, his eyes bright. 'He promised that he'd show me his best catch. I can swing like a mother—'

'Hey! Where did you learn that language?' I demanded.

The schools were breeding grounds for every human vice, always had been.

'Sorry,' he said meekly. 'I got carried away.'

Mr. Foxham – Julian, as I had finally managed to call him without faltering anymore – was just on time. He had a baker's apple pie with him, which I accepted gracefully, putting my hair (which I always let down when I was at home) behind my ear like a shy schoolgirl. I had to put a stop to the butterflies in my stomach.

'Mr. Fox, will you show me how to do a catch? That's still sort of like my weak side.'

'Of course, lad. Let me just have a quick chat with your mother and I'll meet you outside. You practice your swing in the meantime, OK?'

Warren smiled, nodded and disappeared into the backyard as if he'd been put in charge of choosing his own team for the Boston Red Sox.

'So, how are you doing?' he asked me.

'Great! Still high about Warren's performance. My son's an ace! And so is his coach.' I had to stick my finger in it again, didn't I.

Julian smiled. 'He takes after you. By the way, you have a lovely house – very warm and comfortable.'

'It's a mess. There are toys everywhere. It seems for every doll or ball that I pick up, ten more materialize.'

'I find it perfect the way it is. And it's enormous.'

I blushed at the compliment while I loaded the coffee maker.

No point in telling him about the divorce. 'Together we earn enough, Ira and I. But sometimes I wonder if my job is worth it.'

'It is if you manage to get home in time to pick up the kids. I see you every day. You never turn to say hello, though.'

I pushed a hand through my hair again and smiled, embarrassed. 'You got me there,' I admitted.

'Erica, please let me get one thing straight. I don't have any doubts about your parenting skills. I think you're a wonderful mother.'

I had to ask. 'Then why are you here?'

He went bright red. 'Because I wanted to see if your coffee is as good as your cakes.'

'Well, in that case, I have a confession to make. I bought this one. Well, no, that's a lie. I didn't pay for it.'

'You mean you forgot to pay for it?' he concluded gently, his expression unwavering.

'No!' I said with a giggle, and his face relaxed. 'I'm the manager of a hotel – The Farthington?'

'Wow! that posh place. I'm even more impressed.'

'And I didn't have any time to run home and bake a cake like I normally do at this hour on Fridays, so I took one off Jeremy, the in-house baker.'

His eyebrows shot up. 'You *bake* every Friday?'

'Uh-huh. My grandma taught me. I bake a cake, a pizza, and a meat and vegetable dish or lasagne, so I don't have to cook too much on the weekends and I can spend more time with the kids.' The fact that I don't eat any of it in an attempt to get fit is better left unsaid.

He beamed at me. 'You know, Erica, you're the only working mother I know who does that.'

'Really? I've always envied the non-working mothers. You know, the posh ones with the perfect manners.'

He chuckled, shaking his beautiful, beautiful head. Somebody *please* stop me before I reach out and caress his face...

'No, really. I mean, they're so together and elegant and...'

'You think too much, Erica. You look just fine – great, actually – and your kids adore you. You're the woman every man would want to marry. Just enjoy your family time together. Now if you'll excuse me, I promised Warren I'd dedicate some time to him today.'

Which was just as well that he didn't see me fall back onto my chair with a thud. *You are the woman every man would want to marry.* If that was his idea of encouraging parents to do a good job, he'd have to watch it, because he'd soon have dozens of swooning women in his wake just like the Pied Piper, if he already didn't. Because women, no matter what we say, always fall for compliments in an accent. What a charmer.

I craned my neck, to see Warren and Julian playing on the front lawn. And let me tell you – my kid was all googly-eyed for having his very own baseball champion live in his own yard.

And that was exactly how my soon-to-be ex-husband came home to find a six-foot former baseball champion in jeans and a sweatshirt playing the sport he loved more than anything in the world with his only son.

Ira gaped at me, and I said, 'This is the school principal, Mr. Julian Foxham. The other day, Warren won the game for his team.'

Ira strode over to Julian and grasped his hand. 'Mr. Foxham! I'm a *huge* fan!'

'That's very kind of you, Mr. Lowenstein.'

'Call me Ira.' He beamed. 'You must be super famous at school!'

Ira was so enthusiastic, I hardly recognized him. So *that* was what it took to excite him. Maybe I should have had

Paul sew me a little baseball skirt number I could wear to bed. Too late for that now.

As it turned out, Ira was so happy to have met his hero that he invited him and us all out to Le Tre Donne for dinner. Which was a shock per se. Didn't he have a lover to tend to?

'I'm not going out to dinner with you,' I hissed to Ira as Julian played with Warren.

'Come on, Erica. We agreed to keep up the charade until the New Year. Plus, it's a great opportunity for the kids to build a rapport with their principal.'

I crossed my arms. 'You mean *you* want to build a rapport with him.'

'What if? The man's a legend.'

Great. Absolutely friggin' great.

Zia Martina and Zia Monica were serving our table (being family, we normally got our own bread and drinks, etcetera, but tonight my aunts were bent on making a big impression on Julian) and simultaneously gave me a *yum-yum* look.

'*Bellissimo!*' Zia Monica hissed in Italian as she spooned caponata onto my plate. 'Where did you *find* him?'

'In the ladies' room,' I hissed back, enjoying her blank face.

Yeah, even I couldn't understand how he'd come into my life after I'd begged him to take my pants off and security came bursting in, only to apologize. Did *everyone* but me know who he was?

'More vino, Mr. Foxham?' purred my aunt Monica, and I rolled my eyes. She never purred for a guy.

'Thank you. And please – call me Julian,' said Julian.

'Monica,' purred Monica.

As Ira kept Julian and Warren busy with baseball memories, even Zia Maria came out of her temple – the kitchen – to look at him. A long, hard look. Then she looked at me and jerked her head toward the kitchen.

I sighed and excused myself from the table to follow her back to her frying eggplant.

'What?' I hissed.

Zia Martina, who was emptying the dishwasher, raised her eyebrows in another yum-yum expression.

'How old is he?' Zia Maria asked.

I shrugged. 'I don't know.' Of course I knew, but I wanted to hear their thoughts.

'Thirty-seven,' Zia Martina said. 'Monica googled him and Paul told us about how he ripped your pants off because of the spider. He's perfect for you.'

Perfect for me because he'd ripped my pants off? They had a point there.

'What?' I hissed again. Paul – that little runt! 'Are you out of your *minds*? I'm a married woman. And if you don't remember, go back out there and take a look – my husband's sitting right opposite him.'

Zia Maria waved her spatula at me. 'Cut the crap. Paul told us you're getting divorced.'

I looked at all three of them in pretend shock.

I nodded tiredly. 'Not because of Julian. And stop listening to Paul – his love life sucks more than mine.'

There. I'd said it out loud. After years and years of grinning and bearing for the benefit of the family. My love life sucked. Fuming, I turned to go.

'Paul only wants what's best for you – just like we do, sweetheart,' Zia Martina assured.

Even if men like Julian existed out there, it didn't mean they (or he, in this case) were destined to be with a woman like me. I'd never been the happy-ever-after girl with the soppy love story. Men like Julian didn't even know I existed – much less were they interested in getting to know my kind better. Men like Julian were only meant for women like me to ogle at and dream about. And dreaming about him, I had to admit, was becoming the norm.

All I had to do was close my eyes and imagine his strong arms around me, his mouth on mine, whispering in between kisses hot, naughty things I hadn't done in years. And some, I'd never ever done. Just the thought heated my skin and by the time I sat down again opposite Julian, I could hardly look at him.

The meal with Julian and my entire family had been an exception to my constant hunger, although I hadn't managed to swallow much, with Julian's eyes on me most of the time. When he sipped his coffee, his eyes would search for mine over the rim, and I'd blush and wipe Maddy's face or remind Warren not to chew with his mouth open.

If emotionally I was torn to pieces and haunted by images of Julian naked next to me, every night and all night, physically I felt great. Ira's betrayal had been, looking back, what had finally snapped me out of my hibernation. If it hadn't been for his betrayal, I'd never have looked at another man. But now I was looking forward to the rest of my life. If only Julian could be part of it all.

Not with your kids' principal, you can't, you idiot, my

meddling conscience informed me. *You don't want your kids to get too attached. Find someone else.*

Trouble was, I didn't want anyone else, I realized. One thing was sexual fantasies, but truth was, I even enjoyed sitting across from him over coffee. There had never been anyone who had made me feel like Julian. Oh, why couldn't I have met someone who just wanted to have fun, and not my children's chief educator?

16

Hungry Eyes

Tonight was the school Thanksgiving play and both the kids were starring in it, Warren being the Indian chief and Maddy a devoted pilgrim. Despite my courtesy car, Julian offered to drive us and wouldn't take no for an answer. Not that I'd refused vehemently.

So, I was going to see him again.

Another woman's heart would flutter with sheer joy at the thought, but my insides squished and contracted like it was trying to free itself from a vise. The last time I'd felt like this had been over Tony Esposito, whom I loved with a passion all through junior high.

As I always planned everything to death, there was one last thing that I still absolutely needed to do before tonight.

'Lucy, do me a miracle,' I pleaded as I sank into a chair at Lucy's Hair Salon.

This was maybe the second time I'd been here in many, many years. My hair grows slowly and it comes out in curls, which I've been pulling back into a tight bun that hurt my face for years. I'm convinced it really has acted like a face lift. If only I could do that to the rest of my body.

Lucy combed back my wet hair, talking to my reflection in the mirror. 'What'll it be?'

I sighed. 'I don't know. Chop it all off, but don't make me look like an idiot. I have no time to do my hair in the mornings – or on weekends, for that matter.'

When I let it down at the weekends, my hair, finally free, didn't know which way to turn, like prisoners who feel out of place in society once they get out after forty years. 'Or just shave me bald – I don't care anymore. I give up.'

Lucy looked at me for a long minute and then sighed, shaking her head. 'You know how many distress calls like this I get?' she asked. 'You're just having a bad hair week, that's all.'

'More like a bad hair *life*,' I corrected as she ran her hands through my wet, shampooed, heavy mane.

'Naw! Give me an hour and you'll see! Now, what do you do for a living?'

Was she going to charge me according to my earnings? 'I'm a hotel manager.'

'Ah-ha,' she exclaimed, pointing an accusing finger at me. 'So, you gotta look good always, and in no time, am I right?'

Was that not every woman's dream? 'Uh, yes.'

Now I remembered why, among other reasons – like never having the time between making paper dolls with Maddy or doing some baseball swings with Warren – I'd never returned to this place. Lucy was odd. And her assistants were two gossipers. They reminded me of my two youngest receptionists, Lesley and Lindsay – remember them? The ones who missed working in joints? These two were dead ringers for them. Every time their heads joined to exchange some information, Lucy whirled around and gave them a glare very similar to my hairy eyeball. It worked. They parted as if on fire and scrammed back to their stations, busying themselves with rinsing sinks and wiping seats.

She turned back to me and lifted a lock, examining it. 'You never cut it, never style it. Why?'

'No time,' I replied, and she shook her own sleek head.

'Your hair could be so much more beautiful and glossier with a haircut and a protein mask. And your face is so pretty. Why do you let yourself go like this?' she asked as if talking to her best friend and not a customer she hardly ever saw. 'Look at this skin – like a porcelain doll's!'

Yeah, I thought to myself. A doll's head on a stuffed elephant's body. I used to do that to my toys when I was a kid – pull Barbie's head off and stick it on another toy, possibly a fat animal. If I couldn't be slim, then nor should she. Boy, did I come up with freaks of nature. And for punishment, now my head looked like it *belonged* to my body. It served me right.

Lucy clipped and feathered, layered and pulled as I wondered what freak of nature I'd surface looking like. At this point, anything would be an improvement.

When I finally emerged from Lucy's beauty salon, I didn't recognize myself. I actually loved my hair – feathered but full and really glossy. It even made my face look slimmer, classier, as if I had it together and wasn't a delusional maniac constantly searching perfection. If perfection existed, it was my hair tonight. I passed shop windows, barely recognizing myself as I admired the new me. I had to make a point of going out more often.

Paul came over that afternoon more dramatic than his usual dramatic self, and just in time to help me get dressed.

'If this isn't fate, I don't know what is,' he said out of the blue.

Fate? I wondered as Paul adjusted my new blue jersey wrap dress – the one that made me look 20 pounds slimmer. Could he be right? Could it be some mysterious galactic force that had brought Julian and me to the same spot? Could Julian really be interested in me as a woman? But then the usual pragmatic me took over.

'It's just a school play, not the royal wedding,' I groaned, handing him the silver lace shawl Nonna had made me. 'Ira can't come and my car's still at the mechanic's (that much was true), so Julian offered to drive us.' I never mentioned the courtesy car, which was sitting on the driveway in full splendor, with a green 'you break it, we fix it' logo along the sides.

Paul beamed at me as he did my make-up. I knew I hadn't looked this good in a long time. Like hell I could have worn something like this a few months ago. My policy of not eating everything in sight and shaking my ass in tango classes was working nicely, because now I could actually get to the lesson in a vertical position, and I could finally catch Maddy as she shot across the back garden when before I'd only get a few meters in before clutching my spleen. Yes, definitely feeling fitter now.

'What, he's showing up tonight with you and the baggage – no offence to the kids – in front of his whole school?

That's practically professional suicide. Man, he must really have the hots for you, girl.'

The doorbell rang and I jumped. 'It's him! Be a star and let him in. And behave yourself! He already thinks I'm weird.'

'Relax! I got it,' Paul said as he sauntered gracefully down the stairs.

I listened as he opened the door and said in an exaggeratingly polite voice, '*Hello!* You must be *Julian*! I'm Paul – Erica's best friend.'

I cringed because wily Paul had lowered his voice and now they were speaking in soft tones. That was all my kids' principal needed – a pass from his students' very fairy godfather on my behalf. I didn't need a pimp – I could push my own goods. But only if and when I was ready.

I strained to listen, without success, and glanced in the mirror, feeling just a bit guilty as I removed some lip gloss – Paul always exaggerated – and took another look. Dress? Clung perfectly in the boob area, keeping away from the bulges. Hair? Still fresh from this morning. Eyes? Still green, only prettier, with some artfully applied eye shadow that made them look huge. That was the only huge thing I wanted tonight. Except for maybe, umm… No. No thinking about sex. I wasn't going on a date – this was my children's Thanksgiving play. Had I absolutely no shame?

With a deep breath, I scooped up my dainty clutch, so far from my everyday Mary Poppins leather bag, and floated down the stairs to find two gorgeous Latino-looking men at the kitchen table deep in conversation, like they'd known each other forever.

Julian looked amazing in an elegant dark grey suit, a light

grey shirt and no tie. That was him. Elegant but casual. He reminded me a bit of Vince. Not that I'm attracted to guys who look like my brother, mind. We're weird in my family, but not *that* screwed up.

Maddy and Warren were already at the school, so it was just the two of us in the jeep. Convenient, you'd say. I couldn't be more nervous.

'Take care of my doll, Julian, and bring her back in one piece. Or not – whichever way the evening may take you.' Paul giggled.

I turned to spear him with my evil eyebrow, but he just beamed at us and gave me a smack on the rump (oh, God, he was doing his best to embarrass me tonight) and shoved us out my front door.

Being alone with Julian in his jeep was like skating on thin ice with red-hot blades. I knew I was going to go under, capitulate. I made a superhuman effort to drag my eyes away from his strong hands as he caressed the wheel. Sinewy hands. Definitely not a wimp's hands. These were hands that had worked hard. I wondered what it would be like if those hands touched me again, and the thought that he'd actually ripped my pants to shreds simply because I asked him made me shiver all over.

He turned to look at me. God, those long *lashes*.

'Cold?' he whispered.

No, just horny, I imagined answering and shivered again.

He turned a dial and soon it was nice and warm.

'Thanks,' I whispered, and he smiled, his eyes lingering on mine, before he turned his attention back to the road.

*

Even in the theatre hall, during the play, Julian kept stealing me glances in the dark while I fought not to turn round and meet his eyes, which I could almost feel calling me. I clapped as hard as I could at the right times to show him I was totally swept away by the children's performance, when actually I can't remember a single scene (except for when Maddy and Warren appeared onstage).

After a smashing success and rounds of applause, Julian extricated us from the crowd of mums wanting to linger with him (who wouldn't?) and drove the four of us home.

As the kids chattered non-stop, he glanced over at me again, only for longer, the ocean in his eyes flipping my stomach. And I felt a deep, deep shiver coming up from my insides.

'How about a quick bite?' he whispered so the kids wouldn't hear.

Actually, I'd have preferred a slow-burning, full-out tasting, but that wasn't what he meant.

I turned to look at him again. 'Don't you want to go to your own home and get some peace and quiet? I mean, haven't you had enough of us for one evening?'

'Never,' he said and grinned his boyish grin.

'Food it is, then,' I answered with a smile, and the kids in the back shouted a big 'Yay!'

The kids sat at the next table, but I kept a trained eye on them.

'Your children are adorable,' he said, a twinkle in his eyes as he watched them.

So are you, I wanted to add, along with drop-dead sexy. 'Do you have any yourself?' I ventured.

He shook his head wistfully.

'Are you involved with anyone?' Uh-oh. What the hell was wrong with me?

Again he shook his head, blushing. I found that endearing – a chink in his headmaster's armor.

'No.'

Picking at my fries, I looked up and caught him staring at me. I mean really looking hard, as if trying to figure out what he was doing here on a Friday night (it just occurred to me it was a date night) with someone like me.

'Sorry for staring,' he said quickly. 'It's just that since the first time I saw you in that restroom, you seem... different.'

'That would be because I have my pants on,' I giggled, and he grinned. 'And because I've lost some weight,' I added, chomping on my fries with more confidence.

(You'd think I'd eat daintily for his benefit and that I'd learned from my marriage, but that's precisely what I had learned. Don't pretend to be someone you're not – eventually, your nature will catch up with you and the transformation will send him screaming for the hills. And when he comes back, if he comes back, he'll be angry at you for duping him.)

Who cared if he thought I shouldn't be eating fast-food after going to all the trouble of losing weight? A girl's allowed a treat every now and then.

I expected him to say, 'Ah-hah! That's it!' But he didn't. Instead, he looked at me and said, 'Congratulations, but that's not it.'

'No?' I said, remembering to close my mouth.

'I know! It's your hair. It's beautiful.'

I stopped, my mouth full of fries, my hand stealing to the back of my neck. 'Maybe you always see me on my way back from work. I always wear a bun. It makes me look meaner. The staff are scared stiff of me.'

He threw his head back and laughed, his gorgeous eyes crinkling at the corners with tiny wrinkles, and it made my stomach flip every time. Yes, Julian was too dangerous for someone like me. You couldn't just flirt (assuming he'd ever want to with me) with someone like him and go home and forget about it. You'd want more. No question, I was out of my depth. And he was out of my league.

In any case, assuming I had a fling with anyone in the near future, how could I protect the kids from becoming too attached and then get their hearts ripped out by another man leaving my life? I could handle it mainly because of them. Maddy and Warren didn't deserve another disappointment. Their own father had been more than enough. No, my future fling would have to be carried out away from my kids' eyes, when instead all I wanted was to be just like we were now. Even if I couldn't emotionally afford to fall for him.

I looked at my watch and feigned a polite yawn. 'Thanks so much for everything, Julian, but I really have to get these guys home.' Pretending I wanted to end the evening – I should have won an Oscar just for that.

He didn't blink but smiled. 'Sure, Erica. Let's go, kids.'

Once outside my front door, I scooted them out of his jeep, thanked him for a nice evening and said, 'Goodnight, Julian. Take care.'

'You too, Erica. Thanks for your company. I enjoyed it very much.'

And then, to cover the awkwardness of the fact that we were standing around, I said, 'Would you like to come in?' Meaning, can you pretend to have a friendly conversation while my kids fall asleep so we can afterward jump each other's bones like there was no tomorrow.

He stuffed his hands in his pockets and said, 'Uh, it's getting late. I have to go. Goodnight.'

Meaning... What did that mean? I thought he'd been warming up to me. How wrong I'd been.

'Oh. OK. Goodnight,' I said back and closed the door behind him, leaning on it, shaking my head.

Stupid, stupid idiot! Why did you have to invite him in and ruin the great vibes? It was a miracle I hadn't torn his clothes off, horny as I was, but did I have to go and ruin it?

After I put the kids to bed, Paul video-called, surely to gossip about Julian all night.

'Did he kiss you goodnight with that gorgeous British mouth?' he asked with a swoon.

'Haven't you got a good book to read or toenails to varnish?' I quipped, pretending to be bored by the subject.

'Did he kiss you or not?'

'Of course not.'

'He likes you-ou,' Paul sing-songed.

'You're wrong, Paul. Trust me. He thinks I'm some career freak and thus incapable of taking care of my kids. He's keeping an eye on me so I don't end up starving them to death or something.'

'You're a supreme fool, my dear,' he said, and he cupped his mouth to form a pretend megaphone. 'The. Guy. Has. The. Hots. For. You. Big. Time.'

While I was considering Paul's sci-fi tale, I got a 'call waiting' beep.

'Hang on a sec, will you?'

'Don't leave me hanging too long!' Paul hollered as I clicked the phone.

'Hello?'

'Erica. It's Julian.'

Just the man.

'Is it too late for you?'

Was it too late for me? About twelve years too late, but who was counting tonight? 'Oh, hi,' I said, trying to sound calm and collected. And possibly sexy at the same time.

'I wanted to thank you for such a good time.'

I was the one who should have been thanking him. But it sounded too lame to confess. And desperate. 'Likewise,' I echoed shyly.

'By the way, Erica – you looked very pretty tonight.'

No I didn't – not as pretty as the other moms – but my stomach flipped anyway and I grinned to myself as I rolled onto my back and stuck my legs in the air. They looked slimmer that way.

'It's all thanks to Paul. He's an image counselor and make-up artist.'

'He had an easy job with you.'

Flattery had already gotten him into my deepest, darkest fantasies. I knew I'd lie awake yet another night and think about the mess I was getting myself into.

'Erica?'

'Hm?'

'Would you like to go for a cup of coffee tomorrow afternoon?'

If I hadn't been lying down, I'd have fallen over. Now, an invitation for coffee sounded like the perfect way to start something completely inappropriate with your kids' principal. I loved it! But why me? I was ages away from his kind of friends – baseball champions and beautiful girls. I could give him nothing. What could he possibly want from me?

'Er, can you hang on a second? I have an incoming call,' I lied.

'Sure. I won't budge from here.'

'Should I accept Julian's invitation to go for coffee?' I whispered to Paul over the phone as if Julian could hear me. I could almost see Paul jump with glee.

'I knew it! Is the hot principal waiting on the other line?'

I rolled my eyes. 'Should I go or not?'

'Of course you have to go! You can't let him get away from us! He's my impossible dream! You have to keep him around, if only for me to gape at, honey! Plus, I want to know what he's like in the sack.'

'Stop that,' I said. 'He's my kids' principal. And I don't want Ira knowing anything about it.'

'Honey, you're separated, albeit in the same house. How long does Ira need to move out, for Christ sake?'

'Right, I get it. You're so *not* the person to talk to in this situation. Or maybe you are. What do I wear?'

'Ah-ha!' Paul exclaimed in triumph. 'You see, you *are* interested in him! Your green cashmere dress. It brings out your eyes. And makes your boobs look nice but not too revealing. You don't want them to scream, *here we are!*'

I rolled my eyes again, my nerves ready to snap. 'Gotta go. Talk later.'

The green dress. Was it still in the wash? I clicked back to Julian and his suave, deep voice filled me with a strange warmth. This was ridiculous. I wasn't going to continue with this crush on my kids' principal. I was a grown woman. A lonely, separated grown woman. And Julian was too involved in my children's life. So I'd have to forget about him and start seeing someone I'd feel less guilty about. Like a mass murderer.

'OK for the coffee.'

Now all I had to do was figure a way of not jumping his bones the minute he showed up at my door. As much as I wanted to do coffee (among other things) with him, I didn't know how I was going to get through it without confessing to him that instead of sleeping at night, I stare up at the ceiling, wishing I were in another life – one where he'd fall in love with me, have mind-blowing sex with me every night, marry me and finally drag me off to Tuscany. That alone was enough to make any guy never call you again.

'Brilliant. I'll see you tomorrow, then,' he said, and I closed my eyes. 'Erica?'

'Huh?'

'You still there?'

'Yeah,' I answered, nodding vigorously to myself.

'I'll see you tomorrow. Sleep well.'

Sleep well. All he had to do was add a *sweetheart* to that and I'd kill for him.

17

Catharsis

At about the time I should have been out with Julian that day, I had another major fight with Ira. On the phone. Because things weren't going well at his office and there was no one else to take it out on but me, apparently.

His 25-year old secretary, Pristine Maxine (so dubbed by me because she always wore white and had her hair coiffed like Lady D. Someone should have told her the Eighties were over), wanted a raise, but he couldn't afford to give her one, so she'd threatened to leave. I couldn't blame her. Ira could wear out anybody's patience. And now he was taking it out on me, saying if I'd been a good wife all these years, I'd have offered to do her work on the weekends.

I actually had, in exchange for Saturdays with the four of us as a family, and memories of me scrubbing his urinals came back to me on a regular basis while he watched baseball games and pigged out on the office sofa. And his promise to be a Saturday father had quickly died a death, as he simply couldn't be bothered, so he'd hide out at work.

I squared my shoulders and whispered into the phone, 'Those days of me bailing you out all the time are over, Ira,' and hung up.

I was at the end of my tether. And while I was at it, I wasn't doing his laundry anymore, or his dishes. Among other things. I was officially off wife duty.

I rang my zia Maria and ordered a roast chicken and potatoes to go. 'Can you throw some veggies in there, as well?' I asked. 'And a nice big tiramisu?'

'You inviting The Hunk over?' she asked.

'No, of course I'm not – why do you ask?'

'Paul told us you had an invitation for coffee. So it's serious?'

Arrgh, there he went again. I'd have to talk to him about discretion. 'No, there's nothing going on between me and The Hu… my children's principal.'

'Of course there isn't,' she laughed and said, 'Martina, pick up the phone, will you? Erica's got a date with The Hunk!'

I rolled my eyes as Zia Martina squealed 'No way?' somewhere in the background.

'Listen, you two. I'm not going out with Julian Foxham! And that's that!'

'Can I have him, then?' Zia Monica chimed, presumably from a third phone, and Zia Martina snorted.

'Don't take her seriously. She's got the hots for Father Frank.'

'I do not!' she assured.

'Ooh, father Frank's nice – go for it,' I joked. Had we all suddenly lost our morals? Had we all become like Marcy and Judy?

'Erica?' Zia Maria said softly.

I knew that tone. 'What?'

'We're not going to do all that again, are we?'

I groaned. 'All what again?'

'You married Ira because you thought you were too fat for anyone else to marry you. And now that you're a free woman, you won't let yourself love Julian because you're afraid to jump in case you make the same mistake.'

'Actually, I married Ira because I loved him.'

'And because he knocked you up,' Zia Monica sentenced.

'Guys, please…'

'Let me tell you one thing, sweetheart,' Zia Maria said. 'A man like Julian will love you forever.'

I wish.

'And you know what else?' Zia Monica added. 'Nothing should stop you from being happy.'

'Heaven knows you've earned it,' Zia Martina echoed.

'Just how much have you and Paul been talking?' I asked.

'Enough to tell you to get over your paranoia before you sabotage this relationship and the chance to be happy ever again. Now go and enjoy him,' Zia Monica cut in.

'I can't go and *enjoy* him – we're just… acquainted.'

'Honey,' said Zia Martina. 'Remember the day you married Ira?'

Did I ever. Paul had given me six days to leave him – a week before the wedding – and my aunts had told me that even if I was a Catholic girl who had been knocked up, marrying Ira was still a little too much punishment. You see what I mean about them now?

'Right. Gotta go!' I chimed and hung up.

*

As I was getting ready for bed, I tiptoed to the bedroom door, locked it and did something I hadn't done in a while – look at the external me, really up close. I took off my pajamas and scanned my naked body in the mirror. For a long time studying my skin critically. I really was looking so much better, I could see it.

And then, without warning, I started thinking what my junior high crush, Tony Esposito, would say if he saw me now. And imagined him standing behind me, looking at me in the mirror, his hands searching for my boobs like that day a million years ago. In my imagination, he'd grown into a gorgeous man, maintaining the same features that had made him so yummy in my schoolgirl's eyes.

As I watched him, he turned into Peter DeVita, my junior high boyfriend, who moved to Florida right before the year-end dance. Then I imagined Josh, my lifeguard on the English Riviera where I'd learned my trade of managing hotels, and his hands grew bolder, running over my thighs, parting them, his beautiful head ducking to kiss my mouth. For a few weeks of my younger life, I'd wanted him so much I thought I'd die of lust. And all that time I'd only been dying for an orgasm.

And then (there was no point in denying it by now), in my mind Josh turned into Julian, his hair wet from the rain (because I figured he'd look *really* sexy with wet hair). And his arms warm around my waist as he kissed the side of my face and the hollow between my neck and shoulders, sending a tingling shiver down to the soles of my feet, like in the historical romances I'd devoured as a kid.

Julian, so strong yet gentle, sooo not the guy for me, yet a constant thought trickling through my mind when I least expected it endlessly, like a babbling brook. It scared me. I couldn't afford to lose my head. Not now, not ever.

It got so bad I even contemplated changing the kids' school so I wouldn't have to see him anymore, but I knew I couldn't do that to them, so I resolved never to look toward the school while I was picking them up, because he had a habit of waiting outside to greet parents and have a quick chat.

Fantasies over, I finally settled into bed and suddenly realized that in the short pageant of the desirable men in my life, I'd totally skipped Ira.

18

Bullies and Baseball Bats

Finally at home after another grueling day, I was preparing some nice veal and eggplant casserole for dinner. (Ira never had dinner with us anymore now that he had his own life, which was a blessing, and even more so that the kids just assumed he was at work as always.)

Once dinner was in the oven, I'd have about forty-five minutes to have a long, hot shower and change into fresh gym pants and a sweatshirt to do some squats or something and then go fetch Warren from baseball practice. Julian had started a team, which he coached every Monday and Wednesday until six, so that would also give me time to help Maddy with her homework and catch up on my chores.

And while I worked, I thought of the kids and how things were going well lately. I knew their needs, their rhythms, their passions, their insecurities and strong points. I was finally ahead of the game and it felt great. Like I was on top of the world for once.

As I was dicing the mushrooms and scooping them up

– whoops, right against my Sex Pistols 'Anarchy' T-shirt – the doorbell rang.

'Stay put,' I said to Maddy, who had already jumped to her feet from her complicated ballet pose that looked more like a yoga position.

One day, she'd get her long legs all tangled and fall flat on her cute little face, if she took after her mommy.

I dabbed at the brownish stains on my T-shirt as I pulled the door wide open.

'Hi,' Julian said, gloriously sexy in a pair of jeans and a Lacoste designer polo the color of the sky.

Did this guy have an image consultant or something? Weren't men supposed to be color-blind? Forget the grab-me-now smile on his face. Forget the width of his shoulders that seemed to embrace me. Something from inside him leaped out at me and grabbed me by the shoulders, screaming, *you may not know it yet, but we were made to roll on soft beds together!*

'Nice T-shirt. Love the Sex Pistols,' he said, although his eyes weren't smiling.

And again, the tingle down my spine, dammit. Not to mention the state I was in. I wish he'd called. But I played it cool. 'Aren't you supposed to be coaching your little league?' I asked.

'I was, but now I'm on my way to the hospital.'

Oh, God. 'Warren…?' I squeaked, and he lifted his hands. 'He's perfectly alright. But in big trouble. He hit a boy.'

'Oh my God! Is the boy alright?'

'He will be. I've brought Warren home to save you a trip, but I have to run to the hospital now. I'll call you later.'

'Are you sure?' I asked, backing a step into the house,

ready to grab my coat and bag. The story of my life. 'I'll just get Maddy and drive to—'

'No need.'

I searched his face. There was something he wasn't telling me, and then I knew.

'The parents are suing, aren't they?'

Julian sighed. 'I'll see what I can do.'

My eyes swung to his jeep, where I could see Warren crouched, his enormous eyes fixed on me. He was no doubt terrorized.

'Let him out,' I sighed, straightening my shoulders.

Julian gave me a last 'are you going to be OK' look. I nodded and he signaled to Warren. Silently, my son slid out and I stepped aside for him without speaking. I was shaking so badly, I was afraid I'd fall apart.

'Erica?' Julian whispered, his eyes studying me.

I stood up straighter. 'I'm fine, Julian, thanks. Just let me know about the boy, please.'

'Alright,' he said softly, then with one last glance and a meaningful nod to Warren, he got into his jeep and drove off.

So much for me knowing what my children were feeling. I realized I was clueless, after all, and that no, I wasn't ahead of the game. *Just what the hell is the matter with you?* I wanted to scream at him, but held my tongue, because that was exactly how Ira would have reacted.

I only hoped Julian didn't think Warren had learned this behavior from Ira, because Ira couldn't lift a finger to swat a fly out of its misery. With words and vicious expressions, he was great in demeaning you, but in no way was Ira a physical person.

'Maddy, sweetie, why don't you go and color in your bedroom, honey?'

My eight-year-old daughter slid off her chair again and looked at her brother, making a face like *boy, are you in for it*. Which was of course an understatement.

Once alone with him, I sat down at the kitchen table and, my fists supporting my cheeks, I looked at him squarely, unimpressed to say the least.

'Mom...' he began bravely.

I watched him, my eyelids swelling with the tears that were dying to spill, and he watched me back, his own eyes glassy.

Good. Let him cry. He needed a reality check. At this point, I think we both did. I'd never been so disappointed in my whole life.

'Why did you do it?' I asked finally, my voice barely audible.

He drew a deep breath and looked me straight in the eye.

'It doesn't matter why. Just give me my punishment and let's get it over with. I'm sorry.'

And that's when I lost it. 'Sorry?' I cried. '*Sorry?* There's a boy in the hospital because of your actions and all you can say is sorry?'

Warren looked at me with his solemn green eyes and bowed his head.

'Why did you do it?' I demanded, and he flinched. 'Warren!'

My son looked up at me with the eyes of a grown-up and it scared the crap out of me.

'I had to. He said you and Mr. Fox are sleeping together.'

I swear I felt my eyes pop. I hadn't known my

twelve-year-old son had any concept of what sex was. Hell, at thirty-four, *I* still didn't.

'And you believe that garbage?' I barely managed, and he shook his head vigorously.

'Of course not, but you don't know what it's like at school if someone gets on your case.'

I didn't know?

'You always taught me that violence isn't the answer,' he offered.

'Oh, good, I'm glad you remember that – now.' I stood up. The meeting was over. 'You're grounded for a month. No sports, no internet or any computer games.'

I have to tell you, he didn't flinch.

'Yes, Mom,' he whispered, his hands stuffed in his pockets.

I groaned and sat down again, my forehead in my hand. Where had I gone wrong? Maybe if I'd spent less time at work, or less time daydreaming...

'Mom?'

'Yes?'

'I am so sorry I disappointed you.'

'Yes, Warren, so am I. Now go wash up for dinner and help your sister pack her school bag for tomorrow. And don't forget her math book.'

He nodded again and went. I confess I felt a slight pang of sympathy. Warren was like me – he'd sit there and take it without ever lashing out until he could take it no more. But it wasn't an excuse for violence.

My behavior around Julian was obviously reflecting badly on my kids. Not that I was bonking him or anything, but you know people. First, he shows up with me at the Thanksgiving play. And then we go out for a bite in public, where everyone can see us driving off in his jeep. Then he shows up at my home for coffee. Although harmless encounters as they had been, they were attracting the attention of the gossips, while only making me more and more lustful for the guy. He was only being nice and checking on me. I loved being with him, but now, for the sake of my children, I needed to avoid him.

A few hours later when I came out of the bathroom, Julian was there, waiting on the sofa. I sighed and padded into the living room.

'Hi. Warren let me in,' he said.

'He's going to need an ally,' I said as I sat down next to him, my legs tucked under me. 'How's…?'

'Billy. Billy Blackmoore. Eight stitches.'

I sank lower into the sofa, muttering 'Jesus Christ almighty. What have I done wrong?'

Julian's voice was gentle. 'You've done nothing wrong, Erica. Kids can be cruel sometimes, and see filth where there is none.'

I looked up at him. 'So Warren told you what set the fight off?'

'Of course. Warren tells me everything.'

Uh-oh. 'Well, not *every*thing,' I laughed uneasily as my hand went to my wet ponytail.

'Everything,' he said gently.

Did he mean the imminent divorce?

'Like how you drag them across town to take them roller-skating and to the movies and for a hamburger or bowling. And how you always manage to cut yourself or fall.'

'Well, what parent doesn't?' I said.

Julian looked at me strangely. Really strangely.

'What?' I asked. 'Oh, God, is there more?'

Julian cleared his throat, but his voice was very low, almost raspy, his eyes a darker color, but at the same time brighter, more luminous. 'Forgive me for telling you this, but Warren also told me how you cry yourself to sleep under the covers. And Paul told me—'

'About the divorce,' we said in synch as I nodded knowingly.

The little shit had ratted me out to Julian, as well.

'I don't want you to be sad, Erica...'

I looked up at him. His eyes were kind and understanding, almost urging me to let myself go, almost like a physical embrace. An embrace I so needed. And suddenly, I was too tired to keep it all bottled up inside. I felt the tears come in a gush of shame. I tried to stop, but I wasn't very good at anything these days.

'It's so difficult to pretend everything is OK,' I sniffed, and he nodded.

'Nothing is easy, Erica. But you're doing a great job.'

'Yeah, I'm doing a fan-bloody-tastic job,' I snorted, and sniffed loudly into a tissue, but soon needed another one to blow my nose.

Julian leaned over and handed me the tissue box on the coffee table. God, what a sight I must have been, with my trackpants, T-shirt, red-and-white striped socks and wet ponytail.

186

'You're not alone, Erica. Paul loves you like a sister and I'm here to help you in any way I can. *And...*'

I wiped my nose and looked up at him hopefully.

'... good news. The parents aren't suing, provided you foot the medical bills. Billy admitted he was bullying Warren.'

I sputtered in relief. 'Oh, thank God! You're a good principal, Julian. Thank you so much.'

'I have to intensify recess watch. Billy had been badgering him about... us for some time now. I must make my mission statement clearer.'

And speaking of being clear. 'About that... us thing,' I breathed. 'We have to stop these... rumors. I know there's nothing between us, but I can't see you anymore. For my children's sake. And for our reputations.'

Julian lowered his eyes. 'Is there nothing between us, Erica?' he whispered.

'I don't know,' I whispered back. 'But I don't want anybody else to get hurt. I'm very grateful to you and what you're doing for the kids, but this is where I take a step back.'

He took my hand, still not looking at me, and, sighing, nodded. 'Erica... I'm sorry if I've caused you any trouble. But I'm just a phone call away. Whatever you need.'

'OK. And... I'm extremely flattered for all the time you've dedicated to me. You're very generous and selfless,' I said, trying to ignore the fact that we were sitting on my sofa, holding hands, our thighs touching, only a 'yes' away.

'Selfless? No, lately I've been extremely selfish, thinking only about happiness and not worrying about others.

Forgive me, Erica,' he whispered as he took my hand and brought it to his lips, his thick black lashes lowered.

I watched as he kissed my hand, his beautiful mouth on my skin, and I almost melted from the scorching pleasure that ripped through my insides without warning.

He closed his eyes briefly and then shook his head. 'I should go,' he sighed and stood up. 'For both our sakes.'

I nodded and followed him to the door. He gave me one last look, concerned but at the same time full of longing. I leaned against the door, fighting the urge to call him back inside. He'd asked if there was nothing between us. He felt something, too. It would have been so simple just to wrap my arms around him and ask him to stay.

'How come you're seeing so much of Julian?'

I snapped out of my reverie and looked up to see that Ira had pulled up, just in time to see Julian driving off.

'Are the kids having problems at school?'

I crossed my arms in front of my chest. Of course it wouldn't remotely cross Ira's mind that Julian might be attracted to me. I almost wished he were my lover – he was definitely excellent rebound lover material. He was built for sex, that guy, with a smile that would take your panties off in one go. I loved the way he looked at me and the way he spoke to me – the opposite of this jackass here.

There was no way I was telling him that Warren had given me and the school a few problems. Not this time. Ira would only give my little boy a hard time and now that things were OK, I didn't need a major regression.

'We're just keeping a close eye on the kids, that's all.'

'Good. They're good kids, aren't they?' Ira grunted,

already having lost interest as I ducked back inside while he pounced on his mail, which he tore open and read avidly.

'Yes,' I agreed, happy we were managing a conversation. 'Julian's coaching a little league and Warren's in it. He's great.'

Ira kept on reading for a while, a smile forming on his lips. Then he dragged his eyes away from the letter and looked up. 'Yeah? That's great.'

This was the longest conversation we'd had in weeks. When I got to Tuscany, we wouldn't have to converse with him at all. He'd be a long-distance, forgotten memory. The thought made me shiver all over with delight.

19

Losing a Friend?

I told Paul about Warren hitting Billy Blackmoore.

'You can't blame the kid. You must be hot news all over the school.'

'What?' I said, panicking. 'Don't be ridiculous.'

I hoped that we were never really a topic of conversation. I didn't know many other mothers and the few I knew were acquaintances – not people who would pull me aside and discreetly warn me I was regarded as the school slut. But if this episode was anything to go by, we were in shit. Deep shit.

'Erica's in love with the pri-i-i-inci-pal,' Paul sang as he painted my toenails, each one a different color.

I had a high ponytail and my cow jammies on with my matching stuffed cow slippers by my side that even had ears. Or were they horns? If only my fearful hotel staff could see me now, they'd have a field day.

'And the principal's gonna get fi-i-ired because he can only keep it in his pants for so lo-ong!'

'Sto-op,' I said, slapping his arm, giggling.

But the thought of Julian warmed me from the inside, like a glass of brandy. Not that I ever drank any. Paul and I were wine freaks, especially Italian wines, which he brought back from Italy in copious quantities, despite the fact that I always got it for free from Dad's Italian Gift Store.

'What would you do,' Paul said with a cute Kermit the Frog-like burp, 'if Julian rang the doorbell right now and wanted to take you upstairs?'

I stopped munching on a mini Mars bar and stared at him, then slapped his shoulder. 'Why is it always about sex with you?'

'Because I know when I see an interested guy. So say you could make a wish and it happened…'

'Oh, so we're talking *Fantasy Island* stuff, then?'

I didn't have to think about it but pretended to. If that last parting look on Julian's face was anything to go by, he was feeling something, too. But just how far it went beyond friendship remained to be seen.

'That's the worst impersonation of someone thinking I've ever seen,' he said disgustedly. 'Admit it – you like him, too. A lot more than you think.'

'If I admitted that…' I whispered, and he leaned closer.

'Yeah?'

'I'd have to kill you.'

Paul stomped his feet and said, 'I don't care. I know you'd sleep with him. Oh, Erica, he's *so* the guy for us.'

Could he be right?

It was late, the kids were asleep and we were watching some oldies. Paul's choice was *Sooner or Later*.

'OK,' he said. 'You take Julian, I'll take Rex Smith. Man, I lu-u-urve him.'

'He's not gay, Paul. Actually, he's a real ladies' man. Didn't he find out he had a son years ago?'

'Imagine that – finding out you have a son somewhere. That would freak me out,' Paul said with a nod as he guzzled some wine.

'If you'd slept with a woman, I'd be freaked out, too,' I informed him, and Paul took another swig of his wine, swallowed and suddenly went serious.

'God, I still miss Carl, you know?'

He sighed and I stared at him. Ages and battalions of men had gone by since Carl.

'What do you miss about him? You always used to say he was too much of a workaholic.'

He shrugged. 'Dunno. I just do. Life is a bitch without someone to love. Without a family, don't you think?'

I shrugged. 'I have you.' Which was true. No matter what, I'd always be happy with Paul. As long as I had him, my safety net, I'd be fine.

'I wonder what he's doing now,' I asked about Carl.

'Probably still writing scripts. He was good. Maybe I'll be costume designer for one of his movies one day. We'll look into each other's eyes and realize we made a big mistake splitting up.'

I was still staring at him. In all the years I knew him, he'd never got sentimental, except for when Warren and Maddy were born. God, you should have seen old waterworks then. He couldn't pick either of them up without bawling.

'Oh, Paulie.'

'I'm so lucky to have you, Erica. You're my family,' he said flatly. 'And I love you.'

'Sweetheart,' I whispered. 'You've had too much to drink. Let go of the cask now before you keel over.'

He stared back at me with his large dark eyes and burst out laughing and soon, for no reason, we were rolling all over the floor in hysterics.

'OK, I confess,' I managed between cackles of delight. 'If Ricardo Montalbán put a lay around my neck and said "Welcome to *Fantasy Island*," I'd immediately say, "Point me to Julian!"'

'Ha! I knew it. No woman can resist the shoulders on that guy.' Paul shrieked in triumph. 'And have you seen his hands? They're enormous. I say, let's make a toast to his hands.' Paul giggled and jabbed me in the ribs.

And so we made a drunken toast to Julian's hands with our empty glasses before reaching for another bottle.

The next morning at work, the ringing phones sounded like Quasimodo had gone berserk on the church bells of Notre Dame in Paris. Between my ears. Damn the wine.

Clutching my temples, I looked around for Jackie, who was nowhere in sight. Sighing, I distractedly picked up the receiver. 'Yes?'

'Mrs. Lowenstein?'

Not for long, I wanted to answer. I glanced at the display. It was an external line. Someone must have asked for me specifically.

'Yes?'

'A friend of Paul Belhomme's?'

Aw, crap. The bastard had tried to set me up with another one of his rare heterosexual friends again. 'Er, yes?'

'We have your number down as his emergency contact. There's been an accident, ma'am.'

I gripped the receiver. 'Is he alright? Where is he?'

A heavy silence fell, and then I knew.

'He had a car accident.'

My knees buckled and I hit the chair hard. 'This is some kind of joke, isn't it?' I pleaded as they all do.

'No, ma'am.'

Paul. Last night he was painting my toenails, and now he was dead. *Oh, Paul*.

'Ma'am?'

I sat up. 'Yes. Where am I going?'

'Boston County Medical Center.'

'I'll be there as fast as I can.'

I don't remember how I got there, except that I was in an elevator going down to where the morgue was located, according to all the blue signs on the walls. And I suddenly gagged. *Paul*. I couldn't do it. I couldn't face seeing his lifeless body. But if I didn't, who would? I was his best friend. The only friend he'd want here.

I pushed down the frog in my throat as the elevator doors pinged open. The entire floor was tiled white, just like you see in the movies, and all around was a stench of decay smothered in bleach. I pictured him, lying flat on his back, eyes closed, and clamped my hand over my mouth, swallowing the bile of my despair and approaching the woman in the white coat sitting at a desk.

'Excuse me?' I choked and she stood up, her face grave.

'I'm so sorry,' she whispered as if she'd known him.

But she hadn't been that lucky to have him in her life. I swallowed again and clenched my fists to stop them from shaking.

'May I see him?' I asked.

'Of course, whenever you're ready.'

I huffed and wiped away the sweat from my forehead. *Oh, Paul…! Why did this happen to you? Why did you leave me?*

You know the saying, only the good die young? How true was that! Can you think of someone here who should have gone way before everyone else? Someone I'd been sending off for years in my fantasies? It served me right. All this time desiring Ira's death and karma came round to kick me in the ass, taking from me the adult I loved most in the world, more than my own siblings, more than my own parents.

Paul had been everything to me: my friend, my brother, my maid, my cook, my image consultant, my therapist, my life coach, my babysitter. Had he been straight, and assuming he desired me, I would never have needed anyone else. And now this gem of a man was gone from my life for good. How was I supposed to go on without him? How could anything ever be bearable from now on?

'Ma'am?'

'I'm ready.' Which was so not true.

As she beckoned me to follow her, my legs turned to rubber and I swayed. She turned to take my arm.

'Are you OK?' she whispered.

Of course I'm not OK! I wanted to scream. *My best friend is dead and I'll never talk to him again!*

But instead, I squared my shoulders, took another deep

breath and nodded. She nodded back and we approached The Drawers.

She lifted the sheet as I bit my lower lip to keep from screaming.

I screamed.

'That's not Paul!'

She stared at me, then at the old man on the slab. 'Not who?'

'Paul!' I screamed. 'Paul Belhomme, my friend!'

She quickly covered the body with a whispered, 'Oh my God, aren't you Mr. Smith's daughter?'

'No, I'm not! Where's Paul?' I screeched, my whole body shaking, unable to understand what was happening.

'Just one moment – someone must have misplaced him,' she said, her eyes darting everywhere.

'You mean to tell me you've lost him?'

'What's his name again? Paul?'

'Paul Belhomme! B-E-L-H-O-M-M-E!'

She gave me another quick apologetic look as she rifled through her files and then finally picked up the phone.

'He must be in the new morgue. Just one moment, please,' she pleaded, on the verge of tears herself.

I closed my eyes and began to bawl. 'I don't know anything about a new or old morgue. All they did was tell me to come—'

She raised a hand to shush me and I almost grabbed her by the lapels to give her a good shake. They'd lost Paul and now she was *shushing* me?

She put the phone down. 'They're getting back to me in a few moments. I'm so, so sorry. Can I get you some coffee, Mrs. Belhomme?'

I slumped into a chair and let the tears roll. Even in death, he was being mistreated! Why couldn't people respect him for what he was? He was gay. A wonderful, loving gay man who was my anchor. My lifeline. And my lifeline had died in a stupid, stupid *car accident*.

I couldn't catch my breath, wiping at my tears as they appeared, but they were too fast to keep up.

The phone buzzed and she pounced on it but missed her mark as she tripped over the cord and fell under her desk.

'Oi oi…' she moaned.

I leaned over the desk and peered down into her face. 'Are you OK?'

'Yeah,' she whispered, and I stepped over the killer cord to help the poor thing up.

Her nose was bleeding like bloody Niagara Falls.

'Here, hang on to me,' I said as I lifted her bodily (she was practically the size of Yoda in *Star Wars*) and gently placed her on a chair and pulled out some tissues from my bag. I twirled two tiny bits and gently wedged them on the inside of her nostrils like I always did with Warren's nosebleeds. 'There you go, how's that?'

Yoda looked up at me in total misery, her eyes as red as her face. 'Blease doh'd tell addybuddy. Idz by first day here ad I really deed dis job.'

'I won't,' I promised. This day couldn't have got any worse.

The phone on her desk rang and we turned to stare at it, or rather, cower from it. Paul. Where the hell had they put him?

'Shall I answer it for you?' I offered, seeing as she sounded like she was talking from the bottom of the ocean.

'Doh'd, blease doh'd!' she cried and threw herself on the

phone as if her life depended on it. 'Yes?' she breathed and listened. 'Yes. Where? I uddersdad. Thack you.'

'What?' I glared at her as she put the phone down, deadly pale. Paul was already dead, what the hell could be worse?

'He's dot here,' she whispered.

'Not here?' I whispered back. 'What do you mean?'

'He bust be id adudder borgue.'

Another morgue? I stared at her, trying to make sense of her words. 'What? How many morgues are there in Boston?'

'Several. Are you sure it was Bostod City Borgue and dot the Boston County Borgue?' she asked, trying to be helpful.

I stared at her as my mind began to clear. 'Why, which one is this?'

'Dis is the Bostod City Borgue,' she answered apologetically. 'Baybe he's at de Bostod County Borgue.'

Did I detect hope in her voice?

I fell into the chair again, my hands wrapped around my head. This was a nightmare. Not even death was simple anymore.

'Baybe I could call for you, save you the trip?' she suggested politely.

'Why, you think he's taken the bus home?' I snapped, and she blushed and lowered her eyes. 'I'm sorry,' I whispered. 'I'm sorry for being a bitch, but you understand, right?'

Her eyes met mine. 'Of course. I'b sorry, doo. Let be bake dat call.'

I sighed, my insides turning outside in frustration as my cellphone rang. I didn't want to answer it, didn't want to tell anybody about Paul yet, in case it wasn't true, in case I'd dreamed this whole thing up and he was sitting in my backyard waiting for me with a couple of margaritas. I pushed my knuckles into my eyes and answered the damn phone.

'Hello?' I said, trying to clear my throat.

'Hey, sunshine,' came Paul's voice. 'What's keeping you? Are you OK?'

20

Gaining a Lover?

I hated waking up with a headache. My whole face hurt, as well. I yawned, my mouth tasting like Scotch tape.

Above me were the worried faces of a man in scrubs, plus Paul and Julian. What the hell were they doing in my bedroom? Paul could have been a figment of my hopeful imagination and Julian the usual guest star of my dreams. But a doctor?

'Are you OK, sweetie?' Twin voices, one deep and one effeminate, penetrated my foggy brain.

I tried to sit up and Julian supported my shoulders, along with Paul, whose arm was in a sling. Had I been dreaming?

'You scared us for a minute, sunshine!' Paul grinned, taking my head in his good hand and kissing me.

I looked at him, trying to make sense of his words, but my mind was foggy. 'You're not dead?' I squeaked.

'Do I look dead, sunshine? When you didn't arrive,

I thought you'd be, well… somewhere more exciting, so I called Julian's school,' Paul explained.

I looked up, back and forth between them. Clear as mud.

'Paul had a car accident. But you misunderstood and went to the wrong place, thinking Paul had died.' Julian added. 'Why didn't you call me?'

I looked up at the three of them. Paul, here, alive? This wasn't making sense. 'I went to the wrong morgue.'

'Forget it, we'll explain on the way home,' Julian whispered, and I clutched his sleeve.

'Where's Yoda? Is she still bleeding?'

At that, they all laughed.

'You'll be a little loopy for a bit,' the doctor said. 'Let's get you up here.'

Julian bent over and lifted me into his arms and onto the stretcher. Just like that. No huffing and puffing.

'No blowing big houses down?' I asked him, and he looked at me for a second and then grinned.

'Come on, Little Red Riding Hood. Let's get you checked out.'

'Three little pigs,' I corrected them, and they stared at one another.

'Gee, thanks, sunshine. We really needed a compliment after dying,' Paul chuckled.

'I'll huff and I'll puff and I'll blow your house down,' I insisted, and Julian looked at Paul, who nodded.

'A margarita will set her straight.'

'No alcohol,' the doctor said. 'She's still got the dregs of shock. Just keep her warm and get her to lie down.'

'I'm not lying down in a morgue – whether it's Boston

City or Boston County,' I sentenced. 'What's wrong with you guys?'

The doctor checked my blood pressure.

I'm not the one who's had the accident, I wanted to tell him. 'Paul…' I murmured, and he bent over me.

'Nice to know you'd miss me, sunshine, but really! You think I'd die in a car accident and get blood all over my Armani?'

And that's all I remember.

When I woke again, I was in my own bed (I recognized the cow jammies hanging on the back of the door) and Julian, Paul and the kids were there, Maddy curled up in the crook of my arm.

'Mommy's awake!' she hollered into my ear.

I jolted up as Warren checked me out and then hugged me as Maddy tugged on my hand.

'Mommy!'

'Sweetheart,' I whispered, kissing the tops of their heads as my eyes swung to Paul's. He wasn't dead. My darkest fears hadn't materialized today. The idea of losing Paul was something I couldn't stand.

'Oh, boy, am I glad to see you,' I breathed, and, realizing how stupid I sounded, began to sob. Not a loud sob – just a sniffly, teary thing under my breath so the kids wouldn't be alarmed.

'OK, kids, you've seen your mum's alright. Bedtime now,' Julian said in his deep, deep voice that was tender but commanding as well.

Julian in my bedroom. For real this time. Oh, wow. Although this wasn't exactly the way I'd pictured it, with Paul in it as well.

Maddy and Warren gave me one last look and a kiss before they allowed Julian to usher them out.

I sat up and looked at Paul in the lamplight.

'What time is it?' I asked.

'Well, I'm fine, thanks for asking,' he quipped, and I held my forehead.

'Stop, my head is killing me.'

'Serves you right, burying me before my days,' he said as he reached out his hand and caressed my cheek. 'I meant what I said yesterday. You are my family, Erica.'

I nodded and let him hug me as I cried my eyes out on his good shoulder. 'I was a complete idiot. I was so afraid something would happen to you one day and I'd be in real trouble without you. When the hospital called, I thought I'd lost you, Paul.'

'Well, not quite, luckily for me,' he said, patting my shoulder and helping me sit up with his good arm. 'I'm here, sweetie.'

'You know how much you mean to me, right? I can't even think of life without you.'

'You don't need to, sunshine. I'm not going anywhere.'

After a few quiet moments of me leaning contentedly on Paul's good shoulder, Julian came back into the room with a tray full of sandwiches and wraps and fruit and nuts.

'Ooh, yummy,' Paul said and grabbed one as he hopped to his feet and headed toward the door. 'See you later,' he chimed.

I panicked. 'What? Where are you going?'

'I have to see Bobby – I promised him,' he shrugged and wiggled his eyebrows at Julian. 'He'll stay here and take care of you, won't you, Julian?'

'Absolutely,' Julian replied, his eyes tender on me, his face turning red.

'See ya, lovebirds,' Paul sang and closed the door on my protests.

Lovebirds? I glanced at Julian, the most magnificent male in Creation, sitting on the edge of the bed with a tray full of food for me. What else could a woman want from life? I looked away so I wouldn't have to see the look in his eyes.

'I'm so sorry about Paul's innuendos, Julian. As much as I love him, he doesn't have a firm grasp on reality.'

Julian cleared his throat. 'Erica, I think you and I need to have a serious chat.'

Hoo boy. Here it was. 'Well, thanks for being here. I don't even know why Paul called you.'

Julian cleared his throat. 'I brought the kids home.'

'Oh. *Duh.*'

Julian smiled, his eyes studying my face. 'Why didn't you call me? You know I'd have come running.'

I looked up, confused. What was he saying? 'I-I didn't… there was nothing you could have done.'

'I could have been by your side. You should never have been on your own in a moment like that – ever.'

'I'm a big girl, Julian. Everyone can see that,' I said with a giggle when instead I wanted to pull back the covers and jump his beautiful bones, just like I had endless times in my fantasies.

He took my hand and squeezed it. 'Let me be there for you.'

If I was thinking of a fling, this sounded like more. What did I want? 'Don't waste your time on me, Julian.

I'm just a pseudo-suicidal homicidal housewife. Stay away from me.'

He grinned, lifted my hand to his lips and kissed it. I looked into his face as my skin began to tingle. It would have been so easy to lock the door and let him slide under the covers with me. Or rather, it would have been easy for me. For him, not so much, because I'd never let him go again. Ever.

I watched him, long lashes fanning his red cheeks, as his lips touched my hand. And then his eyes searched mine. 'I'm sorry, Erica...'

I nodded. 'It's OK. You don't have to apologize for staying away.'

He shook his beautiful head. 'I'm apologizing, because I don't *want* to stay away. Not anymore. I think you're the most beautiful, kind and caring woman in the world.'

I swallowed to stop my heart from jumping out of my mouth. 'And I think, Julian, that you're absolutely nuts. Go home and leave a poor woman her inner peace.'

Julian lowered his eyes. 'I'm sorry, Erica. I didn't mean to... I don't want...'

He swallowed, his cheeks hot as he gathered my hands in his, bringing them to his heart, palms flat on his chest. I could feel it pounding inside him, could almost see his shirt twitch under the force. He leaned over the tray, his breath shallow, his expression solemn, like I'd never seen him before, and took my face in his hands.

I could have closed my eyes, but I didn't want to miss a thing. I didn't want to miss Julian's beautiful, beautiful lips searching mine. Didn't want to miss the sight of his face an inch from my own, his dark hair falling over his forehead, his incredibly dark eyes…

He kissed me. Delicately. Tenderly, face-to-face, his eyes searching mine. No one had ever, *ever* kissed me like that. And then he kissed me again, only deeper. A real, real kiss.

My head spinning, I broke away and fanned myself. 'Whoa. That was, uhm…'

At that, he silenced me with a third kiss.

I could get used to this kind of treatment, I thought as I finally wrapped my arms around his neck like a drowning woman and kissed him back, all barriers down. And boy, let me tell you, it was the sexiest, most erotic moment of my life.

I let my hands roam over his shoulders and back, enjoying the feel of his strong, lean body against mine, more than aware that I was anything but lean myself. I envisaged him kissing me more, his hands slipping under my shirt and touching my roly-poly body. And I instantly stiffened. I had lost weight, but I wasn't at my best physically yet and probably never would be for him. And if I ever was, it would be time to find myself a toy boy with an expiration date – not my kids' principal, of whom I couldn't stop thinking.

'I think you'd better go now,' I whispered – before I tore his clothes off and he'd have to reciprocate (out of sheer courtesy). 'Thanks for everything. Especially for the kisses. Yum.'

'There's more where that came from,' he promised with a grin and a wink as he gathered my hands in his and kissed them one last time.

When he closed the door, I sat back and let out a huge sigh. I'd have to be very careful. I'd already done the falling in love thing and look where it had got me. Sex? Yes please – and lots of it, thank you. Love? Not happening until I touched Italian ground and an Italian family man.

21

In the Lion's Den

One evening when I got home from work, Ira was on the phone with his Stiletto Girl. He was in the guest room and hadn't heard me come in, but his low, sexy voice was clear in the silence of the house.

Ira laughed. 'I know, honey, I know. I can't wait, either... I miss you, too... I miss that gorgeous body of yours and can't wait to sleep with you in our very own bed.'

I froze.

'Who, Erica? She's probably at work now. All she does is work and stuff her face.'

He hadn't even noticed all the weight I'd lost. It figured. But I didn't care anymore. Nothing I ever did for him went noticed. I was done. Finito.

Without a sound, I slipped out of the house, closing the door gently behind me. I walked and walked aimlessly, but my unconscious was working overtime, because after a while I found myself standing before Clifton Street School, precisely under Julian's illuminated office window. I stood there until the sky turned from dark blue to purple, a golden light still lingering at the fringes above the city. I swung open the gate and sat on a bench – the same bench Julian and I had sat on a million years ago – staring at my swollen, now practically purple feet and finally sinking my head into my shoulders.

It wasn't long before Julian came out and I could tell he was surprised to see me here, sitting under a lamp post, my shoes on the bench beside me. He strode over to me and before I knew what he was about, he lifted me into his arms in one swift movement.

'No,' I said, ashamed. 'I'm too heavy. Put me down.'

'Nonsense,' he whispered and took me to his jeep, placing me in the passenger seat.

I slumped against it, stony-faced and furious with the world. Of all people, he was the last person I'd wanted to see me like this. And yet I'd come here, to him. What did that say about what I really wanted? I was done pretending.

Julian pulled up before a large, elegant house and came round to lift me into his arms again, closing the car door with his hip. I rested my head against his shoulder, absorbing the odd feeling of having him carry me and the sensation of strong, hot male around me. The last time someone had done that I'd been about five and had sprained my ankle. The hero had been my dad. But this time it was Julian, and I enjoyed the guilty pleasure of his body against mine.

I looked into Julian's face, so close I could smell his familiar scent. I'd smelled him before, in his jeep on the way back from the play, in the darkness of the car, and sitting on the sofa next to me. His scent had imprinted itself in my mind.

I fought the urge to kiss him as he simply smiled at me and I knew I must have been a sight, my eyes puffy and my bun coming undone. Why was I always such a mess around him?

'What will the neighbors think?' I whispered, unsure what I meant.

'That I'm a very lucky man,' he whispered back, and still none of it made sense.

Once inside, he peeled off my stockings (one was already around my knees) and bathed my feet in some special solution for athletes then dried them gently, his eyes never meeting mine. I watched him, mesmerized, as the blush seeped into his cheeks, his hands shaking, his breath quick. I was an absolute wreck, too, trembling from head to toe.

'I owe you big time,' I said breathlessly, caressing his face, unable to stop myself.

He shut his eyes tight for a moment, as if suffering from a major migraine, and turned his face in my hand to kiss my palm.

'I'm the one who owes you, Erica.'

For what, I didn't want to know. I reached up and kissed his lips. They were soft but firm and hot. Too hot for a principal's lips. And what if it turned out that he and I didn't click? Like Ira. That the minute he saw me naked, it not only took the wind out of his sails, but brought down the mast, as well?

'I'm not... turning you off, am I?'

'See for yourself,' he said gruffly, taking my hand, guiding it toward... Oh! goodness. From what I could see, it was sails ahoy.

'I did this to you?'

'You did this to me,' he murmured against my mouth. 'You always do and I want you so badly,' he whispered as his mouth left mine to travel down to my shirt buttons and began tugging on them.

I willed him to hurry before my mind figured out what he was about to do.

Ira had never understood or cared to learn my most sensitive spots. I loved my throat to be kissed and nuzzled and nibbled. I loved it as much as I loved everything else, and I was enjoying every moment.

Julian came closer – so close I could see the flecks of gold in his dark eyes. He smelled of soap and I don't know what else, but I knew in an instant that I'd recognize his body in the dark among millions of people. That scent was like a secret code I responded to, like when you touched a live wire or something, only delicious.

His hand rested on the back of my head, almost timidly, watching my face as his mouth descended on my lips, caressing them tentatively as if asking me a silent question. And when I wrapped my arms around his neck and slipped my fingers into his dark hair, something inside me exploded, and I had to hang on if I didn't want to reel off into space. For real.

His mouth was teasing and his kiss made me shoot skyward, higher and higher like in those Mills and Boon romances I'd binged on as a girl, breaking away from the Earth's pull of gravity. I was light, ultralight, and giddy. There wasn't enough oxygen going to my brain. I never remembered kisses being like *that*! I never knew that lip-on-lip contact could make me so hot for a guy.

Usually, it took me a long time to get carbureting, but

Julian's lips were like magic. All they had to do was touch my skin and boom – I was on fire. How the hell had I managed to live without this sensation for so long?

I gasped, coming up for air, my hands still clasping his neck. Whoa. Wow.

'Hello,' he whispered, his voice so deep it made my skin tingle.

'Fancy bumping into you,' I whispered playfully, by now a complete goner.

I imagined that if I'd traveled the world and cherry-picked the best qualities of the best human male specimens and put them all together, I still wouldn't have someone like Julian. He was kind, patient, loyal. He was everything Ira had never been and could never be in a million years. Helpful, optimistic, creative, passionate. And one hell of a kisser.

The next few steps, which would have involved stripping and lying next to him, were a little trickier. No matter how good he made me feel, I'd seen the Google images of the beautiful women on his arm at parties and stuff. I wasn't blind. Soon, he'd tire of the messy, screwball of an odd housewife who had held a challenge for him. But for now, I couldn't help but enjoy what he was doing to me.

And the minute he saw me naked? you might ask.

He didn't run but groaned 'Come here, you.'

No frozen smiles, no eyes bulging out of his head for the shock of seeing a less-than-perfect body, no nervous swallowing, wondering how he was going to approach the mountain of my body. Just his hands running all over me, caressing me, driving me crazy.

And when he moved to lift me on top of him, I cringed, but only for a split second.

'You are so beautiful,' he whispered as he easily lifted me up against his hard body.

He was beyond strong, beyond aroused.

Once I got over the shock of how easy it could be, I began to move as he caressed me, clutching at me and whispering how beautiful I was. I expected to wake any second alone in my bed at home, but here he was, underneath me, and I saw my whole life flash before me like when you die, only I'd skipped that part and gone directly to heaven.

I lay in his arms two orgasms later as he played with my hair.

'Will you tell me what happened to upset you so much today?' he asked gently.

I shrugged. Did he really need to know about Ira? 'Ira and I are divorcing.'

'I know. Are you OK with that?'

I nodded. 'It was time. There hadn't been anything left between us for years. And yet we tried so hard, but it didn't work out. And now Ira's with the Stiletto Girl. I guess he's finally got what he always wanted.'

'What do you mean?' Julian asked.

Again, I shrugged. 'She sends him sexy text messages.'

Julian chuckled. 'I can send you *shamefully* sexy text messages.'

'Yeah, but I'm not Miss Sexy.'

Julian sat up. 'Erica, there's absolutely nothing wrong with you. Ira's the one who doesn't know what he's lost.'

'That's sweet of you, Julian.'

'I'm serious. I'm so happy you're here with me. Truly I

am, and you shouldn't let such a clueless bloke hurt you like this.'

I looked up at him. I was the clueless one, because I didn't have a clue why he was saying such nice things to me. He'd already got me in the sack, what more did he want?

'You're a gorgeous guy. A former baseball celebrity. Why would you waste your time on me?'

'Erica, you have to stop measuring relationships with people's looks or jobs. I slept with women because something in their personality triggered me, certainly not their physical beauty.'

'And I'm your latest bursting-with-personality and non-beautiful woman,' I concluded.

He took my chin. 'No, you're not. You're very beautiful, with your sparkling eyes and this cute dimple on your cheek.'

'But you could have absolutely anybody.'

He grinned. 'I don't want anybody. I want you,' said my tall British and delicious baseball warrior.

'Oh, well. In that case, kiss me.'

'Now you're talking,' he agreed and took my mouth. 'Mmm, you taste wonderful.'

'You're not so bad yourself, Julian,' I offered.

'Here, I want you to have this. Use it whenever you want – no strings attached,' he said, reaching behind him into a bureau and wrapping my fingers around a small metal object.

A key.

I looked up at him. The key to his home?

'Julian, you can't be serious,' I whispered.

His hand curled around mine. 'The alarm code is 190651.'

I buried my face into the hand holding the key. To me, it was more than a house key. It was a *home* key. It was the key to happiness. If only I could use it. I slipped it onto my necklace and beamed at him through my tears.

'Use it any time, day or night, even just to chill out. If I'm not home and you need me, call me and I'll come,' he whispered.

I looked down at the key around my neck. 'Thank you.'

'Will you have lunch with me tomorrow? I know a place that serves fantastic shrimp linguine and the most amazing scallops.'

What do you say to a guy who gives you all you need? Plus scallops…

22

Juan and the Hooch

The next day, as you can imagine, I was walkin' on sunshine, floating above the clouds, beaming at everyone and everything and shamefully happy. I knew it couldn't last all day.

'Uhm… Mrs. Lowenstein?' came my senior waiter's terrified voice behind me, bringing me out of my steamy sex memories, and instantly the hair on the back of my neck stood on end. I needed to announce my change of name.

I turned around in my swivel chair. 'Yes, Mitch?'

'Uhm… we *kind* of have a problem.'

The tone I'd grown accustomed to, but it was the 'uhm' that promised nothing good. I sat forward, planting my still sore feet flat on the ground, pinching the bridge of my nose where a major ache was already developing. 'What is it, Mitch?'

'It's, uhm… Juan.'

Juan, my genius, arrogant and extremely lazy head chef. I swore one day I'd sack him.

'What about him? Is he giving you grief again? Send him in and I'll deal with him.'

'No, ma'am. It's just that he… isn't here.'

I shot to my feet, oblivious to my blisters from the day before, only aware of the fact that it was too close to lunchtime and that we were now in the danger zone. The next question was useless and stupid.

'What do you mean, not here? We have twelve delegates from Europe over for lunch in an hour and Juan's gone AWOL?'

Mitch nodded miserably and squeaked, 'I thought he'd arrive. He's always a little late, but—'

'Mitch, you have to stop defending your colleagues, especially if they're the first to rat on you.' I felt like a bad schoolteacher. And now we were in shit. And then another stupid question. 'Have you tried calling him at home? Maybe his wife knows where he is.'

Mitch shook his head. 'No one is answering.'

I grabbed my bag and coat. 'Have Dieter bring my car up, will you?' I said as I flew out the door and bam into none other than Julian.

Images of him inside me flashed through my mind and I tried to shake them off. What was he doing here?

'Lunch, remember?' he said as he took my outstretched hand as I slipped away.

'Sorry, I can't – emergency!' I called back over my shoulder, but then slowed as I reached the lobby, so as not to make a scene, and to give my blisters a breather. Our hotel was, after all, a chic one.

'Wait, I'll come with you,' he offered, steering me toward his jeep.

This was it. This was my job on the line. I'd never screwed up before. I hadn't monitored my staff. It wasn't a mistake I could afford. The moment I'd slip, as some had wagered, had come. I was screwed. Dead.

And so now I was on my way to Juan's house to salvage the salvageable, Julian at the wheel. I just hoped it wasn't what I thought. Last year, I'd caught Juan guzzling a secret stash of hooch. On the job. The fact that he'd stolen it from the bar was immaterial. I wanted him, needed him to be sober 24/7. I should have fired him at the first sign of weakness. Or better, I should have killed him.

My heart froze at the thought of him passed out on the floor and me holding him by the lapels, shaking him like a madwoman, trying to get his secret recipe for gazpacho Andaluz out of him.

This time, I wouldn't be able to forgive him (unless he was prostrate on the floor with the mortal effect of some rare snake bite). This time, I was deep in it. If my twelve European delegates didn't get their lunch, it would be my butt as well as Juan's.

'He'd better be dead, or else,' I choked. Gone was the broken but horny woman of the day before, replaced by my usual kick-ass efficiency.

'Ira?' Julian asked, glancing at me as I pointed and he turned a corner.

Obviously, he was still following the thread from yesterday.

'My chef, Juan. Turn left here!'

In one second, I'd explained the emergency, jumping out the car before Julian had come to a full stop and pounding my fists on my now ex-chef's front door (I make it my business to know everything about my staff, including where they live), before you could say 'Holy Guacamole.'

Julian went round the back to find another entrance, I presume, or, judging by the look I must have had on my face, to point Juan to the nearest escape.

And then the front door opened and Julian let me in, dragging me by my arm to the bedroom at the back. Juan was kneeling by his bed, as if in prayer, sobbing like a baby. And then I froze. Sprawled among the sheets was a young woman, her eyes unseeing, her naked body wracked with deep, broken breaths. The bastard was sleeping behind his wife's back. I was tempted to leave him here – it would save me firing him – but then I thought of his wife, Rita, and how she needed his benefits package.

'Call 911!' I heard Julian say as he dashed toward the woman and pulled off his own belt and tucked it in between her teeth.

'What's the matter with her?' I cried as I dialed. 'Hello! Yes! Please send an ambulance to 99 Rosecliff Terrace!'

'Ma'am, what's the problem?' came a disembodied male voice that sounded like it belonged to someone picking his nose.

I looked at Julian desperately, and he said, 'It's a seizure.'

I repeated the information to the operator.

The sight of that poor girl made me cringe. Never had I seen someone in such a state, but Julian acted swiftly, like he knew what he was doing. Then she fainted. Or I hoped.

He turned her onto her side and then set her back to give her mouth-to-mouth resuscitation. I stared at him as he touched her throat for a pulse, lowered his face to her naked breasts and listened, then began all over again. After a moment, he placed one hand on top of the other on her chest and pushed in short, rapid shoves.

Juan still lay sprawled in the corner on the floor, still bawling like a baby. That sure was a deterrent from betrayal to anyone.

'Juan, what's her name?' Julian demanded, but all Juan could do was hold his head in his hands.

'Juan!' he shouted. 'Her name!'

'I don't know!' he exclaimed. 'I think she said Lola.'

Holy crap. Juan, whom everyone thought was happily married. He even had children, for Christ's sake. And he'd brought her into his own home? What the hell was happening to the world? I should listen to my instincts more often. And now here I was, having to clean up after his marital indiscretions, as if I didn't have my own problems. I only hoped this poor girl would make it. And that Rita would be strong enough to face this.

After what seemed like forever, the wail of an ambulance filled the air and in no time, paramedics spilled into the house with a stretcher, asking Julian all kinds of questions, which he promptly answered.

'Sir, you may have well saved this woman's life,' one informed him gravely.

'So she's going to be OK?' I asked.

The poor girl looked wasted. I cringed at the thought of her mother receiving the news.

'She's coming to,' one of the paramedics said as they hauled the gurney into the back of the ambulance and disappeared.

Julian turned to me and I sagged with relief. Juan went back inside and threw himself on the sofa in his droopy underwear. Not a good sight. And to think that this man had served me food.

'Thank you, Julian,' I moaned as I pulled him close to kiss him smack on the mouth.

He tasted yummy – good enough to eat. And then I remembered my Europeans.

'Crap!' I screamed. 'I have to go take care of my twelve guests!'

It was like The Last supper, or at least it would be for me if I couldn't pull this off. I whipped out my cellphone and started barking orders at my sous-chef, Walter.

'Get Hank in pronto. Tell him Juan's ill and he's got ten minutes to get his butt to the hotel, otherwise it's his job! And get Marie and Angie to start dicing vegetables. And make sure you pull out the right cut of meat.' Then I hung up and huffed.

Julian was looking at me.

'Sorry,' I said. 'But the show must go on.'

Julian escorted me back to his jeep and closed the door for me.

'Lucky for you, I'm a great cook.' He grinned.

We barely made it. The delegation was fifteen minutes late, which gave us the time we needed. As it turned out, Julian really was a good cook – and fast, too. He expertly cut the meat and seasoned the vegetables as I ran around giving my staff orders. Still, I didn't miss his furtive glances at me. I couldn't tell if he was scared or impressed. This was one side of me he'd never seen. But he, too, was extremely efficient. He worked quickly and quietly, except to communicate his timing. Gordon Ramsay would have loved him.

'You're hired,' I beamed, and he smiled and shrugged. 'How can I ever repay you?'

He grinned. 'There is one thing.'

'Done!' I exulted.

'Seriously. I'd like to learn how to cook Italian food. Would you teach me?'

'You want me to teach you to cook Italian food?'

'I told you - my real mother was Italian and I feel I've missed out on so much while growing up. You're a real Italian. Would you do that? It would mean so much.'

It also meant a form of commitment. Would I spend hour after hour while Italian food slowly cooked in my oven, this delicious man standing by my side? Is the pope an old geezer? He was asking me if I minded having it all. Being happy. All I wanted was to be around him, bask in the heat of his sensuality, laugh at his jokes. Be his woman.

Was that what he'd asked me? Was I his woman? I had his house key, didn't I? And now he wanted me to teach him to cook Italian food. He wanted to learn my culture, to appreciate it. Ira could never have cared less, but Julian was finding ways for us to spend more and more time together. Was he really ready to take me on... in a real relationship? Was he ready for commitment? Was I?

And what about Tuscany? I couldn't forgo that, never in a million years. Maybe I was building all this up in my mind. Something that was turning out to be too deep for me. A fling was what I needed, not to be salivating after a guy like Julian. Why didn't I just take what life gave me instead of trying to have it all at the same time?

Because for twelve bloody years I'd missed out on so much happiness, that's why. And, dammit, didn't I deserve some happiness? But standing before this beautiful man, I didn't want to ruin whatever this was we had.

I swallowed. 'Learning to cook takes a lot of time. Are you sure you can spare it? I mean, you'd be spending hours on end with me.'

'I already spend every night with you.'

I looked up, confused, and he grinned.

'I lie awake at night thinking about you.'

'Sold,' I grinned back, and he leaned over and kissed me. Smack dab in the middle of The Farthington kitchen crawling with my staff. How was that for commitment?

23

Birthday Suit (Stilettos and Panties)

The day before my birthday I decided to give myself a little carefree present, precisely a pair of red stiletto heels and a pair of lace panties, just like Ira's lover. Only my target wasn't Ira. It was to be able to have sex playfully, not just as a chore as it had been with Ira. No, from now on there would be fun in my (or Julian's) bed. To hell with my good resolutions about finding another guy. I didn't want anyone else.

I pulled out my old trench coat to make sure it didn't smell like mothballs, my heart beating like a schoolgirl's. I knew it was cheesy, maybe even ridiculous, but played right it could be fun. I'd always wanted to do something like this, but Ira never let me get away with it.

But, if I could start off my relationship with Julian on a sexy, playful note, I'd already have a better relationship than I'd ever had with my husband. If Julian was game, I was home free. And if not, simple – the kids could still be happy at a new school!

★

Of course I had some back-up clothes in the car, but for now, I wrapped the trench coat tightly around me and rang Julian's doorbell. His jeep wasn't there, but I rang all the same out of courtesy. After all, it was his house. Nothing. I bent to fit the key around my neck into the lock, punched in the code and stepped over the threshold.

My feet, still blistered from the other night, were killing me already with the new shoes. Maybe I wouldn't have to wear them until he got back... I shrugged out of my coat and looked in the hall mirror, my naked breasts glowing white in the dying light.

'You have completely lost it, lady,' I said to the woman in the mirror, and burst into a hysterical laughter.

I wasn't a raving beauty, but Julian was right – I did have beautiful breasts and my curves were generous. I liked generous. He liked generous. So why was I so friggin' panicky? Wasn't this what I'd always wanted?

I found a beautiful chaise by one of the living room windows – a room we'd bypassed on my first visit – and adjusted myself on it like a Hollywood star. Waxed within an inch of my life and as fresh as a rose, I leaned back, my too-tight stilettos dangling from my toes, my long hair all on one shoulder, looking sultry and relaxed on the outside while on the inside I was having multiple mini-strokes by the minute.

There was still time for me to get up, go home and save my dignity. I didn't have to go through with it. But I really wanted to. At thirty-five (minus one day), this might well be my last chance to have sex like a young woman without looking pathetic (if I didn't already). As a sudden wave of panic washed over me, I bolted back to the mirror, checking my B-side and all the other sides to make sure I didn't have anything gross on me like a major pimple or wart. Was I really doing this? Damn right I was.

I heard a car door close and then recognized Julian's car alarm bleep. Dashing back into the living room, I slipped my feet (ouch) into my red stilettos and spread myself out on the chaise, saying a silent prayer. It was do or die. I held my breath for my surprise exhibition.

'Erica?' he called as he came down the hall.

Shit. My Kia was in the damn driveway, wasn't it? Some surprise.

'Sweetie, where are you?'

He appeared on the threshold, still as a rock, his jaw dropping open, speechless. Which was the effect I'd been going for. But in the slanting rays of the sunset, I made out another figure. A woman. When realization hit, I screamed and dashed behind the chaise longue, lacy butt momentarily exposed, clutching at the upholstered back like a drowning woman to a raft in the storm. Julian had brought a *woman* home? Why the hell had he given me his key, then? They both stared at me with enormous eyes and the silence was so thick, you could have cut through it with a knife.

'Erica?' he choked, then coughed politely. 'I, um, this is my mother, Maggie Foxham.'

His mother? His *mother*? Wanting to fall through the floorboards, I stuck my head out from behind the back of the chaise just long enough to show half my face and raised my hand. 'Hello, Mrs. Foxham, it's so... *nice* to meet you.

Sorry about the… ah…' And then I simply shut up. What would you have said?

Her eyes swung to Julian's as she tried to stifle a laugh and warmly waved from the hall.

'Hello, pet. I've heard so much about you. I'm glad I finally got a chance to meet you,' she said graciously in Julian's same British accent, then kissed Julian on the cheek. 'We'll do the papers some other time, dear. No hurry.' And then she turned to me once more and smiled. 'Hope to see you again soon, Erica,' she said and was gone.

Preferably with my clothes on, I cringed to myself as Julian saw her to the door. What a classy lady. Cool as a cucumber.

When Julian came back in, I was fumbling around on all fours for my trench coat. Where the hell had I put it? Damn, was I a total loser or what? Never had I done something more disastrously embarrassing than that. It was a sign. I had to scram. If I could just…

'Looking for this?' he asked, my coat hanging from his index finger, a strange look on his face.

'I'm so, so sorry,' I mumbled. 'I wanted to surprise you and—'

'Well, you certainly did,' he agreed, chewing on the inside of his cheeks to stop from laughing. 'What were you planning?' he whispered as he came into the room slowly, like a panther stalking a big, juicy rabbit.

'I-I… nothing,' I said, reaching for my trench coat.

'I'd like you to continue where we interrupted you,' he said, his eyes now hooded.

I swallowed. 'You would?'

He nodded, taking his own coat off and throwing it aside with mine.

'Lie down again,' he directed me, 'just as I found you.'

As I obeyed, he kneeled between my feet.

'Open your legs,' he whispered.

Oh, boy! This was suddenly looking up. I obeyed, my heart pounding in my ears.

'I'm going to love you now from head to toe,' he growled softly.

And with that, he took my stilettos off (thank God) and gently brought my foot to his mouth, kissing my toes, one by one. As I watched through half-closed lids, he kissed my ankle, my shinbone, traveling up my leg and thigh, his eyes never leaving mine. Before he reached my panties, he pulled himself up and kissed me on the mouth, deep and hard, as I melted into a puddle at his feet.

'Erica, before we go any further, I have to be honest. I lied to you.'

My eyes snapped open, alarmed. 'What? You're married?'

He chuckled. 'No, silly. I'm single. But this,' he said, his mouth easing its way back down to our target, thank God, '*does* come with strings attached.'

I frowned. 'Strings… what do you mean?'

His mouth swept over me right there and I lurched like a bolt of lightning had hit me, almost knocking a nearby lamp over.

'I simply mean that this comes with dinners, dates, movies. The works.'

'Oh!' I exhaled in relief.

Julian sat up, his hands keeping my thighs apart. 'I mean it, Erica. I don't want to be just your rebound boy.'

I stared at him. 'Rebound? What are you talking about?'

'That I don't want you to start this if in your heart you know I can't be more for you. I'm serious, Erica.'

Yes, lately my world had fallen into the twilight zone, no doubt about it.

I opened my mouth to say something, but nothing came out, so I simply nodded, feeling like the most beautiful woman in the world as he bent over me once again. He made love to me on that chaise and somewhere in the middle, I remember him carrying me to his bedroom upstairs, where it started all over again. Bless the Brits.

24

Ti Amo

As I was climbing into my car after work the next day (not that I'd got much done, as you can imagine), Julian appeared out of the blue, waving, running toward me. Julian. I almost hadn't recognized him with his clothes on, so branded in my mind was the image of his beautiful, statuesque, naked body. Face flushed and excited, he made his way over as my heart lurched. God, why was he so sinfully gorgeous?

'Erica, am I glad I caught you!' he exclaimed, his other arm pinned behind his back.

'Julian – is everything OK?' Did he want to call it off? Had I not performed well enough?

He produced a giant bouquet of red roses and planted a delicious kiss on my mouth that almost bowled me over.

'Happy birthday, my girl.'

Wait, how did he even know about my birthday? Had he checked the school files? Sneaky, sneaky fox!

'*Old* girl, you mean,' I gushed, taking the flowers from him. 'Thank you so much, Julian.'

'Old? You're luminous. Brilliant. Besides the fact that you look sexy as hell sprawled naked on my living room chaise.'

I liked the sound of that, although I was unfamiliar with the concept. I nodded finally and Julian took my hand.

'Come on, let's go.'

'Uhm, I can't. I have to go home to the kids.'

'That's where we're going,' he assured.

'You want to come home with me?'

'I thought you'd never ask,' he said with a devilish grin.

I stared at him, trying to recover, and finally nodded, realizing my mouth was still open. 'OK, but I need to go to the supermarket to get some stuff first.'

'Cool.'

So I let him come grocery shopping with me on my birthday – in my car.

'Until you take me on board as your cooking student, you'll have to settle for a British meal,' he informed me when we got in.

I turned to him. 'You're cooking me a meal?'

He grinned his hallmark sexy grin – the one that made me want to jump over the kitchen island in one swing and pull his clothes off.

'It was the least I could do – plus, it's your birthday. You shouldn't have to cook on your birthday.'

Madeleine and Warren had taped balloons and crepe paper all over the living room and kitchen. Julian's roast beef with potatoes and vegetables and the works was delicious. Just like him. The kids had got me a gift – a beautiful make-up set – with Warren's money from his paper run and

Maddy's allowance (and I suspect with a little help from the school principal). Julian had taped a Happy Birthday sign high up on the wall, framed with balloons of every color.

'Ready for my gift?' he asked and winked at the kids.

I widened my eyes. 'There's *more*?'

He handed me an envelope. Inside was a ticket to Paris and a booking for a five-star hotel, l'Athénée! *And* free entry for a week to the Musée d'Orsay – my favorite Impressionist museum in the whole world.

'I saw your books on painting,' he grinned. 'And I've seen your own lovely work hanging around the house.'

Lovely work? Did he see what I saw in my paintings? Did he see the yearning for a dream landscape, my craving for freedom that dotted every corner of my home?

I gaped. 'Are you crazy? I can't accept such an expensive gift!'

'Of course you can.'

There was no way I was going to fly to Paris courtesy of another man and give Ira any ammunition in a court room. I shook my head at Julian, opening and closing my mouth, not wanting to ruin the moment.

'I don't know what to say.'

Except for that I was dying to use that ticket, and fly to Paris and roll over and over on a French mattress with him. I remembered my aunts telling me to go for it, Paul telling me to go for it, Julian's *eyes* telling me to go for it. So why wasn't I going for it?

'Say thank you, Mommy!' Maddy exclaimed, her beautiful eyes shining.

I looked over at Julian and blushed. 'Thank you, Julian.'

Then *he* blushed. 'You're very welcome, Erica.'

With Julian, all I had to do was close my eyes and feel him, even when he was on the other side of town. Once you've slept with a guy you like and the sex is mind-bashing, he's virtually inside you (or me, in this case) forever.

So how the hell was I not going to get hurt again? I'd survived Ira. I definitely wouldn't survive Julian.

Sure, he was great to the kids and me, but how did I know he really cared for me as a woman and that he simply didn't suffer from Superman syndrome, thinking he could save me from all forms of evil and danger, myself included? And sure, he made everything perfect, but how did I know he wasn't going to lure me off my straight path, into his bed for a painfully brief spell, and then lose interest in me once he woke and realized he wasn't a superpower, and that, as much as he wanted to, he couldn't solve my issues?

I mean, let's be honest here. He was a gorgeous ex-baseball star. I was an overweight, under-loved wife and mother of two who, when at home, dressed like Ernie from *Sesame Street* on her better days. I was still slowly getting back in the saddle. We had nothing in common. Could you even remotely see us together? So could I.

25

Free to Be

You know those days at work when it looks like it's going to be a breeze, when you can link your hands behind the back of your neck for a minute or two and relax because this might finally be the day everything will go, at least for a couple of hours, reasonably smooth? If you do, then I envy you.

I'd just flown in from San Francisco, California and was sitting at my desk with a thumping headache, trying to fight jet lag. It was pointless going home, as the kids were in school and I didn't want to be there alone. Plus, I was actively avoiding Clifton Street Private School to avoid running into the other moms.

My stomach felt queasy and my legs hollow, and if I hadn't known better, I'd have thought I was pregnant. There was no point in denying the deeply buried truth that Julian and I were, in a sense, lovers. And it felt great.

Let's be honest. I'd married Ira out of fear of remaining single. All my life I'd lived in the shadow of gorgeous women like Marcy and her sisters. If all three of my gorgeous, intelligent and talented aunts were still on the shelf, what hopes exactly had I had?

Oh, why the hell did I have to go and get a schoolgirl crush on my kids' principal? Why did he have to be so damn sweet and sexy and inaccessible? And where the hell had he been twenty years ago when I was looking for a boyfriend? But this wasn't *Fantasy Island* and I wasn't fifteen anymore.

And what was worse, in my dream I kept experimenting with these amazing sex positions I never knew existed (and I'm sure I must have invented a couple), and felt such intense climaxes that I'd wake up aroused, my heart pounding, my body more than ready. I needed another Julian fix pronto. I knew this was going to happen. Not that he'd want to sleep with me but that I wouldn't be able to stop.

Jackie craned her neck into my office. 'Honestly, I don't know whether to laugh or cry,' she managed, dabbing at her eyes with a Kleenex tissue.

'What now?' I groaned.

'Better go see for yourself. Room 1312. It's been like that for hours.'

I gave her my famous hairy eyeball and got to my feet. There were some days I really wished I'd stayed at home.

The occupant of Room 1312 was Mr. Dupré, a businessman from Chicago, Illinois. I stopped just outside his door, listening to the bed springs squeak and heave, squeak and heave, non-stop. Either he and his mysterious partner in there were going at it like jackhammer rabbits or there was a real problem.

I knocked discreetly. 'Mr. Dupré?'

'Come in!' came an imperious voice.

I wish I hadn't obeyed, because there he was, in his undershirt and boxers, jumping up and down on the bed. What the…

'Hi!' he exclaimed as he thumped away.

I crossed my arms. 'Hello…?'

'Don't mind me,' he said. 'I can't stop.'

'The springs in our mattresses are that good?' I asked nonchalantly.

'It's just that I had breakfast this morning, you see.' *Thump, thump.*

I sighed. Something told me this was going to be a long day. 'Yes?'

'And by mistake…' *Thump, thump.* 'I had regular coffee.'

'Right.'

'But I can only drink decaf… because *this*'—*thump, thump*—'is what it does to me!'

'It makes you want to test all the mattresses you sleep in?' I couldn't help saying.

'It charges me with this nervous adrenaline!' *Thump.* 'And this is the only way I can get rid of the caffeine in my system!' *Thump, thump, thump.*

The way I saw it, I had two alternatives. Either shoot him down or let him deal with it as he thought best. He wasn't doing anyone any harm, only trying to flush something out of his system. I made a mental note to make sure the bed was OK once he'd checked out. And maybe even try it myself. It looked like fun. I smiled and left him to deal with it his own way.

★

I wanted to call Julian, to tell him about the crazy man. I picked up the phone, knowing (or at least hoping) I was one of the few mothers who had his personal number. And then I put the phone back down.

If I called him, it would only mean one thing. Let's pick up where we left off. Wasn't my life complicated enough? *Hell, no.* Even if I was still the betrayed wife, part of me demanded the right to be myself, but only with a little more enjoyment, a tiny moment for Erica Cantelli, if not downright, every now and then, fun.

Besides, how long could straw lie next to a burning fire before it burst into flames again? How could I resist a possible round three?

26

Love Stinks

I was diligently working away on my laptop, grateful that we were having a quiet day at The Farthington. As my mind began to wander to what I'd be cooking that evening, I became aware of a low buzzing sound, like a cellphone alarm vibrating. I looked around me, but all was normal. The noise became louder until I found myself investigating in the front office, where I almost fainted dead away.

At the center of our posh gilded reception, surrounded in a circle created by our elegantly dressed and distinguished guests, was no less than a catfight.

Dr. Hendricks and Dr. White, both blonde and Barbie-doll-like, were rolling on the plush carpeting, in a swirl of yellow-and-turquoise designer suits, pulling on each other's hair while grunting and squealing. The same ones, as far as I could tell, I'd secretly envied the day before, all immaculately dressed in their labels. The kind who had made me feel like the big fat toad in the fairytale – ugly and unwanted.

And now dresses rode high over thighs, exposing lacy and fleshy bits. And I'd wanted to be like them, thinking they'd looked like supermodels. And you wouldn't believe the language. Some people you can't take the trash out of, degree or no degree.

But the horrific part was that no one was intervening. The busboys and the rest of the male staff watched in admiration as these two 'ladies' clawed at each other, pushing the other's chin back, scratching each other's eyes out, not to mention uprooting clumps of peroxide blonde hair.

I wrung my hands. I'd never been so ashamed of my gender in all my life.

'Call security!' I hissed to Lesley, my main receptionist, who, wide-eyed, scurried toward the phone.

'I'll teach you to steal my man!' the yellow Barbie said to the turquoise one.

'He's not your man – he can't stand you!'

Oh, God. If all these people were doctors, brain surgeons and shrinks, what hope did the rest of us have? It was too much. I couldn't wait for security to get off their fat asses while these two women destroyed what I represented.

Without thinking, I ran over to them, trying to part them, but only managed to get my eye punched and my cheek scratched. It was like having an enraged lion swiping at you with French manicured claws. I licked my lips and tasted blood on my face.

Now if I'd been anywhere else and not on the job, I'd have lost it like a bull taunted by a red cape and licked them real good, but being in my position, I had to carry myself gracefully, whatever the situation. So I smothered a few of my own foul four-letter faves and ran to the corner of the hall, where I grabbed one of the fire extinguishers and let them have it – the whole damned thing.

As the foam started to envelop them, they squealed, trying to get up, but slipped, over and over, clutching at the floor, losing their shoes in the process, as if they'd stepped into a giant cake. Their hair, make-up and clothes were one humongous mess. When they finally desisted, I watched them, my chest heaving from the exertion (they should make these contraptions a bit easier to handle), my eyes shooting daggers.

'Get someone to clean this mess up,' I said to Lindsay and turned, glad to have put the scene behind me. 'And bill them for the damages.'

The hilarious part, if there was any, was that the guy in question hadn't even stepped forward to split them up. I'm sure he was here, because everybody else sure was, cheering them on. In my posh hotel.

After having written a personal report about the incident and emailed it to Mr. Farthington, I called it a day. I was, after all, working only until three now.

At five, my doorbell rang. I opened the door and started. Julian, loaded with grocery bags. I'd totally forgotten about our cooking lesson.

'Hi, Erica. I got some lean *filetto* and some articho—'
I shot him a glance as I stepped aside to let him in.

His eyes widened, then narrowed. 'What happened?' he asked as his hand caressed my cheek.

I flinched at the pain and his mouth formed a grim line.

I led him into the kitchen, almost resigned that we were going nowhere all too fast. I enjoyed his company. He was a good cook, willing to learn, fun, confident and had an aura of security around him that attracted me like a magnet.

He gently took my arms and made me sit on a stool by the island and peered down into my eyes. 'Who did this to you?' he said gruffly.

'Catfight at work,' I replied.

He fetched a terry cloth (good thing I'd just changed them) and got some ice from the freezer, coming to crouch in front of me, his fingers gently dabbing at my bruised face.

'You always seem to be in the right place at the right time,' I whispered, wincing at the cold contact, but he said nothing, his eyes searching mine, so close I lost myself in his dark eyes.

Long moments passed before he whispered, 'How's that?'

And I whispered back, 'Better, thanks.' But he wouldn't stop studying me. 'I'm OK, Julian. Really.'

'*OK?* You got *hurt*. What happens when he really picks up that baseball bat? You wouldn't survive that one, Erica.'

I blinked. 'What are you talking about? You think Ira did this to me? No, I told you – I tried to break up a catfight. At work. Couple of brain surgeons, believe it or not, fighting over a male colleague.'

He looked at me gravely, with a mixture of anger and doubt, but finally exhaled, his mouth tight.

'OK,' he said, his voice so gentle I wanted to cry.

He stuffed his hands in his pockets and looked me square in the face, his expression softening. There we were. This was it. Something was happening and I couldn't stop it.

'Hi, Mr. Foxham. Like Mom's shiner?' Warren asked as he walked in, not surprised, or disturbed, in the least to see his principal there for the umpteenth time.

Rumors at school must have stopped, because Warren seemed much happier now.

'You keep an eye on your mum, alright?' he said softly, and Warren nodded.

I ruffled Warren's hair and he put his arms around me. One of his rare moments. I sat still and enjoyed the feeling as Julian watched us.

I turned to him. 'Come on, you. Wash your hands. I want to see you doing justice to this fantastic food. You're making stuffed artichokes and *filetto* in mushroom sauce.' I could get used to having my own personal chef at home.

Julian eyed me, then the kids, and finally reached into the grocery bags.

In thirty minutes, he managed to get the food in the oven.

'Why do you think you need lessons?' I asked, suddenly suspicious.

He checked the timer. 'I told you. I've wanted to learn all my life. And now that I've found an expert—'

'I'm no expert. Zia Maria is.'

'She's great,' Julian agreed. 'But I'm only interested in you.'

'So it was just an excuse for round three?'

He grinned. 'You make it sound like a fight.'

I sighed. Sex with Ira had been a fight – a war. But with Julian it was easy to feel something good. If only I could talk to him about Tuscany.

Are you nuts? My alter ego snapped at me. *You barely know the guy and you want to drag him all the way to Europe? Don't you think you're taking a lot for granted?*

Maybe, I snapped back. *But if I don't risk it, how will I ever know?*

You're in for a big crash, it countered. *You talk to him about the future, especially in another country, and you're going to scare the crap out of him. Your own husband and father of your children wouldn't follow you – what makes you think Julian would? At least wait a while before you drop that bomb on him.*

Well, my conscience was certainly right about that. I couldn't do that to him so early in the relationship. But sooner or later, if this continued, it would have to take some direction, right? But for now, I'd take what life gave me. Which was countless orgasms a week. Not that I was complaining, mind you.

'Erica, you're amazingly sexy,' Julian whispered against the side of my face, and then down between my breasts as his hands traveled over and over my butt.

Oh boy. If he kept that up, we'd be doing it among the artichokes.

But how exactly was I sure this could lead to Tuscany? There was no way I was ready to trust a man again just yet. Not even Julian. But the sex, I could enjoy and milk forever. Until he got sick of me and would break the heart I professed had been closed for business. Not to mention the kids – they adored him. What if he broke their hearts, too? This was something I couldn't accept.

I kissed him back and he sighed.

'What?' I asked.

'I told you, Erica. I don't just want this to be about sex.'

'Why don't we take one day at a time, huh?' I whispered softly lest the kids came back downstairs and then I'd have one hell of a task explaining why Mr. Foxham had his hands down Mommy's pants.

He ran a hand through his gorgeous black hair and nodded. 'OK, we'll do it your way. For now.'

Which to me sounded not like an ultimatum, but a promise.

27

Irreconcilable Differences

One rainy afternoon, Julian asked me to meet him at his home. Was he going to dump me? Or move our sex relationship up to the next level, with maybe leather straps and chains? Hell! If I knew what was going on between us, really.

At first, I'd said yes (to meeting him at home – not the chains), but by the time I was due there, I chickened out and went to my local coffee shop for a cappuccino instead and watched the streets flood under the sudden downpour. There were a thousand things that I still worried about.

Due to my healing self-confidence, and also thanks to Julian's reactions to me in and out of bed, my weight was no longer an issue for me anymore. Sure, I wasn't Barbie, but I was no longer obese. Big? Sure – but happy, too. I'd taken to seeing myself as Julian did – curvy and sexy. And that, in a normal woman's mind, should only have been the start of a happy ending. But you know me and my obsessive fears.

What if he suffered from Superman syndrome and eventually got fed up with saving me? He'd break my heart and the kids'. I knew I was being a chicken, but I had the horrible feeling that I'd fallen in love with him after, what – a couple of months? On what planet had I allowed that to happen? And to boot, I was still worried about Tuscany.

What person in their right mind would upheave their entire life to follow someone they barely knew halfway across the world? I knew Julian loved his job, his home, his parents. Why the hell would he leave all that for me? It wasn't like he'd said he loved me or anything, right?

'Julian?' I said into my cellphone, my heart in my throat as the rain beat against the large windows of the café. And then I told him why I wouldn't be keeping our date, all in one breath, before I could change my mind. That I wasn't ready for another relationship, especially with my kids' principal. Yeah, it sounded lame to me, too, but when you're chicken, you're chicken.

He sighed softly. 'Where are you?'

I swallowed. No way I was telling him. 'In the coffee shop round the corner from my home.' Shit. 'Don't come,' I added lamely.

'I'll be there in five.'

'Don't! I won't be here,' I warned. But who was I kidding?

Exactly five minutes later, he poured into the shop, his jacket flying in the wind behind him, his hair wet from the downpour. He looked damn sexy, all wet from head to toe. What the hell did he want with a woman like me? I had baggage – physical, emotional and lately, even under my eyes.

And I'm passing this guy up? I asked myself, bewildered. I could at least *ask* him if he liked Tuscany, no?

Julian slid into the seat opposite me without a word, his eyes caressing me, so warm my skin began to heat.

He put his hand on mine, his eyes liquid. 'Hey...'

I closed my eyes and swallowed. He sighed.

'It's become way too obvious that this is serious stuff, sweetheart. Maybe neither of us expected this to happen. But is has and there's no denying it.'

Sweetheart. I laughed bitterly at the sound of the endearment. I wasn't used to hearing it from my husband's lips, let alone from another guy. And if I could think of a billion reasons to go with him back to his house, I could think of two billion for not doing it – now, as the rain pelted the scurrying passengers outside, forcing them to run for cover. Were they going to meet their lovers, too, or were they going home to their families, where I should have been as well, getting a nice roast ready instead of flirting around?

Who was I kidding? I'd never been able to flirt in my whole life. I was a total loser in the romantic field. And to the point where here I was, caught in one of those pathetic scenes you only see on really bad daytime TV.

I lowered my head, feeling the top of the ketchup bottle pressing into my forehead. That would leave me a nice round red mark for all to see. K is for ketchup and kissing.

As hard as I tried, I couldn't tear my hand away from beneath Julian's hot, protective touch. He'd have to do it for me and pronto, because my body was dying to reach out and grab him by his coat and beg him to stay. Forever, if he was crazy enough.

'Do you like Boston?' I blurted.

He stared at me and then grinned.

'Love it. Why?'

Fan-bloody-tastic. 'Just wondering. And what's your second favorite city? Or country?'

He groaned. 'Jesus Christ, Erica – just answer this question. Do you still love your husband? Is that what's stopping you?'

I looked up, raising my eyebrow. 'Hello? Have you not been listening to a word I've said since we met?'

As much as I'd wanted Julian, who represented all that had been denied to me previously, the truth was, I was terrified of admitting this *want* if he was going to refuse to move to Tuscany with me. It was way too early in the relationship to ask him, yet the right time in my life. I'd always put others – namely Ira – first. Wasn't it time to think about the kids and me?

Julian suddenly beamed at me, his finger reaching down to touch the sore spot where the ketchup cap had carved itself into my forehead.

'I'm happy when I'm with you and you're happy when you're with me,' he said.

Huh. Simple as that. Concise but true.

I nodded. 'But don't you care about your reputation? Or your job?'

'Not as much as I care about you, no,' he said, holding onto my hand, stroking the back of it.

How quickly our dutiful principal had morphed into a lovesick puppy. At least he looked like one, though I knew all he wanted was to get into my pants again. Which earned him oodles of brownie points.

'So, you'd leave your job if you had to?'

'Erica, nothing is going to happen to my job because I'm sleeping with you.'

Just then, my eyes faltered and caught sight of his dark juicy lips. The lips I was dying to kiss again. The temptation was killing me. He was so close. What harm could one kiss possibly do? Just one.

'Technically, you're sleeping with a married woman, you know that?'

He shrugged. 'You're divorcing him.'

'And I have two kids.'

Julian took my chin in his hands. 'The kids adore me. Erica, work with me here. What are you afraid of? That I'll leave you?'

'Technically, we're not even together yet,' I said, and he rolled his eyes.

'My chaise and bed don't agree with you. Besides, my mum's curious to see what you look like with your clothes on. Even though I prefer you naked.'

I gawked at him. 'You want to introduce me to your mom?'

'Well, technically you've already met.'

'Did she ask you who I was?'

Julian laughed, his eyes twinkling. 'She already knew.'

'Oh.'

'But you're right. We'll take it slow until you and the kids are ready to go full throttle.'

Which would give him time to understand his feelings before making such a monumental decision like leaving the USA. 'Thank you,' I whispered.

★

As I came in through my front door later that evening, I heard unfamiliar noises. The kids were having a sleepover at Paul's, so who could it be? A burglar? There was no sign of forced entry that I could see. Gathering my guts, I inched my way down the hall and stopped at the foot of the stairs, making an effort to breathe quietly, something that my burglar wasn't doing. I slipped into the kitchen and grabbed my cleaver from the top cabinet.

As stealthily as I could, I crept up the stairs, avoiding the seventh step that always creaked. It was coming from my bedroom. The thought of someone helping himself to the contents of my safe filled me with rage and I had to restrain myself to not fling the door open and kill the guy by simply jumping on him. But if this guy was armed, I'd be in trouble, so I peered round the corner and through the chink in the door. And my jaw dropped open.

Ira and a woman. They were emptying his drawers, shoving the carefully ironed and folded clothes into a small suitcase.

The woman turned her head to the side and our eyes locked. Pretty young face. A familiar face. She screamed.

Ira jumped back and turned to see me – weapon in hand. I'd forgotten all about it, as dazed as I was by the sight of my husband and his lover. The husband I'd tried so hard to sex up – the marriage I'd tried to save. The cleaver felt heavy in my hand, my hand felt heavy on the end of my arm, but I couldn't let it drop to the floor. Could I use it? Was I finally going to realize my dreams of killing him? Only this time I'd be the betrayed wife who had flipped.

I gave the young woman a closer look. And then it dawned on me. 'Maxine? Is that you?'

Ira's young secretary ran past me like the bed had caught fire.

'Erica, what the hell!' Ira yelled as if I'd walked in on him using the toilet. 'Put that down! What are you? Nuts?'

But all I could do was stare at him. Wow! Boss screws secretary. The same cliché repeats itself. Hadn't I been knocked up by him when he was my boss? And then I started to laugh. Real ROFL, rolling on the floor, laughing. Maybe I was nuts. For having renounced my own dreams all this time. For having tried all these years to stay faithful to a man who didn't deserve me. For a man who had no respect for me or my home. I leaned against the door and cackled, holding my sides until I couldn't breathe anymore.

They dashed past me (I'd never seen *him* move that fast) and a few seconds later, the door slammed and their car took off like a shot. I went downstairs, grabbed the keys from the island, closed the door behind me and slid into my Kia van. I turned the ignition and drove away from my pain.

28

The Amazing Erica

I drove for hours, recklessly, aimlessly, risking a few scrapes here and there, almost willing myself to crash into something. *Sue me, ruin me, destroy me, all of you. Get in line behind my husband. See if I care.*

I drove out of Boston, through several other smaller towns I didn't recognize for hours on end, until the gas tank marked empty and the car jumped and heaved its last sigh in the middle of absolutely nowhere. I was surrounded by pitch-blackness. I had no idea where I was. I hadn't seen any gas stations for the last few miles, or at least I couldn't remember. My mind was so fogged up it was a wonder I hadn't run anyone over. Had there even been anyone on the streets? How long had I been driving?

As the night wrapped me in its cold grip, I began to shiver in my coat inside the car. I knew the kids were safe at Paul's and that nothing bad would happen to them. Right now, I was worried about me, stranded out in the sticks.

Say I was found by some idiot with a weapon? Fear

began to lick its way up my legs and into my stomach. I'd never been religious, but I found myself praying.

Please, God, keep me safe tonight until I can get back into my own warm bed. But the thought of my bed, Ira's and my bed, made my eyes burn. For months I'd been trying to make it work: trying to save my marriage, save my family, keep things normal. And then I'd met Julian, possibly the best thing that had ever happened to me, and all I'd done was push him away. When would I finally get it once and for all?

Sprawled across the passenger seat, I forced myself to be calm and not worry about the children's future and where our life was going. I had to rev up my one-year plan to less than six months. By the summer, I had to get the kids to Tuscany. It was already December.

I rummaged through my bag for a Kleenex, blew my nose and checked my cellphone. Ten missed calls and a message:

Is everything OK? I'm worried about you. Please call me.
Julian.

I burst into tears. That amazing man was *worried* about me, while my own husband hated me.

I woke with a jump, confused to find myself in my car parked in the middle of nowhere, under a pitch-black sky. And then the previous afternoon played itself out in front of my eyes and I began to bawl all over again. All these years, chasing a dream of happiness. Sacrificing myself for my family, my husband. And what did that leave me with now if not an empty bed and a broken heart? And even if I had met Julian, why did all this still hurt? Why, like a miracle cure, could I not just wipe the past out of my mind? Because pain always left scars, no matter what joys you experienced afterward.

I caught another glimpse of myself in the mirror. Jesus, did I look *rough*. I *felt* rough. I felt dead. Actually, I really didn't feel anything. I felt no pain, no anger. Just a big empty spot in my soul. But I'd always felt empty. That's why I ate.

I called a taxi and gave the driver Julian's address, silent tears gushing down my face. All I needed now was to be with him, to lie back and let him sink into my soul, to be loved. Because I deserved it. I deserved Julian and I also deserved a shot at Tuscany. I finally understood that now. And he'd either come with me or not.

This time I didn't use my key but rang his doorbell once. A quick buzz. If he didn't answer, it was a sign that I shouldn't even be here, but he opened the door after a few moments, his chest bare and his hair mussed. He was wearing jeans and smelled of clean warm bed and man. I looked up at him, his image blurred by my tears.

'Erica...? What happened?' he whispered as he took me in his arms.

'I'm sorry for not calling,' I croaked. 'Can I crash here?'

'Of course. Are you OK? Where are the kids?'

'They're having a sleepover at Paul's.'

He put a hand on my chin, lifting my eyes to his, but I couldn't look at him.

'Please tell me what happened, sweetheart.'

I shut my eyes tight and shook my head. 'Bed,' I whispered. 'With you. Please.'

There was a long silence. I'd die if he'd changed his mind.

Instead, he took my hand and led me upstairs, my eyes hungrily watching his exquisite Levi's butt.

He stopped on the threshold and looked back at me, as if to give me time to retreat if I still wanted. His bed was unmade and in the light of the nightstand, it looked like a sea of warmth.

As he watched me, still unsure, I reached for his unbuckled belt and pulled him toward me, kissing him on the lips. He responded immediately, wrapping his arms around me and lifting me up against his hard body. I heard his breath catch in his throat, could feel the banging of his heart under my lips as I ran my mouth over his pecs.

He traced my cheekbones with his thumbs and looked into my eyes, his own hooded. I unbuttoned his jeans and pulled them off his thighs and then he lifted me onto his bed. I closed my eyes and hung onto him as he pulled my dress over my head, raining kisses all over me, washing away the pain and replacing it with pleasure. Deep, uncontrollable pleasure.

I remember the thump-thumping of my heart and the way my skin tingled all over like a live wire when he lowered his lips to my neck, my weak spot. In twelve years of marriage, I hadn't been able to bring myself to tell Ira I wanted him to kiss me there, and Julian instantly hit the nail on the head. And now I clutched at him, his kisses hot and amazingly sexy as he nibbled at my throat, caressing it with his tongue, searing it with his mouth.

'Erica…' he groaned as I pulled him to me.

The moonlight shone silvery through the window and

seemed to bounce off his abs. He looked like a ripped silver god floating on a silver sea. And he was all mine. For now, at least.

I swallowed, reached out a tentative hand, and in the silence of his unfamiliar bedroom, my fingers traveled over his chest that seemed ready for the most intense exertion.

As my fingers fell below his waist, a low growl escaped his lips and his hand came up my thigh, closing around the wide stretch of my hip.

I lowered myself and kissed the area around his belly button, and he groaned. Not in annoyance, like Ira, but with want. God, he was so gorgeous, lying there just for me.

'Erica…'

'Shh…' I whispered, getting bolder, and he took me in his arms and kissed me. Deeply. Like no one ever. The fireworks had begun.

I watched his beautiful jaw clench over and over as he brought us together. Had I been wrong! When there was chemistry between a couple, lights *did* go off in your brain, and you did soar through the universe at light speed, and, believe it or not, I did clutch at him – not for fear of falling off the edge of the Earth this time, but of literally passing out. The preliminaries went on and on, topped by such a strong orgasm I almost thought I'd die.

Four hours and two sets of multiple orgasms later, he reached out and wrapped an arm around my waist, his other hand playing with my hair. We both watched in the sunlit room as he unraveled a lock of my hair and let it snap like a spring. Then back again, curling it round his fingers. I never knew my curls could be so bouncy if I just let them be.

'How's my girl?' he whispered, nuzzling my neck.

'Great. Can I ask you a question?'

'Shoot.'

'Why don't you play anymore?' I blurted.

At that, he stiffened slightly, and then finally sighed. 'Many things have changed since then, Erica.'

I propped myself up on my elbow. 'Meaning?'

He shrugged, caressing my thigh. 'I'm not a champion anymore. Who cares what I do?'

'Who cares? Just about everybody who meets you, Julian. You're a big name. If you don't play anymore, you could at least do something. Maybe write another book or something. Didn't you like it?'

He looked at me and I read nostalgia in his eyes. 'I loved it.'

'So why not continue? Just because you don't play pro anymore doesn't mean you can't talk about your experience or teach a punk or two what it's like to work so hard for your dreams.'

Julian huffed. I'd never seen him huff until now. This thing was obviously a thorn in his side.

'Can we forget the compliments and go straight to my favorite part, where you let me make love to you again?'

'But I don't understand. You're a talent.'

'Sweetheart, really. Come a little closer, will you?'

I nestled in the space between his arm and his hip, determined to use sex to ply him. If it worked, I could get away with murder here.

'Up until now, you've been helping me,' I began.

'I like helping you,' he argued softly.

'I know and I'm so, so grateful, Julian. But I want to help you back.'

'By pushing me to write another book?'

'By reminding you that you love sports and writing. Hell, even *I* loved your last book and I absolutely hate sports.'

At that he chuckled and squeezed me.

'I'm not joking, Julian. You're an amazing writer. Why waste your talent looking after a bunch of unruly schoolkids?'

He eyed me dubiously. My magic was starting to work.

'Anybody could be a principal. Well, almost anybody, but you're way too talented.'

He sighed, almost as if to say, *I know you're right, but I don't want to admit it.*

I caressed his strong chin. Every day I knew him a little more and it dawned on me that he was wasted here. 'Just promise me you'll think about a new book. Then, if it doesn't come, it doesn't come. Think about yourself, how you started out and all your dreams. Think of how you'd inspire and help rising talents.' Man, I was good.

'It's not all a bed of roses, Erica. There are a lot of dangers following a sport like mine. Doubts. The prospect of drugs and booze and you have no idea.'

'That's why you need to have your say. If I could have my say, I'd boast about how cool it is to sleep with a champion,' I giggled. 'A sex champion.'

Julian grabbed his opportunity to get out of dodge and get back to more impelling issues – in other words, sex. So I let go of my bone. For now.

'It's nice to sleep with a redhead,' he grinned.

'I'm sure you've had lots of redheads in your past.'

'Not real redheads.' He grinned again, and I slapped him playfully on the arm.

'Some gentleman you are, spilling the ladies' secrets.'

'I'll tell you a secret,' he said, pulling me close.

'Your hair is died, too?' I offered, and he whispered into my ear.

'*Ti amo*, Erica. I love you.'

And I love you, I wanted to say. If I could do that, it would be like the first breath I'd taken since I was born, as if I'd been living my life underwater. Just one last obstacle and I'd have broken the surface.

'Really? Since when?'

'Ever since you fell off the chair in my office.'

Wow. And to think I even had a stuffy nose that day, on top of that horribly thick brown dress and that awful coat. But I needed to believe this whole wonderful Julian thing was true.

What would happen now to Julian's spontaneous 'I love you' when I started snoring or thrashing around like, as Ira was often fond of saying, a pig on a spit? That would certainly be the last of him. And then what would happen to *my* 'I love you'? I wasn't wasting any of those on a man again. At least not until I was good and ready. Until I knew for sure where he stood and how far he would come with me. Literally.

But for now, I'd enjoy the sex and try not to fall asleep at work. It was going to be a long life of sleepless nights if Julian and I were going to be doing this on a regular basis. For once in my life, sleepless nights were a good thing.

'What are you thinking?' he whispered into the hollow of my collarbone.

I hesitated. Did Julian need to know everything that passed through my mind? Probably not. But the mistake I'd made with Ira was that he knew nothing of my thoughts, nor I of his. I'd find a happy medium this time, however long (or short) this relationship lasted.

'You really don't want to know.'

'I do if it's bothering you,' he answered softly.

'I was thinking about… my sleeping habits. I'm a real earthquake.'

I felt him grin against my neck as he pulled me closer. 'I wouldn't worry about it. I sleep like a log.'

'No, I mean it. I talk in my sleep.'

'So do I.'

'You do?'

'Real long monologues. It was time I had someone to have a chat with.'

I grinned. 'Ira didn't like to chat in bed. He'd always fall asleep when I talked to him.' A bit too much information?

'That won't be a problem seeing that you and I are both perfectly capable of continuing our conversation in our sleep,' he said, his voice mirthful.

'Silly,' I whispered.

'Tell you what. Whichever one of us falls asleep first has to do the dishes the next evening. How does that sound?'

'Like a dream,' I grinned, caressing his chest.

The next day, as I helped my aunts do some prep work during a brief visit to the restaurant, I filled them in on Julian, minus the sex, obviously.

'It's a sign.' Zia Maria leaned into me as I helped her dice red peppers for tonight's special, caponata.

'Absolutely,' Zia Martina chimed in, lifting her face from the sink she was happily scrubbing away at. 'Now she can finally think about her own life with Julian.'

'Will you two stop it?' said Zia Monica as she came into the back kitchen and dropped her bag on a bench then stormed into the pantry. 'If she's not ready, she's not ready.'

'What's eating you?' I asked as she whooshed by.

'Monica's in love,' Zia Martina teased, and my eyebrows shot up. 'Major crush on Father Frank.'

I poured the peppers into the pan with frying onions and potatoes, ready to add the capers. 'Father Frank? You're kidding?'

'I wish I were,' Zia Martina said. 'She's been miserable for a while now.'

Both sisters shrugged.

'It's a big secret,' Zia Maria said. 'We're not supposed to know.'

As if love were a shameful thing that needed to be hidden. Boy, did I know a thing or two about that.

As I walked into my kitchen at home to retrieve my Christmas shopping list, Ira came out of the spare room with another suitcase. He'd been packing like a madman since I'd discovered him with his lover. One more week and he'd be out. One more week to prepare the kids and I still didn't know how I was going to do it.

'I'm leaving now,' Ira said, his voice barely audible.

My whole body was traversed by icy claws that racked

my legs, ripped into my stomach and my lungs, squeezing real hard while my entire world, which was already pretty much off its axis, started to spin drunkenly.

Now? He had no idea how much pain and unhappiness he'd caused me during all our years together, but leaving us on the day before Christmas Eve? What the hell was wrong with him? Wasn't he thinking about his children at all?

'We've already had this conversation. You're supposed to wait until *after* Christmas,' I said.

Ira lowered his eyes and sighed. 'We open the gifts after dinner tomorrow and then I go.'

'Tomorrow is Christmas Eve. You can't abandon them on Christmas Eve – you're going to scar them for life. You owe it to Maddy and Warren.'

He only shook his head. 'I can't. I already don't know what to tell them.'

I shrugged, feeling numb. 'The truth. That you've found someone more important to you than them.'

'Erica, let's at least be civil, OK?'

Civil? For years he'd treated me like I didn't exist, sighing in frustration at the mere sight of me, and now he wanted to be civil? I pushed my chin out and straightened my hair. My messy hair that he'd used to put behind my ear. But that was long gone. Gone too were the caresses, the laughs, the evenings we couldn't keep our hands off each other. That was a long, long time ago. Now, we were two total strangers hardly able to look each other in the eye and who couldn't wait to go separate ways.

'Are you picking up the kids from your mom's?' he asked.

I sighed. 'They're at Paul's. He's bringing them back later today.'

He nodded. 'OK. I have to go now,' he said. 'I'll be back tomorrow.'

'Yeah, whatever.'

I waited for him to clear the driveway, then I drove to the supermarket, determined to cook the best meal ever, so that years from now the kids would remember this Christmas for the amazing turkey, sweets and gifts and not because their dad had left them. I'd protect them from the pain, the heartache.

As I ambled through the bright red-and-white aisles lit like Santa's sled, through the merry music, the colors, the bright lights, happy snowmen and Santas climbing chimneys and Rudolphs jumping over roofs, I wished we'd officially told the kids about us so we could spend this Christmas all together. But hopefully, there would be more Christmases ahead of us.

29

Jingle Bell Hell

Paul and I made it back to the house at the exact same time, the kids dancing around me like I were a campfire.

'Alright, you two. Go wash up and change.' I forced a laugh as I gave them both a quick peck.

Paul took a few bags off me and followed me into the kitchen.

'Well? Did you do it? How was he? Tell me!'

'Thanks for picking up the kids,' I said as I put the food away.

Paul waved his hand in the air. 'Never mind them. Spill!'

'First things first. I caught Ira and his secretary here the other day.'

Paul's jaw fell open. 'What? Screwing here?'

'No, just packing. Anyway, it's Maxine.'

Paul gasped, his eyes wide. 'Pristine Maxine? No!'

'Yeah. She's at least twelve years younger. And yes, I slept with Julian. But last night wasn't our first time.'

Paul hugged me, jumping up and down as if he'd won

the lottery. 'Oh, Erica, you dark horse, you. This is amazing! Tell!'

'Some other time. For now, I have to deal with the fact that Ira's leaving on Christmas Eve. The kids will be devastated.'

Paul waved a hand in the air. 'They'll get over it. We both know you're all better off without him. Forget Ira – you've got yourself a real man now. What's he like in bed? I *have* to know.'

I stopped and placed some ready-made dough on the counter and thought about it. What was Julian like in bed? Hot. Tender. Sexy. Extremely selfless. 'It was out of this world,' I gushed.

'Good for you!' Paul whooped. 'Is he big?'

'Paul!'

'Oh, get off your high horse. Details!'

I beamed at him. 'He's absolutely perfect.'

Paul punched the air. 'Hallelujah! The amazing Erica is back!'

She certainly was. And an hour later, the new Erica went out and bought herself a new bed. And shopped for gifts. And cleaned like crazy – even the windows – and baked the best food, including cookies and cakes.

In only a few hours, the hour of my children's loss of their innocence, I'd take pictures of the kids and their father so they wouldn't miss him too much. But deep down, I knew that he wouldn't be all that missed. His presence in the house consisted only of his computer and his gazillion shirts and suits hanging in the closet. The wooden model planes hanging in Warren's room were my effort, just like the fairy wings hanging on the back of Maddy's bedroom door. And then I realized. Ira was leaving *nothing* to his children – no kind memories, no afternoons of laughter. Bupkes.

So it was settled. I was selfishly looking forward to coming up for air after years of apnea. I bought the biggest tree I could find. Warren and Maddy helped me decorate it with all their artwork and my grandmother's old decorations and Nativity scenes, and when we finally plugged it in, Maddy gasped in awe. Such a cute 'ohhh', her big green eyes wide, while Warren grinned sheepishly. He was still a little boy, although he tried to be tough sometimes. My heart hurt for them.

Lunch with my entire family on the 24th was my last obstacle. After that, I wouldn't have to pretend that everything was thumbs up. Zias Maria, Martina and Monica were there every year, beautiful and cheery. God, what I wouldn't have given to be like one of them. No man in sight (except for maybe Father Frank) and they didn't appear to have a care in the world.

Lunch went by very festively, contrary to my expectations. My nephews and nieces branched off to play with Warren and Madeleine as Vince helped me make coffee in the kitchen.

Later, Judy helped me with the dishes. Mom, as always, kept a strategic distance, lounging on the sofa, my dad massaging her feet. Poor old fool that he was, hopelessly in love with the beauty goddess who had blessed him with her attention and an 'I do' so many years ago, making him the proudest, if not the happiest man alive. Good for them. I wondered how they did it.

'So, how's Trey, your new toyboy?' I asked Judy, drying my wet hands on my apron. 'Are you and Steve splitting up after Christmas, too?'

'Shush,' she hissed. 'Steve doesn't know about him! And what do you mean, "too"?'

I went back to my sudsy sink, ignoring her, and she sucked in her breath as she reached a conclusion. The wrong one.

'Shut up! You're finally leaving *Ira*?'

I turned to look at her and shook my head. 'He's leaving me, tonight after we open the presents,' I managed, wiping my eyes on a tea towel.

I wasn't crying for me. Hopefully, I had Julian to console me and a new life ahead. It was the kids I felt sorry for.

Again, she gasped. 'He's leaving *you*? What's the matter with you? *You* should have left him long ago! I swear, Erica, I don't recognize you anymore!'

'A little louder, please. Marcy hasn't heard you yet,' I croaked.

Judy sat me down. 'Honey, this can't be right. Why would he leave you?'

'I caught him with his secretary.'

'I don't believe it,' Judy muttered. 'Oh, well, his loss, honey. Just make sure he pays you alimony. Now, dry your eyes and let's bring these desserts out, huh? Trey is going to have to work me out like crazy to shift these extra calories.'

And that was my sister's entire contribution to my personal tragedy.

★

Hours later, the dreaded Christmas dinner with the four of us was quiet but for Madeleine chatting happily, seating herself – like she used to when she was a toddler and things were very different – on Ira's leg, giggling shyly and unaware of the tragedy that was about to strike her. I swallowed back the tears as I watched my little angel rest her head on his chest. The place I'd rested against so many times when I was younger. I hated him for being unable to keep our family together.

If Ira had given me that extra time, I'd have come up with a way to soften the blow. I'd have somehow suggested that this was going to be their last Christmas with both parents. I don't know what I'd have done. Whatever it was, I hadn't done it and now it was too late.

As we sat around the fire, I sensed the moment was dangerously near. *No. Please, not yet*, I pleaded with him silently with my eyes, but, as always, he wasn't looking at me.

I jumped up to get my camera. These would be the last pictures of us all together. Ira pulled Maddy and Warren close as I sat next to them, grinning – or rather squinting, to keep from crying – into the lens as the auto-shoot clicked, blinding me.

'We'll frame that one and put it on the mantel,' I said cheerfully, when all I wanted was to hang Ira instead – hang him upside by his big toes from the highest branch of our Christmas tree, for all to see what a useless piece of shit he was.

Warren kept stealing Ira and me glances as if he knew what was coming.

'Stay until tomorrow morning. You can tell the kids then,' I whispered when I caught him alone in the kitchen, my heart in my mouth, knowing it was imminent. I couldn't bear it.

Ira stared at me and for a moment he seemed to give in, like someone under hypnosis.

He ran his hands over his face and looked at me. 'I'm sorry, Erica. I've made up my mind. One more night isn't going to change anything. I'm sorry. I don't love you.'

'But it's not about *us*, you idiot!' I insisted to his back as he turned and left me there.

You can imagine what happened at the stroke of eleven, after Warren and Maddy opened their presents. I won't even bother putting you through it. Suffice to say that when he sat them down to tell them their parents were splitting up, Maddy started to cry, I mean really bawl, and begged him to stay.

'I can't,' he answered, biting his lip.

Apparently, he'd promised Maxine he'd be there by the stroke of midnight. That was his only explanation.

Warren sat quietly, eyeing me, then him. 'You're nothing but an asshole!' he bellowed suddenly, knocking his chair over as he shot to his feet. 'We're sooo much better off without you!' he continued, breathing hard, his face flushed. 'So go! You're nothing but a loser anyway!'

'Warren…' I said, thinking how similar my kid was to me. I was, to be honest and horrible, so proud of him.

'Dead weight!' Warren finished. 'We don't need you! Mom is a perfect mother *and* father!'

Before Ira could react, Warren scooped up Maddy and said, 'We're going to bed. This is the last time I want to see you. Ever again.' And up he went, his sobbing little sister's legs wrapped around his waist.

Having packed his clothes, there was nothing left for Ira – or me – to do or say.

'My lawyer will be in contact with yours,' he said.

'Yep, *ciao*,' I said without looking at him and closed the door after him, catching his heel in my haste to close that chapter.

I tiptoed to the kids' rooms, but they were pretending to be asleep. I wasn't worried. I could deal with that tomorrow. The important thing was that Ira was gone for good. Everything else would be easy from now on.

I went to the kitchen, poured myself a very large glass of *inzolia* wine and then sank into a nice warm bubble bath, breathing deeply – deeper than I had in years.

On Christmas morning, Warren and a sniffling, listless Maddy got up to set the table for me without my even having to ask. It was going to be tough on them, but I knew in the end we were going to be just fine.

After we'd all opened our presents, Paul handed me a big box with a card that read:

Something to look forward to. It's never too late for anything, sunshine. Merry Christmas.

Love Paul.

I tore at the packaging and gasped at the sight of the pale burgundy chiffon. I hadn't seen this dress in years. And even if I had to appreciate the irony of how that dress had marked the beginning and the end of my marriage, that wasn't why it meant so much to me. It was important because Paul had remembered our youth and our lifelong friendship. And he'd recognized that I'd made so many efforts to fit back into a similar dress. I never thought he'd get it back for me. Paul. My best friend. My only friend. *If you didn't count my lover, Julian.*

[faint text bleed-through from previous page, illegible]

30

New Year's Revolution

'Why on earth would you even consider going back to Italy when your grandparents made so many sacrifices to move all the way here?' my mother asked.

I sighed. Years of dealing with her and still she didn't understand me. I had to learn to pick my battles with her.

'Because I think my family would be very happy there,' I said simply.

'You can't run away from your problems, Erica.'

Said by the woman who had always been sheltered from life.

'I'm not leaving my problems behind. Only Ira.' Which was technically the same thing.

'Ask him back.'

There she went again, like the Sicilian saying went: as crazy as the March wind.

'Have you been drinking, Marcy?' It certainly wouldn't be the first time.

'Erica, let's look reality in the face, shall we? A single

working mom hasn't got it easy nowadays. You need a man next to you.'

Any more platitudes from sharp Marcy and I'd be howling in pain. Besides, I had a man. Sort of. And I was trying to find the guts to ask him to come with me.

The holidays came and went, but I didn't have the heart to take the tree and decorations down. All through the house festive cinnamon-scented candles still burned, there were still candy canes hanging over the mantelpiece and I made all the kids' favorite dishes, trying to prolong Christmas for as long as possible. We watched movies and played board games and many evenings I sat with Maddy making paper dolls.

I cut out a whole cardboard posse of them, blondes, redheads and brunettes, while Maddy drew their dresses and colored them in. She'd inherited my mother's sense of fashion, no doubt. I drew one that was slightly chubbier just to see her reaction and she looked at me but said nothing. But that doll's clothes were darker and longer. A bit like mine, funnily enough. It seemed she'd also inherited Marcy's critical sense.

Maddy asked me only once if her father was coming back and when I told her that he probably wasn't, she simply replied, 'OK.'

Later, when I was out of her brother's earshot, I'd tell her the usual lies of how her daddy loved her so much, because Maddy deserved no less than a real loving family. If nothing, I'd give her the illusion of one. There was plenty of time for her to grow up and see the world as it could sometimes be.

Warren seemed to have transformed into a gentleman overnight. No more wars over his homework, no more arguments about his messy room. I daresay due to Ira's vanishing and overwhelming influence. It was as if suddenly a veil had dropped from before Warren's eyes and he was seeing me for the first time. He also knew things could only get better, now the house didn't boom with the disapproval of Ira's voice in the evenings.

With dinner in the oven, I sat down to read all the Christmas cards we'd received and that the kids had strung above the fireplace in the living room. There were even presents for me that I hadn't opened. One from my parents, one from Judy and one from Vince (the card was in his wife Sandra's writing). Then I spotted one that made my heart quiver. It was from Julian, and it was enormous. How did it even get there? Warren, surely. He was becoming Julian's inside trader. I tore the card open.

Merry Christmas, Erica. All your dreams can still come true.

Love, Julian.

Love. 'Love,' I whispered, trying to taste the word on my tongue.

Under the shiny red wrapping paper and a beautiful ribbon with holly and ivy, I found a large book of glossy photographs of Tuscany. I didn't have this one, which surprised me, because I thought I had them all. I flipped through the pages. *Your dreams can come true. Tuscany. Happiness. Love.*

Love? I sat there and thought about it. Could this be a

sign? A sign that Tuscany and Julian could happen in the same lifetime? Assuming he really, really did love me with a capital L, if I told him my dreams, would he follow?

Because I *loved* him. Deeply, helplessly, and it couldn't have happened at a better time. It couldn't have happened at a worse time. Because I couldn't possibly give up my Italian dream. I'd made too many sacrifices for a man before and where had that got me? Exactly.

When I phoned him to thank him, he simply said, 'I heard about Ira.' I also noticed he didn't say he was sorry.

'Who told you?' I choked, although I already knew the answer.

'Warren. I wanted to give you a little time.'

I didn't answer. It figured Warren would go to Julian. This, too, was a sign. They were becoming close. Was it a good thing? A bad thing?

'Are you OK?' he asked gently.

'Sure,' I said, baring my teeth into the phone. 'Of course.'

So much for my bravado the past few weeks. Now, I was feeling misplaced, like someone had tossed me into the air and told me to flap my wings. But flap my wings I would, even if it would be a long time before I could fly again.

Financially I was OK. I was organized. The kids were growing up and I with them. Eventually, I'd catch up with them some day.

'Are you still there?' Julian asked.

'Of course.'

'Then open the door.'

So I did. He was standing there with a large bouquet of orchids.

'Hi.'

'Hi.'

He hesitated. 'Long time no see.'

'I know,' I whispered. 'I'm sorry.'

He sighed and said softly, 'I don't even want to think what it must be like for you right now.'

'Do you... want to, uhm, come in?'

Julian stepped over the threshold. 'These are for you,' he whispered, giving me a deep kiss.

I had to hang onto him just so I wouldn't fall over. God, I'd missed him. But he'd done the right thing, giving us some time to digest it on our own. But now that we had, I was hungry again. Not for food but for a new life.

'Hello,' he grinned, and I grinned back.

I nodded to his big bag. 'What's in there?'

'A very late Christmas prezzie for the kids.'

'Thank you, that's very kind of you. They're at soccer and ballet.'

'Aren't you supposed to be at your tango class?'

'Paul's arm is acting up again. He must have sprained it real bad in the accident. He's really accident prone.'

Julian looked at me, his grin disappearing, his hand reaching for mine. 'Then let me be your partner, Erica.'

Partner. Dance partner... or life partner? 'You a tango champion as well?' I quipped.

He grinned. 'No, but hey, I can always learn. How about it?'

'Cool,' I grinned, and he grinned back.

'Cool.' And then he pulled out a beautiful gold-wrapped and cream-colored box. 'For you.'

'Julian, you already gave me a Christmas present, which

was lovely, by the way. And I didn't get you anything. I'm sorry.'

He shrugged. 'I've got all that I need.' And then he looked into my eyes, I mean really looked into them, and added, 'Almost.'

I looked down and unwrapped his gift. A Burberry designer set of perfume, soaps and shower gel.

'My favorite fragrance. How did you know?'

'I recognized your scent. I'd recognize it anywhere.'

'You're so romantic,' I smiled. 'I love romantic.' And I love *you*, I almost said.

'Come out to dinner with me. Tonight. I'll take you anywhere you like.'

'On one condition.'

He raised an eyebrow at me. He learned fast.

'Oh-K...?'

'I'll come out to dinner with you if you tell me about your new book.'

'Erica, I don't have a new book.'

'Yes, you do. The young baseball players all over America who are just starting out *need* you.'

At that he laughed – a hardy, heartfelt laugh. 'You never give up, do you?'

'Please? I guarantee you it'll go through the roof.'

'I don't have a book in me, sweetheart.'

'Of course you do! Where there's one there are many more!'

He laughed, his eyes twinkling. Good. I was getting somewhere.

'So you'll think about him?' I prodded.

'Him?'

'The young athlete who needs your help.'

'I'll think about it.'

'You're not saying it just to shut me up?'

'That too,' he said with a grin, and I reached over and kissed him hard.

So that evening I went out on a real date with him rather than just have wild sex. We were waiting to be seated at my favorite Indian restaurant, when who do you think we bumped into? Exactly.

'Oh, crap.'

'What's wrong?' Julian asked, squeezing my hand.

'Ten o'clock, my ex-husband, enter the scene: new lover.' It was impossible even to fathom the two words together in the same sentence, let alone see it live, but there they were, hand in hand like two love puppies. Pretty much like Julian and me.

'Oh, crikey,' Julian whispered.

As we watched, Ira took Maxine's hands to his lips with a coy smile. And now he was smiling at her, with *my* smile – the one he'd used on me years ago. Somewhere between the stomach bypass I'd passed up and tango lessons, I'd lost him. Thank God.

Maxine was young, single and a bit naïve, seeing as she believed Ira could actually love someone besides himself. Boy, was she in for a reality check. I almost felt sorry for her.

'Too late – they've already seen us. Chin up, kiddo.'

He was right. Maxine gawked at us as Julian (still holding my hand, by the way) followed the waiter to the nicest table. Ira stared, too, then sullenly buried himself into his menu, refusing to acknowledge my presence any longer.

I had to hand it to Julian – our first date and the ex-husband was already in the way, but he was cool and quiet, just happy to be sitting across from me, staring into my eyes. Actually, we looked like it wouldn't be long before we hit the carpet in the throes of passion.

'I want you now, among the samosas and chicken vindaloo,' I said out of the blue.

Julian laughed and Ira threw him one of his killer glances. I couldn't believe that once upon a time, I'd loved that man so much – enough to give up my dreams and have his babies. It's the mistake lots of women make. Husband-wise, not baby-wise. I wouldn't change Warren and Madeleine for any other kids in the world.

As they (finally) passed us on their way out, Maxine attempted a hello. Julian and I looked up from the tangle that was our hands and fingers and smiled politely.

Ira wasn't jealous, I knew. Only annoyed at having his evening ruined by his ex-wife's happiness. Me, I wouldn't let him bother me anymore. From now on I'd concentrate on the good stuff. Like the hunk of man sitting opposite me, holding my hands.

To prove a point, he heaped my plate up with a delicious chicken curry and poured me a glass of wine, leaning over to kiss me – 'Bon appétit!' – leaving me stunned. So we really were doing the public displays of affection as well? Cool.

He smacked his luscious lips and murmured, 'Mmm-hmm! Raspberry.'

You don't know how hard it was to drag my lips away from his. Or even to close my mouth.

'Just how many women have you had exactly?' I asked.

'Less than… what's-his-name – that good-looking guy who plays for the New York Knicks?'

He took a sip of his wine. 'That's basketball, and no, not even close. I'm a monk by comparison.'

'Huh?' Somehow, the image of a monk didn't quite fit my idea of him. 'What about Moira what's-her-face? The one who owns the magazines. And all those models I read about.'

He blushed. 'That was a long time ago, Erica.'

A long time ago or not – you just can't sleep with a model and then want to be with me, can you? was what I wanted to say, but instead asked: 'So what's your next best-seller about?'

Julian rolled his eyes. 'You don't let go, do you?'

'Never. I'm a bloodhound with a big, juicy bone.'

'Actually, I have been thinking about it,' he conceded.

'Great! So tell.'

He shrugged. 'I'm still mulling it over.'

I beamed. 'This is fantastic news. Not only have I slept with a champion, but I'll soon be sleeping with a best-selling author. How gratifying can this be for me? Just one thing…'

'What's that?'

'Don't use any of our sex material, huh?'

'That would be a capital sin for a writer.'

'It would also be your last living day.'

Julian laughed.

As if once wasn't enough, the very next day I met Maxine again at the supermarket. Go figure! I hadn't seen her in years and then bam – she was practically everywhere.

'Hi again, Mrs. Lowenstein,' she chirped, oblivious of the pain she was causing me, poor little idiot.

Apparently, she'd got over the 'knife in my bedroom' moment. Kids were like that. Because as grown up as she thought she was, she was still very naïve of the ways of the world.

'I'm so sorry about your split-up,' she offered. 'But the two of you just weren't working out, right?'

I turned to face her and blinked. I was so surprised, I didn't even think not to say, 'Is that what he told you? That we weren't working out?'

At this she looked uncomfortable.

'I just want to say no hard feelings. We can still be friends.'

I sighed. 'Maxine, I don't think that's a good idea.'

Her face red, she stepped back. 'I'm sorry you feel that way. In any case, I wanted to warn you.'

Warn me? The nerve of this kid! Was she that insecure? If so, their relationship couldn't be much better than ours had been.

My brow shot up and I snorted. 'Oh, you won't be getting any trouble from me. You can keep him.'

She stared at me, a strange expression on her face. Almost earnest.

'Erica, please listen to me, for your own good. Ira's decided to go for full custody of Maddy and Warren.'

Down went my potatoes, my detergent, my popcorn and chocolate, one by one, plop, plop, plop, onto the floor, along with my heart. She instantly bent on her thin haunches to retrieve them for me and I watched the top of her head without really seeing it, the clanging of her charm bracelets enough to make my head explode. No court on *Earth* would award him full custody, not after what he'd done to us. Impossible.

'Ira's determined to keep the kids. I've tried to dissuade him. I think you're a good mother.'

'I'm sure,' I snapped, taking my items from her as if she'd stolen them. 'You just don't want them in your life. Well, that's one thing we agree on.'

'No, that's not true. I'm looking forward to spending time with Maddy and Warren and getting to know them…'

My blood pressure must have suddenly hit the roof, because I was seeing spots.

'But I also think kids should stay with their parents, particularly with their mothers.'

Here was another one of Marcy's acolytes, God help us.

'My advice is you get a lawyer fast. I won't tell Ira I told you. I'll try to stall him in the meantime and convince him to reason.'

And then I think I passed out, because when I opened my eyes there were shelf-loads of hairspray on the ceiling, with Julian under them, his face hovering close to mine.

'Erica? Sweetheart, talk to me. Are you OK?'

I scrambled to my feet. 'I'll kill him! He wants my children!'

Julian turned to Maxine and said, 'She's fine now.'

He helped me up, guiding me through the throng of people who had cordoned around me and were now starting to disperse once the drama was over. Over for them, maybe. Because for me it was only just unfurling.

'Maxine told me she has no interest whatsoever in taking the children away from you,' Julian offered.

'No shit,' I mumbled. 'It would ruin her weekends of sex.'

Once outside in the parking lot, I grabbed my cellphone and dialed my lawyer. Julian waited quietly as I calmly explained the situation and made an appointment to see him. Then I clicked the phone shut and buried my face in my hands. This could not be happening. For years Ira couldn't have cared less, and now he wanted to take them away from me?

'Let me drive you home, then I'll come back and get my car,' he said softly.

'Thanks.' I was still feeling a bit woozy, so I was grateful for the help. 'Who called you anyway?'

Julian grinned. 'Maxine.'

'But how did she get your number?'

'I have no idea.'

'Yeah, well, let's hope that homewrecker stays away from you,' I blurted without thinking.

He grinned and wrapped an affectionate arm around my neck to draw me in for a kiss.

'Jealous, huh?' he said. 'That means you care.'

'Of course I care,' I said. Only I hadn't told him exactly how much.

31

Separate Lives

Tonight I was having my first tango lesson with Julian.

'Hey! look at you,' Julian whistled as I hung my coat on a peg in the dance hall – revealing my Elaine Richman tango dress, with cleavage – and hesitantly faced him on the dance floor.

I'd been to Lucy's Hair Salon too, for one of her special blow-dries that always made me feel good.

'You're so beautiful, Erica,' he said simply.

'I'm not,' I laughed, slapping his arm playfully, embarrassed – yet desperate for more.

He took my hand and spun me before the mirror. 'Of course you are. Look at yourself in the mirror. How can you not know that?'

I did look at myself but got distracted by the beauty of the man holding me. Up close, he seemed bigger. I'm a tall girl, but he was at least a head taller than me, so my eyes came up to his throat, which was gorgeous, the Adam's apple covered in just-shaven stubble, giving him that five o'clock shadow surrounding dark-fleshed, well-defined lips that were now curved up in a smile.

'Shall we give it a go?' he said.

I swallowed and nodded.

'OK now, people, listen up!' our instructor called. 'Gentlemen, put your right hand on the small of your lady's back.'

Julian obeyed and I felt my whole spine tingle.

'Take her hand in your left one.'

Julian did as he was told.

'If your lady is in your height range there will be a better physical understanding.'

I glanced around and realized I was, as always, the tallest woman.

'No shrimp for me,' Julian murmured with a wink.

My whole body was shaking so badly just from having his eyes focused on mine – imagine when he'd have to pull me into a hot tango embrace...

'You there – the tall girl,' the instructor called.

I turned. 'Yes?'

'Don't stand like you're terrified of touching him. Your hips have to touch; it's a love dance, not a soldier's march. Meld the hips, communicate through your bodies! Tango is *sex*,' he continued, and above me, I could literally feel Julian smile.

'Just pretend you're alone with him in your bedroom'—as if I hadn't done that a gazillion times—'and let yourself go.'

'OK,' I whispered with a determined huff and a nod.

'And you – husband...'

Julian turned, grinning, enjoying every moment of my discomfort, the cad.

'Yes?'

'Hold her a little closer. She won't break, you know?'

Which was true. I'd passed the dummy crash test against his headboard several times before, he-he.

'That's more like it. Now, ladies. Point your toes and push your right leg out, rubbing it against the outside of his thigh. This is when being the same height comes in handy.'

I was nowhere near his height, but I can guarantee you, my legs found his thigh like it was second nature.

'Good... now, gentlemen, when she does that, you tilt her back over your arm and bury your head into her breasts.'

What?

'Like this...'

And with that, he grabbed his own partner, who was wearing a red dress like mine, only so much smaller that it looked like a mere splinter off mine. The girl threw her head back joyously as he lowered his head to her inexistent breasts.

'Bend back, Erica,' Julian whispered as I grabbed his forearms instinctively.

'No – wait.'

He caught me, eyes searching mine. 'What's wrong?'

'I'm... too heavy for you,' I said meekly.

'You must be joking,' he chuckled, trying to lean me over again, but I resisted, my arms now around his neck.

'Please.' It was so humiliating, I wanted to cry.

'Sweetie, I'm not going to let you fall. Promise.'

I bit my lip. Could this man really catch me if I fell?

In response, he tilted his head to look into my eyes. 'Let me show you something.'

'What?'

'Do you trust me?'

'Yes.' Truly, I did.

'Put your hands on my shoulders now, OK?' he said, placing his hands on my waist, and I cringed inwardly, more than aware of the flab.

I nodded, cursing last night's cannoli.

'Look into my eyes,' he whispered, and I obeyed as he slowly and delicately lifted me off the floor – at least three feet – until I was looking down at him, clutching at his shoulders for something solid to hold onto. 'See? Easy as pie. I could hold you like this forever.'

'Oh, Julian...' I moaned and reached down to kiss him as I slid back down his body. I wanted to wrap my legs around his waist and...

'Hey, Dirty Dancers,' came the instructor's voice behind us. 'You follow *my* moves. Improvisation classes are down the hall!'

Julian put me down with a wink and I could feel my face boiling. He'd lifted me. Just like that. And he wasn't even hyperventilating or anything.

'Trust me to hold you now?' he asked, and I nodded instinctively.

'OK now, ladies and gents, we're doing this again on three!' the instructor hollered.

Soon we were learning more steps to string together and he was dipping me backward, his soft black hair tickling my collarbone as he bent forward, his hand strong and firm as

I curved my back. When I came up, I giggled, and he smiled at me and lifted me again.

'That's not part of the steps,' I said, and he grinned.

'I just like holding you,' he said with a shrug. 'You feel good.'

'You mean I feel abundant.'

'I don't like bony women. I want to touch as much woman as I can. And you're the most feminine I've ever met.'

'Of course. I'm two at the price of one.'

'Silly.'

'It's true. Ira always said he should have traded me in for two size tens.' *Way to go, dummy. Now he knows you were once a size twenty.*

He ducked until our foreheads were touching. 'I wouldn't change you for ten size *twos*.'

And with that, he brought me close and kissed the top of my head before letting me slide safely back to my feet, savoring every inch of the way down his body. I was so excited I saw spots. His hand lingered on my back.

'Are you OK?' he whispered.

It turned out Julian knew how to tango. Why else would he have agreed if he was going to make a fool out of himself? After our instructor gave us some final pointers and the music began, Julian put one hand at the back of my waist, pulling me up against him but not in a blatant, rude way, and held my hand in position. And I was in his arms, with no place to go and no place to look, except for his shoulder.

My brain, or what was left of it, registered the familiar masculine scent of his lean body, the feel of his chest underneath his shirt, the whiteness of his teeth and *all* the stuff we'd done in his bed. A slow flame of panic began to rise inside me. Yes, I was a free woman now, but what could happen from his moment on was a mystery.

Julian had a raw, primitive sexual pull on me. Forget tango, forget our manners. I wanted him here and now. Who cared if my classmates and instructor gasped at the sight of our writhing, naked and sweaty bodies on the wooden parquet, and at the sound of our pleasure-howls echoing in the dance studio, draining out the loud music… So much for keeping my distance.

But that was my alter ego talking and not me, because as Julian's hips gyrated expertly and neared mine, grinning a sexy grin, I feared I wouldn't be able to cope, but then he whispered, 'So far, so good? I just hope I don't step on your dainty little toes with my size twelve hind paws here,' and I giggled. 'You've got such a beautiful smile, Erica,' he said. Yep. I was toast – no doubt about it.

And later, under the sheets, or rather, on top of them, I proved it to him.

'Man,' he gritted his teeth, eyes flashing. 'You've got me totally wrapped around your finger.'

'Have I now,' I drawled as my lips traveled down his chest to deeper, darker seas.

'Absolutely. I'd do anything for you, Erica…'

I stopped. Was now the time to mention Tuscany? Hell no! Why ruin a perfectly good evening?

To compensate my hesitance to speak, I once again passed the dummy crash test against his headboard that night – several times.

★

'I have to show you something.' He pulled out a sheaf of papers as we were lounging around in bed an hour later.

'What's this? A lawsuit?'

He laughed. 'Are you ever serious?'

'I'm always serious.'

'It's my new book.'

I jumped up. 'You're kidding me!'

'It's just a rough draft, of course. I pounded it out over the Christmas holidays. I figured time without you shouldn't be a total loss, so—'

'But that's fantastic! Oh my God, Julian!'

He let me hug him tight and plant kisses all over him.

'Wait until you read it,' he laughed.

'It's amazing, I'm positive. Give me that. I'm not stopping until I finish it.'

I slid out of bed and he caught me around the waist.

'You're not planning *any* breaks?' he murmured into my ear.

'Are you kidding? But if it's as good as I know it is'—I wrapped my arms around his neck—'you get an extra bonus.'

It didn't take all night, but man was it *good*. The book, you dirty mind! And it was beautiful. Poignant, funny, honest, sharp, insightful. Just like Julian. Where the hell had I found this man? What had made him what he is today? All I had was the end product, but why did he turn out to be so much better than the average man who burped and farted proudly and always left the toilet seat up? What made him so special?

We discussed his book, made love again, discussed it some more over a midnight snack of leftover lasagne (which he'd made while I was reading, constantly asking me, 'What part are you at? Did you get to the darkest moment yet?') and finally fell asleep around 3 a.m. At least he did.

I was on a mission to satisfy my morbid curiosity, so while Julian slept, I logged onto Google and typed in Red Sox and Foxham. And there he was. Julian Nigel Foxham, alias The Red *Fox*, former baseball champion for the Red Sox. He'd been defined 'The Diamond of the Diamond'.

But what had been a promising career had been brutally interrupted due to an arm injury received during a game. After a total refusal of sports, he'd thrown himself into dating practically every girl in a label – and especially out of it – from actresses to models to sports stars.

The list was endless. And it never lasted more than a week. I wonder how many notches he had on his bed post… I'd have to make a point of counting them. I read on:

After having suffered a major injury to his batting arm, Julian Foxham retired from the sports scene. He's currently writing his second book on his experience with the Red Sox, entitled, *The Woman in Red Sox*.

Woman in red socks? Who was she? A former lover? His first title had been *My Love Affair with the Red Sox*.

He had been a few years younger. Always those kind but sexy eyes.

Things between Julian and me were going great. The sexual tension gave no sign of dying out and we'd done it oodles of times – in his bed, in my bed, on his chaise longue (that was a favorite of ours), on my sofa, on his sofa, in my shower (another favorite), in his shower. On my kitchen counter (Paul had the kids), among flour and chocolate (which I strongly recommend, as Julian's got a shamefully sweet tooth).

The only place we hadn't done it was our cars or our offices, but we'd pretty much covered the geography of our lives.

32

The Return of Ira?

One February evening as I was waiting for Julian to take me out on another dinner date, I got a little visit from Ira. He was standing on the doorway, pale and unshaved. He looked horrible.

'What are you doing here?' I demanded as that old feeling of resentment rose in me as if on cue.

'I need to talk to you.'

'I'm on my way out. You should call.'

'Where are the kids?'

'With my sister Judy and Steve.'

'Where are you going?'

'That's none of your business.'

And just then, Julian pulled up in his jeep and got out, carrying a box of pastries and a bottle of wine. His smile disappeared like an elastic band that had been stretched and flung far away.

'Julian, you remember my soon-to-be ex-husband, Ira,' I

said, baring my teeth. And then I added, 'Ira, you know my boyfriend, Julian.'

'Uh, hello, Ira,' Julian managed.

'Go on in, Julian. Ira was just leaving.'

Ira stared at him, then at me, as if he still couldn't fathom how the hell someone like Julian Foxham was with someone like me when I wasn't even good enough for my own husband.

'Tell the kids I'll come by tomorrow evening,' he snapped and left, driving off with a screech as Julian watched him go, then turned to me again, his eyes still huge.

'I'm sorry about the boyfriend, Julian – it just came out. I wanted to hurt him.'

'Is that the only reason why?' he asked softly, placing my gifts just inside the entrance, under the mirror, leaving me a moment to think that one over without him breathing down my back. 'Or does it feel good to say it out loud?'

He was so sweet, it scared me. I turned to look at him. Was he asking me for himself or for me? I could no longer keep him hanging. It wasn't fair on him.

'Ah... well,' was all I could say, not being one for words when talking about private stuff.

And then there was an awkward silence, which I knew he was waiting for me to fill. But then he took my hand, guiding me to his jeep, where he opened the door, helped me in, closed it and grinned at me.

I swallowed. I wasn't used to having someone looking at me so intensely. Then he leaned in and took my chin in his hand. I closed my eyes and he dropped a smackingly delicious kiss on my mouth. I moaned and wrapped my arms around his neck, almost pulling him in through the window.

'I think you know how I feel about you,' I murmured into his ear.

He shivered, squeezing my upper arm. 'Do I...?'

As I was putting away some groceries the next day, the doorbell rang. It was Ira again, his face drawn and his eyes sunken, as if suffering from a severe illness.

'I'll call the kids down,' I managed, grinding my teeth. 'Be nice.'

'I-I need to talk to you first, Erica.'

I opened the door wider to let him in against my better judgment. 'What is it?'

He nodded his thanks and sat down on the sofa, fidgeting with his tie like a rookie at his first job interview. I sat opposite him, my heart racing. What could he possibly *want* still?

Then he took a deep breath and said it. 'I want to come back home, Erica.'

I shot to my feet and instinctively headed for the kitchen. Why, I don't know. It was the place I felt safest in the house. The place where I excelled. It hadn't certainly been the bedroom, according to him.

He followed me into the kitchen – another first – where I continued to pull the groceries out of the bags. It had always been obvious to me from day one that Maxine wouldn't last long, but *come on*. It wasn't even Easter yet.

And now he realized that he was alone with a

twenty-something year-old who was completely clueless about the sacrifices of being in a relationship. Now he knew what he'd lost, leaving us – a strong, sturdy presence – behind him. A family.

'Listen, I already told you that you can see the kids anytime you want,' I said, but Ira shook his head, taking the milk carton out of my hands and stilling me so I was looking straight into his eyes.

The eyes that I had once loved so passionately. So hopelessly. Now, they just made me sick.

'I know, but… can't we work it out?'

I pushed him away. 'No, we can't, and for the record, don't even dream of applying for full custody.' Years and years of dreaming murder would come in handy if he went down that road.

'No, Erica – I don't want full custody. Listen to me, please. I'm so, so sorry. I miss you – not just the kids. I miss *you*, my wife.'

I stared at him stupidly as he said the words I'd waited to hear for twelve years. Ira still loved me. Ira wanted me back. What a bunch of *bull*.

I buried myself in the fridge, stacking my dairy products. Milk, cheese, butter, yogh…

'Erica, honey…'

That *honey* could have been useful while I was trying to win his heart, once upon a billion years ago.

I faced him again, the blood flooding into my cheeks, and let it all out in one breath. 'What happened? Was Pristine Maxine too high-maintenance for you? Doesn't she want the kids around? Good, because guess what? They're not interested in hanging around her, either, or any of your poor victims.'

'Please, Erica. Forgive me,' he said softly, his hand on my shoulder. 'I made a big mistake. I need you. You give my life a meaning. You're my rock. I love you.'

I flung his arm off me and moved away. 'No, you don't, Ira. You don't treat people you love like you've treated me and your children all these years.'

He stepped closer, his fingers tightening around my wrist. 'No – you don't understand. I need your support.'

'I do understand. You think you made a mistake, but you haven't. You left because you didn't love me. Or the kids.'

There was a long, heavy silence, as if he was considering my words, wondering how true they were.

I sighed. 'You can go now. I'm busy. I have a guest for dinner.'

At that, Ira's chest puffed out. 'A guest? Of course – Julian Foxham. The two of you were already sleeping together, weren't you?'

I crossed my arms in front of my chest. 'Are you pretending to be jealous? Didn't you once tell me there was no way a man could ever be interested in someone like me? Aren't I too fat to attract a man, let alone a champion like Julian Foxham?'

But Ira ignored my words, struck by a bright light bulb in his deviant little mind. 'You were sleeping with him way before I started seeing Maxine. And you even brought him here, in my own home! You should be paying me alimony!'

At that, he turned and headed for the stairs. I followed him.

'What are you doing?' I demanded as he strode into our – *my* – bedroom.

He yanked the bed away from the wall and retrieved his baseball bat, sweating and red-faced, his eyes flashing.

33

Ira and the IRS

I blinked, frozen to my spot as Warren and Maddy skidded to a halt on the landing, Warren's face ashen.

'Ira, put that down! You're scaring the children!' I hissed.

'I just want you to listen to me, goddammit!' he yelled. 'I'm over a hundred thousand dollars in debt and I don't know what to do!'

Maddy began to cry and I swiftly moved downstairs so Ira would move away from them. But to my horror, they followed, as well.

'Get out of here, now!' I yelled.

'You're paying me alimony!' he repeated. 'Give me the money or I swear—'

'Dad!' Warren said, puffing his chest out bravely, but his lips were quivering. 'Put that bat down. *Please.*'

'Warren,' I managed. 'Daddy isn't going to hurt anyone, I promise.'

Ira whirled around to stare at me. 'Of course I'm not – what do you think I am, Erica? A psycho or something?'

Looking at him wielding a baseball bat, insanity did come to mind. I stared into Ira's eyes as I spoke to Warren. Calm but firm.

'Warren. I need you to take your sister upstairs again. Now. Can you do that for me? Daddy and I need to talk. Please, sweetheart.'

Warren gave his father a look of hatred mixed with fear, scooped Maddy up into his strong arms and headed upstairs. After a moment, I heard a chair dragged across the floor and presumably propped up against the door knob. I breathed a silent prayer of thanks. As long as they were safe, nothing else scared me.

I bunched my fists. 'What the hell do you think you're doing, coming into my home and scaring the kids? You left us, remember?' I cried, fighting back the tears. 'What the hell do you want from me now?'

'I want you back.'

Tears were streaming down his cheeks too, and he was babbling incoherently, but I had no pity for him. In fact, I felt nothing for this man whom I'd once loved.

'You don't want me, Ira. Nor do you care about the children. You just want the cushy life you led in this home while you basked in the warmth of our love, without ever giving any back.'

He raised his bat, his eyes huge. 'This is my house, too, and I'm coming back!'

'And you're trying to convince me by threatening us with a *baseball bat*?' I spat.

'I'm not threatening you with anything,' he boomed. 'I just want you back.'

'But I don't want you,' I cried. 'I don't love you anymore. Now get out – you're terrifying my children!'

'Our children!' he screamed, and swiped the photos off the mantelpiece with one sweep of the bat. 'They're mine, too!'

I screamed. An angry scream. 'What are you *doing*? Stop it!'

'I don't want a divorce,' he bawled.

'Too late!' I bawled in turn. 'I loved you for years, Ira. For both of us. I can't do that anymore,' I cried.

In response, he swung the bat out again, knocking the lamp off the side table. I protected my face as the shards flew around my head. This was not the way I'd envisaged it. In my mind, I'd always been the one to attack. I'd always been the one killing *him*. How ironic that it would be him to have the violent reaction. And now, he was advancing on me, his eyes burning with something I'd never seen before, as if he'd completely lost all connection with reality.

Another set of baubles flew off the other side table, its pieces exploding even closer to me. I stepped away, looking around for an escape, or a weapon, but he was now standing between me and the kitchen, where I kept my knives. Not that I'd really use it on him to hurt him, unless he headed upstairs for the kids.

As I was trying to figure how to get between him and the staircase leading upstairs to the kids if he turned that way, a loud bang shook the house. I whirled around to see Julian's face in the front door window.

'Erica!' he yelled, pounding on the wood.

I turned as Ira neared me, his eyes unfocused.

Julian punched a fist through the front door window and stuck his arm in to unlock the door. Once inside, he took in the smashed lamp and looked at me, paling instantly.

'Are you OK?' he demanded, and I nodded.

Ira whirled around, his wild eyes focusing on Julian, who raised his hands.

'Mr. Lowenstein – Ira,' Julian continued. 'Please put that down. You're scaring everybody.'

'You!' Ira spat, coming forward. 'Baseball champion!'

'Please, Mr. Lowenstein, before somebody gets hurt.'

'You want my family? Come and get it!' And then he dropped the bat, throwing himself on Julian, who easily wrestled him to the ground.

Julian didn't look at me, but his voice was low. 'Erica, get me some duct tape. The police are on their way.'

And as if on cue, there was a loud bellow from the front door. 'Everybody, hands up!' And only then did I see the blue, white and red lights of the police car swirling around the living room walls like a giant psychedelic star-spangled banner.

To an outsider, Julian would still have seemed the aggressor, crouching down to keep Ira still, huge and panting, as Ira crouched in the corner, sniveling.

'You alright, ma'am?' asked one of the agents.

Ira let himself be handcuffed and taken to the car, his eyes burning through me. I'd never forget the sheer hatred in his eyes. It was much more intense than all my murder fantasies put together.

'Ma'am, you need to come down to the station with us.'

I had no choice but to leave the kids with my neighbor, Mrs. Oldman, who shuffled them in through her front door, as I called my parents. Who called my lawyer.

Who found out that Ira was being hunted down by the IRS, Inland Revenue Service. The bastard wanted to get back with me to minimize the chances of my testifying against him. Some love.

I refused to press charges against Ira. But I had a restraint order issued against him.

At the station, Julian held my hand. Neither of us spoke. It was enough just to have him near me.

In three hours, we were back home. Paul opened the door, pale and shaken as he opened his arms for us. My family had come and gone, offering to stay the night, and even Mrs. Oldman next door offered to keep the kids overnight, but I refused. I needed to keep things as normal as possible.

The broken lamp and pictures had been removed. Maddy and Warren, who were still shaking under the blanket I'd put over us, refused to go upstairs to bed lest their father return to finish us all off.

So Julian temporarily patched up the window he'd broken earlier and Paul cooked us a meal, while I lay on the sofa with Maddy in my lap and an arm around a still trembling Warren. I only hoped it was from shock and not rage. Shock subsides in time, while rage only grows like a well-fed fire.

'You did the right thing, calling Mr. Foxham,' I whispered

as I kissed the top of his head, and he nodded against my chest, snuggling up to me like when he was little, only now his arms rested around me protectively.

'He was going to kill you, Mom.'

'Oh, honey, Daddy would never hurt us,' I said. 'He's just not well at the moment, but he'll get better soon, you'll see.' Ira needed both financial and psychological help.

'Good thing Julian came,' Warren said.

I wondered fleetingly when Warren had started calling his principal by his first name.

'Julian's cool,' Warren whispered.

And as if summoned, Julian and Paul appeared with steaming trays of spaghetti and meatballs, grilled vegetables and cake. Plus a glass of red wine for me.

As I watched, Julian cut up Maddy's spaghetti for her with a spoon, just the way she liked it. How did he *know*? Maddy took her bowl and he tickled her until she giggled.

Julian had managed to reach their hearts in no time, so starved were they for a father figure. Julian was the alpha male. The protector. He'd sure won me over. Not only was he kind and considerate, but he was also warrior-like. Which was so, so sexy.

'I always knew Ira was a shit,' Paul whispered to Julian, who tilted his head to listen and nod.

I glared at them and jerked my head toward the kids.

'As if they didn't know,' Paul said and got to his feet. 'Sunshine, you're in good hands here. Get some sleep – preferably in this gorgeous man's arms, huh?' he whispered in my ear and kissed my cheek. 'I'll call you in the morning.'

Julian and Paul swatted each other across the back like gorillas and nodded, then Paul headed for the door.

Sitting on the sofa with my children, I watched Julian's back as he whispered something else to Paul. It was probably about Ira, but now I didn't have to worry anymore. For tonight at least, there was someone taking care of me. I wanted to pull Julian to me and feel the stubble of his cheek against my face again. To be with him all the time.

'Hey, Warren,' Julian said as he came back into the living room. 'You were very brave today. You're a real champ, you know that? Want to do some throws tomorrow?'

'Sure,' Warren said, all proud of himself. And then added, 'Can you stay the night? Please?'

'Aw, champ, I don't think—' Julian began, and I said, 'Stay, Julian.'

I didn't care what people thought. From now on, I'd do things my way and not worry about others. This was our life now.

'You're sure?' Julian asked dubiously.

'We'd be happy to have you.'

'In that case, I'll be happy to stay.'

'Cool.' And with that, Warren, exhausted from all the emotion but knowing he was safe, was asleep on the sofa within minutes.

Julian grinned.

As we lay sprawled with my children between us, I listened to their breathing.

'You hanging in there?' Julian whispered, placing a finger under my chin to look into my eyes.

The unexpected contact made me shiver and I nodded.

NANCY BARONE

'Thank you,' I whispered back, my eyes never leaving his face.

His own were solemn and dark in the evening glow of the fire he'd built. In our house it was always me who made the fire. Ira had never stuck around long enough to enjoy its warmth and now the flames seemed to be caressing me.

'Thank you – for everything you've done for us.'

'I want to do more,' Julian whispered back.

I slowly eased myself out of the tangle of my kids and then Julian brought Warren upstairs while I placed Maddy in her bed, my love fiercely gushing out of every pore. I'd kill anyone who hurt them.

I sat there for a few moments until Julian came back from Warren's bedroom, then I crept downstairs into the kitchen and away from Julian. My face was hot and I was trembling. Julian's presence in the house was reassuring me, but his nearness was overwhelming. I felt drawn to him like no one ever before. I wanted to reach out and touch him, smell the shampoo scent of his hair, touch the tautness of his skin. I wanted him to put his arms around me and tell me everything was going to be alright, because *he* was here.

There was no denying it. I wanted him to be my man for good. I wanted him to be part of my Tuscan dream.

Julian took my empty mug from my fingers and set it on the counter and before I knew what was happening, he pulled me into his arms. I felt the stubble of his face against my cheek, and my body and soul filled with so much longing, I moaned. He pulled me closer and I wrapped my arms around him, my hands climbing up his back, gripping

306

his shoulder blades. The feel of his strong, lean frame against mine was so invigorating, and it scared me, the way my body reacted. Like never before.

He stroked the back of my head and neck, and I could hear his breathing, feel the warmth of it against the side of my face.

'You're so brave, Erica,' he whispered, his voice deep, hoarse. Breathless, almost.

'What *are* you talking about? I'm a total loser. Can't you see the mess my life is?'

He put his hands on my shoulders and looked down at me in surprise. 'No. I see a strong woman whose kids love her to pieces because she's a wonderful mother,' he said softly. 'I see a kick-ass manager who makes things work. And a sexy, intelligent woman. And the way you faced Ira – I don't know anyone who wouldn't have cowered in a corner, but you... you are amazing and I...' Then he went silent, busying himself with our coffees.

I rubbed my face against his chest and he squeezed my shoulders, his eyes hooded, then turned to the coffees again. I had to hand it to him. He was a real gentleman. I knew he wanted to take this further, but he respected the situation I was in. Later, once we were all settled, I'd show him exactly how grateful I was.

'You're the amazing one,' I said finally. 'And so was your meal. You and Paul could rival Le Tre Donne.'

'You're my teacher. You know, we should ditch our jobs and open an Italian restaurant somewhere,' he whispered, and I felt my cheeks go hot.

Now would have been the perfect time to investigate.

The coffeemaker pinged and he poured me a cup.

'Thank you,' I whispered as he handed me a full mug. 'What you did today – you saved our lives. Ira could have seriously hurt you as well.'

'Well, he didn't, and you won't have to be afraid anymore. Now, you're free of him.'

Free. I'd never be totally free until I landed on Italian soil. And until I could confess my Italian desires to Julian.

34

Carpe Diem

Morning caught me unprepared. I opened my eyes to find myself on the sofa – in Julian's arms under a throw, his lips against my temple, his body hot against mine. Would I never tire of this man?

'Morning,' he murmured, his voice languid, caressing me just as languidly, and just like that, I wanted him, right here, right now.

Here was our chance. It was early and all was quiet. I shifted so I was straddling him. Ooh, that felt nice.

'Morning, your highness,' I whispered with a giggle. 'Or should I say your hardness?'

'Kids are fast asleep,' he informed me, kissing my lips. 'Come here,' he rasped as he grabbed my hips and placed me on his...

'Ah...' I moaned. 'That's... that's *good*...'

'Perfect fit,' he moaned back as he removed our clothes under the throw, his mouth bending to my bare breasts, and I gripped his shoulders.

And we took each other home in record time. Fast (that was a first), hard, urgent. I loved it. I loved any way we did it.

'Mommy?' came Maddy's voice from somewhere at the back of my consciousness.

I turned and threw on my jeans and T-shirt before she made it downstairs. That had been close. The kid was already scarred for life – the last thing she needed to see was her mommy buck naked lying on the sofa with her principal.

'Yes, sweetie?' I whispered.

'Warren's wet his bed,' she whispered back.

'That's OK, sweetie. You go back to your room and get dressed before breakfast, OK?'

'OK,' she said, obeying.

I crept up into Warren's room and halted on the threshold. He'd already removed the sheets, his eyes lowered.

'Hey, Warren, I'm changing the bed sheets today. I've already got mine and Maddy's. Can I have yours, too?'

He nodded, still not looking at me. I felt for the little fella.

Julian appeared at the bottom of the stairs, fully dressed. 'Hey, champ, want to come down and shoot a few hoops before breakfast?'

Warren shot to his feet gratefully. 'Coming,' he called, then turned to me, his eyes pleading. 'Please don't tell him.'

I crossed my heart and took the sheets from him.

'Thanks, Mom.'

I lingered, looking out his window as he reached Julian outside. I watched them play. I knew he'd be fine. Thanks to some time with a fine man.

After the game, I invited Julian to stay for lunch.

'What did you say to him?' I asked when we were alone.

'That it happened to me, too.'

'Did it really, or were you just trying to make him feel better?'

'I wish. It happened when I was thirteen. I'd just discovered I'd been adopted.'

'Oh, right.'

'It's no big deal,' Julian said. 'My adoptive parents have always loved me like their own.'

'As if anyone could not love you,' I whispered, and he grinned.

'Plus, I have you – and you're all that a bloke could ever want.'

Thinking that someone had abandoned him only made me realize how strong Julian was and how much more I still needed to learn about this magnificent man.

I don't know when I fell asleep again, but the next thing I was aware of was the last rays of the day streaming across my face and the joyous laughter of the kids. I'd never slept for so long in my life.

I rubbed my face and padded into the kitchen, where I peered out the window over my (still flourishing, by the way) succulents. There, in the back garden, Julian and Warren were rolling around in the sandpit, pure glee on their faces, while Maddy was perched daintily on the edge, clapping her hands in delight.

As I watched, Julian stood up, and tons of sand spilled from his pockets and pant legs.

I wiped the sleep out of my eyes and the cobwebs out of my brain, the night before coming back to me with a vengeance, with the horror of Ira's violence, the hatred in his eyes as he begged me to take him back. It hadn't been a bad dream, but it still didn't make sense. Until I factored in the money aspect. He was not only hoping to bring me back round to him, but also banking on squeezing some more dough out of me.

In all probability, Ira's company really was sinking, only he gave priority to Maxine's needs. Whenever I'd asked him about Tech.Com, he'd sighed and said, 'I'll take care of it.' Which he hadn't, obviously. Now, I understood what had made him crack – not the fact that he missed us, but that he needed money and needed it fast. You don't screw around with the IRS.

So yes, it was really time to go away. I'd sell the house and invest in a smaller farmhouse I could afford, and do it up little by little. There was no way Ira would get joint custody now and in a sense, I was doing him a favor. He'd never really wanted the burden of having children. I wrapped my sweater around me. Outside it was still cold, but it was nothing compared to the icy fingers gripping my heart. Now, I had to look out for the light at the end of the tunnel. Nothing else mattered.

That night after Julian left, I couldn't fall asleep, so I dialed Paul's cellphone.

'Sunshine,' Paul said softly, 'things aren't going to get better if you stay up all night.'

'I know, but everything is such a mess,' I sobbed, then sniffed. 'How did you know it was me?'

'Because you're the only fool who would be up at this ungodly hour? Besides, I have caller ID, silly, remember?'

'Right,' I said as I dashed the back of my hand into my eye. 'I forgot.'

'So, what's up?'

'I'm so, so tired of all this. I just want to go now. I'm still looking for a place in Tuscany, possibly near your place.'

'Tell you what. I'll ring up my good friend Roberto Luzzi again and give him a kick up the ass, OK?'

I swallowed. 'OK. Nothing too expensive. I don't have a big budget.'

'Just send me an email with your specifics and I'll forward it to him. OK?'

'OK,' I answered.

'Have you told Julian you want to go?'

I sighed. Never more than a step behind me, my Paulie. 'Not yet, but I will.'

He sighed. 'The guy's crazy for you. He's got a right to know.'

'I know, but what if it doesn't last?' I whispered, feeling sad and grateful and hopeful at the same time. I was so afraid to let myself go to someone and ruin it all over again.

'Honey, he's friggin' perfect for you.'

I smiled and swiped at a tear. Julian *was* worth the risk.

'Don't waste any more time, Erica. Nab him now before

somebody else does.' He yawned. 'Now go get some shut-eye. You've got a long day ahead of you and I need my beauty sleep.'

I smiled into my phone. 'OK,' I answered. 'See you tomorrow?'

'You betcha, baby,' he said and made kissing noises. 'Now, get off the phone and go to bed!'

I hung up. Bless his soul.

35

Seduction/Abduction

March melted into April, defined by the poet T.S. Eliot as 'the cruelest month'. I guess he must have known what April had in store for us. And still I hadn't asked Julian, my excuse being I wanted the relationship to grow a little more before I sprung this on him. I wanted to have *some* sort of history behind us before I blew us to smithereens.

'Erica, Maxine Moore on the phone for you on line two,' Jackie informed me from my office door.

Jesus! not bloody Pristine Maxine again. I hadn't seen her since the supermarket episode. 'Tell her she can go to hell.'

'She says it's urgent.'

'Just hang up on her, Jackie.'

'I can't do that.'

'Here, give me the phone, then,' I snapped, and clicked it shut.

As soon as I disconnected, Jackie said, 'Erica, your principal on line three.'

'He's not *my* principal,' I muttered as I reached for the phone, but something very warm washed over me, making me feel real good. Now *he* was someone I'd gladly talk to anytime. 'Hey, Julian,' I chimed.

'Sweetheart, your cellphone's off.'

Sweetheart. That felt even better. Would I ever get used to it? 'Oh. I'm sorry. What's up?'

'Ira came to the school this morning.'

'Oh my God. Did he make a scene?'

I heard him hesitate.

'No, he wasn't looking for me. He told one of the secretaries he was taking Maddy to her dentist appointment. They let her go with him.'

I sat up, my heart in my mouth. 'I'm on my way.'

'You'll find me at the police station near the school.'

'Where is she? Where is she?' I couldn't help crying as I exploded through the front doors of the police station and into the hall where Julian was waiting for me with a policeman.

'Erica, this is Detective Roker. He's dealing with Maddy's—'

'Abduction?' I whispered in a broken voice. On the way over, I'd dialed Ira's cellphone a million times in vain. Oh, my sweet, sweet little girl!

The detective led us into a private room, where he sat us down, explaining that because the abductor was a parent, it would be more difficult to trace them, and was I absolutely sure that my husband understood he had to check decisions with me first...

'Yes, yes!' I practically screamed. 'He was never interested in seeing them!'

'Ma'am, can you give us a picture of your ex-husband and your daughter and a description of his car?'

With shaky hands, I fished in my wallet and retrieved a copy of the picture I'd taken on Christmas Eve, minutes before he'd abandoned them.

'Uhm, a blue Ford. Boston plates: AB17-2427,' I informed him, imagining the police swooping down on him with a helicopter and shooting him on sight.

Never too soon for me. I didn't care if one day he really did bludgeon me with his baseball bat, but my kids were sacred. When I got my hands on him...

'I'm going to kill him, Julian,' I rasped as the detective went to answer a phone call in the next room.

'That won't be necessary, Erica. A warrant has been issued for his arrest. We're talking abduction here. I could kill Miss Simpson. She knew she wasn't allowed to release either of the kids to anyone but you.'

I wanted to kill Miss Simpson, too, because her stupidity was limitless. 'What if he tries to get Warren as well?'

Julian frowned. 'I doubt it, Erica. Have you blocked the airports?' he asked the returning detective.

'Yes, but it's difficult to determine where they may be headed.'

'Colorado!' I cried, and they looked at me. 'He might try to get to his parents' summer lodge!'

'Alright,' the detective said. 'Call your in-laws and alert them.'

I did as he asked but no one was home, so I left a message and sank into my chair, my mind mush and my body liquefied with fear as it really began to sink in and the shock began to wear off. *Maddy!* Where else could Ira have taken her? And what was going through his deviously twisted mind? He didn't know anything about her – her tastes, her interests, nothing! And she'd be petrified of him after the baseball bat episode.

It seemed impossible, but it was true. Ira was doing this just to make me suffer for God knows what sins I'd committed against him. I'd always been a patient, loving wife. How could he do this to me? To Maddy? And how the hell was I going to break it to Warren?

'Anywhere else he could be?' Julian asked me, and I shook my head.

'Ira doesn't have any friends. He spends all his time at his office.' *With his secretary.*

When we were free to go, Julian took me down to Tech. Com, just north of the highway. There was only one car in the private parking lot – the janitor's.

'Where's Mr. Lowenstein?' I demanded of him in my brisk business manner to avoid falling apart.

'He left a couple of hours ago.'

The man shrugged as he continued to mop the floor and I remembered when I used to clean Ira's offices for him. And do his bookkeeping.

'Where's Maxine?'

'You mean his wife, Mrs. Lowenstein? They left together.'

I felt a tingling, odd sensation at the back of my head, like someone was creeping up from behind me. Julian glanced at me.

'Why are you here so early?' I asked him. 'It's only four thirty.'

Again, he shrugged. 'I've been coming at this time for a year. When everybody's gone.'

I felt the blood drain from my face as I tripped out of the office and into the parking lot to vomit on the tarmac. A year. They'd been together for a year. And instead of coming home to his family, he'd gone home with *her*. Spending at least eight hours per evening there. *On top* of the entire day. Ira didn't have just a mistress. He'd been leading a double life.

Julian caught up with me and held my hair away from my face as I puked.

'No – go away,' I sobbed, pushing him away, but he didn't move.

I straightened up and dashed my hand over my drenched eyes with a moan. A year. One whole year of sleeping with his secretary. No wonder he came back in the wee hours. No wonder he'd always left his dinners half-eaten. No wonder he'd built a barricade in our bed and avoided turning in for the night at the same time I did. It was easier to pretend to be asleep, easier to use the same excuse every single night, or, as he'd done, to give no excuse at all, besides the fact that I made him sick.

'Think, Erica,' Julian said. 'Where could they have gone? Where does she live?'

'It should be here, on file,' I suggested, going back into the office to rifle through the file cabinet.

Maxine Moore lived on the seventh floor of a new condo in a nice area overlooking Harbor Islands. My heart was in my mouth as we rode up in the elevator, Julian opposite me. The detective and his men had taken the previous one. I looked up at him, and he squeezed my hand and kissed my forehead. He opened his mouth to say something, but the doors pinged open and we jumped out.

As expected, no one answered the door, so the detective used the search warrant he'd obtained in record time and pushed his way into Maxine's empty apartment, and I catapulted myself in behind him, calling Maddy's name.

The apartment echoed with its emptiness and I felt the walls closing in on me. I ran to the bathroom and hurled again.

After I'd finished and rinsed my face, I caught sight of a stack of baseball magazines on the side of the toilet and the bathtub. Old habits die hard for a baseball freak.

Hanging on the wall was a picture of Maxine and Ira, happy and in love on a beach. She was wearing Ira's New Jersey City University shirt. I recognized it because it bore an ink stain I hadn't been able to remove. So *that* was where it had gone.

Steadying myself, I opened the medicine cabinet. There was a bottle of prescription vitamins – B9, to be exact. Folacin, or Folic acid. I'd taken them, as well. When I was pregnant.

And then I saw a file on the bathroom counter. She must have forgotten it in her haste to leave. It was the complete file of her pregnancy. This was her first. She was eight months along.

I sat down on the edge of the tub next to Ira's magazines and held my head. Eight months! For eight months and more he hadn't loved me. He'd loved someone else. Fathered another *child*. Ira didn't even love his own family and he was starting another one? You can do that with your *knitting*, or a bad book because it's not good enough to hold your interest, because it bores you. You can put it down and start something new. There's nothing wrong with that. But you couldn't put a family away in the drawer when you tired of it.

On shaky legs, I returned to the living room, where Julian was waiting for me.

'Are you alright?' he asked.

I shook my head and handed him the folder. He went pale as he read.

I opened the front door to leave Maxine's apartment, wanting to throw myself off her balcony instead. 'Tell the detective to call his men off the airports. She won't be flying,' I said over my shoulder on my way out, but the detective followed me into the corridor.

'Mrs. Lowenstein?' came Detective Roker's voice.

I turned to see him holding another folder as he beckoned us in again.

'Were you aware of any family funds missing from your joint account?' he asked softly.

I shook my head. 'No. I check my balance every week.'

'Well, based on these documents, this apartment has been rented for a few years by Ms. Moore. But three days ago, it was purchased by your husband.'

I gasped as Detective Roker leafed through the folder he'd found and nodded apologetically.

'There's a record here of one hundred thousand dollars paid by Mr. Lowenstein in person – as a down payment for this apartment.'

I walked back to Julian's jeep, not feeling my legs, as if I were drunk, not feeling my body or seeing my surroundings, as if I were dead. Ira had stolen my money – money that my nonna Silvia had made sacrifices to give to me for my future. Money that I'd kept in a separate account for my children's college funds. Not only had he ruined my whole goddam life, but he'd also taken from his children, which shouldn't have surprised me. And yet, I couldn't believe the man I'd married had managed to hate me so much to do this to me. If I could have pushed a button to make him disappear from the face of the earth, I would have.

36

April Fools and Irises

Maddy's Minnie Mouse model, hanging from her bedroom ceiling, seemed to be suspended miles above me. I had the sensation I was lying, stuck, at the bottom of the ocean, under a periscope that was focused on the Disney character. Minnie. Mickey. Goofy. Maddy loved them all.

'Minnie and Mickey Mouse,' I murmured with a smile as Julian's face came into focus at the top of the periscope. He'd come to bring me back to the surface. 'Disneyworld…'

'Poor thing,' I heard a familiar voice say. Marcy. 'She thinks she's a little girl again. She wants to go to Disneyworld.'

'Bullshit,' came another familiar voice. Judy. 'She's always hated Disneyworld, Marcy, don't you even *remember*?'

'Disneyworld!' came Julian's voice again as I heard him click his phone open. 'Detective Roker? Block all the roads to Florida! Erica thinks they may be headed for Disneyworld.'

'Thank you,' I whispered, but it was already dark again.

*

I woke to the sound of Maddy's voice.

Had I dreamed it? Or was she downstairs playing in the living room, as usual?

I jumped out of bed and flew down the stairs, where my parents and Detective Roker were watching a family video of Maddy's sixth birthday party. I turned away, tears running down my cheeks as Julian was coming in through the open door.

'Mom!' I heard, and whirled to see Warren as he catapulted himself into my arms.

I clung to him desperately, wishing I could take his fears and pain away. Wishing I could dissolve his anger and hatred. They'd never done *me* any good.

'Warren, sweetheart!' I cried, nearly strangling him. 'She's OK, you'll see.'

'I know it,' he answered, his lips trembling. 'Dad doesn't hate her. Even if he doesn't care. Right?'

I hoped Ira cared for Maddy a lot more than he hated me. I nodded and he threw his arms around me again.

I glanced at Julian. His eyes were red and his face had the shadow of a beard. How much time had elapsed since Maddy had gone? How many hours had she been begging Ira to take her back home? Did Maxine have the sense to take care of her properly? Oh, God, I didn't even want to think of what I'd do when I got my hands on both of them. Death wasn't enough. I had something more twisted in mind, like re-enacting all my murderous dreams on him – all at the same time.

'Get some sleep, Julian,' I said, bringing myself back from my murderous thoughts. 'Don't worry about me. I'm going to be sitting on the phone until the damn thing rings.'

But instead, Julian produced a box of muffins and coffee from Starbucks. 'Eat. You need to keep your sugar levels up.'

He was the only man who had ever said that to me.

Marcy had the gall to gasp and say, 'Why don't I just get you some yoghurt or something?'

Julian turned and incinerated her with a look that was worse than my evil eye, and she stepped back. If I hadn't been so terrified for Maddy, I'd have laughed. Old Marcy had finally found a man who didn't succumb to her charms.

As I was upstairs getting dressed, Julian's cellphone rang.

'Erica!' he called, flying up the stairs.

On the landing, he grabbed my arms.

'It's Maxine! She's called the police and Ira's under their custody. Maddy's with her and they're on their way over with a squad car!'

I covered my mouth with my hands. *My baby was coming home!*

When she came in through the door, whimpering 'Mommy, Mommy!', I couldn't keep my tears back any longer, clawing at her, squeezing her so tight I thought I'd break her.

'Baby!' was all I could say over and over for the first few minutes. Then I cleared her face of her pretty reddish-blonde curls and whispered, 'It's alright, Maddy. Mommy's here and I'm never going to let anything happen to you, OK?'

She nodded fiercely and threw her little arms around me again. 'Maxine bought me some toys. She said she was going to take me home because Daddy was crazy again.'

Warren threw himself at us and I caught a glimpse of

Maxine in the corner, talking to some police officers. Her stomach was huge now.

Julian watched us, his eyes shiny and red. Maddy looked up, noticing him.

'Hey, sweetie pie,' he whispered, and she flew into his arms, burying her face in his stomach as he bent to kiss the top of her head, whispering comforting words to her before lifting her. And she rested her head against his, just happy to be there.

'I'm glad Maxine didn't forget your number, after all,' I muttered, wiping my eyes.

Maxine whispered, 'I'm so sorry. I didn't know he'd *abducted* her. He said you and Julian were going away somewhere. He said you were on better terms now and—'

'It's OK, Maxine. Really.' I nodded at her, indicating the sofa for her to sit down.

I wasn't angry at her anymore, because now she was a victim, too, and I was just grateful she'd brought my daughter back to me before Ira became dangerous again.

'I don't know what happened to him,' she sniffed as she slowly lowered herself next to me. 'One minute he was fine and the next, he just lost it because we had to go to the bathroom. Only then did I realize that something was very wrong. He'd changed practically overnight, mentioning debts and the IRS being on his case. And then I knew it was dangerous for us to stay with him. So I locked Maddy and myself in the bathroom at a gas station and called the police.'

'You saved my baby's life. Thank you,' I whispered. 'And I'm sorry that you had to go through that. Ira isn't the man he was when I met him twelve years ago.'

She looked up into my face. 'I'm so, so sorry for what we did to you. It was wrong. I thought you were the bad one. He kept saying that you were a horrible mother and wife, and I believed him. But I didn't know that the money was yours.'

'It's OK, Maxine,' I repeated, wondering how I could ever repay her for what she'd done.

'I need to speak to him,' I said to the detective as Ira was ushered into a private office, paler, scrawnier and skinnier than he'd ever been.

There was a strange light in his eyes that I didn't recognize and it scared me. The Ira I knew, I could handle. This Ira was someone I'd never seen before.

'Yes, ma'am. There will be an officer in there with you at all times for your safety.'

'Do you want me to come in with you?' Julian asked softly.

'I can do it, thanks.'

He nodded and whispered, 'That's my girl.'

I smiled wanly and sat in the chair facing the bullet proof glass. But it sure wasn't hatred- proof. I hated him so much, I was trembling, but I had something to say to him.

'Maxine never wants to see you again, ever. Neither do I, or my children. If and when you ever get out of here, I suggest you steer clear of us, because with one phone call, you'll be back here – for good,' I informed him and turned on my heel.

★

That night, after my family had come and quickly gone, as they always did when I was in trouble, I turned to Julian as he was climbing into his jacket.

'Julian, I don't want you to have to leave every night. I want you to be a part of this family.'

In response, he took my face in his hands and bent to kiss me on the lips. 'It's not an April Fool's joke, is it?' he asked. 'Are you serious?'

Julian drew me into the circle of his arms and hooked his thumbs into the belt around my jeans.

'I'd be the fool to let you go,' I murmured as he lowered his delicious mouth to mine. 'I love you, Julian,' I finally whispered, and it felt like going home.

At work, things were always hectic, just the way I liked it. And sometimes I even got little satisfactions. Mr. Simmons, a very annoying guest whom I'd handled brilliantly, turned out to be the owner of a rival hotel in New England, The Pilgrim. He'd offered me a position over at his chain and I realized that his increasing difficulty as a guest had simply been him running me through his tests. Apparently, I'd passed with flying colors. I was flattered but politely refused. Soon I was going to be in Italy, if I had any say in it.

And... I'd managed it. My irises were finally starting to bloom in my now beautiful garden. Swallows began to circle the yard out back, diving to catch any insect stupid enough to hang around. I leaned out the window, my elbows on the sill, and sighed with what I believe was contentment after a very long time. It had been an endless winter. But having survived it, I knew we could survive anything.

37

Truth is Freedom

The next day, I got a call from my zia Monica to stop by at Le Tre Donne.

'Hello?' I called to the empty dining hall. 'Zia Maria? Martina? Monica?'

Silence, and then a burst from the kitchen and three happy women bearing gifts. Never trust three happy Italian women bearing gifts.

'*Vieni qui*, Erica, come and sit down. We have something for you,' said Zia Maria as the other two huddled around her, their faces red with excitement.

'What's up? Why is the shop closed?' The last time one of my family closed a shop was when Nonna had died. I bolted to my feet again. 'Is someone ill?'

'*Zitta, zitta!*' They silenced me, looking around.

Zia Monica locked the door and pulled down the blinds. 'Everything is fine.'

'So why do I feel like we're in a mob movie and I'm

going to get a half-moon stuck in my throat?' I chuckled. Sometimes they could be so dramatic, it was sweet.

'We were cleaning out the storage room and found some of Nonna's stuff that she left for you,' Zia Maria said. 'It's time you had it.'

'Had what?' I asked, curious and intrigued by the whole setting: the empty restaurant, the air of secrecy and the bright eyes.

Out of a large cardboard box hidden under the table, they each pulled out a packet as I eyed them, confused. Then they passed me an envelope.

I stared at them and Zia Monica rolled her eyes. 'Come on, will you? I'm dying to see your face!'

'Why? What is it? Stocks? Bonds? Are we suddenly rich?'

Still eyeing them, I carefully opened the envelope addressed to me. It was wrinkled and grey. I froze as I recognized the writing:

My Dearest granddaughter, Erica, light of my life,

Although I probably won't be there to celebrate you coming into womanhood, I want to leave you four gifts.

The first is for your own home one day.

The second is for your matrimonial bed.

The third is for you personally.

The fourth will free you.

You were not blessed with a good mother and we have all tried to make up for her faults. Use your strength to get through life and to keep it light. And think of love – the possibility of real love – when you are down.

I love you with all my heart,

Nonna Silvia Bettarini.

When I finally managed to see through my tears, Zia Maria nudged me softly.

'Go on, open it,' she whispered, her voice shattered, her eyes red.

On either side of her, my aunts nodded.

The first gift, the one for my own home one day, was a large set of white linen hand-embroidered curtains, enough for an entire house, signed at the bottom in linen thread by Nonna herself.

I stared up at my aunts, who were now in tears, patting me. This stuff was worth thousands and thousands of dollars. But to me it was priceless, because I knew what an endless feat it was once you started the work, assuming you had the talent to do so. I lightly touched the linen, waves of sorrow passing through me. *Nonna*. My one and only Nonna.

'Go on – this one next,' Zia Martina said, passing me the medium-size parcel.

I opened it to find a matching linen sheet, pillowcases and coverlet, again all hand-embroidered. The linen was smooth and the embroidery flawless. As a child I'd seen this stuff in my nonna's Italian magazines. I also remembered that year in, year out I'd seen her working on them. But I hadn't realized they were for *me*.

'And now for your third gift,' Zia Monica whispered, sniffling.

'But what did I do to—'

'You don't know?' Zia Maria chuckled. 'You're one of us, Erica. Absolutely nothing like Marcy. And Nonna wanted you to know that.'

'But I'm not! I'm nothing like you!' I protested under my

breath, and they all laughed at me, patting me on the back and handing me the smallest parcel that fit in my hands.

Despite my doubts, I tore at the plain brown paper and stared. Inside was a rectangular blue velvet box. With tight lips and shaky hands, I opened it and peered inside. It was a beautiful pearl necklace, identical to the ones my aunts – and Nonna Silvia – wore on special occasions, but with a gold E hanging from the clasp at the back. Zia Monica slipped it around my neck and the cool pearls nestled under my collarbone.

'E for Erica,' I choked, and my aunts all looked at one another.

I sat there like an idiot, trying to make some sense of what had happened, as if from one day to another I'd magically become someone else, someone who deserved something so precious, something so rare.

'There's still your fourth gift, Erica,' Zia Monica said softly, glancing at her sisters, who winced. 'Well, we have to. Don't you remember the pact?'

Zia Martina nodded and sighed. 'I knew this was going to happen.'

'Pact? What pact?' I asked, raising my eyebrow. Was it true that they really were sorceresses or fairies of some kind? I always knew there was a special magical bond there and that Nonna Silvia was at the heart of it.

'Well, we thought Marcy and your father would have taken care of it by now,' Zia Maria explained.

'Well, they didn't,' Zia Monica answered and then turned to me, a hand on my knee. 'Your Nonna must have forgotten to do this. She wasn't well toward the end and it must have slipped her mind.'

'What? What must've slipped her mind?'

At that point, Zia Maria reached into the box and pulled out another parcel. I unwrapped it to find an old leather-bound family album. One I'd never seen before. Now pictures of Marcy I've seen a *million* times, but family pictures, where they were all together, were a rarity, because Nonna had always taken them but never been in them. But she was in many here, I noticed with satisfaction as I flipped through the album.

There were pictures of a beautiful medieval town, San Gimignano, from where the Bettarinis had originated. I recognized the old towers that the most powerful families had built to assert their commercial and financial prowess among their rival families.

There were pictures of their large farmhouse, the stables and stalls, the cheeses and hanging prosciuttos. A family that had been doing well. And then the war had come, taking my grandfather away from Nonna, leaving her no choice but to sell up and go.

But something made me stop and go back to page one, as if I already unconsciously knew that there was more. One particular picture had caught my eye. The women were there in their Sunday best, all pretty and frilly, between five and fifteen years of age, standing on the steps of an old medieval church in Tuscany. I smiled, recognizing younger versions of Marcy (whose name back then was Marcella), Zia Maria, Zia Monica, Zia Martina and... Marcy again?

I looked back at the Marcy on the left, then at the Marcy on the right. It was an old photo that had been folded and had a crease down the middle to show for it. Had the image on the left bled onto the background of the right-hand side, producing a copy of Marcy?

I now know that in my mind, I was trying to come up with the easiest, less painful solution.

I took a closer look. There was no mistaking it. There *were* two Marcys. *Twins.*

'What's going on here?' I asked my aunts, who were all holding their breath. 'How come we were never told we had another aunt? Where is she now?'

'Her name was Emanuela. And she had a baby.'

I stared at them. 'We have a cousin and we didn't know? Where do they live? In Tuscany?'

'Manu... Emanuela died,' Zia Maria croaked as if difficult for her to speak. 'She was your mother's twin. They were physically identical, but on the inside, they couldn't have been more different. Manu was sweet, selfless, a hard worker. She had excellent grades. And a young man who loved her and was going to marry her. But she got pregnant before that and died during labor.'

Oh my God. 'Where's the child? Was it a boy or a girl?'

They turned to stare at me sadly and I understood. 'It died, too?'

Zia Martina shook her head slowly, her eyes never leaving mine, until I got this real creepy-crawly itch at the back of my neck where the gold E hung. And then I understood. This was her necklace – Emanuela's.

I am the daughter of Emanuela Bettarini. My mother's dead twin. I was never Marcy's daughter.

'I'm Emanuela's baby,' I whispered, and Zia Maria sobbed, reaching for me as the other two hugged me and stroked my hair.

Dumbstruck, my mind on pause, frozen in time, I tried to thaw the concept, to accept it into reality.

I was Emanuela's daughter. I wasn't Marcy's. And that, precisely, was why she'd never loved me. Not because I was unlovable or unworthy of a mother's love, but because I didn't *belong* to her. I never had and never would.

I swallowed and looked up at my aunts' beaming faces. 'And my father? My real father?'

'Edoardo *is* your real father, sweetie. He was Manu's husband-to-be. He loved her completely. And still hasn't gotten over it.'

My father, in love with another woman. In love with my real mother. That certainly explained my father's melancholic sweetness.

'Marcy had been in love with your dad for years,' Zia Monica explained. 'And when he chose Manu, she was heartbroken. But when Manu died—'

'Marcy saw her chance to swoop in,' I finished for my aunt, who nodded and bit her lip. I finished the sentence for her. 'The only catch was she had to take care of me. Jesus, what a price to pay for a husband, huh?' As if I hadn't known.

All this time... all this time she'd resented me because I'd been the deal-breaker in her marriage. If she wanted my dad, which she did, she had to take me on as her daughter. A child she'd never wanted. I looked up at my aunts through a swell of tears.

'We were there, every step of the way, you know that,' Zia Maria said defensively. 'All of us. That's why you lived in the same building as us. So we could all keep an eye on Marcy and—'

'And love me like she never could?' I whispered and, after a few moments, they all nodded simultaneously.

That was why Marcy never appreciated her sisters but heavily depended on them all the same to take me to school and back, help me with my homework, growing pains and... life in general. They'd represented, in Marcy's little mind, a necessary evil. But she got away when she could, with what she could, by ignoring me most of the time. Living under the same roof so that everyone would think she was acting as my mother. Everyone, I'm now sure, knew the truth. Everyone from Bartolo, the butcher, to Mirella from Mirella's *merceria* knew my family's story. The story of how I was born. Everyone except me.

It all finally, *finally* made sense. I looked down at the album and leafed through some more while they each told me stories about my real mother, of how she loved my father and how he almost went crazy after her death. Emanuela.

She'd been the smartest in her class. She loved sports (I sure hadn't inherited that from her), painting (which I did) and was training to get a junior flying license. Now that was something I'd love to do myself.

And now suddenly, I didn't know who I was anymore. And I'd thought I'd been doing just fine with the divorce thing. Being strong and determined and all. And now I felt... lost.

I gathered my things and stood up slowly, feeling a hundred years old.

'Are you OK?' Zia Monica asked.

'Leave her,' Zia Maria ordered. 'She needs time now.'

I nodded. 'Time.' I knew exactly what I needed.

*

A couple of hours of brooding later hadn't been enough, so I went to my parents' home and used my key. Thinking of Marcy as my non-mother was surprisingly easy. And uplifting.

She was lying in bed, leafing through a magazine. The pose that I'd always remember her in. She looked up, startled.

'Erica, what are you doing here?'

No, *Hi, sweetheart, how nice to see you.* It was yet another piece that fit the puzzle.

'Why didn't you ever tell me you had a twin sister?' I whispered.

Her eyes widened, then narrowed. 'Where did you get that crazy idea from?'

'From this,' I managed, shoving the album in her face.

Marcy pushed the album away from her nose to focus and suddenly paled.

'Well?' I prompted.

'I'm sorry you had to find out this way. We wanted to tell you, your dad and I, but no time ever seemed right.'

I rubbed my face in exhaustion. Why, oh why was everything always so difficult?

'Sit down, sweetheart. It's time you knew.'

Sweetheart? *Now* she called me sweetheart. 'I already know. I want to know why you never told me. Why the big secret? Why have we never seen any pictures?'

To which Marcy sighed. 'Your dad has tons of them, only he keeps them to himself. I don't interfere with his lost dream.'

I was surprised Marcy could admit defeat so easily. 'He loved her very much and I was nothing.'

'I find that hard to believe. Dad treats you like a princess and he always has.'

She looked up at me. 'Because I'm weak, Erica. I'm not like you. You're like my mom's side of the family. You're all strong. Fighters.'

Marcy admitting her weaknesses? Had I somehow ended up on *The Twilight Zone*? This was getting weirder and weirder.

She groaned softly, as if in pain, and I suddenly realized how painful it still was for her, too. Knowing you were never someone's first choice hurt. I knew what that was like.

But on the other hand, the only feeling I could muster was relief. Relief that my mom didn't love me like mothers love their children simply because she *wasn't* my mom and not because I was unlovable or that there was something very wrong with me, as I'd believed my whole life. All those years of begrudging me a single ounce of affection and now I finally knew why. I represented Marcy's failures and weaknesses. Just like I represented Ira's failures. A part of them both would always resent me for being stronger, more capable.

I tried to feel anger as was my second nature, but still relief flooded my heart, over and over, like a fresh spring rain washing over me, cleansing me inside and out. All the times when she didn't praise me or encourage me or cheer me on – all those moments I couldn't justify or explain – now made sense, in a Marcy-logic sort of way.

Any other woman would have been moved by her dead sister's newborn, taken it in (especially after having married my dad) and loved it twice as much. But not Marcy. In Marcy's heart there was no room for anything but her grief and herself. Because she was weak and had no choice but to cover herself with lies, which she also told others every day.

Like all those stories about him choosing her because she was the prettiest. Marcy had been heartbroken surely when Dad had chosen my real mother. But when all that ended, Marcy had foisted herself upon him and he'd agreed, with the proviso that everyone else would stick around to help take care of me. And now I was no longer trapped in a relationship with an unloving mother.

I thought of Emanuela – Manu. She'd have been exactly like Marcy on the outside, only loving. Undoubtedly, she'd be running Le Tre Donne with her sisters while Marcy skulked around at home in her shiny kimonos with her sleepy eyes.

'All these years I've had to stay on my toes to keep up with Emanuela's memory,' Marcy whispered. 'It was no contest from the start. There was no way I could ever be as important to your father as you were. So I simply gave up.'

I searched her face, understanding her for the first time.

'I gave up because I knew whatever I did wouldn't change the facts. But your father is a good man. He dedicated extra attention to me so I wouldn't feel left out. But no matter how many flowers and gifts I got, we both knew it was to fill a great big gap that could never be filled.'

My eyes blurred. 'It must have been difficult looking me in the face every day. I wondered why you didn't love me...'

At that, Marcy sat up. 'Oh no, Erica! Never think that I didn't *love* you. I do. But you understand you represented for me the greatest hurdle for a woman's pride.'

Boy, did I know a little something about hurdles. But I'd evolved, moved on, while Marcy would be forever stuck in this rut if she didn't get over it once and for all.

And to think many times during my childhood I'd found my mother standing, or rather slumped, her red eyes lost on the expanse of the back lawn. And for many years I couldn't figure out why she was so afflicted and what dark acid was consuming her. While growing up, I always thought that if I had Marcy's looks, her clothes, her husband and her home, I would have been happy and managed to love myself.

And now I knew. I didn't need anything but my loved ones and my own inner strength. And that would always be my starting point in life, no matter what happened to me.

'Can you forgive me?' Marcy whispered, big tears plopping down onto her purple-and-black kimono.

I looked into her face, slowly riddling with wrinkles. I saw the vacuity of her eyes, the decent person she was trying to be despite her fragility. She'd never be my mother. But maybe we could bury the hatchet now that I knew I was the stronger one. Now, it was my turn to act the grown-up.

'Silly Marcy,' I said, and she smiled up at me. 'There's nothing to forgive. Now get up, have a shower and let's go out to lunch. My treat, OK?'

She nodded and smiled, like a little girl who had been promised a lollipop if she stopped crying over her scratched knee.

I smiled back and silently slid to my feet, holding onto her hand briefly before I slipped from the room. Now no longer trapped by false ties, maybe one day we'd be friends.

★

Once back in the security of my own home, I crept up the stairs as quietly as I could and opened Warren's door. He was fast asleep, lying on his back. As I watched, he rolled over and mumbled something about baseball. I kissed his soft cheek and tiptoed out the door to Maddy's room.

Her fairy light was on, projecting images of gossamer wings around the walls. Pink reigned everywhere, from her coverlet to her rug to her curtains. Hanging on her door, the angel wings I'd made for her (with Zia Martina's help, of course) out of tulle on a thin wire frame. Oodles of starch kept it in shape. Maddy. My little fairy. My little angel.

And then, inevitably, I was in front of my own bedroom door. I pushed it open and smiled down at my spider-whisperer, more gorgeous than ever and fast asleep. I slowly undressed and sank into the space next to him as he murmured and pulled me into the circle of his arms. I breathed in his familiar manly scent and let him hold me. Tomorrow I'd share my news with him. But tonight, all I wanted was to be held. To belong.

38

A Woman's Wait

For Warren's birthday on the eighth of May, we planned a picnic on the beach. Before we left home, Julian gave him his very own first professional baseball glove that still bore his initials, J.N.F. And it was personally autographed.

'Julian, no. It's too much,' I protested.

'Mo-om!' Warren pleaded.

'Warren, please go out and play for a minute.'

He knew better than to object.

'Julian, that glove is worth a fortune – much too much for a thirteen-year-old. You're too generous.'

Julian waited until the back door closed and got up, holding out his hand to me.

'Erica, sweetheart. It's time you and I had a talk. A serious one.'

Uh-oh. 'Look, Julian. You're great. But if you want the kids to love you, just be yourself.'

'And what do I have to do to make *you* love me?' he whispered, pushing back a strand of hair behind my ear, and I felt my cheeks redden. 'Mmm? Am I that unlovable, Erica?'

I looked up. 'Of course you are – lovable, I mean,' I assured.

'I want to be your man, Erica.'

'You are my man,' I said, and stopped in surprise. 'And I love you. Gee, that sounded good. Can I say it again?'

'Please do,' he murmured, taking my mouth.

'I love you, Julian. Mmm, this is much more fun than sports,' I whispered.

'Come on, lazy bones,' Julian sighed, pulling me out the door. 'Warren's waiting for his picnic.'

The Harbor Islands were visible in the distance. Julian and I were sitting on a picnic blanket as the kids chased the waves. Getting away for even a couple of hours was pure bliss.

I bit into a peach and looked at my rolled-up pants, wondering if I'd get them wet. Sure, it would be nice to stroll hand in hand along the shore and look like characters out of a Rosamunde Pilcher book. But in the end, I'd be stuck with sopping pant legs sticky with sand. Not so romantic, especially if after the romantic moment you're planning a sexy one.

Julian pulled me up and dragged me down the beach, and up into his arms in a face-to-face piggyback. I gasped in surprise, enjoying the feeling of my legs around his hips, his hands under my thighs. Those hands, so well-meaning yet intimate, burned into my skin.

I'd let him be with me in Tuscany if I thought that he'd be happy with me. Did he just think he was? Had Julian only been guided by the sufferings of a family in distress? He'd seen the signs early on. Only he shouldn't have allowed himself to get personal. With all our baggage, my family could only weigh a single, optimistic man like Julian down. And then he'd start to resent me like Ira had. Even if he was a gentleman extraordinaire with a heart of gold and the patience of Job.

But whichever way you put it, Maddy and Warren would never be his kids, and he could never love them the way… I was going to say *the way a biological parent could*. Hah. Served me right. I think Julian already loved Warren and Maddy much more than Ira ever had. I could see that.

When we got home, Julian put on a pot of coffee. We'd dropped the kids off at Paul's for a couple of hours as they loved spending time with him, and it gave Julian and I time to be alone together. It had been a warm day, but I still welcomed the feeling of hot coffee trickling inside me.

I sipped and murmured with pleasure. Julian took my face in his hands and sucked the drops of coffee that clung to my lips, lingering, tasting, tantalizing.

I nearly fell over, had it not been for his hands on my hips, lifting me onto the kitchen counter behind me, my feet dangling – which was just as well, because I couldn't feel my legs anymore. As if in a trance, my eyes remained wide open, taking in the sight of his long, long lashes, the stubble on his lean cheeks, the way his eyes finally opened and found mine in a soul-searing smile. I'd literally forgotten to breathe and fanned myself with my hand.

'Oh, wow,' I managed, and swallowed before he enfolded me in his arms and sucked on my lips. *Oh, God.*

'I've got to tell you something,' he whispered, excited like a young boy.

'I'm all ears,' I said, running my fingers through his soft hair.

'I've almost finished my new novel. And it's all thanks to you.'

I gasped and covered my mouth, my heart bursting with joy. 'Julian, that's amazing! Oh my God, we have to celebrate! This is fantastic.'

'There's only one way I want to celebrate,' he whispered with a grin, reaching for my zipper.

'Done,' I agreed.

'Now you're in trouble...' he growled softly between our kisses, bringing our bodies closer until my breasts were flat against his chest and I felt his arousal.

And a very big arousal at that. This hunk of a man wanted me.

'I'm going to flatten you out on this counter and feast on every delicious inch of you...'

Which is precisely what he did.

39

While You See a Chance…

'What is this?' I asked the next day, eyeing the small velvet box in Julian's hand as he came in through the front door and kissed me.

I was a stone's throw away from a coronary. It was too big to be a ring. Unless it was a big ring. I had big fingers. Maybe a can opener…

'Open it,' he answered simply.

Duh.

I did so with one eye closed, ready to shut the box again if it was something that scared me. I couldn't believe it. A tennis bracelet. With – gulp – real diamonds?

'It's to thank you for getting me off my ass and writing again. Man, you don't know how good it feels.'

'I'm glad, but are you crazy or something? This kind of stuff is expensive.'

'I can afford it,' he smiled.

Was this thank-you gift just a thank-you gift? It looked more like a commitment gift. And if so, shouldn't I have told him about Italy by now? I was being beyond dishonest. It was unfair and cruel to all of us. I'd been dishonest with Julian, the man who had single-handedly changed the way I saw life and myself. I owed him way more than I'd given him.

I burst into tears. 'I'm sorry – I can't accept it.'

Julian pulled away to look into my eyes. 'Why not?'

'Because... I've been dreaming of moving to Tuscany...' I blurted.

'I know.'

Of course he knew. All I ever did was talk about Italy. But talking was one thing. I swallowed.

'And I always wanted to buy a farmhouse and rent out accommodation so I could give up my job and stay home with the kids.'

I watched his face as he watched me back, wondering what could be so terrible. The fact was that it wasn't terrible for me. It was what I'd always wanted. If I could have him, too, my whole life would be made.

'I've been looking for years. At first Ira was OK with it. Then he changed his mind.'

'Go on.'

I let it out in one breath. 'I want to sell my home and move to Tuscany and get a mortgage. I want to move there and start my own bed and breakfast.'

I'd said it all in one go, unable to look into his eyes, and now he was silent. Did he care for me that much, that the thought of losing me did this to him? *Please, God, let it be so*.

'Wow,' was all he could say. 'That's one hell of a life-changing decision.'

'So is divorcing and starting all over again. But I love Tuscany, and my children. I believe I'm making the right decision for my family. I'm sorry.'

He sighed loudly and said, 'No. *I'm* sorry. Fuck this.' And without another word, he strode out the door, leaving the bracelet there. Just like that.

I'd never heard him say a dirty word except for in between the sheets, which was always linked to happiness. This wasn't.

And I watched him go, without saying a word, like those tragedies that you see happening on movie in slow motion, where you don't miss a moment but you can't move or react. Like when my grandma was teaching me to flip an omelet with the use of a lid. On my first try I let it slip into the sink from beneath the lid, while she was exclaiming, 'Hurry, don't let it slide!' And I just stood there, unable to move. My life was the omelet that I didn't know how to flip.

So I called, 'Julian! Come back! Please don't be offended!' But it was too late. He'd already driven off – tires screeching – officially out of my life.

I was a fool. There he'd gone, a beautiful, beautiful man, inside and out, who had claimed to love me, although I just couldn't see how he could, in only a short space of time, when for years I'd tried to win my husband's love and never managed.

In another time, way back into the depths of my past, I'd have clung to someone like Julian and never let him go. Hunky, interested in my well-being *and* hot for me? What was the *matter* with me?

So I did what I do best. I baked myself a cake and ate

it. Who says you can't do that? And I ate *all* of it, licking the icing off my fingers, tasting the sweet chocolate and my salty tears at the same time. It's a combination I'm very familiar with but don't recommend.

When I was done, I spread myself on the couch, remote in hand, and, would you believe it, *The War of the Roses* was showing. I sat there and watched with growing trepidation as husband and wife offended each other, broke each other's most prized porcelains, and killed what was left of their love and their lives. I shut my eyes so I wouldn't have to see the end.

No, I couldn't go through that again, see in the eyes of a man who once loved me a newfound hatred, because I didn't correspond to his ideal of beauty, simply because I was me and refused to be someone else.

And while I was thinking about it, my stomach began to give me huge jolts, as if there were angry sharks swimming in there, threatening to find their way back up through my throat. I managed to drag myself to the toilet bowl just in time as I heaved out the cake, the icing, my last meal and all my misery.

I threw up Ira, my life with him and the countless nights I'd snuggled up to him only to be refused and rebuked. I brought up my childhood, my mom's depression, my grandma's death, Maddy's abduction and finally, Julian's hasty retreat. Talk about undigested issues.

I could feel the veins in my temples bulging as I hung onto the toilet bowl, pressing the side of my head into the coolness of the ceramic surface. Oh, God, never again. Please let me survive this night and I'll never touch chocolate or refuse happiness again…

If you want to cleanse your mind and soul, I highly recommend chocolate cakes (minus the tears). It took me a whole one to put me on the path of soul-searching and assertiveness. And although I was done for now, I knew this was only the beginning.

Emptied and limp like an old, fading hot-water bottle, I lay on my stomach on the bathroom floor. Maybe I could stay here all night and they'd find me dead in the morning. Anything was better than this.

The sound of a car in the drive did nothing to stir me. I was already dead, only waiting for them to come and bury me. I was dead in my body and dead in my heart. And semiconscious as well, I think.

Then a car door slammed and the doorbell rang.

I felt like I had two heads. 'I'm not in,' one called, while the other felt like a bell was clanging inside it, right between my ears.

'Erica, open up.'

Julian's voice. I opened an eye and my body jerked as if I'd been touched with a live wire. Or at least I thought it had, but I was still plastered to the floor.

'I know you're in there.'

Come in! I wanted to shout, but no sound came out. *I do see you as my man! Please forgive me, but I'm really crap at this!*

'I'm sorry,' I managed to yell as I peeled myself off the floor. 'I'm so sorry, Julian!'

I flung the door open and threw myself at him, babbling about what an idiot I was but could he be patient with me because I did love him, even if I'd never understand what he saw in me and...

He took both my heads in his hands and I found myself staring into his dark, dark eyes.

'Now you listen to me, you nutter.' He was serious.

I swallowed, not knowing what to think or say, so I just listened.

'You gave me the encouragement I needed to get back in the saddle with my books. Without you, I'd still be feeling sorry for myself.'

Now *that* had come as a surprise. All this time he'd supported and cheered me on, when he had his own little traumas, which he hid very well.

'But besides that, I love you. Very much. And I want to make you and the kids happy. How could you—'

'I'm sorry,' I repeated, tears coming into my eyes. 'Especially because I love you. And I've been rehearsing ways to ask you to come, but I know your life and career are here. I'm sorry to do this to you now.'

He sighed and pulled me onto his lap.

'Erica, please let me finish. How could you even think for a moment that I wouldn't follow you if you wanted me to?'

I gaped at him, although you and I both know I was banking on him coming. 'You want to come?'

'Do you *want* me to come?'

'Would you?'

He nodded. 'Of course. You think I'm going to let someone else snatch you up? You must be crazy.'

I felt a smile coming on. Not a teeth-baring one, but a real smile. 'Cool!' I breathed.

'Cool,' he agreed.

'But what about your job? You studied so hard to be principal after your injury.'

He shrugged. 'I think it's time for you to be happy with me and for me to be happy with you.'

Which should have been more than enough, but you know good old practical me. 'So while I run the B & B, you're going to write your book?' I asked.

Again, he shrugged. 'I'd also like to breed horses.'

I grinned. 'Books and horses it is.'

'But first...' Julian said, pulling out a small velvet box this time.

'Uhm... what's that?' I asked.

'It's a goddam ring. To spell it out to you.'

It *was* a goddam ring. A big chunk of a rock, all shiny and pure. I looked at it and back at him, my eyes misty again.

'This is not a marriage proposal,' he warned me.

I forgot my tears as my jaw dropped in disappointment. 'It's not?'

'No. Because I know you're not ready yet, and I understand. But I don't want to lose you, so I'm hoping you'll wear this to scare off other men.'

'Oh, I've never needed a ring for *that*. They run the minute they see me,' I laughed as I dashed a hand over the new gush of tears running down my face.

He laughed and cupped my chin, delivering me a whoppingly delicious kiss on the lips.

'Chocolate?'

My one weakness. I nodded. 'I ate the whole thing,' I giggled and bawled at the same time.

He chuckled and murmured, 'Silly you...' as he tucked me into his arms.

I rested my face against his warm chest, enjoying the feel of his lean body through his blue cotton polo shirt. It was almost summer now and I hadn't realized it, so cold had I been inside.

Oh, how much easier my life would have been if I'd met Julian instead of Ira thirteen years ago. He took the ring out of the box and slipped it onto my finger, rolling my hands between his, his beautiful face flushed and excited like a young boy's.

'You, Erica Cantelli, are a magnificent woman. I love everything about you – your wacky sense of humor, your strength, your intelligence, your smile, these beautiful shoulders, your curves'—his hands slid down from my arms to my (ooh) butt—'your skin, the twinkle in your eyes, the sound of your voice, the way you play with your hair, the way you—'

'OK, I think I get it,' I giggled. He really was smitten. 'And you're really willing to wait, until I'm ready?'

'I swear. No pressure,' he promised.

Wow. Something in me had definitely changed, if a guy like Julian was willing to wait for me, let alone *look* at me. So I decided to push my luck. Why the hell not? 'And you won't try to take over my life? You don't mind me keeping my spaces?'

'I can handle that as well. As long as you don't run off with some Italian lover.'

I snorted. 'They're not exactly banging on my door, you know. Which is why you should reconsider while you still can.'

'I want to be in your life, but if and when you don't, I need to know.'

'Cool. But FYI, I'm not easy to live with. I'm bossy, arrogant, and I can be a real pain in the ass.'

'Don't I know it,' he grinned.

Things had really changed for me. A man like Julian was handing himself to me on a silver platter and I was no longer shocked.

40

Coming Up for Air

Julian decided to sell his home and put the money toward buying a farmhouse with me and some guest annexes to open our business. He'd also added a pool, paddocks and a tennis court to his wish list. It blew my budget out of the water.

'This is to show you how much I care,' he said, kissing me. 'This is my commitment until you decide to let me walk you down the aisle.'

'And you can really afford to buy all this?'

'Of course. Am I not a former sports celebrity?'

'So you're loaded?' Not that I hadn't noticed his house was a tad beyond a principal's salary.

He grinned. 'Let's say you won't have to worry about anything for the rest of your life.'

'Hello, have we met? I always worry about everything.'

'Not anymore, you won't.'

I pulled his face to mine and delivered him a whopper of a kiss. 'I love you, and not because you're filthy rich,'

I whispered, feeling my eyes burn and moisten. Enough crying. After twelve years, I was finally happy again. I felt like friggin' Cinderella.

We threw a leaving dinner party. It was mostly my family, but he invited a couple of colleagues from school and his old agent, Terry Petersen, who was salivating at the idea of another book. Also his father, Tom, a real British gentleman, just like his son, and his mother, Maggie, who was thrilled to see me in my clothes this time and to chew the breeze with me. She didn't seem the least perturbed her favorite son was leaving the continent to live with a flasher like me.

'You're doing the right thing, Erica,' my dad said as he kissed my cheek. '*Follow your dreams*, a wise woman once said to me, *no matter what shape they may take*.'

I smiled. 'Nonna told you, too? Did you listen to her?'

'No, unfortunately – I married your mother.'

'I heard that,' Marcy drawled as she slurped on her third Martini.

Dad shrugged his shoulders and winked.

41

Old Continent, New Life

Paul's Tuscan friend, Roberto Luzzi, sent some more listings for Julian and me to view, with the additional extras Julian had asked for. I turned around in my chair to look at my man.

'House-hunting is so much more fun with you.'

He bent to kiss me on the lips. 'See? You should have asked me sooner.

'Oh!' I cried as I flipped the pages. 'Look at this one!'

It was in Castellino, in the province of Siena near the border with Umbria, and it looked perfect.

In the space of one week, Julian and I had packed our belongings into a container. Well, not quite *all* of them.

I walked into the back garden and threw all my big old clothes into an enormous heap and lit a match. Bonfire time. Here I was, shedding my old skin for a new one. I watched as my heavy past turned to ashes and lifted into the air in tiny embers riding on the early evening breeze. It was going to be a colorful summer. In every way.

NANCY BARONE

I had a new killer wardrobe (Paul's advice had finally stuck after all those years), with smaller-sized sexy black items, and reds, blues, greens, whites – lots of them – all light textures, because the winter was far from my mind. I'd never worn white pants in my life because black was more slimming. It was also more depressing.

I lifted out of the garbage bag the coat and brown dress I'd worn the day I'd met Julian again, in his office. I brought it close to my face and breathed in the smell of mothballs, remembering that day a million years ago and how it really did look like shit on me. The texture – thick and stiff – was all wrong. Plus, it belonged to another time, in a galaxy far, far away. So I plopped it onto the fire.

By week three, Julian and I had both miraculously sold our houses (someone up there was rooting for us), and resigned from our jobs, not without a bit of gossip in the teachers' lounge, nor a bit of a fight from Harold Farthington. My boss hugged me and told me if I ever wanted to come back, I was welcome because I was the best manager he'd ever had, and if I was thinking of starting a rival company, he'd kill me. I smiled and hugged him back.

On week four we left the kids with my sister and together Julian and I flew to Sant'Egidio Airport in Umbria, for a quick recon visit to the best farmhouses of the batch and immediately made our decision. It was the house we'd seen in Castellino and it was love at first sight- just like when I'd first met Julian.

The farmhouse was tasteful – expensively tasteful – and extremely well-kept, from the gardens to the orchards to the olive groves to the vineyards. It had several fully renovated annexes and a couple more rustic. It also had two swimming pools, one for us and one for the guests. It looked like something out of a magazine. Better – out of a dream – my dream. And at the entrance, a beautiful, thriving, healthy rosebush. I couldn't wait to tell Maddy and Warren. It was perfect. But for one minor detail.

I turned to Julian. 'It's two bloody million euros!'

'Just go with it,' he said, putting his arm around me.

'But if you've got that kind of money lying around, why do I have to open a B & B? Why don't we just piss off somewhere, never to be found?'

'Because I know you. You'd get all itchy again and I'd have to put up with you.'

'True,' I sighed. 'What did I ever do to deserve this house?'

'You mean to deserve *me*.'

'That, too. What have I ever done for you?'

'You need to ask?'

'Uh, ye-eah?'

Julian took my face in his hands. 'You brought me back to life, kicked me out of my hibernation, pushed me to believe in myself again. If it hadn't been for you, I'd never have written another book. Or learned to cook Italian. And...' He kissed me so softly on the lips, I could almost taste his soul on them. 'I'd still be a very lonely man without you. You've made my life, Erica.'

'And you mine,' I whispered back. 'And of course, there's the farmhouse, as well.'

He smacked my bottom and grinned.

That same afternoon, we put in an offer, which was accepted. We'd be back in one month's time (which was fast for Italy) to sign the deeds and cough up the dough. The kids would be thrilled.

We slept in a hotel, or rather, made love and ate, made love and plans all night long, all day, for three whole days.

On the final morning of our stay, he wrapped a blindfold over my eyes.

'Mmm,' I murmured. 'That's a side of you I didn't know.'

He chuckled. 'Come on, insatiable. Come with me.' And led me to our rental.

I felt the steep incline as we went uphill. What the hell was he planning?

'OK, princess, step out. Keep the blindfold on. Easy – take my hand.'

The sun was warm, but the air was much breezier up here.

'You haven't followed me all this way across the world to push me over a cliff, have you?'

'OK, step up – one step, that's it. When I say so, you open your eyes. Got it?'

I could hear the joy in his voice. 'Got it.'

'OK! Open your eyes now.'

I obeyed. And almost had a coronary on the spot.

We were standing inside a hot-air balloon, bright red and filling up with gas.

Inside there was an easel, sketching material and paints.

'Oh my God,' I whispered over and over. 'I can't believe you did this for me...' I turned in his embrace and faced him, covering him with loud kisses.

'Ready, then?'

Ready? I was excited, anxious, not knowing where to feast first. 'Oh, yes!' I breathed. 'I didn't know you knew how to pilot one of these things, Julian.'

'I don't. But *you* do.'

'How did you know?'

'I have my secret informers.'

I watched him as he secured the door and leaned back.

'Ready when you are, then,' he said. 'Fly me to the moon.'

I looked at him blankly. 'You trust me?'

'Of course. Why wouldn't I? I have every confidence in you, Erica.'

'Cool!'

'Cool,' he agreed.

Though unaccustomed as I was to a similar statement, you can imagine how gratifying it was for me. With one last glance in his direction, just to make sure he wasn't turning green, I began my maneuvers. He stood back and watched me, his hands behind his back, probably to fight the instinct to jump out.

Once upon a time, I'd have joked that I was a basket case in a basket. Or a blimp in a blimp. But from now on, I'd be kinder to myself and ease a little on the self-effacing sarcasm.

It was heaven, soaring above treetops and fields ranging from yellow to green to brown, weightless for once in my life, not having to worry about how many people were allowed in the elevator or how many kilos it held. And Julian by my side. What a beautiful country we'd chosen to live in.

Then I felt him move. I turned to look at him and saw his face was flushed as he bent over. My God, he was ill and hadn't said anything.

'Julian? Julian, are you OK?' I asked, tugging at him to pull him up.

'I'm fine,' he said, bending to his knee, another little box in his hand. Yuh-oh.

I swallowed as the wind whipped at my face. 'Are you proposing this time?'

'Uh-huh…' he said, radiant.

'In a balloon? Cool.'

'Not so cool if you don't say yes this time.'

I didn't need to think about it. I looked at him and he became serious. 'Do I get to keep both rings?' I quipped, and he laughed.

'Yes, you do!'

I threw my arms around his neck and kissed him as hard as I could. 'I love you so much,' I whispered. 'You won't mind if I keep my maiden name? Not that Foxham isn't nice, but—'

'OK, OK,' he chuckled, and cupped my chin to kiss me.

I'd always loved Erica Cantelli. Only I didn't know it.

I remembered my Nonna's words. *Don't let go of your dreams, Erica – whatever shape they take, just hang onto them…*

Julian had helped me realize three of them (I'd postponed my ticket to Paris and bought three more for the next August).

I was flying over the Tuscan countryside in a balloon with a box of paints at my feet, and I had someone to share it all with.

And the joy of it was that, after all the heartache and diets, I'd managed to be myself again and steer my life where I wanted it to go. After all this time, I'd finally realized that my best diet had been love.

Epilogue

Julian had been right – he really was a heavy sleeper, so he never complained about my snoring or midnight monologues. But if I needed him awake at say, 3 a.m., which was basically always for one reason, all I had to do was pull the right chord – yes, *that* one – and he'd be instantly alert.

Ah, the joys of sex in the wee hours. It's the best – you're rested, relaxed and warm, and then you can go back to sleep again without worrying about rushing off to work. Not that I'd be rushing anywhere in Tuscany. We even arranged for the school bus to pick the kids up, starting the new school year. Year. Wow. I hadn't known Julian for a year and here we were. I must have been nuts.

And guess what – I wasn't grinding my teeth or having my apnea episodes anymore. Even my migraines were gone. It just goes to show you what a bit of serenity can do. No longer did I wake in the middle of the night gasping for breath – unless Julian's tongue was running down my body.

We give ourselves completely in the hope of being happy. But sometimes, no matter how hard we try, it all goes wrong. Too many commitments, too many sacrifices, the growing apart emotionally thing, etcetera. We invest the best years of our lives to pursue this dream. But in the meantime, we' also forget who *we* are and what our original aspirations were.

Only lucky people get all their love back and live the dream of a great relationship. And if you're really lucky, like me, there's enough love to spare for yourself, as well.

Oh, and if you're *still* wondering who left those flowers and that anonymous love note on my front door on Quincy Drive a thousand years ago, look up to the sky and you'll see him kissing the luckiest girl in the world in a hot-air balloon.

Caveat

To all so-so husbands out there: Pick up your socks, because your Erica might find a Julian.

To all Ericas: Have faith. You don't have to put up with it. Julians do exist out there if you believe in yourself.

To all Julians: You make life worth living. Keep up the good work, lads!

Apology

The medieval town of Castellino is fictional, and for one specific reason. Please enjoy Castellino as a summary of all good things that make Tuscany such a great place to live. Why not hop onto a plane and see for yourself? Or, alternatively (and much cheaper), you can wait until my next book to see what Erica gets up to in Tuscany.

Thank you,
Nancy Barone

About the Author

NANCY BARONE grew up in Canada, but at the age of twelve her family moved to Italy. Catapulted into a world where her only contact with the English language was her old Judy Blume books, Nancy became an avid reader and a die-hard romantic.

Nancy stayed in Italy and, despite being surrounded by handsome Italian men, she married an even more handsome Brit. They now live in Sicily where she teaches English. Nancy is a member of the Romantic Novelists' Association and a keen supporter of the Women's Fiction Festival at Matera where she meets up with writing friends from all over the globe.

Acknowledgements

Dear Readers,

Thank you once again for spending time with me. Choosing a book is also an investment of time and feelings. I hope you have enjoyed Erica's journey enough to join us on her whacky Tuscan adventures in the sequels!

I'd also like to thank my amazing publisher Aria and my lovely editor Martina Arzu who is never too busy for me.

The same goes for my super-duper talented agent Lorella Belli, the fantastic lady who made all of this happen. Thank you!

Of course my DH, my family and friends who support and bear with me deserve their names in lights, but you'll have to settle for a dinner!

See you all in Tuscany!